THOMAS HARDY was born in a cottage in Higher Bockhampton, near Dorchester, on 2 June 1840. He was educated locally and at sixteen was articled to a Dorchester architect, John Hicks. In 1862 he moved to London and found employment with another architect, Arthur Blomfield. He now began to write poetry and published an essay. By 1867 he had returned to Dorset to work as Hicks's assistant and began his first (unpublished) novel, *The Poor Man and the Lady*.

On an architectural visit to St Juliot in Cornwall in 1870 he met his first wife, Emma Gifford. Before their marriage in 1874 he had published four novels and was earning his living as a writer. More novels followed and in 1878 the Hardys moved from Dorset to the London literary scene. But in 1885, after building his house at Max Gate near Dorchester, Hardy again returned to Dorset. He then produced most of his major novels: *The Mayor of Casterbridge* (1886), *The Woodlanders* (1887), *Tess of the D'Urbervilles* (1891), *The Pursuit of the Well-Beloved* (1892) and *Jude the Obscure* (1895). Amidst the controversy caused by *Jude the Obscure*, he turned to the poetry he had been writing all his life. In the next thirty years he published over nine hundred poems and his epic drama in verse, *The Dynasts*.

After a long and bitter estrangement, Emma Gifford died at Max Gate in 1912. Paradoxically, the event triggered some of Hardy's finest love poetry. In 1914, however, he married Florence Dugdale, a close friend for several years. In 1910 he had been awarded the Order of Merit and was recognized, even revered, as the major literary figure of the time. He died on 11 January 1928. His ashes were buried in Westminster Abbey and his heart at Stinsford in Dorset.

TIM DOLIN teaches English at the University of Newcastle, New South Wales. He has published articles on Dickens, Gaskell, Charlotte Brontë and Hardy, and is the author of *Mistress of the House: Women of Property in the Victorian Novel* (1997). He is working on a study of Dickens and Victorian art, and an electronic edition of *The Early Life of Thomas Hardy, 1840–1891*. He is also the editor of the Penguin editions of *The Hand of Ethelberta* and *Tess of the D'Urbervilles*.

PATRICIA INGHAM is General Editor of all Hardy's fiction in the Penguin Classics Edition. She is a Fellow of St Anne's College, Reader in English and *The Times* Lecturer in English Language, the University of Oxford. She has written extensively on the Victorian novel and on Hardy in particular. Her most recent publications include *Dickens, Women and Language* (1992) and *The Language of Gender and Class: Transformation in the Victorian Novel* (1996). She has also edited Elizabeth Gaskell's *North and South* and Thomas Hardy's *The Pursuit of the Well-Beloved and The Well-Beloved* and *The Woodlanders* for Penguin Classics.

THOMAS HARDY

Under the Greenwood Tree

A RURAL PAINTING OF
THE DUTCH SCHOOL

Edited with an Introduction and Notes by
TIM DOLIN

PENGUIN BOOKS

PENGUIN BOOKS

Published by the Penguin Group
Penguin Books Ltd, 27 Wrights Lane, London W8 5TZ, England
Penguin Putnam Inc., 375 Hudson Street, New York, New York 10014, USA
Penguin Books Australia Ltd, Ringwood, Victoria, Australia
Penguin Books Canada Ltd, 10 Alcorn Avenue, Toronto, Ontario, Canada M4V 3B2
Penguin Books (NZ) Ltd, Private Bag 102902, NSMC, Auckland, New Zealand

Penguin Books Ltd, Registered Offices: Harmondsworth, Middlesex, England

First published in 1872

This edition published in Penguin Books 1998
3

Introduction and Notes copyright © Tim Dolin, 1998
General Editor's Preface and Chronology copyright © Patricia Ingham, 1998
All rights reserved

The moral right of the editors has been asserted

Set in 10/12.5pt Monotype Baskerville
Typeset by Rowland Phototypesetting Ltd, Bury St Edmunds, Suffolk
Printed in England by Clays Ltd, St Ives plc

CONTENTS

ACKNOWLEDGEMENTS

The excerpt from Thomas Hardy, *The Life and Work of Thomas Hardy*, ed. Michael Millgate, is reproduced with the kind permission of the publisher Macmillan, London.

Research for this edition, undertaken at the Dorset County Museum, Dorchester, and the British Library, London, was funded in part by the Research Management Committee of the University of Newcastle, New South Wales. Microfilm copies of texts were purchased from funds made available by the Department of English at the University of Newcastle. I received invaluable assistance from Richard de Peyer and his staff at the Dorset County Museum, my colleagues at Newcastle (especially Christopher Pollnitz, Dianne Osland and Karen Ractliffe), and Mary Rimmer at New Brunswick. I would like to acknowledge in particular the expertise and the knowledge and generosity of Michael Millgate and my editor, Patricia Ingham.

This edition of *Under the Greenwood Tree* is dedicated to Laurence Dolin and Daniel Dolin.

GENERAL EDITOR'S PREFACE

This edition uses, with one exception, the first edition in *volume* form of each of Hardy's novels and therefore offers something not generally available. Their dates range from 1871 to 1897. The purpose behind this choice is to present each novel as the creation of its own period and without revisions of later times, since these versions have an integrity and value of their own. The outline of textual history that follows is designed to expand on this statement.

All of Hardy's fourteen novels, except *Jude the Obscure* (1895) which first appeared as a volume in the Wessex Novels, were published individually as he wrote them (from 1871 onwards). Apart from *Desperate Remedies* (1871) and *Under the Greenwood Tree* (1872), all were published first as serials in periodicals, where they were subjected to varying degrees of editorial interference and censorship. *Desperate Remedies* and *Under the Greenwood Tree* appeared directly in volume form from Tinsley Brothers. By 1895 ten more novels had been published in volumes by six different publishers.

By 1895 Hardy was sufficiently well-established to negotiate with Osgood, McIlvaine a collected edition of all earlier novels and short-story collections plus the volume edition of *Jude the Obscure*. *The Well-Beloved* (radically changed from its serialized version) was added in 1897, completing the appearance of all Hardy's novels in volume form. Significantly this collection was called the 'Wessex Novels' and contained a map of 'The Wessex of the Novels' and authorial prefaces, as well as frontispieces by Macbeth-Raeburn of a scene from the novel sketched 'on the spot'. The texts were heavily revised by Hardy, amongst other things, in relation to topography, to strengthen the 'Wessex' element so as to suggest that this half-real half-imagined location had been coherently conceived from the beginning, though of course he knew that this was not so. In practice 'Wessex' had an uncertain and ambiguous development in the earlier editions. To trace the growth of Wessex in the novels as they appeared it is necessary to read them in their original pre-1895 form. For the 1895–6 edition represents a substantial layer of reworking.

Similarly, in the last fully revised and collected edition of 1912–13, the Wessex Edition, further alterations were made to topographical detail and photographs of Dorset were included. In the more open climate of opinion then prevailing, sexual and religious references were sometimes (though not always) made bolder. In both collected editions there were also many changes of other kinds. In addition, novels and short-story volumes were grouped thematically as 'Novels of Character and Environment', 'Romances and Fantasies' and 'Novels of Ingenuity' in a way suggesting a unifying master plan underlying all texts. A few revisions were made for the Mellstock Edition of 1919–20, but to only some texts.

It is various versions of the 1912–13 edition which are generally available today, incorporating these layers of alteration and shaped in part by the critical climate when the alterations were made. Therefore the present edition offers the texts as Hardy's readers first encountered them, in a form of which he in general approved, the version that his early critics reacted to. It reveals Hardy as he first dawned upon the public and shows how his writing (including the creation of Wessex) developed, partly in response to differing climates of opinion in the 1870s, 1880s and early 1890s. In keeping with these general aims, the edition will reproduce all contemporary illustrations where the originals were line drawings. In addition, for all texts which were illustrated, individual volumes will provide an appendix discussing the artist and the illustrations.

The exception to the use of the first volume editions is *Far from the Madding Crowd*, for which Hardy's holograph manuscript will be used. That edition will demonstrate in detail just how the text is 'the creation of its own period': by relating the manuscript to the serial version and to the first volume edition. The heavy editorial censoring by Leslie Stephen for the serial and the subsequent revision for the volume provide an extreme example of the processes that in many cases precede and produce the first book versions. In addition, the complete serial version (1892) of *The Well-Beloved* will be printed alongside the volume edition, since it is arguably a different novel from the latter.

To complete the picture of how the texts developed later, editors trace in their Notes on the History of the Text the major changes in 1895–6 and 1912–13. They quote significant alterations in their explanatory notes and include the authorial prefaces of 1895–6 and 1912–13. They also indicate something of the pre-history of the texts in manuscripts where these are available. The editing of the short stories will be separately dealt with in the two volumes containing them.

Patricia Ingham
St Anne's College, Oxford

1840 2 June: Thomas Hardy born, Higher Bockhampton, Dorset, eldest child of a builder, Thomas Hardy, and Jemima Hand, who had been married for less than six months. Younger siblings: Mary, Henry, Katharine (Kate), to whom he remained close.

1848–56 Schooling in Dorset.

1856 Hardy watched the hanging of Martha Browne for the murder of her husband. (Thought to be remembered in the death of Tess Durbeyfield.)

1856–60 Articled to Dorchester architect, John Hicks; later his assistant.

late 1850s Important friendship with Horace Moule (eight years older, middle-class and well-educated), who became his intellectual mentor and encouraged his self-education.

1862 London architect, Arthur Blomfield, employed him as a draughtsman. Self-education continued.

1867 Returned to Dorset as a jobbing architect. He worked for Hicks on church restoration.

1868 Completed his first novel *The Poor Man and the Lady* but it was rejected for publication (see 1878).

1869 Worked for the architect Crickmay in Weymouth, again on church restoration.

1870 After many youthful infatuations thought to be referred to in early poems, met his first wife, Emma Lavinia Gifford, on a professional visit to St Juliot in north Cornwall.

1871 *Desperate Remedies* published in volume form by Tinsley Brothers.

1872 *Under the Greenwood Tree* published in volume form by Tinsley Brothers.

1873 *A Pair of Blue Eyes* (previously serialized in *Tinsleys' Magazine*). Horace Moule committed suicide.

1874 *Far from the Madding Crowd* (previously serialized in the *Cornhill Magazine*). Hardy married Emma and set up house in London (Surbiton).

They had no children, to Hardy's regret; and she never got on with his family.

1875 The Hardys returned to Dorset (Swanage).

1876 *The Hand of Ethelberta* (previously serialized in the *Cornhill Magazine*).

1878 *The Return of the Native* (previously serialized in *Belgravia*). The Hardys moved back to London (Tooting). Serialized version of part of first unpublished novel appeared in *Harper's Weekly* in New York as *An Indiscretion in the Life of an Heiress*. It was never included in his collected works.

1880 *The Trumpet-Major* (previously serialized in *Good Words*). Hardy ill for many months.

1881 *A Laodicean* (previously serialized in *Harper's New Monthly Magazine*). The Hardys returned to Dorset.

1882 *Two on a Tower* (previously serialized in the *Atlantic Monthly*).

1885 The Hardys moved for the last time to a house, Max Gate, outside Dorchester, designed by Hardy and built by his brother.

1886 *The Mayor of Casterbridge* (previously serialized in the *Graphic*).

1887 *The Woodlanders* (previously serialized in *Macmillan's Magazine*).

1888 *Wessex Tales*.

1891 *A Group of Noble Dames* (tales). *Tess of the D'Urbervilles* (previously serialized in censored form in the *Graphic*). It simultaneously enhanced his reputation as a novelist and caused a scandal because of its advanced views on sexual conduct.

1892 Hardy's father, Thomas, died. Serialized version of *The Well-Beloved*, entitled *The Pursuit of the Well-Beloved*, in the *Illustrated London News*. Growing estrangement from Emma.

1892–3 *Our Exploits at West Poley*, a long tale for boys, published in an American periodical, the *Household*.

1893 Met Florence Henniker, one of several society women with whom he had intense friendships. Collaborated with her on *The Spectre of the Real* (published 1894).

1894 *Life's Little Ironies* (tales).

1895 *Jude the Obscure*, a savage attack on marriage which worsened relations with Emma. Serialized previously in *Harper's New Monthly Magazine*. It received both eulogistic and vitriolic reviews. The latter were a factor in his ceasing to write novels.

1895–6 First Collected Edition of novels: Wessex Novels (16 volumes), published by Osgood, McIlvaine. This included the first book edition of *Jude the Obscure*.

1897 *The Well-Beloved* (rewritten) published as a book; added to the Wessex Novels as vol. XVII. From now on he published only the poetry he had been writing since the 1860s. **No more novels**.

1898 *Wessex Poems and Other Verses*. Hardy and Emma continued to live at Max Gate but were now estranged and 'kept separate'.

1901 *Poems of the Past and the Present*.

1902 Macmillan became his publishers.

1904 Part 1 of *The Dynasts* (epic-drama in verse on Napoleon). Hardy's mother, Jemima, 'the single most important influence in his life', died.

1905 Met Florence Emily Dugdale, his future second wife, then aged 26. Soon a friend and secretary.

1906 Part 2 of *The Dynasts*.

1908 Part 3 of *The Dynasts*.

1909 *Time's Laughingstocks and Other Verses*.

1910 Awarded Order of Merit, having previously refused a knighthood.

1912–13 Major collected edition of novels and verse, revised by Hardy: The Wessex Edition (24 volumes). 27 November: Emma died still estranged. This triggered the writing of Hardy's finest love-lyrics about their early time in Cornwall.

1913 *A Changed Man and Other Tales*.

1914 10 February: married Florence Dugdale (already hurt by his poetic reaction to Emma's death). *Satires of Circumstance. The Dynasts: Prologue and Epilogue*.

1915 Mary, Hardy's sister, died. His distant young cousin, Frank, killed at Gallipoli.

1916 *Selected Poems*.

1917 *Moments of Vision and Miscellaneous Verses*.

1919–20 Mellstock Edition of novels and verse (37 volumes).

1922 *Late Lyrics and Earlier with Many Other Verses*.

1923 *The Famous Tragedy of the Queen of Cornwall* (drama).

1924 Dramatized *Tess* performed at Dorchester. Hardy infatuated with the local woman, Gertrude Bugler, who played Tess.

1925 *Human Shows, Far Phantasies, Songs and Trifles*.

1928 Hardy died on 11 January. His heart was buried in Emma's grave at Stinsford, his ashes in Westminster Abbey. *Winter Words in Various Moods and Metres* published posthumously. Hardy's brother, Henry, died.

1928–30 Hardy's autobiography published (on his instructions) under his second wife's name.

1937 Florence Hardy (his second wife) died.

1940 Hardy's last sibling, Kate, died.

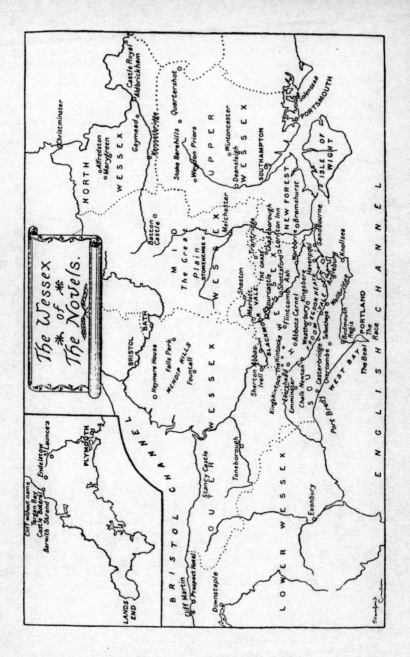

This map is from the Wessex Novels Edition, 1895–6

BIBLIOGRAPHICAL NOTE

The following abbreviations are used for texts frequently cited throughout the edition.

Collected Letters: Richard Little Purdy and Michael Millgate (eds), *The Collected Letters of Thomas Hardy*, 7 vols. (Oxford: Clarendon Press, 1978–88)

Creator: Simon Gatrell, *Hardy the Creator: A Textual Biography* (Oxford: Clarendon Press, 1988)

Firor: Ruth A. Firor, *Folkways in Thomas Hardy* (New York: A. S. Barnes and Co., 1962)

Life: Thomas Hardy, *The Life and Work of Thomas Hardy*, ed. Michael Millgate (London: Macmillan, 1989)

Notebooks: Richard H. Taylor (ed.), *The Personal Notebooks of Thomas Hardy* (New York: Columbia University Press, 1979)

Pinion: F. B. Pinion, *A Hardy Companion: A Guide to the Works of Thomas Hardy and their Background* (London: Macmillan, 1968)

Purdy: Richard Little Purdy, *Thomas Hardy: A Bibliographical Study* (Oxford: Clarendon Press, 1954)

Taylor: Dennis Taylor, *Hardy's Literary Language and Victorian Philology* (Oxford: Clarendon Press, 1993)

'It may be thought that there is enough, and to spare, of a meditative quality' in Thomas Hardy's fiction, declared Lionel Johnson in 1894: 'surely, summer suns might have shone in them more brightly, and winter winds blown through them more freshly! there is but one *Under the Greenwood Tree*'.[1] For most readers, *Under the Greenwood Tree* is indeed that one book of Hardy's that knows no enemies but 'winter and rough weather'.[2] It is an early novel, his second, published in 1872 when he was thirty-two years old and known only as the author of an undistinguished sensational melodrama, *Desperate Remedies* (1871). Stung by the spectacular commercial and critical failure of that first novel, but heartened by a couple of reviews that had at least singled out its little rustic sketches for praise, Hardy decided to follow it up with a full-length prose idyll of rural life. Despite poor sales at first, *Under the Greenwood Tree* was warmly received, and quickly became a popular favourite, establishing 'the true romance of country life' as Hardy's 'own ground'.[3] For all its popularity, though, which grew in proportion as Hardy's later novels alarmed and alienated some readers, *Under the Greenwood Tree* has never been taken very seriously by critics, as if it were neither quite good enough nor quite bad enough to be much bothered with. Perhaps in deference to Hardy's affection for it and his high opinion of it (he includes it among the pre-eminent 'Novels of Character and Environment' in the 1912 Wessex Edition[4]), it is granted a shrugging respect as 'the light-weight among his masterpieces' – 'unforgettable in its sweet good humour' and 'charming in its direct naturalness'.[5] Often called the 'best-loved' of the books, and nearly as often the 'most perfect' of them, this 'little "Dutch picture"' of country life'[6] is also, as Johnson's remarks suggest, somehow the least Hardyan: the happiest, and therefore the least interesting, of almost anything he wrote.

Why such faint praise? The Mellstock of *Under the Greenwood Tree* is surely at the heart of Hardy's Wessex, set as it is in the South-West of England in the 1840s, when Hardy himself was growing up in a village only a couple of miles from Dorchester, the county town of Dorsetshire. In fact, though, *Under the Greenwood Tree* was incorporated into Wessex only in 1896, when Hardy revised the book for the first Wessex Novels collected edition. Only then did he include elements from his own childhood past, linking Mellstock and its environs with Stinsford and the hamlets of Higher and Lower Bockhampton. When it first appeared in 1872 (the version republished here), Wessex had not been devised and Mellstock was more or less a generic English village (notwithstanding the distinctive West Country dialect). Moreover, everything that Wessex came to represent in the great tragic novels seems absent here. The familiar woodlands and hamlets, farms and churchyards ring unfamiliarly, even eerily, with Christmas good will, wedding bells and the laughter of villagers, as if the air of 'remembered happy childhood'[7] carried only the faintest echoes of darker stories to come. We scour the text for evidence of romantic irony shadowing the Mellstockers' innocence, as if Mellstock itself were only a sort of backdrop, a preparatory space, and to that extent an empty space: a clearing in the woods for the later, more consequential, dramas of Flintcomb Ash or Little Hintock. But as one early critic of Hardy's remarked, while *Under the Greenwood Tree* 'makes a great advance in the art of setting', it 'is so largely wanting in the interest both of plot and of character that we are inclined to look upon it hardly in the light of a novel; and we pass on at once to . . . *A Pair of Blue Eyes*'.[8]

And *Under the Greenwood Tree* does look slight next to other Wessex novels. It is barely half as long as any of them, and this modest length along with a fine stylistic unity and economical plot are for many readers the plainest evidence of Mellstock's emptiness. This 'most nearly flawless'[9] of the novels seems to carry none of that resistance in the language so characteristic of Hardy's great work, none of those fluctuations and lapses in style that John Bayley calls his peculiar 'vulnerability'.[10] Readers accustomed to this style, with its inflections of the archaic, the idiomatic, the literary and the prosaic, and its recycled bits and pieces of the cultural heritage, find here a marked air of constraint. This is in part because, I think, Hardy meant *Under the Greenwood Tree* to be a corrective to the thickly allusive melodrama of *Desperate Remedies*. In the latter his 'search for a method' had hit upon the distinctive idiosyncratic use of phrases, part-phrases, lines of verse, biblical quotations and misquotations, allusions and echoes, a method he was to exploit in later fictions. But the manuscript of *Under the Greenwood Tree* shows him exercising what looks like discipline: a number of chapter titles that make use of quotation are cancelled, one from Wordsworth (discussed below), others, virtually illegible, from ballads or, possibly, verses by William Barnes. This pared-down text is very effective, but it conveys a rural England radically simplified and insulated from the wider culture. Knowing what we know of Hardy's Wessex, that simplification may seem merely youthful or it may seem somewhat contrived, as though something were being withheld from us. The *bonhomie*, the mood of forgiveness and forbearance, the happy marriage ending: it is all a little well turned-out, on its best behaviour, as though some complication, ambivalence or anxiety were being kept just out of sight, like a family secret.

As Hardy grew older, he too came to feel the emptiness of Mellstock. *Under the Greenwood Tree* was the only novel to which he did not retain the copyright, with the consequence that the version of 1872, with its 'chapters penned so lightly, even so farcically and flippantly at times' (1912 Preface) remained in print throughout his life, continuing to be sold alongside the carefully revised and newly prefaced editions of later years. Abashed by its facetiousness and nonchalance, but powerless to suppress it, he simply disowned the 1872 version as the careless work of his youth. But he did not by any means disown the novel altogether. He simply wished that he had written it all down differently, though whether the novel he never wrote could have been a novel at all, or what a later Preface called a 'study of another kind' – perhaps a study along the lines of his 1883 essay 'The Dorsetshire Labourer' – is unclear. In any event, over the years, *Under the Greenwood Tree* became more and more important to him as a document about a past that had been lost to him, and lost to England. Although he stressed in his autobiography that there was 'no family portrait in the tale',[11] he took pleasure in matching up characters with people he and his family had known and loved, and in the *Life* he expressed regret that in 1872 he had not memorialized these village-folk with the dignity that was their due. Accordingly, he strove in later revisions (he revised it again in 1912) to draw out the intimate associations with his own childhood, subtly altering the topography of the first edition to secure them: tranter Dewy's cottage, for example, is converted only in 1896 into the larger 'cottage' that many readers would recognize as Hardy's birthplace in Higher Bockhampton. These adjustments cannot be too much relied upon as biographical or historical evidence, however, since Hardy here, as elsewhere in his work, slyly encourages and resists the tourist's game of real-life correspondences. Nevertheless, he did succeed in transforming *Under the Greenwood Tree* from an idyll set in some indeterminate pastoral realm into a novel of Wessex (these changes are discussed in Appendix II), and it duly took its place in the collected editions.

A novel of Wessex, perhaps, but *Under the Greenwood Tree* resisted all its author's efforts to convert it into what we think of as a 'Wessex novel'. These efforts were principally focused on the imbalance he perceived in the two competing (one might even say rival) stories, one telling of the supersession of a group of church musicians by a single organist, and the other telling a conventional tale of love and marriage. Hardy consequently set out to reinstate the choir as the leading men in later editions. The dominant love romance of 1872 was a paltry confection for subscribers to circulating libraries, he implied. His original conception had been a vigorous and celebratory tale that immortalized the doings and (mostly) sayings of the village musicians, but this had promised insufficient dramatic interest in its own right. From the evidence of the manuscript, it is clear that Hardy had indeed reshaped the novel quite late in the initial process of its composition during 1871. Probably on the advice of Macmillan's reader, John Morley, he emphasized the plot of rival suits for Fancy's hand and cut out considerable material relating to the choir (see 'A Note on the History of the Text'). But there is no evidence that he originally intended to call the novel 'The Mellstock Quire' as he later asserted. This title is written at the head of the manuscript and cancelled out, but it has been added later in different-coloured ink.[12] In any case, as he enigmatically remarked in 1912, 'circumstances would have rendered any aim at a deeper, more essential, more transcendent handling unadvisable', and even had the novel taken the deposition of the choir as it central event, it would have remained a simple rural story which draws its characters 'humorously, without caricature'.[13]

To compensate for the novel's seemingly implacable triviality, Hardy used the occasion of the appended Prefaces to the revised editions of 1896 and 1912 to direct his readers' attention to its underlying project of historical recovery and its deep personal significance for its author. In the 1896 Preface, for example, he calls it 'a fairly true picture, at first hand, of the personages, ways, and customs which were common among such orchestral bodies in the villages of fifty years ago', anticipating in the rhetoric of social documentation the argument of the 'General Preface' to the Wessex Edition of 1912, in which he would describe his fiction as a whole as 'a fairly true record of a vanishing life'. Forgotten, or concealed, is the novel's own history. It did not evolve from an unprompted urge to preserve 'personages, ways, and customs' in village Dorset, but from Hardy's immediate response to his two preceding efforts at fiction: the unpublished *The Poor Man and the Lady*, and *Desperate Remedies*. George Meredith, who read *The Poor Man* for Chapman and Hall, felt that its pronounced antagonism towards the ruling classes would irreparably damage the young novelist's reputation, and he discouraged Hardy from pursuing its publication, suggesting instead that he try a novel in which plot predominated. The mostly devastating reviews of *Desperate Remedies*, the 'unfortunate consequence' of Meredith's advice,[14] scared Hardy away from such elaborately constructed 'artificial' fictions and encouraged him to 'try his hand' at a story with almost no plot. Paradoxically, he already had plenty of material for such a story in the discarded *Poor Man*, which included the early Christmas Eve scenes at the Dewys'. Around these scenes he developed a pastoral story, explaining to Malcolm Macmillan that 'It seemed . . . upon the whole . . . the *safest* venture.'[15] This is the young author speaking cautiously as an inexperienced man of business, determined to succeed financially at fiction, and be saved from an unpromising career as a provincial architect. And this is the impression we have of *Under the Greenwood Tree* – of a safe novel, calculated to seem 'natural': effortless and artless.

If the novel of 1872 was not, as it became, the deeply personal remembrance of Hardy's own past, therefore, but the product of a conscious decision to dissociate himself from *Desperate Remedies* and demonstrate his versatility, no project could have suited him better than a pastoral story, traditionally a mode that was sophisticated and artful whilst striving to seem natural and spontaneous. He had various materials ready-to-hand for just such a project. He was living with his parents in Dorset, and his assiduous self-education had already schooled him thoroughly in the classical idyll, and in English pastoral and anti-pastoral.[16] In an early notebook he had jotted down an idea for a poem which compared 'Theocritus & the life at Bockn when I was a boy'.[17] In addition, he drew upon his knowledge of various historical conventions of rural painting, gleaned from visits to the National Gallery when he was working as an assistant architect in London,[18] and he studied up on local dialects and customs. Family stories; Shakespearian rustics; the genre paintings of Wilkie and Teniers mentioned in the *Spectator*'s review of *Desperate Remedies*; the Loamshire tales of George Eliot mentioned in the *Athenaeum*'s review;

historical romances and ballads of old England; the new interest of urban readers and tourists in dying rural customs and rituals: Hardy made good use of them all to produce a novel that is deeply satisfying to many readers, if also a little disquieting to some. *Under the Greenwood Tree* is a very successful pastoral story indeed.[19]

As Michael Millgate observes, the conflict between pastoral modes and the social realities he knew from his own childhood 'troubled Hardy all his life', yet in *Under the Greenwood Tree* he chooses not to explore it. For the only time in his career, it would seem, he is allowing us a country holiday away from the pressing and depressing claims of a rural England blighted by social change.[20] Of course, Hardy 'loved the art of concealing art',[21] and this is no artless optimistic work of his youth, so we should be cautious even of its 'relative innocence', an innocence 'which in his later fiction becomes blighted with knowledge'.[22] Geoffrey Grigson perceptively reminds us that Hardy wrote 'Neutral Tones' (1867), with its 'God-curst sun' and its 'few leaves . . . on the starving sod', long before *Under the Greenwood Tree*, and many readers detect in the serene complacency of Mellstock life dark hints of the Hardy to come, 'the tragedy that always underlies Comedy if you only scratch it deeply enough'.[23] But is it worth the scratching? Grigson remarks that to 'look for intimations of the "ghast and grim" of human relationship in the light mix of *Under the Greenwood Tree* wouldn't be very sensible',[24] and few readers bother, beyond acknowledging a mild irony here and there.[25] Even if this is not 'the only one of Hardy's successful works in which the love story ends in unqualified sunshine',[26] it seems barely troubled by its many unresolved intimations of discontent: Fancy's 'secret she should never tell'; Mrs Day's obsessional housekeeping; Enoch's hostility; the routine unhappinesses and vexations of the older married couples; or the distant miseries of Mrs Leaf, mother of eleven dead children and one living congenital imbecile, Thomas. Most readers decide, as Simon Gatrell does, that these elements 'are all accommodated within (or subordinated to) the larger images of social integration, and the most inclusive of these is the dance under the shade of the greenwood tree at the end of the novel, which shows the whole community celebrating the union of Dick and Fancy'.[27]

Little wonder, then, that the villagers can afford to 'fleet the time carelessly', as Charles tells Oliver in Shakespeare's *As You Like It*, the play from which Hardy's title derives. Like all pastorals, this one has removed to a world outside the gates of the world, seeking in the highly elaborate ceremonies and conventions of the forest – courtship and marriage, music and dance, eating and drinking, fellowship and community – patterns of meaning and opportunities for reconciliation unavailable in the *polis*. We look on indulgently as the Mellstockers admire their own fine old-fashioned craftsmanship and good husbandry (though work does not have the central place here that it usually does in Hardy's Wessex tales), and we feel that even in this inconsequential world there is leisure enough for us to wait upon the lingering courtship of Dick and Fancy. We know from *As You Like It*, however, that such rare good fun cannot last for ever. The green world is a temporary world: Mellstock is only, as Simon Schama says of Arden, 'an upside-down world',[28] a reorientation of Victorian rural and industrial England, not a remote, pre-industrial Eden.

The presence of that England is perhaps most strongly elicited, paradoxically, when readers are determined to celebrate Mellstock's emptiness. *Under the Greenwood Tree* came to be associated with a nostalgic simplification of rural England early in its interpretive history, which is partly why it has remained at such odds with Hardy's other work, including, even, relatively happy 'pastoral' novels like *Far from the Madding Crowd* (1874). This association perhaps accounts in part for Hardy's strong objection in later years to the title from Shakespeare, and his insistence that the authentic title was 'The Mellstock Quire'.[29] The allusion to *As You Like It* was a powerful reminder of the central position the novel occupied and continues to occupy in 'a national literature with Shakespeare at its centre'.[30] In this role *Under the Greenwood Tree* helped (where other more troublesome Hardy novels failed) to fit Wessex to the development of the powerful myth of 'English Heritage' later in the century. It also helped to reconcile Hardy's problematic and unpredictable opinions with those of a culturally expansive Imperial Britain. The title's allusion to the 'greenwood', additionally, links the 'perished band' (1896 Preface) with another band of exiled Saxon commoners under siege, and links Mellstock with 'the sylvan habitat of Merrie England' where 'nightingales sing, the ale is heady, and masters and men are brought together in fellowship by the lord of the jest: Robin Hood'.[31]

So while the drowsy village seems to admit 'scarcely a murmur of the world outside',[32] the novel itself, published in London for Londoners, has frequently been put to profoundly worldly uses, and it was this wieldiness that Hardy found so difficult to counter in his attempts to integrate *Under the Greenwood Tree* into the Wessex novels. Its pastoral nostalgia is so effective that the novel did not respond under revision to the method he had developed for probing the 'interaction between general forces and personal histories – that complex area of ruin or survival, exposure or continuity', as Raymond Williams described it in *The Country and the City*.[33] We are simply not convinced that this poignant pocket-handkerchief drama of a village choir's extinction plays out, just as the grim plots of later novels do, momentous and traumatic shifts and transitions in the social and economic conditions of rural communities. But this is not to say that Hardy has no interest here in those 'general forces', or those shifts and transitions. Rather, it is literary and pictorial conventions, not personal histories, that are exposed to convulsions in rural class structures in the 1840s – convulsions both minute and broadly felt – and that become vulnerable to stirrings of national feeling in the 1870s. The pastoral space in this novel, the space under the greenwood tree, cannot, therefore, be seen in the 'sentimental terms' of a contrast between 'an internal ruralism and an external urbanism'.[34] Nor is it a refuge for social reintegration, a stay against the forces of change that Williams identified as already at work inside rural communities at the mid-century. The real conditions of English country life in the 1840s and of English rural and national life in the 1870s are not excluded from *Under the Greenwood Tree*; they are just not present as realism. At no stage does the narrative attempt a baldly mimetic representation of the social world in this novel; rather it filters its representation through a number of distinct and even contradictory representational conventions, making use of pictorialism, dance-steps, musical forms, ballads, Romantic stereotypes, dramatic tableaux, and more. As John Goode has observed, *Under the Greenwood Tree* is 'as naturalistic but as distanced . . . as a still life', and we are 'invited to think of it all the time as a work of art'.[35]

There are, however, moments when we are invited to think of it as a work of art that is very far from naturalistic. The opening scene provides a striking example of a self-consciousness about aesthetic modes and social meanings which pervades the novel. 'On a cold and starry Christmas-eve', in the pitch-black woods, voices hail and respond to each other across the darkness of a winter landscape. These are the 'dwellers in a wood', introduced to us (feeble dwellers in a city) as aboriginal beings with amazing powers: a primitive race exhibited as anthropological curios, who can identify any species of tree on the darkest night by its sound alone. Our eyes strain to adjust to these dark forms passing along a dark lane against a dark sky, their disembodied part-song heard before they can be picked out, as Dick's lively ballad in 'a rural cadence' is taken up by Michael Mail's ' "Ho-i-i-i-i-i!" ', Robert Penny's vigorous oath, and Joseph Bowman's cheerful exclamation. As these figures grow in definition, the scene wavers on the edge of the picturesque, threatening to arrange itself at any moment into a conventional sylvan nocturne in the manner of Ruysdael or Teniers. But Hardy, wary of the naturalizing power of his 'rural painting of the Dutch school', accordingly introduces contradictory pictorial elements. Dick's portrait, for example, is described as that of a young man with an 'ordinary-shaped nose, an ordinary chin, an ordinary neck, and ordinary shoulders', but it suddenly takes the form of a fashionable silhouette: he is not a man who drives a horse and cart for a living, but 'a gentleman'. Likewise, the five men 'of different ages and gaits' shuffle out like Shakespearian players from the darkness. They have 'lost their rotundity' and advance against the sky 'like some procession in Assyrian or Egyptian incised work'. A cold pastoral for a cold night, these men are suddenly not quaint misshapen rustics but noble ancients fixed in stone. In the revisions of 1896, Hardy emended this description to a 'processional design on Greek or Etruscan pottery', thereby fixing the allusion to Keats's urn, upon which the poet reflects, appropriately enough in this context: 'When old age shall this generation waste,/Thou shalt remain, in midst of other woe' (*Ode on a Grecian Urn*, ll.46–7).

The detailed patterns of lines and flat planes pictured by Hardy's prose organize this spectacle of a lost past coming back to life into a compelling abstract design, as if the landscape is only one of many aesthetic effects; as if the past, preserved like a Keatsian artefact, is another; and as if we are another. The converging pathways, verbal echoes and ascending figures 'rising against the sky' in a kind of ramshackle unison lead us in to the splendid scenes of the night's carol-singing, but we enter this landscape through a process intended to alienate us from it. We are self-conscious, unsure of the light. We feel as if we might be tourists, or visitors to a museum or diorama, or spectators at a theatre, seated before a chorus of sobbing trees and a blacked-out stage. We read 'the dark interior of the grove' as the dark interior of a grave, and the choir as illumined figures in a Stanley Spencer resurrection, clearing their throats and greeting each other in readiness for a final Christmas Eve recital. We recognize from the start, I think, that these men are long dead, and that all this is long past. Gone for good, they can now only be called up into a work of art, which only really speaks to something lost from the reader's world, some way of seeing and knowing rural England not as it is or ever was, but only as it can be represented. The Mellstock woodland and its shivering dwellers are in one sense mere reflexes of the city – again, the city upside-down.

The really remarkable thing about this opening chapter is that it manages to suggest at one and the same time that Mellstock is a place where nothing ever changes, where everything has changed inexorably, and where everything is perpetually in the process of changing. We sense that these villagers are being reincarnated before our eyes into a past that we know is past, simply that they may re-enact for us the drama of their passing. As Michael Mail says, '"Times have changed from the times they used to be . . . I've been thinking, we must be almost the last left in the county of the old string players."' Already Hardy is focusing on the precise moment of a rural English community's death as social reality and rebirth as representation, the moment when the old choir dies as social fact and is reborn into a timeless rustic yesterday, where lives are governed by the cycle of the seasons, Christian rituals and the agricultural calendar, and where men and women are born into parishes, court each other in local country dances, give birth to children, and are buried in the churchyard. The Mellstock choir is a vestige even in its last surviving days, casting the characteristic mood of resignation over proceedings which caused the *Spectator* to remark incredulously, 'Did ever a village choir submit to its fate so mildly?'[36] In keeping with this mood, the characters express at intervals a certain wry consciousness of their own pastness and their curiously anomalous representational status. They behave as if they are sensible of their complete anachronism, and as if they have long since happily passed from active participation in the social life of the parish, content to live out their days as figures in a landscape. They stare vacantly into space as though casting their minds back to an earlier state of being, and even as they do so are half-aware of composing themselves for our benefit into picturesque groupings or studies in rustic quaintness. Their idiosyncratic tendency to lapse into abstractedness accords unexpectedly with the pleasure they take in their own pictorial abstraction, as they contemplate each other's shapes framed in doors and windows or cast against a low sun or a bright fire.

Diminished by the picturesque, these whimsical men of the choir seem as archaic as shepherds, or as earthy as peasants. But we need to be careful, for they are not even agricultural labourers. In fact, the labouring classes are more or less absent from *Under the Greenwood Tree*, represented, rather dubiously, by the smocked village idiot Thomas Leaf. Hardy explained the reason for this in 1926: 'down to the middle of the last century' villagers 'were divided into two distinct castes, one being the artisans, traders, "liviers" (owners of freeholds), and the manor-house upper servants; the other the "work-folk", i.e. farm-labourers ... The two castes rarely intermarried, and did not go to each other's house-gatherings save exceptionally.'[37] The choir allows the work-folk along as 'supernumeraries', but they are never described other than by their smocks and are certainly not invited to the tranter's party or the wedding of Dick and Fancy (with the exception of Leaf, on whom the choir takes pity). The higher caste of villagers, where the Dewys, Robert Penny and the rest of the central group of players belong, is, of course, only in the middle ranks of the village hierarchy. As well as the labourers, the squire, too, is absent (he is unnamed in this edition but later identified as the Earl of Wessex). In the squire's place, Parson Maybold is the most socially elevated character in the novel. Below him are Shinar, the gentleman farmer; the socially ambitious (though in this edition still quite lowly) keeper Geoffrey Day and his equally ambitious daughter, Fancy; then the players themselves, and the scant labourers.

The importance of the parson in a village without a resident aristocracy at this time is crucial in this social organization, especially since Maybold represents the new Anglican order in the English countryside in the 1840s. A product of the radical reform of the clergy at this time,[38] he takes over the parish from Mr Grinham, the ' "right sensible parson" ' who never bothered his parishioners ' "from year's end to year's end" ' and never put anyone ' "to spiritual trouble" '. The ' "hearty borus-snorus ways" ' of Maybold, on the other hand, vex the choir and the parish: ' "there's this man never letting us have a bit of peace; but wanting us to be good and upright till 'tis carried to such a shameful pitch as I never see the like afore nor since!" '. According to Alun Howkins, a clergyman like Maybold was 'a key figure in the recreation of paternalism'[39] in the absence of the aristocracy in English villages in the mid-century. This paternalistic authority is suggested in the villagers' awkward deference towards their vicar, as well as in his institution of an efficient core of lay workers, including the churchwardens. But most of all it is felt in the matter of the deposition of the choir on the very day of the Harvest

Festival, a key communal ritual co-opted into the Anglican liturgy at this time.[40]

It is tempting to read this moment of crisis as typical of the introduction into the country of corrupting forces of change from the city. After all, the vicar brings with him a new organ, despised and feared by the choir and, in its efficient, mechanical way, as insidious to them as the threshing machine in *Tess*. In the 1896 Preface Hardy lamented this development, arguing that the 'control and accomplishment' of the 'isolated organist' tended to 'extinguish the interest of parishioners in church doings'. As the novel makes clear, only old William Dewy takes what could be called a spiritual interest in the music-making or the life of the parish. The others are ' "Good, but not religious-good" ', as Mr Penny remarks of the departed Sam Lawson. There are, however, inklings that the choir's future is already under question even before Maybold's scheme is revealed. Not only is it the last surviving string-choir in the county, but its youngest member, Dick, is clearly not as committed to the music as the older generation, who are themselves not as committed as old William, their guiding spirit and conscience. As if to suggest this, when the novel opens Dick is singing his own tune softly to himself, and is reproached in a friendly way by Michael Mail for not stopping for ' "fellow-craters – going to thy own father's house too, as we be, and knowen us so well" '. Like Fancy, Dick has been educated – sent ' "to a school so good that 'twas hardly fair to the other children" ' – and like her he speaks standard, not dialect, English. These two are early versions of Hardy's returned native, representative in their modest ways of what Raymond Williams called 'the problem of the relation between customary and educated life'.[41] Later the same Christmas Eve, Dick does go his own way, literally breaking away from the choir on their rounds and doubling back to stare lovelorn into Fancy's window. The woman's seductiveness is implicated in his distraction, of course: Fancy is a prime agent of social disruption in the parish, far more visibly disruptive than the timid Maybold, who uses her vanity and sexual charm to win over the parishioners to his new liturgical order. Around her focal singing and playing, moreover, lurks the decided menace of 'united woman' ranged competitively against the precarious clubbishness of the choir.

But Fancy or no, Dick is a ready accomplice in Maybold's vision of a new social hierarchy in the parish. His attraction to a young woman is part of the natural order of things, of course, and his diffidence about the choir can be put down to ordinary generational conflict. He does not, as Fancy is apt to do, automatically object to the old ways of the village on the grounds that they are unfashionable. He feels pulled away from the community of men, but he goes along with most of the traditions and habits of the village in his complaisant way, and looks forward to nothing so much as a nice wedding and a nice family life, an outcome that at least promises certain rewards for him as a man. But the world in which he has grown up is at once 'rooted and mobile, familiar yet newly conscious and self-conscious'[42] and part of that self-consciousness is the faint recognition in the novel that the supposedly timeless pattern of communal life may be nothing more than a pastoral myth. This is adumbrated in a handful of important references to time and timelessness in the novel. In the front room of Day's cottage in Yalbury Wood, for example, two clocks restlessly compete against each other for the honour of being Fancy's wedding gift. Dick's successful courtship, likewise, is framed in the same terms: he becomes 'a man of business and . . . strong on the importance of time'. As if to emphasize this, on the Christmas Eve rounds Dick disappears at a significant moment, when the players have stopped for their midnight meal of hot mead and bread-and-cheese in the belfry of the parish church. Unaware that Dick is not with them, the older men listen as the 'direct pathway of Time' passes above them in the 'little world of undertones and creaks' in the 'halting clockwork' of the tower clock. Suspended outside the onward mechanical movement of time, the choir are gathered up in the structure of the seasons, and their demise is made an occasion for nothing more than melancholy. But there are hints everywhere in *Under the Greenwood Tree* that the cyclical rituals in which so much store is set, might be oppressive, not reintegrative – and not only to the restless young people, but to others as well. And that the great celebrations of village solidarity and harmony, most especially the centre-piece dances, might in fact be coercive and stifling.

The first sign of trouble in paradise occurs in the opening paragraph, which is set apart from the narrative proper like a kind of proem:

To dwellers in a wood, almost every species of tree has its voice as well as its feature. At the passing of the breeze, the fir-trees sob and moan no less distinctly than they rock; the holly whistles as it battles with itself; the ash hisses amid its quiverings; the beech rustles while its flat boughs rise and fall.

And winter, which modifies the note of such trees as shed their leaves, does not destroy its individuality.

The suppression of individuality by society had long interested Hardy. In the mid-1860s, he had read and copiously annotated the chapter on individuality in John Stuart Mill's *On Liberty* (1859),[43] and it is in this context that the troubling, discordant songs of the trees painfully and violently asserting their individual voices can perhaps best be understood. In his copy of Mill, Hardy marked with double lines the argument that 'Human nature is not a machine to be built after a model, and set to do exactly the work prescribed for it, but a tree . . . a living thing.'[44] This seems most immediately relevant to Hardy's critique in the 1896 Preface to *Under the Greenwood Tree* of the wholesale introduction of mechanical and centralized music-making in the village communities: the barrel-organ with its limited repertoire of Tate and Brady psalm tunes taking over from the imperfect but 'organic' choir. But to read further in Hardy's underlinings, markings and marginal annotations of Mill is instructive, because the social 'machines' that destroy individuality are found in unexpected places. 'Customs,' Mill writes, 'are made for customary circumstances, and customary characters.'[45] They may be good in themselves, but they severely restrict an individual's right to make a choice. Thus, 'He who does anything because it is the custom, makes no choice'; and (in a memorable phrase which Hardy later incorporated into *Jude the Obscure* 'He who lets the world, or his own portion of it, choose his plan of life for him, has no need of any other faculty than the ape-like one of imitation.'[46]

   Seen in this light, the round of customs and rituals in *Under the Greenwood Tree* is despotic, in Mill's sense. If this seems far-fetched, consider all the secret signs, fleeting grimaces, and silent, angry semaphores that point to a barely suppressed mood of intransigence. Significant glances and enigmatic facial expressions abound in this novel, which focuses conspicuously on forms of arcane gesticulation. When Shinar, for example, hung over, abuses the choir on Christmas Eve, the tranter exhorts his fellow musicians to play ' "fortissimy, and drown his spaking!" ' Effectively drowned out, Shinar wildly flings 'his arms and body about in the form of capital Xs and Ys', appearing 'to utter enough invectives to consign the whole parish to perdition'. The choir, however, unexpectedly find itself drowned out in church the very following morning by a group of insubordinate school-girls, who refuse to be 'humble and respectful followers of the gallery'. This assault upon the choir's authority, which alludes to the pastoral convention of the song contest,[47] is a portent, but it also reveals a deep vein of aggression and insurgency beneath the surface of the community. When the choir visits the vicar to plead for a decent leave-taking, its members draw blood: it is only a shaving cut which 'busts out' when Maybold bends to retrieve his pen at a very awkward moment in the proceedings, but it suggests, however comically, a certain latent animus. The tranter admits that the vicar is the boss, and will have his way in his own workshop. But he really believes all along that he has in fact 'managed' Maybold rather well, and, never one to resist an opportunity to turn an aphorism, he advises his friends that ' "Everybody must be managed. Queens must be managed: kings must be managed; for men want managing almost as much as women, and that's saying a good deal." '

The irony, of course, is that the vicar – the source of benevolent power in the village – has nicely managed the choir, and that Fancy nicely manages the vicar, Dick manages Fancy, and so on. The villagers are perhaps not so pliable after all, but concede control with an unshaken belief in their real authority over the victor. But then neither is the village such a benign community. Social power struggles are being incessantly played out there, and the deluded weak are being constantly defeated. When 'equality of social views' might in fact be 'damaging to the theory of master and man', as in the relationship between Geoffrey Day and his trapper, Enoch, the latter ends up in the stocks. Shouting angrily at the wedding party like an evil omen, 'a brown spot far up a turnip field', Enoch's distant replies are stretched out of shape, and drowned out.

Enoch is not the only 'mastered' man absent from the final celebrations, however. The long-forgotten rival, Shinar, is missing too, banished from paradise for his contempt of the community. As well as abusing the choir, he refuses to follow the rules of the dance at the tranter's, makes a nuisance of himself at Geoffrey Day's honey-taking, and swaggers around eyeing Fancy and wearing too much gold and silver. He is the epitome of that modern type, the parvenu. As his name indicates (and, significantly, Hardy changed its spelling to 'Shiner' in later editions to make the point more transparently), he represents the primacy of money over tradition. His superiority and self-confidence, like Day's, lie not in his land or his name but in his ostentatiously displayed personal wealth. The novel frames him as Dick's patent rival, but he is effectively no rival at all, and after the honey-taking he drops out of sight, superseded by the real rival, Maybold.

In fact, Shinar is actually too much like Dick and Fancy to prove a distinctive antagonist in the love triangle. He is vain about his personal appearance, wears jewellery, is capricious and self-important, and does not hold with customs that are followed just for their own sake: attributes also associated with Fancy. And though Dick is contemptuous of Shinar's vulgar wealth, it is ironical that he, too, likes to think of himself as something of a modern type. He energetically plans to expand the family business in a manner unheard of in the village by introducing a conspicuously modern marketing idea, business cards (Mr Penny, remember, does not even have a sign over his workshop). Dick's stirrings of interest in the new social order promised by money and its accumulation is borne out in Thomas Leaf's epithalamial story, which occupies such a strangely central place in the wedding scene:

'Once . . . there was a man who lived in a house! Well, this man . . . said to himself, as I might, "If I had only ten pound, I'd make a fortune." At last, by hook or by crook, behold he got the ten pounds! . . . In a little time he made that ten pounds twenty. Then a little time after that he doubled it, and made it forty. Well, he went on, and a good while after that he made it eighty, and on to a hundred. Well, by and by he made it two hundred! Well, you'd never believe it, but – he went on and made it four hundred! He went on, and what did he do? Why, he made it eight hundred! . . . yes, and he went on and made it A THOUSAND!'

Leaf's fable announces a new kind of ritual – the ritual multiplication of wealth. It is virtually bereft of plot: 'a bad story, lacking form and point', as Barbara Hardy argues.[48] But this little capitalist romance takes on the shapely structure of a story of accumulation without labour. It is as pleasurable in its own way as a dance-step, gradually mounting not in narrative interest but in compound interest, as it reaches towards the gratification of the climactic sum. It is almost the novel's last word.

But it is Fancy who has the last word in the novel, and the last dance. Whatever pleasure we take in *Under the Greenwood Tree* is largely a pleasure of deferral: we enjoy waiting upon an ending as inevitable as that of Leaf's story, just as the choir take a kind of communal pleasure in their last months, and Fancy lingers on in her triumphant maidenhood, putting off the inescapable wedding as long as possible. Courtship is given as her natural state: she is radiant and fulfilled – an angel, as Dick calls her so often. But to the men and women of the village (and the narrator) she looks decidedly less promising as a wife, and there are many hints that the otherworldly pleasures of courtship will soon enough pass to the cynical worldliness of marriage, the drudgery of conjugal obedience, the pains of childbirth and infant death, and the mediocrity of domestic life. In a memorable phrase that Hardy reworks from Wordsworth's 'She was a Phantom of Delight', Fancy is described by the narrator as 'less an angel than a woman', and she herself is alert to the scornful inflections in a man's praise of womanhood. In another borrowing from Wordsworth's poem, Dick calls her ' "You perfect woman" '; but she replies, ' "Yes; if you lay the stress on 'woman' " '. When she defines the nature of womanhood, therefore – ' "to love refinement of mind and manners" ' and ' "elegant and luxurious" ' surrounding – she is catching nicely the sense of her own passionate ambition and everyone else's sense of a woman's inevitably venal desires.[49] The nature of womanhood is conceived by the men of the novel, and the narrator, as something almost incomprehensible but also something grimly essential and material. There is no gainsaying it: a woman is a woman, and the plan of a woman's life, to return to Mill, is laid out for her. *Under the Greenwood Tree* expresses powerfully the sense of the inconsequentiality, almost the invisibility, of this grim material future that waits in hiding for Fancy, only faintly felt in the charged sexual atmosphere of courtship. Her choice of partners may be the last choice of any significance she makes, her last expression of individuality. Courtship is so delightful to Fancy because it is a stay against custom, an authorized resistance, a way of prolonging herself.

Of course she must give in and bring this happy period of courtship to a close, not least because it is the function of the romance plot to heal the damage done by the decimation of the choir: to provide the spring following that winter. But though social conflict has been successfully re-routed into sexual conflict, that must now be resolved, and its resolution marks the end of an epoch, for Fancy and for Hardy. Pastoral as post-ponement: herein lies the key to *Under the Greenwood Tree* and Hardy's insistence upon its status as a 'Novel of Environment'. As he later wrote in 'The Dorsetshire Labourer', 'it is among such communities as these that happiness will find her last refuge on earth, since it is among them that a perfect insight into the conditions of existence will be longest postponed'.[50] All of Hardy's great novels are essays in the postponement of perfect insight. It afflicts their protagonists and it shapes their narratives.

Fancy's acceptance of Maybold's unexpected marriage offer triggers the events that bring *Under the Greenwood Tree* to a close. This late romantic development is obviously far more problematic than the earlier and more prolonged flirtation with Shinar, for behind it, and now unnervingly close at hand, looms the spectre of her undistinguished afterlife as Dick's wife. Maybold promises a more glamorous future, but it is obvious to her almost immediately that she is not good enough for him, and, worse still, that she does not love him. As John Goode has pointed out, Dick and Fancy are not punningly named for no reason,[51] and during the courtship their relationship, and our interest, is sustained by considerable sexual tension. Readers of Hardy's later fiction recognize that such strong physical attraction leads only to entrapment, but this prospect is lightly passed off in *Under the Greenwood Tree*. Still, we are left feeling uncertain whether Fancy's wedding is a comic triumph or an ominous portent of her thwarted and injured life. Even the festive mood of the last chapter, which depicts the wedding celebrations spread out as ever under the fertile shade of the 'ancient beech-tree', is faintly mocked by the narrator. The symbolic greenwood tree has been home to generations of birds, 'tribes' of rabbits, and 'countless families of moles and earthworms', but the grass-plot under it, on which the wedding revels take place, is pointedly described as 'a healthy exercise-ground for young chicken and pheasants'. Meanwhile, 'the hens, their mothers' are 'enclosed in coops . . . upon the same green flooring'. The novel ends with the newlyweds disappearing into the distance through Wilderness Bottom, and Fancy's last word is perhaps wistful, but just as likely defiant: ' "O, 'tis the nightingale," murmured she, and thought of a secret she should never tell.' We think here, perhaps, of Tess's terrible secret, and understand Fancy's silence. So too, perhaps, do we applaud her final indifference to the old ways of the wood, the surest sign that she will go on resisting the cramping circularity of the pastoral mode, in which a woman's will is only errant and disruptive, bringing on the storms of winter and the end of all contentment until it is folded safely back into the community with the coming of spring and matrimony. We may suspect that Fancy will do just as she likes in her new life, but we look anxiously forward, to Bathsheba Everdene, Eustacia Vye and Sue Bridehead. Yet perhaps that is not really fair. After all, there is but one *Under the Greenwood Tree*.

Notes

1 Lionel Johnson, *The Art of Thomas Hardy* (1894; New York: Haskell House, 1966), p. 119.

2 Amiens's song ('Under the Greenwood Tree'), *As You Like It* (II, v, 7).

3 R. G. Cox (ed.), *Thomas Hardy: The Critical Heritage* (London: Routledge and Kegan Paul, 1970), p. 9.

4 For this edition Hardy grouped his fiction into three categories and appended a 'General Preface' in which he explained the distinction between the 'Novels of Character and Environment' (those that 'approach most nearly to uninfluenced works'), the 'Romances and Fantasies' (a 'sufficiently descriptive definition') and the 'Novels of Ingenuity' (the ' "Experiments" . . . written for the nonce simply').

5 David Cecil, *Hardy the Novelist: An Essay in Criticism* (London: Constable and Co., 1954), p. 31; Samuel C. Chew, *Thomas Hardy: Poet and Novelist* (New York: Alfred A. Knopf, 1928), p. 27; Harold Williams, 'The Wessex Novels of Thomas Hardy', in Cox (ed.), *Thomas Hardy: The Critical Heritage*, p. 422.

6 A. J. Butler, 'Mr. Hardy as a Decadent', in Cox (ed.), *Thomas Hardy: The Critical Heritage*, p. 285. 'To this day, *Under the Greenwood Tree* has been the best-loved if not the most highly regarded of Hardy's novels' (David Wright, Introduction to *Under the Greenwood Tree* [London: Penguin, 1978], p. 18). Havelock Ellis, writing in 1896, called it 'the most perfect and perhaps the most delightful of Mr. Hardy's early books' ('Concerning *Jude the Obscure*', in Cox [ed.], p. 304), a claim much repeated: see, for example, Peter J. Casagrande, *Unity in Hardy's Novels: 'Repetitive Symmetries'* (London: Macmillan, 1982), p. 81.

7 Wright, Introduction to *Under the Greenwood Tree* (1978), p. 17.

8 Joseph Warren Beach, *The Technique of Thomas Hardy* (1922; New York: Russell and Russell, 1962), p. 36.

9 Michael Millgate, *Thomas Hardy: His Career as a Novelist* (London: The Bodley Head, 1971), p. 50.

10 John Bayley, *An Essay on Hardy* (Cambridge: Cambridge University Press, 1978), pp. 10–11.

11 *Life*, 95.

12 Simon Gatrell suggests that 'The first two lines are cancelled, but they are written in such a way as to suggest the possibility that they were an afterthought of uncertain date, rather than the original first element in a composite title' (Introduction to *Under the Greenwood Tree* [Oxford: World's Classics, 1985], p. xi). In *Thomas Hardy and the Proper Study of Mankind* (Charlottesville: University Press of Virginia, 1993), p. 11, he amends 'possibility' to 'probability'.

13 Hardy to Macmillan and Co., 7 August 1871, *Collected Letters*, I, 11.

14 *Life*, 66.

15 17 August 1871, *Collected Letters*, I, 12.

16 On the influence of Crabbe's anti-pastoral poetry on Hardy, see note 1 to I, vii. On pastoral and anti-pastoral, see Raymond Williams, *The Country and the City* (London: Chatto and Windus, 1973).

17 'Poetical Matter' Notebook; quoted in Michael Millgate, *Thomas Hardy: A Biography* (Oxford: Oxford University Press, 1982), p. 34.

18 See the 'Schools of Painting' Notebook, in *Notebooks*.

19 On *Under the Greenwood Tree* as Victorian pastoral, see Lawrence Jones, '*Under the Greenwood Tree* and the Victorian Pastoral', in Colin Gibson (ed.), *Art and Society in the Victorian Novel: Essays on Dickens and His Contemporaries* (London: Macmillan, 1989), pp. 149–67.

20 The *Life* records a speech of Hardy's given before a dramatic performance of *Under the Greenwood Tree* in 1910, in which he remarks that 'tonight, at any rate, we will all be young and not look too deeply' (p. 381).

21 *Life*, 328.

22 Gatrell, Introduction to *Under the Greenwood Tree* (1985), p. xxiii.

23 *Life*, 474.

24 Geoffrey Grigson, Introduction to *Under the Greenwood Tree*, New Wessex Edition (London: Macmillan, 1974), p. 24.

25 Peter Casagrande argues that 'elements of disorder, implacable and immune to human means of remedy, are simply kept beneath the surface, though they threaten to break through at every turn' (*Unity in Hardy's Novels*, p. 85).

26 Cecil, *Hardy the Novelist*, p. 30.

27 Gatrell, *Thomas Hardy and the Proper Study of Mankind*, p. 17.

28 Simon Schama, *Landscape and Memory* (London: Harper Collins, 1995), p. 141.

29 The subtitle was not added to the novel until 1906, however.

30 Peter Brooker and Peter Widdowson, 'A Literature for England' in Robert Colls and Philip Dodd (eds.), *Englishness: Politics and Culture, 1880–1920* (London: Croom Helm, 1986), p. 120.

31 Schama, *Landscape and Memory*, p. 141. *Under the Greenwood Tree* was one of only ten books shipped around the world by the Carnegie Endowment for International Peace 'to introduce foreign-language readers to the Anglo-Saxon mind' on the eve of the Second World War. (Reported in Christopher Morley, 'The Bowling Green', *Saturday Review of Literature* [26 March 1938], p. 13. Curiously, the representative Shakespeare play on the list is *The Merchant of Venice*. Morley remarks that this choice 'might seem a little dubious, in some nations, as a textbook of pacification'.)

32 Millgate, *Thomas Hardy: His Career as a Novelist*, p. 51.

33 Williams, *The Country and the City*, p. 209.

34 Ibid., pp. 209–10. David Wright, for example, argues that the novel's main theme is 'the clash between agrarian and urban ways of life, between traditional rural culture and that of the new metropolitan déracinés' (Introduction to *Under the Greenwood Tree* [1978], p. 18).

35 John Goode, *Thomas Hardy: The Offensive Truth* (Oxford: Basil Blackwell, 1988), p. 12.

36 *Spectator*, xlv (2 November 1872), p. 1403.

37 *Journal of the English Folk Dance Society*, second series (1927), p. 54. Hardy refers vaguely to the 'ecclesiastical changes' that precipitated the end of the Stinsford choir in the *Life*. See Appendix IV.

38 Alun Howkins argues that 'attacks from inside and outside the church on latitudinarian theology, moral laxity, worldliness and above all pluralism had assumed an all-pervasive character' by the mid-century (*Reshaping Rural England: A Social History, 1850–1925* [London: Harper Collins, 1991], p. 67).

39 Howkins, *Reshaping Rural England*, p. 70. 'This is not to argue that they were radicals in a political or social sense, rather that they sought to re-establish certain kinds of paternal relationships within their villages which involved not only control but also the creation of positive identification of the interests of the rural poor with the established social order while stressing the naturalness and inevitability of "rank".'

40 Ibid., p. 72.

41 Williams, *The Country and the City*, p. 198.

42 Ibid.

43 In the *Life* Hardy quotes a notebook entry of 1 July 1868 in which he had named 'On Individuality' as one of his [c]ures for despair' (p. 59). Later he transcribes a 1906 letter to *The Times* in which he recalls seeing Mill on the hustings in 1865, and remarks that at that time 'we students' knew *On Liberty* 'almost by heart' (p. 355).

44 John Stuart Mill, *On Liberty* (London: 1867), p. 34.

45 Ibid.

46 Ibid. It is Sue Bridehead who quotes this passage to Phillotson in pleading for her freedom in *Jude the Obscure* (IV, iii).

47 Hardy also alludes to the song contest in the musicians' discussion on their Christmas Eve rounds of the relative merits of various instruments. The competition between Fancy and the choir to control the church music-making also invokes the song contest, of course.

48 Barbara Hardy, *Tellers and Listeners: The Narrative Imagination* (London: The Athlone Press, 1975), p. 205.

49 On Fancy's venality, see Patricia Ingham, *Thomas Hardy* (Hemel Hempstead: Harvester Wheatsheaf, 1989), pp. 29–30.

50 'The Dorsetshire Labourer', in Harold Orel (ed.), *Thomas Hardy's Personal Writings: Prefaces, Literary Opinions, Reminiscences* (New York: St Martin's Press, 1966), p. 169.

51 Goode, *Thomas Hardy: The Offensive Truth*, p. 12.

FURTHER READING

Danby, J. F., 'Under the Greenwood Tree', *Critical Quarterly* 1 (1959), pp. 5–13

Gatrell, Simon, *Hardy the Creator: A Textual Biography* (Oxford: Clarendon Press, 1988)

Goode, John, *Thomas Hardy: The Offensive Truth* (Oxford: Basil Blackwell, 1988)

Hardy, Barbara, '*Under the Greenwood Tree*: A Novel about the Imagination', in Anne Smith (ed.), *The Novels of Thomas Hardy* (London: Vision, 1979), pp. 45–57

Howard, Jeanne, 'Thomas Hardy's "Mellstock" and the Registrar General's Stinsford', *Literature and History* 6 (Autumn 1977), pp. 179–202

Ingham, Patricia, *Thomas Hardy* (Hemel Hempstead: Harvester Wheatsheaf, 1989)

Jones, Lawrence, '*Under the Greenwood Tree* and the Victorian Pastoral', in Colin Gibson (ed.), *Art and Society in the Victorian Novel: Essays on Dickens and his Contemporaries* (London: Macmillan, 1989), pp. 149–67.

Millgate, Michael, *Thomas Hardy: His Career as a Novelist* (London: The Bodley Head, 1971)

—*Thomas Hardy: A Biography* (Oxford: Oxford University Press, 1982)

Spector, Stephen J., 'Flights of Fancy: Characterization in Hardy's *Under the Greenwood Tree*', *ELH* 55 (1988), pp. 469–85

Tolliver, H. E., 'The Dance Under the Greenwood Tree: Hardy's Bucolics', *Nineteenth-Century Fiction* 17 (1962), pp. 57–68

This text of *Under the Greenwood Tree* is based on the two-volume first edition, published by Tinsley Brothers, London, in June 1872. It has been collated with the fair-copy manuscript (located in the Dorset County Museum, Dorchester); Tinsley's one-volume cheap edition of 1873; Osgood, McIlvaine's 1896 Wessex Novels edition (the first to be revised by Hardy); and the Macmillan 1912 Wessex Edition. The holograph emendations pencilled into Hardy's own study copy of this last edition (destined for the 1920 Mellstock Edition) have also been noted.

In addition, sample collations have been undertaken on Henry Holt's 1873 first American edition; later impressions and editions of Tinsley's 1873 edition, published under the imprint of Chatto and Windus, who acquired the copyright in 1877 and were still issuing the novel in the 1920s; and later impressions of the 1896 Osgood, McIlvaine edition, including the Harper and Brothers editions (current 1896–1900), the Macmillan Uniform Edition (current 1903–38), and Pocket Edition (current 1906–29).

Lastly, three editions published since Hardy's death have been consulted. Macmillan's New Wessex Edition, edited by Geoffrey Grigson (1974), and David Wright's Penguin English Library edition (1978) are both based on 1912 and incorporate Hardy's study-copy emendations. Simon Gatrell's Oxford World's Classics edition (1985), on the other hand, 'uses as its basis the manuscript of the novel, to which are made all the alterations which are probably or certainly Hardy's own' (p. xxiv).

To produce a correct and authoritative text based on 1872, typographical errors have been silently corrected and the use of ellipsis and the hyphenation of words (styles inconsistently adopted by the printers – see below) have been standardized. I have also made five substantive emendations: in I, iv, the manuscript 'High Stoy' was incorrectly set as 'High Story' which was not picked up by Hardy in proof; in the final paragraph of I, ix, I have added the definite article erroneously omitted from before 'Angel'; in II, iii, I have substituted a full stop for the question mark which appeared as a typographical error after 'on the subject of children'; in II, vi, the word 'steamed' was mistakenly set as 'streamed' in 1872, and is corrected here; and following Simon Gatrell's 1985 edition, I have reversed the names of the clocks in V, i (see note 4).

Discussed below are the manuscript, the 1872 edition, selected impressions and new editions, and the two major revised editions of 1896 and 1912. The substantial changes to the novel's topography in 1896 and 1912 are discussed in the Introduction and summarized in Appendix II. Other significant or interesting variants are dealt with in detail in the notes.

CHOICE OF COPY-TEXT

In general, this series chooses the first volume edition of Hardy's novels as copy-text (see the General Editor's Preface), and there is a particularly strong case for making the first edition of *Under the Greenwood Tree* available again. Most modern editions are based on the text last revised by Hardy (1912), but as Simon Gatrell has argued,

to call *Under the Greenwood Tree* a novel of 1872 . . . ought to mean amongst other things that the text embodies Hardy's intentions for his novel at that date – something that the 1912 version of the novel in some ways emphatically does not, since it has shed a number of the characteristics of 1872 and been wrapped in others of forty years later.[1]

The distinction between the novels of 1872 and 1912 is, however, complicated by the unique textual history of *Under the Greenwood Tree* during those forty years. This is the only book of Hardy's over which he retained no copyright control. In April 1872 he agreed to the sale of the copyright to the publisher William Tinsley, who had offered 'the sum of thirty pounds to be paid one month after publication'.[2] It was a decision he later deeply regretted for many reasons, not just because he signed away any profits, but also because Tinsley, and later Chatto and Windus, who purchased the copyright for £100 in 1877, were under no pressure from a popular author to lay out the considerable expense of publishing a new edition. Tinsley did propose that Hardy correct printer's errors when the new illustrated edition was being planned in 1875, but this was scarcely satisfactory to Hardy, who replied that he found no serious misprints, or anything that could be set right by slight changes such as you mention. But I do see many sentences that I should rewrite or revise, supposing I had an opportunity, & could thoroughly examine the book, & were not bound at all by the stereotype plates. If at any future time an edition from entirely new type should be desirable, this could be done of course, though at present I could not give it the necessary attention.[3]

This edition from 'entirely new type' did eventuate in 1892 when Chatto replaced the worn plates, but Hardy was apparently not consulted at this time. His chance came when Osgood, McIlvaine embarked on the first collected edition in 1894. Negotiations with Chatto resulted in a separate royalty agreement for this novel, and Hardy set about revising it for the first time in more than twenty years.

Hardy's revisions for this edition as a whole were meticulous and thorough, but finally quite conservative (especially when compared, for example, with the extent of Henry James's revisions for the New York Edition). Though 'much rewriting was done',[4] Hardy did not, in Michael Millgate's words, 'make any fundamental alterations to structure, story, characterization, or theme, nor attempt any shifts of emphasis beyond increasing or decreasing the use of dialect by certain characters'.[5] *Under the Greenwood Tree* was no exception. Printers' errors and earlier oversights were corrected, and Hardy finally attended to problems identified by the original reviewers in 1872.[6] As in the rest of the edition, however, his principal concern was to embed the novel in the fictional realm of Wessex (which he had not conceived in 1872 but 'independently introduced in successive novels and stories over the years').[7] Thus, the most numerous adjustments and refinements were made to the topography and dialect.

Whether Hardy was tempted at this time to undertake more sweeping changes to *Under the Greenwood Tree* is doubtful, given what we know about his approach to revision,[8] but he must have felt deeply ambivalent about the novel as he approached the difficult task. Since 1872 he had grown more interested in the Mellstock Quire, with its strong associations with his distant Stinsford childhood. Yet he had also become more and more dissatisfied with *Under the Greenwood Tree*, which remained exactly in the form he had written it as an ambitious young novelist. Unlike his other early books, it did not evolve through interim revisions between the first edition and the first collected edition during that crucial twenty-year period, and nothing short of a complete rewriting would have transformed it into the book that he now wished he had written. Such a project would have made unacceptable demands on a novelist intent on quitting fiction and, in any case, Chatto's versions of 1872 remained in print, and Hardy may have felt that he risked upsetting readers already devoted to the novel as it stood.

Recognizing that 'artistic errors ... cannot be altered',[9] Hardy developed other indirect ways of indicating his matured intentions for the novel. The topographical changes, for example, turn out to be very significant in this regard. The continuity they extend between this novel and the rest of Hardy's Wessex – a continuity achieved principally through consistent place-names and topographical orientations – serves in practice as an extremely effective reconceptualization of the novel, linking it to a number of important parallel texts in which Mellstock and its Quire *are* thoroughly overhauled. Hardy's principal 'revisions' of *Under the Greenwood Tree*, that is to say, were undertaken outside of, or on the margins of, the text: in the two Prefaces to the 1896 and 1912 editions (Appendix I); in key passages in the *Life* (Appendix IV); and in later appearances of the 'Mellstock Quire' poems (Appendix III). The Prefaces effaced (in 1896) and then openly discredited (in 1912) the 1872 version. In 1896, for example, *Under the Greenwood Tree* is described as 'a fairly true picture, at first hand' of 'orchestral bodies in the villages of fifty years ago'. But in 1912 Hardy rejects this strategy, projecting the novel in terms of its inadequacies ('the realities out of which it was spun were material for another kind of study'), while reinvesting it with the value that is bestowed on rare objects or extinct rituals, however imperfect. It is precious because it is 'the only extant' exhibition of the Mellstock Quire, 'except for the few glimpses ... in verse elsewhere'. The process of revision is indirectly continued in those 'glimpses', which appeared steadily in the volumes of poetry published throughout the last decades of his life. Later, too, in the *Life*, Hardy sketched in the rudiments of that 'other kind of study' he had in mind when he reconstructed the Mellstock choir on the model of its 'original', the Stinsford choir (see Appendix IV). These collateral emendations stress the personal and social significance of the passing of the Mellstock choir, and are the more poignant because as a young man Hardy had failed, as so many of his protagonists and speakers do, to recognize its significance. The 1872 edition, lost to his control when he sold the copyright, became the material reminder of this failure, representing to him a fraudulent past being remade as authentic over and over again.[10]

It is the purpose of this edition, therefore, to recover a text largely unread in 1872 (only 500 copies of the first edition were produced) yet very widely read subsequently, a text that is not just 'a novel of 1872' but one that circulated as a parallel text independently of its author's altered sense of its personal significance and its place in the emerging, and later entrenched, Wessex canon.

MANUSCRIPT

The surviving manuscript of *Under the Greenwood Tree*, described in detail in Purdy[11] and discussed at length in *Creator*,[12] has given rise to some controversy over Hardy's implied intentions regarding punctuation and paragraphing. The manuscript punctuation is conspicuously light, lending a liveliness and subtlety to the rhythms of the narration and the characters' speech; and it seems more so because of the slavish and stilted normalized accidentals of the first edition. The most common styling changes introduced by the compositors are as follows: paragraphs are divided or consolidated; manuscript colons are changed into semi-colons (where they are used in lists); Hardy's abundant dashes are commonly made over into exclamation points, commas, or semi-colons; many compound words written either as separate words or as one word are hyphenated, although not always consistently; and the manuscript 'further' becomes 'farther' (it is changed back in 1896).

It should be said, however, that the manuscript is not by any means carefully or consistently punctuated. Hardy regularly omits opening or closing speech marks, possessive apostrophes, and other punctuation marks, and is inconsistent in the use of commas. It is impossible, then, to decide with any finality whether he has simply left the pointing to the compositors or has deliberately used the lighter punctuation and for some reason let it stand when he corrected the proof-sheets. The truth may well lie somewhere between these two extremes. If the surviving manuscript is the fair copy, Hardy obviously expected the intervention of house-styling and possibly lacked the time or the confidence to challenge it when the proofs were returned for checking. Certainly the revisions for the 1912 edition include the substantial removal of unwanted commas, which indicates that the manuscript does to some degree represent Hardy's partiality for lighter pointing.[13]

Of significance too is the double numeration scheme Hardy employs in the manuscript. It is numbered 1–203 in the top right-hand corner, but consists of only 194 leaves: 'though the MS is complete as printed, many leaves are fragmentary and 9 are wanting altogether . . . suggesting extensive cancellations'.[14] The clue to the cancellations and reorganization of leaves and fragments of leaves can be found in the primary 'working numeration' scheme in the top left-hand corner of the manuscript. When correlated with the final numbering, we can surmise what Hardy removed, added and shifted as he worked on the story. As Gatrell argues, 'throughout Hardy's early writing of the novel, and even during his fair-copying of it, *Under the Greenwood Tree* was a narrative which focused almost entirely on the characters making up the Mellstock choir, and on the loss of their church music-making'.[15] But the manuscript Tinsley received was quite different: *Under the Greenwood Tree* had become a novel about the courtship of Dick Dewy and Fancy Day, in which the choir was shifted to the background to act as a kind of comic chorus. Considerable dialogue between members of the choir is cut out, and to Maybold's role as their nemesis is added the role of rival suitor for Fancy's hand. The modifications and insertions Hardy needed to make to earlier passages to prepare for this new plot element were considerable, but he manages the belated integration skilfully, making use of Shinar's role as suitor and (later) churchwarden to link the two plots whilst allowing them at the same time to run on as if placidly independent of one another.

What prompted Hardy to make these late changes? Probably it was the response of Macmillan's reader, John Morley, who read a version of the novel in October 1871, fully six months before Tinsley asked to see it. Morley had written favourably about the rural scenes in Hardy's first effort at fiction, *The Poor Man and the Lady*, which he read in 1868. Though Macmillan rejected that novel, which was never published, Morley wrote that 'the opening pictures of the Christmas eve in the Tranter's house are really of good quality; much of the writing is strong and fresh'.[16] Hardy accordingly worked these scenes up, lifting material directly from the *The Poor Man and the Lady* and incorporating it into the new rural story.[17] He must have been dismayed at Morley's response, three years after he submitted *The Poor Man*, to these very scenes: 'The opening scenes at the cottage on Xmas Eve are quite twice as long as they ought to be, because the writer has not enough sparkle and humour to pass off such minute and prolonged description of a trifle – *This part should decidedly be shortened*.'[18] The overall response of Macmillan, however, though indecisive, was quite favourable, and it is typical of Hardy's early willingness to respond positively to suggestions for change that he should have written to assure the firm that the scene could 'be shortened as suggested'.[19] Clearly, though, Morley's criticism and Macmillan's equivocation – the direct cause of that decision to alter the focus of the novel from the choir to the love-story which Hardy so bitterly regretted in later years – disappointed and angered him. Indeed, he recalled in the *Life* that he had more or less given up on *Under the Greenwood Tree* when Tinsley met him by chance in London and inquired after any new projects, Hardy claiming even to have forgotten where he had left the manuscript.

1872: TINSLEY BROTHERS

Hardy made a number of changes to the novel at proof-stage for the first edition, the most significant of which are discussed in the explanatory notes. These include the addition of the full text of the carol 'Remember Adam's Fall' (I, iv); the alteration of the slightly risqué 'Solomon's Song lay in Solomon's ink-bottle afore he got it out' to 'Old Ecclesiastes' (II, ii); the addition of several narrative clues to Fancy's real feelings for Dick in the critical scene where they declare their love in III, i; the description of Dick as a 'clever courter' in III, iii; an added clause explaining Fancy's distaste for Dick's rain-soaked figure in IV, vi; and the addition of the reference to Dick as his bride's property in V, i.

1873: TINSLEY BROTHERS

The corrections of the 1872 proofs were the last changes of Hardy's for twenty-three years, but in 1873 Tinsley produced the first reprint of the novel, a cheap one-volume edition. As Purdy and Gatrell note, the 1872 types were reset.[20] Typographical errors are corrected, though some substantive errors in 1872 ('Angel' not 'the Angel' in I, ix, for example) pass uncorrected, and in the process of resetting, other significant errors and changes to both substantives and accidentals are inevitably introduced. The most significant substantive changes occur in I, ii, in the description of the codlin-trees 'hanging above' (1872) the cottage (in 1873 and in all subsequent editions, they are 'hanging about'), and in IV, vi, when Fancy jumps to the floor from her window-seat as Maybold unexpectedly knocks, flinging off in the process 'the shawl and bonnet' (1872). In 1873 this is reset as 'her shawl and bonnet', which it remains. Of the numerous changes to accidentals in this edition, commas are removed and inserted in various places, and there are also other less predictable alterations to the punctuation.

MISCELLANEOUS EDITIONS AND IMPRESSIONS, 1873–92

The only editions of *Under the Greenwood Tree* to appear before Tinsley produced the illustrated 1876 edition (published Christmas 1875) were Asher's Collection of English Authors edition, published in Berlin in 1873,[21] and Henry Holt and Company's first American edition, published in June 1873. The latter was the first of Hardy's novels to appear in America, and the first anywhere to include his name on the title-page. There is no evidence, however, that Hardy revised *Under the Greenwood Tree* for Holt as he did *Desperate Remedies*, for example, in response to Holt's request in 1874.[22] Sample collations reveal only differences in normalized accidentals – punctuation, spelling and house-styling. (Interestingly, though, the copy of the Holt edition in the Sanders Collection in the Dorset County Museum is dated 1873 on its title-page, but includes an advertisement which lists *Far from the Madding Crowd* among other works 'By the Same Author', indicating that it is either a later impression or was bound from the original sheets after 1873.)

The 1876 illustrated Tinsley edition, with a frontispiece, thirteen plates and a closing vignette by R. Knight, became, under the Chatto and Windus imprint, the standard edition until 1896. In 1891 Chatto added a portrait of Hardy to the frontispiece, and in 1892 they reset the novel, introducing the substantive error, 'log-wood' for 'leg-wood' (I, iii).

1896: OSGOOD, MCILVAINE WESSEX NOVELS EDITION

The principal changes in 1896 were in four areas: topography, dialect, the social status of the principal characters, and the widening of the interval between the action and the narration. The topographical alterations are discussed in Appendix II. Changes to dialect can be divided into two kinds: those which correct villagers' speech considered too sophisticated by some reviewers in 1872 (including Horace Moule); and those which help to transform the generic pastoral of 1872 into a Wessexian pastoral by rendering some of the villagers' speech as Dorset dialect. Gatrell points out that 'about a hundred dialectal forms were added and nine removed' in 1896.[23]

Changes to social status are closely related to both of these two areas: the transformation of the Dewys' cottage, for example, discussed in I, ii, is linked with Hardy's wish to specify more precisely their social standing; and slight changes to the balance of standard and dialect English in the Dewys' speech, both in 1896 and 1912, effectively reveal the ambiguity of their position, which is neither that of the traditional village craftsman, such as Penny, nor that of a parvenu like Shinar. Critically, however, when Hardy tinkers with the Maybold love plot in 1896, he introduces an uncharacteristic element of dialect into Dick's speech (in IV, vii) to emphasize Maybold's social superiority.

Hardy also removed some of the more facetious observations of the narrator in 1896, in line with the general playing down of the comic grotesqueness of 1872, and in 1896 and 1912 he shifted the narration forward to coincide with the historical time of the revisions, so that the events of 'less than a generation ago' (1872) occur after 1896 only 'within living memory'. This distancing lends the novel a certain gravity and poignancy. In 1912, Hardy repeats this strategy: for example, the 'mixed midday meal of dinner and tea, which is common among cottagers' (in II, vi) becomes 'was common'; and the narrator finds it necessary to point out in IV, vi that silk umbrellas were 'less common at that date than since'.

The other major change for this edition is the renaming of IV, vii ('A Crisis') as 'Second Thoughts'.

MISCELLANEOUS EDITIONS AND IMPRESSIONS, 1898–1908

The Wessex Novels edition was published simultaneously in New York by Harper and Brothers, and when in 1898 Harper's took over Osgood, McIlvaine, this edition appeared in London under the Harper imprint.

Between 1903 and 1938, Macmillan issued under their own imprint impressions of the Osgood, McIlvaine/Harper edition, variously known as the 'New Edition', 'Uniform Edition' and 'Pocket Edition'. The Pocket Edition of 1906 was the first to bear the subtitle 'The Mellstock Quire'.

In 1907, meanwhile, Chatto and Windus produced a sixpenny edition, and in 1908 a 'fine paper' edition, both of them impressions from 1892.

1912: MACMILLAN WESSEX EDITION

Hardy's changes to 1912 fall into four groups: topographical refinements; further modifications of dialect; the reimposition of his distinctive 'lighter' punctuation (briefly considered above in the discussion of the manuscript); and the small number of significant changes which widen the interval between narration and narrated events (discussed under 1896 above).

Gatrell argues that in 1912, in contrast to 1896, Hardy 'standardized around a hundred and thirty-five dialect expressions and formulated no new ones'. In consequence, he suggests, 'though the upwardly mobile Keeper Day has his regional expression slightly diminished in 1912, so too does the tranter, and even Michael Mail; and no conclusions can be drawn about the relative social standing of the characters from this kind of evidence'.[24]

In 1912, the key word 'choir', spelled thus in 1872 and 1896, takes on the preferred spelling of the subtitle ('quire'). I,iii is accordingly renamed 'The Assembled Quire', and other examples of the standard spelling are changed in 1912.

As with other Wessex novels, bowdlerized oaths are restored in 1912: thus, 'D—l' in I,ii is printed as 'Devil'.

HARDY'S STUDY COPY OF 1912

Hardy marked seven further corrections in his personal study copy of the Wessex Edition of *Under the Greenwood Tree*, held in the Dorset County Museum. Five of these, written in pencil, 'are sent to be made in reprint of this edition'. Two others, written in green, are 'those that, in addition to the above, are sent up for the Mellstock edn, but were not considered of sufficient importance for type-shifting that they wd. necessitate'. Where these corrections are of particular importance or interest, they have been included in the Notes to this edition.

Notes

1 *Creator*, 221.

2 *Collected Letters*, I, 16.

3 Ibid., 39.

4 Purdy, 281.

5 Michael Millgate, *Testamentary Acts: Browning, Tennyson, James, Hardy* (Oxford: Clarendon Press, 1992), p. 13.

6 Hardy retained copies of early reviews, and would have been especially careful to incorporate suggestions originally made in the review written in 1872 by Horace Moule.

7 Millgate, *Testamentary Acts*, p. 112.

8 See Millgate, *Testamentary Acts*, pp. 110–38.

9 Hardy to Florence Henniker, 22 August 1911 (*Collected Letters*, IV, 168).

10 Sometime after 1896, for example, Hardy presented his sister Mary with a copy of the Osgood, McIlvaine edition of the novel (now in Dorset County Museum). On the title-page, between title and subtitle, Hardy carefully printed the words 'OR THE MELLSTOCK QUIRE' in neat block capitals formed to resemble the type that surrounds them. This curious private intervention of the author into the printed text emphasizes Hardy's wistful regret at not being in control of the novel.

11 Purdy, 6–7.

12 *Creator*, 7–14.

13 See also Simon Catrell, 'Hardy, House-Style, and the Aesthetics of Punctuation', in Anne Smith (ed.), *The Novels of Thomas Hardy* (London: Vision, 1979), pp. 169–92; and Robert Schweik and Michael Piret, 'Editing Hardy', *Browning Institute Studies* 9 (1981), pp. 15–41.

14 Purdy, 6–7.

15 *Creator*, 8.

16 Quoted in Charles Morgan, *The House of Macmillan 1843–1943* (London: Macmillan, 1943), pp. 87–8.

17 There is persuasive stylistic evidence that Hardy borrowed freely from *The Poor Man* in his early novels. See *Creator*, pp. 12–14; Pamela Dalziel, 'Exploiting the *Poor Man*: The Genesis of Hardy's *Desperate Remedies*', *Journal of English and Germanic Philology* 94 (1995), pp. 220–32. On the textual history of *An Indiscretion in the Life of an Heiress* and its origin in *The Poor Man*, see Pamela Dalziel's edition of Thomas Hardy, *The Excluded and Collaborative Stories* (Oxford: Clarendon Press, 1992), pp. 66–154.

18 Morgan, *House of Macmillan*, p. 97.

19 *Collected Letters*, I, 13.

20 Purdy, p. 8; Gatrell, Note on the Text to *Under the Greenwood Tree* (Oxford: World's Classics, 1985), p. xxv.

21 Tauchnitz also published English-language editions of Victorian novels and distributed them widely on the Continent, but they never published *Under the Greenwood Tree* because Chatto owned the copyright. No novel of Hardy's appeared in this edition until *The Hand of Ethelberta* (1876), after which Tauchnitz published virtually everything he wrote, usually a year or so after its English release. Hardy was a shrewd businessman and knew the value of these editions.

22 See the Note on the History of the Text to *Desperate Remedies*, ed. Mary Rimmer (London: Penguin, 1998).

23 *Creator*, 181. Examples include 'voot' for 'foot, 'ye' and ''ee' for 'you', 'sommat' for 'something', 'spak' for 'speak', 'onseemly' for 'unseemly', 'zeed' for 'seed', ''ooman' for 'woman', 'vlock' for 'flock', 'mid' for 'might', 'arrant' for 'errand', 'choked off' for 'finished off,' and 'thik gr't stone' for 'that large stone'. Mr Spinks's 'hev', for example, reverts to 'has' in 1912 (I, ii) and 'martel' reverts to 'mortal' in Tranter Dewy's speech in I, v. Mr Penny's 'quaint humorous' last in I, ii is 'queer natered' in 1896, but 'queer natured' in 1912; 'nate' is changed to 'neat', 'naibours' to 'neighbours', 'crater' to 'creature', 'tribble' to 'treble', 'shillens' to 'shillings', 'wimmen' to 'women', 'sich' to 'such', 'maning' to 'meaning', 'rale' to 'real', 'spak' to 'speak', and 'feymel' to 'female'.

24 Ibid.

UNDER THE

GREENWOOD TREE

A

Rural Painting of the Dutch School.

BY THE

AUTHOR OF 'DESPERATE REMEDIES.'

IN TWO VOLUMES.

VOL. I.

LONDON:

TINSLEY BROTHERS, 18 CATHERINE ST. STRAND.

1872.

CONTENTS

PART I: WINTER

PART II: SPRING

PART III: SUMMER

PART I

Winter

CHAPTER I

Mellstock-lane

To dwellers in a wood, almost every species of tree has its voice as well as its feature. At the passing of the breeze, the fir-trees sob and moan no less distinctly than they rock; the holly whistles as it battles with itself; the ash hisses amid its quiverings; the beech rustles while its flat boughs rise and fall. And winter, which modifies the note of such trees as shed their leaves, does not destroy its individuality.[1]

On a cold and starry Christmas-eve less than a generation ago,[2] a man was passing along a lane in the darkness of a plantation that whispered thus distinctively to his intelligence. All the evidences of his nature were those afforded by the spirit of his footsteps, which succeeded each other lightly and quickly, and by the liveliness of his voice as he sang in a rural cadence:

> 'With the rose and the lily
> And the daffodowndilly,
> The lads and the lasses a-sheep-shearing go.'[3]

The lonely lane he was following connected the hamlets of Mellstock and Lewgate, and to his eyes, casually glancing upward, the silver and black-stemmed birches with their characteristic tufts, the pale gray boughs of oak, the dark-creviced elm, all appeared now as black and flat outlines upon the sky, wherein the white stars twinkled so vehemently that their flickering seemed like the flapping of wings. Within the woody pass, at a level anything lower than the horizon, all was dark as the grave.[4] The copsewood forming the sides of the bower interlaced its branches so densely,[5] even at this season of the year, that the draught from the north-east flew along the channel with scarcely an interruption from lateral breezes.

At the termination of the wood, the white surface of the lane revealed itself between the dark hedgerows, like a ribbon jagged at the edges;[6] the irregularity being caused by temporary accumulations of leaves extending from the ditch on either side.

The song (many times interrupted by flitting thoughts which took the place of several bars, and resumed at a point it would have reached had its continuity been unbroken) now received a more palpable check, in the shape of 'Ho-i-i-i-i-i!' from the dark part of the lane in the rear of the singer, who had just emerged from the trees.

'Ho-i-i-i-i-i!' he answered with unconcern, stopping and looking round, though with no idea of seeing anything more than imagination pictured.

'Is that thee, young Dick Dewy?' came from the darkness.

'Ay, sure, Michael Mail!'

'Then why not stop for fellow-craters – going to thy own father's house too, as we be, and knowen us so well?'

Young Dick Dewy faced about and continued his tune in an under-whistle, implying that the business of his mouth could not be checked at a moment's notice by the placid emotion of friendship.

Having escaped both trees and hedge, he could now be distinctly seen rising against the sky, his profile appearing on the light background like the portrait of a gentleman in black cardboard.[7] It assumed the form of a low-crowned hat, an ordinary-shaped nose, an ordinary chin, an ordinary neck, and ordinary shoulders. What he consisted of farther down was invisible from lack of sky low enough to picture him on.

Shuffling, halting, irregular footsteps of various kinds were now heard, coming up the hill from the dark interior of the grove, and presently there emerged severally five men of different ages and gaits, all of them working villagers of the parish of Mellstock. They too had lost their rotundity with the daylight, and advanced against the sky in flat outlines, like some procession in Assyrian or Egyptian incised work.[8] They represented the chief portion of Mellstock parish choir.

The first was a bowed and bent man, who carried a fiddle under his arm, and walked as if engaged in studying some subject connected with the surface of the road. He was Michael Mail, the man who had hallooed to Dick.

The next was Mr. Robert Penny,[9] boot- and shoe-maker, a little man, who though rather round-shouldered, walked as if that fact had not come to his own knowledge, moving on with his back very hollow and his face fixed on the north quarter of the heavens before him, so that his lower waistcoat-buttons came first, and then the remainder of his figure. His features were invisible, yet when he occasionally looked round, two faint moons of light gleamed for an instant from the precincts of his eyes, denoting that he wore spectacles of a circular form.

The third was Elias Spinks, who walked perpendicularly and dramatically. The fourth outline was that of Joseph Bowman, who had now no distinctive appearance beyond that of a human being. Finally came a weak lath-like form, trotting and stumbling along with one shoulder forward and his head inclined to the left, his arms dangling nervelessly in the wind as if they were empty sleeves. This was Thomas Leaf.[10]

'Where be the boys?' said Dick to this somewhat indifferently-matched assembly.

The eldest of the group, Michael Mail, cleared his throat from a great depth.

'We told them to keep back at home for a time, thinken they wouldn't be wanted yet awhile; and we could choose the tuens, and so on.'

'Father and grandfather William have expected ye a little sooner. I have just been for a run to warm my feet.'

'To be sure father did! To be sure 'a did expect us – to taste the little barrel beyond compare that he's going to tap.'

''Od rabbit it all! Never heard a word of it!' said Mr. Penny, small gleams of delight appearing upon his spectacle-glasses, Dick meanwhile singing parenthetically,

'The lads and the lasses a-sheep-shearing go.'

'Neighbours, there's time enough to drink a sight of drink now afore bedtime,' said Mail.

'Trew, trew – time enough to get as drunk as lords!' replied Bowman cheerfully.

This argument being convincing, they all advanced between the varying hedges and the trees dotting them here and there, kicking their toes occasionally among the crumpled leaves. Soon appeared glimmering indications of the few cottages forming the small hamlet of Lewgate, for which they were bound, whilst the faint sound of church-bells ringing a Christmas peal could be heard floating over upon the breeze from the direction of Mintfield parish on the other side of the hills. A little wicket admitted them to a garden, and they proceeded up the path to Dick's house.

CHAPTER II

The Tranter's[1]

It was a small low cottage with a thatched pyramidal roof, and having dormer windows breaking up into the eaves, a single chimney standing in the very midst.[2] The window-shutters were not yet closed, and the fire- and candle-light within radiated forth upon the bushes of variegated box and thick laurestinus growing in a throng outside, and upon the bare boughs of several codlin-trees hanging above in various distorted shapes, the result of early training as espaliers, combined with careless climbing into their boughs in later years. The walls of the dwelling were for the most part covered with creepers, though these were rather beaten back from the doorway – a feature which was worn and scratched by much passing in and out, giving it by day the appearance of an old keyhole. Light streamed through the cracks and joints of a wooden shed at the end of the cottage, a sight which nourished a fancy that the purpose of the erection must be rather to veil bright attractions than to shelter unsightly necessaries. The noise of a beetle and wedges and the splintering of wood was periodically heard from this direction; and at the other end of the house a steady regular munching and the occasional scurr of a rope betokened a stable, and horses feeding within it.

The choir stamped severally on the doorstone to shake from their boots any fragment of dirt or leaf adhering thereto, then entered the house, and looked around to survey the condition of things. Through the open doorway of a small inner room on the left hand, of a character between pantry and cellar, was Dick Dewy's father, Reuben, by vocation a 'tranter,' or irregular carrier.[3] He was a stout florid man about forty years of age, who surveyed people up and down when first making their acquaintance, and generally smiled at the horizon or other distant object during conversations with friends,[4] walking about with a steady sway, and turning out his toes very considerably. Being now occupied in bending over a hogshead, that stood in the pantry ready horsed for the process of broaching, he did not take the trouble to turn or raise his eyes at the entry of his visitors, well knowing by their footsteps that they were the expected old acquaintance.

The main room, on the right, was decked with bunches of holly and other evergreens, and from the middle of the huge beam bisecting the ceiling hung the mistletoe, of a size out of all proportion to the room, and extending so low that it became necessary for a full-grown person to walk round it in passing, or run the risk of entangling his hair. This apartment contained Mrs. Dewy the tranter's wife, and the four remaining children, Susan, Jim, Bessy, and Charley, graduating uniformly though at wide stages from the age of sixteen to that of four years – the eldest of the series being separated from Dick the firstborn by a nearly equal interval.

Some circumstance having apparently caused much grief to Charley just previous to the entry of the choir, he had absently taken down a looking-glass, and was holding it before his face to see how the human countenance appeared when engaged in crying, which survey led him to pause at the various points in each wail that were more than ordinarily striking, for a more thorough appreciation of the general effect. Bessy was leaning against a chair, and glancing under the plaits about the waist of the plaid frock she wore, to notice the original unfaded pattern of the material as there preserved, her face bearing an expression of regret that the brightness had passed away from the visible portions.[5] Mrs. Dewy sat in a brown settle by the side of the glowing wood fire – so glowing that with a doubting compression of the lips she would now and then rise and put her hand upon the hams and flitches of bacon lining the chimney, to reassure herself that they were not being broiled instead of smoked, – a misfortune that had been known to happen at Christmas-time.

'Hullo, my sonnies, here you be, then!' said Reuben Dewy at length, standing up and blowing forth a vehement gust of breath. 'How the blood do puff up in anybody's head, to be sure, stooping like that! I was just coming athwart to hunt ye out.' He then carefully began to wind a strip of brown paper round a brass tap he held in his hand. 'This in the cask here is a drop o' the right sort' (tapping the cask); ''tis a real drop o' cordial from the best picked apples – Horner's and Cadbury's[6] – you d'mind the sort, Michael?' (Michael nodded.) 'And there's a sprinkling of they that grow down by the orchard-rails – streaked ones – rail apples we d'call 'em, as 'tis by the rails they grow, and not knowing the right name. The water-cider from 'em is as good as most people's best cider is.'

'Ay, and of the same make too,' said Bowman. 'It rained when we wrung it out, and the water got into it, folk will say. But 'tis on'y an excuse. Watered cider is too common among us.'

'Yes, yes; too common it is!' said Spinks with an inward sigh, whilst his eyes seemed to be looking at the world in an abstract form rather than at the scene before him.[7] 'Such poor liquor makes a man's throat feel very melancholy – and is a disgrace to the name of stimmilent.'

'Come in, come in, and draw up to the fire; never mind your shoes,' said Mrs. Dewy, seeing that all except Dick had paused to wipe them upon the door-mat. 'I be glad that you've stepped up-along at last; and, Susan, you run across to Gammer Caytes's and see if you can borrow some larger candles than these fourteens. Tommy Leaf, don't ye be afeard! Come and sit here in the settle.'

This was addressed to the young man before mentioned, consisting chiefly of a human skeleton and a smock-frock,[8] and who was very awkward in his movements, apparently on account of having grown so very fast, that before he had had time to get used to his height he was higher.

'Hee–hee–ay!' replied Leaf, letting his mouth continue to smile for some time after his mind had done smiling, so that his teeth remained in view as the most conspicuous members of his body.

'Here, Mr. Penny,' continued Mrs. Dewy, 'you sit in this chair. And how's your daughter, Mrs. Brownjohn?'[9]

'Well, I suppose I must say pretty fair,' adjusting his spectacles a quarter of an inch to the right. 'But she'll be worse before she's better, 'a b'lieve.'

'Indeed – poor soul! And how many will that make in all, four or five?'

'Five; they've buried three. Yes, five; and she no more than a maid yet.[10] However, 'twas to be, and none can gainsay it.'

Mrs. Dewy resigned Mr. Penny. 'Wonder where your grandfather James is?' she inquired of one of the children. 'He said he'd drop in to-night.'

'Out in fuel-house with grandfather William,' said Jimmy.

'Now let's see what we can do,' was heard spoken about this time by the tranter in a private voice to the barrel, beside which he had again established himself, and was stooping to cut away the cork.

'Reuben, don't make such a mess o' tapping that barrel as is mostly made in this house,' Mrs. Dewy cried from the fireplace. 'I'd tap a hundred without wasting more than you do in one. Such a squizzling and squirting job as 'tis in your hands. There, he always was such a clumsy man indoors.'

'Ay, ay; I know you'd tap a hundred, Ann – I know you would; two hundred, perhaps. But I can't promise. This is a old cask, and the wood's rotted away about the tap-hole. The husbird of a feller Sam Lawson –

that ever I should call'n such, now he's dead and gone, pore old heart! – took me in completely upon the feat of buying this cask. "Reub," says he – 'a always used to call me plain Reub, pore old heart! – "Reub," he said, says he, "that there cask, Reub, is as good as new; yes, good as new. 'Tis a wine-hogshead; the best port-wine in the commonwealth have been in that there cask; and you shall have en for ten shillens, Reub," – 'a said, says he – "he's worth twenty, ay, five-and-twenty, if he's worth one; and an iron hoop or two put round en among the wood ones will make en worth thirty shillens of any man's money, if – "'

'I think I should have used the eyes that Providence gave me to use afore I paid any ten shillens for a jimcrack wine-barrel; a saint is sinner enough not to be cheated. But 'tis like all your family were, so easy to be deceived.'

'That's as true as gospel of this member,' said Reuben.

Mrs. Dewy began a smile at the answer, then altering her lips and re-folding them so that it was not a smile, commenced smoothing little Bessy's hair; the tranter having meanwhile suddenly become oblivious to conversation, occupying himself in a deliberate cutting and arrangement of some more brown paper for the broaching operation.

'Ah, who can believe sellers!' said old Michael Mail in a carefully-cautious voice, by way of tiding over this critical point of affairs.

'No one at all,' said Joseph Bowman, in the tone of a man fully agreeing with everybody.

'Ay,' said Mail, in the tone of a man who did not agree with everybody as a rule, though he did now; 'I knowed an auctioneering feller once – a very friendly feller 'a was too. And so one day, as I was walking down the front street of Casterbridge,[11] I passed a shop-door and see him inside, stuck upon his perch, a-selling off. I jist nodded to en in a friendly way as I passed, and went my way, and thought no more about it. Well, next day, as I was oilen my boots by fuel-house door, if a letter didn't come wi' a bill in en, charging me with a feather-bed, bolster, and pillers, that I had bid for at Mr. Taylor's sale. The slim-faced martel had knocked 'em down to me because I nodded to en in my friendly way; and I had to pay for 'em too. Now, I hold that that was cutting it very close, Reuben?'

''Twas close, there's no denying,' said the general voice.

'Too close, 'twas,' said Reuben, in the rear of the rest. 'And as to Sam Lawson – pore heart! now he's dead and gone too! – I'll warrant, that if so be I've spent one hour in making hoops for that barrel, I've spent fifty, first and last. That's one of my hoops' – touching it with his elbow – 'that's one of mine, and that, and that, and all these.'

'Ah, Sam was a man!' said Mr. Penny, looking contemplatively at a small stool.

'Sam was!' said Bowman, shaking his head twice.

'Especially for a drap o' drink,' said the tranter.

'Good, but not religious-good,' suggested Mr. Penny.

The tranter nodded. Having at last made the tap and hole quite ready, 'Now then, Suze, bring a mug,' he said. 'Here's luck to us, my sonnies!'

The tap went in, and the cider immediately squirted out in a horizontal shower over Reuben's hands, knees, and leggings, and into the eyes and neck of Charley, who, having temporarily put off his grief under pressure of more interesting proceedings, was squatting down and blinking near his father.

'There 'tis again!' said Mrs. Dewy.

'D—l take the hole, the cask, and Sam Lawson too, that good cider should be wasted like this!' exclaimed the tranter excitedly. 'Your thumb! Lend me your thumb, Michael! Ram it in here, Michael! I must get a bigger tap, my sonnies.'

'Idd it cold inthide te hole?' inquired Charley of Michael, as he continued in a stooping posture with his thumb in the cork-hole.

'What wonderful odds and ends that chiel has in his head to be sure!' Mrs. Dewy admiringly exclaimed from the distance. 'I lay a wager that he cares more about the climate inside that barrel than in all the other parts of the world put together.'

All persons present put on a speaking countenance of admiration for the cleverness alluded to, in the midst of which Reuben returned. The operation was then satisfactorily performed; when Michael arose, and stretched his head to the extremest fraction of height that his body would allow of, to restraighten his bent back and shoulders – thrusting out his arms and twisting his features to a mere mass of wrinkles at the same time, to emphasise the relief acquired. A quart or two of the beverage was then brought to table, at which all the new arrivals reseated themselves with wide-spread knees, their eyes meditatively seeking out with excruciating precision[12] any small speck or knot in the table upon which the gaze might precipitate itself.

'Whatever is father a-biding out in fuel-house so long for?' said the tranter. 'Never such a man as father for two things – cleaving up old dead apple-tree wood and playing the bass-viol.[13] 'A'd pass his life between the two, that 'a would.' He stepped to the door and opened it.

'Father!'

'Ay!' rang thinly from round the corner.

'Here's the barrel tapped, and we all a-waiting!'

A series of dull thuds, that had been heard through the chimney-back for some time past, now ceased; and after the light of a lantern had passed the window and made wheeling rays upon the ceiling inside, the eldest of the Dewy family appeared.

CHAPTER III

The Assembled Choir[1]

William Dewy – otherwise grandfather William – was now about seventy; yet an ardent vitality still preserved a warm and roughened bloom upon his face, which reminded gardeners of the sunny side of a ripe ribstone-pippin; though a narrow strip of forehead, that was protected from the weather by lying above the line of his hat-brim, seemed to belong to some town man, so gentlemanly was its whiteness. His was a humorous and gentle nature, not unmixed with a frequent melancholy; and he had a firm religious faith. But to his neighbours he had no character in particular. If they saw him pass by their windows when they had been bottling off old mead, or when they had just been called long-headed men who might do anything in the world if they chose, they thought concerning him, 'Ah, there's that good-hearted man – open as a child!' If they saw him just after losing a shilling or half-a-crown, or accidentally letting fall a piece of crockery, they thought, 'There's that poor weak-minded man Dewy again! Ah, he'll never do much in the world either!' If he passed when fortune neither smiled nor frowned on them, they merely thought him old William Dewy.[2]

'Ah so's – here you be! – Ah, Michael and Joseph and John[3] – and you too, Leaf! a merry Christmas all! We shall have a rare leg-wood[4] fire directly, Reub, if it d'go by the toughness of the job I had in cleaving 'em.' As he spoke he threw down an armful of logs, which fell in the chimney-corner with a rumble, and looked at them with something of the admiring enmity he would have bestowed on living people who had been very obstinate in holding their own. 'Come in, grandfather James.'

Old James (grandfather on the maternal side) had simply called as a visitor. He lived in a cottage by himself, and many people considered him a miser: some, rather slovenly in his habits. He now came forward from behind grandfather William, and his stooping figure formed a well-illuminated picture⁵ as he passed towards the fireplace. Being by trade a mason, he wore a long linen apron reaching almost to his toes, corduroy breeches and gaiters, which, together with his boots, graduated in tints of whitish-brown by constant friction against lime and stone. He also wore a very stiff fustian coat, having folds at the elbows and shoulders as unvarying in their arrangement as those in a pair of bellows: the ridges and the projecting parts of the coat collectively exhibiting a shade different from that of the hollows, which were lined with small ditch-like accumulations of stone and mortar-dust. The extremely large side pockets, sheltered beneath wide flaps, bulged out convexly whether empty or full; and as he was often engaged to work at buildings far away – his breakfasts and dinners being eaten in a strange chimney-corner, by a garden wall, on a heap of stones, or walking along the road – he carried in these pockets a small tin canister of butter, a small canister of sugar, a small canister of tea, a paper of salt, and a paper of pepper: the bread, cheese, and meat, forming the substance of his meals, hanging up behind him in his basket among the hammers and chisels. If a passer-by looked hard at him when he was drawing forth any of these, – 'My larders,' he said, with a pinched smile.

'Better try over number seventy-eight before we start, I suppose?' said William, pointing to a heap of old Christmas-carol books on a side table.⁶

'Wi' all my heart,' said the choir generally.

'Number seventy-eight was always a teaser – always. I can mind him ever since I was growing up a hard boy-chap.'

'But he's a good tune, and worth a mint o' practice,' said Michael.

'He is; though I've been mad enough wi' that tune at times to seize en and tear en all to linnet. Ay, he's a splendid carrel – there's no denying that.'

'The first line is well enough,' said Mr. Spinks; 'but when you come to "O, thou man," you make a mess o't.'

'We'll have another go into en, and see what we can make of the martel.

Half an hour's hammering at en will conquer the toughness of en; I'll warn it.'

''Od rabbit it all!' said Mr. Penny, interrupting with a flash of his spectacles, and at the same time clawing at something in the depths of a large side pocket. 'If so be I hadn't been as scatter-brained and thirtingill as a chiel, I should have called at the school-house wi' a boot as I cam up-along. Whatever is coming to me I really can't estimate at all!'

'The brain hev its weaknesses,' murmured Mr. Spinks, waving his head ominously.[7]

'Well, I must call with en the first thing to-morrow. And I'll empt my pocket o' this last too, if you don't mind, Mrs. Dewy.' He drew forth a last, and placed it on a table at his' elbow. The eyes of three or four followed it.

'Well,' said the shoe-maker, seeming to perceive that the sum-total of interest the object had excited was greater than he had anticipated, and warranted the last's being taken up again and exhibited, 'now, whose foot do ye suppose this last was made for? It was made for Geoffrey Day's father, over at Yalbury Wood. Ah, many's the pair o' boots he've had off the last! Well, when 'a died, I used the last for Geoffrey, and have ever since, though a little doctoring was wanted to make it do. Yes, a very quaint humorous last it is now, 'a b'lieve,' he continued, turning it over caressingly. 'Now, you notice that there' (pointing to a lump of leather bradded to the toe) – 'that's a very bad bunion that he've had ever since 'a was a boy. Now, this remarkable large piece' (pointing to a patch nailed to the side) 'shows an accident he received by the tread of a horse, that squashed his foot a'most to a pomace. The horseshoe cam full-butt on this point, you see. And so I've just been over to Geoffrey's, to know if he wanted his bunion altered or made bigger in the new pair I'm making.'

During the latter part of this speech, Mr. Penny's left hand wandered towards the cider-cup, as if the hand had no connection with the person speaking; and bringing his sentence to an abrupt close, all but the extreme margin of the boot-maker's face was eclipsed by the circular brim of the vessel.

'However, I was going to say,' continued Penny, putting down the cup, 'I ought to have called at the school' – here he went groping again in the depths of his pocket – 'to leave this without fail, though I suppose the first thing to-morrow will do.' ·

He now drew forth and placed upon the table a boot – small, light, and prettily shaped – upon the heel of which he had been operating. 'The new schoolmistress's!'[8]

'Ay, no less; Miss Fancy Day: as nate a little figure of fun[9] as ever I see, and just husband-high.'

'Never Geoffrey's daughter Fancy?' said Bowman, as all glances present converged like wheel-spokes upon the boot in the centre of them.

'Yes, sure,' resumed Mr. Penny, regarding the boot as if that alone were his auditor; ''tis she that's come here schoolmistress. You knowed his daughter was in training?'

'Strange, isn't it, for her to be here Christmas-night, Master Penny?'

'Yes; but here she is, 'a b'lieve.'

'I know how she d'come here – so I do!' chirruped one of the children.

'Why?' Dick inquired, with subtle interest.

'Parson Maybold was afraid he couldn't manage us all to-morrow at the dinner, and he talked o' getting her jist to come over and help him hand about the plates, and see we didn't make beasts of ourselves; and that's what she's come for!'

'And that's the boot, then,' continued its mender imaginatively, 'that she'll walk to church in to-morrow morning. I don't care to mend boots I don't make; but there's no knowing what it may lead to, and her father always comes to me.'

There, between the cider-mug and the candle, stood this interesting receptacle of the little unknown's foot; and a very pretty boot it was. A character, in fact – the flexible bend at the instep, the rounded localities of the small nestling toes, scratches from careless scampers now forgotten – all, as repeated in the tell-tale leather, evidencing a nature and a bias.[10] Dick surveyed it with a delicate feeling that he had no right to do so without having first asked the owner of the foot's permission.

'Now, naibours, though no common eye can see it,' the shoe-maker went on, 'a man in the trade can see the likeness between this boot and that last, although that is so deformed as hardly to be called one of God's creatures, and this is one of as pretty a pair as you'd get for ten-and-sixpence in Casterbridge. To you, nothing; but 'tis father's foot and daughter's foot to me, as plain as houses.'

'I don't doubt there's a likeness, Master Penny – a mild likeness – a far-remote likeness – still, a likeness as far as that goes,' said Spinks. 'But *I* haven't imagination enough to see it, perhaps.'[11]

Mr. Penny adjusted his spectacles.

'Now, I'll tell you what happened to me once on this very point. You used to know Johnson the dairyman, William?'

'Ay, sure; that I did.'

'Well, 'twasn't opposite his house, but a little lower down – by his pigsty, in front o' Parkmaze Pool. I was a-walking down the lane, and lo and behold, there was a man just brought out o' the Pool, dead; he had been bathing, and gone in flop over his head. Men looked at en; women looked at en; children looked at en; nobody knowed en. He was covered in a cloth; but I catched sight of his foot, just showing out as they carried en along. "I don't care what name that man went by," I said, in my bold way, "but he's John Woodward's brother; I can swear to the family foot." At that very moment, up comes John Woodward, weeping and crying, "I've lost my brother! I've lost my brother!"'

'Only to think of that!' said Mrs. Dewy.

''Tis well enough to know this foot and that foot,' said Mr. Spinks. ''Tis something, in fact, as far as that goes. I know little, 'tis true – I say no more; but show *me* a man's foot, and I'll tell you that man's heart.'

'You must be a cleverer feller, then, than mankind in jineral,' said the tranter.

'Well, that's nothing for me to speak of,' returned Mr. Spinks solemnly. 'A man acquires. Maybe I've read a leaf or two in my time. I don't wish to say anything large, mind you; but nevertheless, maybe I have.'

'Yes, I know,' said Michael soothingly, 'and all the parish knows, that ye've read something of everything almost. Learning's a worthy thing, and ye've got it, Master Spinks.'

'I make no boast, though I may have read and thought a little; and I know – it may be from much perusing,[12] but I make no boast – that by the time a man's head is finished, 'tis almost time for him to creep underground. I am over forty-five.'

Mr. Spinks emitted a look to signify that if his head was not finished, nobody's head ever could be.

'Talk of knowing people by their feet!' said Reuben. 'Rot me, my sonnies, then, if I can tell what a man is from all his members put together, oftentimes.'

'But still, look is a good deal,' observed grandfather William absently, moving and balancing his head till the tip of grandfather James's nose was exactly in a right line with William's eye and the mouth of a miniature cavern he was discerning in the fire.[13] 'By the way,' he continued in a fresher voice, and looking up, 'that young crater, the schoolmistress, must be sung to to-night wi' the rest? If her ear is as fine as her face, we shall have enough to do to be up-sides with her.'

'What about her face?' said young Dewy.

'Well, as to that,' Mr. Spinks replied, ''tis a face you can hardly gainsay. A very good face – and a pink face, as far as that goes. Still, only a face, when all is said and done.'

'Come, come, Elias Spinks, say she's a pretty maid, and have done wi' her,' said the tranter, again preparing to visit the cider-barrel.

CHAPTER IV

Going the Rounds[1]

Shortly after ten o'clock, the singing-boys arrived at the tranter's house, which was invariably the place of meeting, and preparations were made for the start. The older men and musicians wore thick coats, with stiff perpendicular collars, and coloured handkerchiefs wound round and round the neck till the end came to hand, over all which they just showed their ears and noses, like people looking over a wall. The remainder, stalwart ruddy men and boys, were mainly dressed in snow-white smock-frocks, embroidered upon the shoulders and breasts, in ornamental forms of hearts, diamonds, and zigzags.[2] The cider-mug was emptied for the ninth time, the music-books were arranged, and the pieces finally decided upon. The boys in the mean time put the old horn-lanterns in order, cut candles into short lengths to fit the lanterns; and a thin fleece of snow having fallen since the early part of the evening, those who had no leggings went to the stable and wound wisps of hay round their ankles to keep the insidious flakes from the interior of their boots.

Mellstock was a parish of considerable acreage, the hamlets composing it lying at a much greater distance from each other than is ordinarily the case. Hence several hours were consumed in playing and singing within hearing of every family, even if but a single air were bestowed on each. There was East Mellstock, the main village; half a mile from this were the church and the vicarage, called West Mellstock, and originally the most thickly-populated portion. A mile north-east lay the hamlet of Lewgate, where the tranter lived; and at other points knots of cottages, besides solitary farmsteads and dairies.

Old William Dewy, with the violoncello, played the bass; his grandson Dick the treble violin; and Reuben and Michael Mail the tenor and second violins[3] respectively. The singers consisted of four men and seven boys, upon whom devolved the task of carrying and attending to the lanterns, and holding the books open for the players. Directly music was the theme, old William ever and instinctively came to the front.

'Now mind, naibours,' he said, as they all went out one by one at the door, he himself holding it ajar and regarding them with a critical face as they passed, like a shepherd counting out his sheep. 'You two counter-boys, keep your ears open to Michael's fingering, and don't ye go straying into the treble part along o' Dick and his set, as ye did last year; and mind this especially when we be in "Arise, and hail." Billy Chimlen, don't you sing quite so raving mad as you fain would; and, all o' ye, whatever ye do, keep from making a great scuffle on the ground when we go in at people's gates; but go quietly, so as to strik' up all of a sudden, like spirits.'

'Farmer Ledlow's first?'

'Farmer Ledlow's first; the rest as usual.'

'And, Voss,'[4] said the tranter terminatively, 'you keep house here till about half-past two; then heat the metheglin and cider in the warmer you'll find turned up upon the copper; and bring it wi' the victuals to church-porch, as th'st know.'

Just before the clock struck twelve, they lighted the lanterns and started. The moon, in her third quarter, had risen since the snow-storm; but the dense accumulation of snow-cloud weakened her power to a faint twilight, which was rather pervasive of the landscape than traceable to the sky. The breeze had gone down, and the rustle of their feet, and tones of their speech, echoed with an alert rebound from every post, boundary-stone, and ancient wall they passed, even where the distance of the echo's origin was less than a few yards. Beyond their own slight noises nothing was to be heard, save the occasional howl of foxes in the direction of Yalbury Wood, or the brush of a rabbit among the grass now and then, as it scampered out of their way.

Most of the outlying homesteads and hamlets had been visited by about two o'clock: they then passed across the Home Plantation toward the main village. Pursuing no recognised track, great care was necessary in walking lest their faces should come in contact with the low-hanging boughs of the old trees, which in many spots formed dense overgrowths of interlaced branches.

'Times have changed from the times they used to be,' said Mail, regarding nobody can tell what interesting old panoramas with an inward eye, and letting his outward glance rest on the ground, because it was as convenient a position as any. 'People don't care much about us now! I've been thinking, we must be almost the last left in the county of the old string players. Barrel-organs, and they next door to 'em that you blow wi' your foot,[5] have come in terribly of late years.'

'Ah!' said Bowman, shaking his head; and old William, on seeing him, did the same thing.

'More's the pity,' replied another. 'Time was – long and merry ago now! – when not one of the varmits was to be heard of; but it served some of the choirs right. They should have stuck to strings as we did, and keep out clar'nets, and done away with serpents. If you'd thrive in musical religion,[6] stick to strings, says I.'

'Strings are well enough, as far as that goes,' said Mr. Spinks.

'There's worse things than serpents,' said Mr. Penny. 'Old things pass away, 'tis true; but a serpent was a good old note: a deep rich note was the serpent.'

'Clar'nets, however, be bad at all times,'[7] said Michael Mail. 'One Christmas – years agone now, years – I went the rounds wi' the Dibbeach[8] choir. 'Twas a hard frosty night, and the keys of all the clar'nets froze – ah, they did freeze! – so that 'twas like drawing a cork every time a key was opened; the players o' 'em had to go into a hedger and ditcher's chimley-corner, and thaw their clar'nets every now and then. An icicle o' spet hung down from the end of every man's clar'net a span long; and as to fingers – well, there, if ye'll believe me, we had no fingers at all, to our knowledge.'

'I can well bring back to my mind,' said Mr. Penny, 'what I said to poor Joseph Ryme (who took the tribble part in High-Stoy Church[9] for two-and-forty year) when they thought of having clar'nets there. "Joseph," I said, says I, "depend upon't, if so be you have them tooting clar'nets you'll spoil the whole set-out. Clar'nets were not made for the service of Providence; you can see it by looking at 'em," I said. And what cam o't? Why, my dear souls, the parson set up a barrel-organ on his own account within two years o' the time I spoke, and the old choir went to nothing.'

'As far as look is concerned,' said the tranter, 'I don't for my part see that a fiddle is much nearer heaven than a clar'net. 'Tis farther off. There's always a rakish, scampish countenance about a fiddle that seems to say the Wicked One had a hand in making o'en; while angels be supposed to play clar'nets in heaven, or som'at like 'em, if ye may believe picters.'

'Robert Penny, you were in the right,' broke in the eldest Dewy. 'They should ha' stuck to strings. Your brass-man, is brass – well and good; your reed-man, is reed – well and good; your percussion-man, is percussion – good again.[10] But I don't care who hears me say it, nothing will speak to your heart wi' the sweetness of the man of strings!'

'Strings for ever!' said little Jimmy.

'Strings alone would have held their ground against all the new comers in creation.' ('True, true!' said Bowman.) 'But clar'nets was death.' ('Death they was!' said Mr. Penny.) 'And harmoniums,'[11] William continued in a louder voice, and getting excited by these signs of approval, 'harmoniums and barrel-organs' ('Ah!' and groans from Spinks) 'be miserable – what shall I call 'em? – miserable –'

'Sinners,' suggested Jimmy, who made large strides like the men, and did not lag behind like the other little boys.

'Miserable machines for such a divine thing as music!'[12]

'Right, William, and so they be!' said the choir with earnest unanimity.

By this time they were crossing to a wicket in the direction of the school, which, standing on a slight eminence on the opposite side of a cross lane, now rose in unvarying and dark flatness against the sky. The instruments were retuned, and all the band entered the enclosure, enjoined by old William to keep upon the grass.

'Number seventy-eight,' he softly gave out as they formed round in a semicircle, the boys opening the lanterns to get a clearer light,[13] and directing their rays on the books.

Then passed forth into the quiet night an ancient and well-worn hymn, embodying Christianity in words peculiarly befitting the simple and honest hearts of the quaint characters who sang them so earnestly.[14]

'Remember Adam's fall,
  O thou man:
Remember Adam's fall
  From Heaven to Hell.

Remember Adam's fall;
How he hath condemn'd all
In Hell perpetual
    Therefore to dwell.

Remember God's goodnesse,
    O thou man:
Remember God's goodnesse,
    His promise made.
Remember God's goodnesse;
He sent his Son sinlesse
Our ails for to redress,
    Our hearts to aid.

In Bethlehem he was born,
    O thou man:
In Bethlehem he was born,
    For mankind's sake.
In Bethlehem he was born,
Christmas-day i' the morn:
Our Saviour did not scorn
    Our faults to take.

Give thanks to God alway,
    O thou man:
Give thanks to God alway
    With heart-felt joy.
Give thanks to God alway
On this our joyful day:
Let all men sing and say,
    Holy, Holy!'

Having concluded the last note, they listened for a minute or two, but found that no sound issued from the school-house.

'Forty breaths, and then, "O, what unbounded goodness!" number fifty-nine,' said William.[15]

This was duly gone through, and no notice whatever seemed to be taken of the performance.

'Surely 'tisn't an empty house, as befell us in the year thirty-nine and forty-three!'[16] said old Dewy, with much disappointment.

'Perhaps she's jist come from some noble city, and sneers at our doings,' the tranter whispered.

''Od rabbit her!' said Mr. Penny, with an annihilating look at a corner of the school chimney, 'I don't quite stomach her, if this is it. Your plain music well done is as worthy as your other sort done bad, a' b'lieve souls; so say I.'

'Forty breaths, and then the last,' said the leader authoritatively. ' "Rejoice, ye tenants of the earth," number sixty-four.'

At the close, waiting yet another minute, he said in a clear loud voice, as he had said in the village at that hour and season for the previous forty years:

'A merry Christmas to ye!'

CHAPTER V

The Listeners[1]

When the expectant stillness consequent upon the exclamation had nearly died out of them all, an increasing light made itself visible in one of the windows of the upper floor. It came so close to the blind that the exact position of the flame could be perceived from the outside. Remaining steady for an instant, the blind went upward from before it, revealing to thirty concentrated eyes a young girl, framed as a picture by the window-architrave, and unconsciously illuminating her countenance to a vivid brightness by a candle she held in her left hand, close to her face, her right hand being extended to the side of the window. She was wrapped in a white robe of some kind, whilst down her shoulders fell a twining profusion of marvellously rich hair, in a wild disorder which proclaimed it to be only during the invisible hours of the night that such a condition was discoverable. Her bright eyes were looking into the gray world outside with an uncertain expression, oscillating between courage and shyness, which, as she recognised the semicircular group of dark forms gathered before her, transformed itself into pleasant resolution.

Opening the window, she said lightly and warmly:

'Thank you, singers, thank you!'

Together went the window quickly and quietly, and the blind started downward on its return to its place. Her fair forehead and eyes vanished; her little mouth; her neck and shoulders; all of her. Then the spot of candlelight shone nebulously as before; then it moved away.

'How pretty!' exclaimed Dick Dewy.

'If she'd been rale wexwork she couldn't ha' been comelier,' said Michael Mail.

'As near a thing to a spiritual vision as ever I wish to see!' said tranter Dewy fervently.

'O, sich I never, never see!' said Leaf.

All the rest, after clearing their throats and adjusting their hats, agreed that such a sight was worth singing for.

'Now to Farmer Shinar's,² and then replenish our insides, father,' said the tranter.

'Wi' all my heart,' said old William, shouldering his bass-viol.

Farmer Shinar's was a queer lump of a house, standing at the corner of a lane that ran obliquely into the principal thoroughfare. The upper windows were much wider than they were high, and this feature, together with a broad bay-window where the door might have been expected, gave it by day the aspect of a human countenance turned askance, and wearing a sly and wicked leer. To-night nothing was visible but the outline of the roof upon the sky.

The front of this building was reached, and the preliminaries arranged as usual.

'Forty breaths, and number thirty-two, – "Behold the morning star,"' said old William.

They had reached the end of the second verse, and the fiddlers were doing the up bow-stroke previously to pouring forth the opening chord of the third verse, when, without a light appearing or any signal being given, a roaring voice exclaimed:

'Shut up! Don't make your blaring row here. A feller wi' a headache enough to split likes a quiet night.'

Slam went the window.

'Hullo, that's an ugly blow for we artists!' said the tranter, in a keenly appreciative voice, and turning to his companions.

'Finish the carrel, all who be friends of harmony!' said old William commandingly; and they continued to the end.

'Forty breaths, and number nineteen!' said William firmly. 'Give it him well; the choir can't be insulted in this manner!'

A light now flashed into existence, the window opened, and the farmer stood revealed as one in a terrific passion.

'Drown en! – drown en!' the tranter cried, fiddling frantically. 'Play fortissimy, and drown his spaking!'

'Fortissimy!' said Michael Mail, and the music and singing waxed so loud that it was impossible to know what Mr. Shinar had said, was saying, or was about to say; but wildly flinging his arms and body about in the form of capital Xs and Ys, he appeared to utter enough invectives to consign the whole parish to perdition.

'Very unseemly – very!' said old William, as they retired. 'Never such a dreadful scene in the whole round o' my carrel practice – never! And he a churchwarden!'[3]

'Only a drap o' drink got into his head,' said the tranter. 'Man's well enough when he's in his religious frame. He's in his worldly frame now. Must ask en to our bit of a party to-morrer night, I suppose, and so put en in track again. We bear no martel man ill-will.'

They now crossed Twenty-acres to proceed to the lower village, and met Voss with the hot mead and bread-and-cheese as they were crossing the churchyard. This determined them to eat and drink before proceeding farther, and they entered the belfry. The lanterns were opened, and the whole body sat round against the walls on benches and whatever else was available, and made a hearty meal. In the pauses of conversation could be heard through the floor overhead a little world of undertones and creaks from the halting clockwork, which never spread farther than the tower they were born in, and raised in the more meditative minds a fancy that here lay the direct pathway of Time.

Having done eating and drinking, the instruments were again tuned, and once more the party emerged into the night air.

'Where's Dick?' said old Dewy.

Every man looked round upon every other man, as if Dick might have been transmuted into one or the other; and then they said they didn't know.

'Well now, that's what I call very nasty of Master Dicky, that I do so,' said Michael Mail.

'He've clinked off home-along, depend upon't,' another suggested, though not quite believing that he had.

'Dick!' exclaimed the tranter, and his voice rolled sonorously forth among the yews.

He suspended his muscles rigid as stone whilst listening for an answer, and finding he listened in vain, turned to the assemblage.

'The tribble man too! Now if he'd been a tinner or counter chap, we might ha' contrived the rest o't without en, you see. But for a choir to lose the tribble, why, my sonnies, you may so well lose your . . .' The tranter paused, unable to mention an image vast enough for the occasion.

'Your head at once,' suggested Mr. Penny.

The tranter moved a pace, as if it were puerile of people to complete sentences when there were more pressing things to be done.

'Was ever heard such a thing as a young man leaving his work half done and turning tail like this!'

'Never,' replied Bowman, in a tone signifying that he was the last man in the world to wish to withhold the formal finish required of him.

'I hope no fatal tragedy has overtook the lad!' said his grandfather.

'O no,' replied tranter Dewy placidly. 'Wonder where he've put that there fiddle of his. Why that fiddle cost thirty shillens, and good words besides. Somewhere in the damp, without doubt; that there instrument will be unglued and spoilt in ten minutes – ten! ay, two.'

'What in the name o' righteousness can have happened?' said old William still more uneasily.[4]

Leaving their lanterns and instruments in the belfry they retraced their steps. 'A strapping lad like Dick d'know better than let anything happen onawares,' Reuben remarked. 'There's sure to be some poor little scram reason for't staring us in the face all the while.' He lowered his voice to a mysterious tone: 'Naibours, have ye noticed any sign of a scornful woman in his head, or suchlike?'

'Not a glimmer of such a body. He's as clear as water yet.'

'And Dicky said he should never marry,' cried Jimmy, 'but live at home always along wi' mother and we!'

'Ay, ay, my sonny; every lad has said that in his time.'

They had now again reached the precincts of Mr. Shinar's, but hearing nobody in that direction, one or two went across to the school-house. A light was still burning in the bedroom, and though the blind was down, the window had been slightly opened, as if to admit the distant notes of the carollers to the ears of the occupant of the room.

Opposite the window, leaning motionless against a wall,[5] was the lost man, his arms folded, his head thrown back, his eyes fixed upon the illuminated lattice.

'Why, Dick, is that thee? What's doing here?'

Dick's body instantly flew into a more rational attitude, and his head was seen to turn east and west in the gloom, as if endeavouring to discern some proper answer to that question; and at last he said in rather feeble accents,

'Nothing, father.'

'Th'st take long enough time about it then, upon my body,' said the tranter, as they all turned towards the vicarage.

'I thought you hadn't done having snap in the belfry,' said Dick.

'Why, we've been traypsing and rambling about, looking everywhere like anything, and thinking you'd done fifty horrid things, and here have you been at nothing at all!'

'The insult lies in the nothingness of the deed,' murmured Mr. Spinks.[6]

The vicarage garden was their next field of operation, and Mr. Maybold,[7] the lately-arrived incumbent, duly received his share of the night's harmonies. It was hoped that by reason of his profession he would have been led to open the window, and an extra carol in quick time was added to draw him forth. But Mr. Maybold made no stir.

'A bad sign!' said old William, shaking his head.

However, at that same instant a musical voice was heard exclaiming from inner depths of bedclothes,

'Thanks, villagers!'

'What did he say?' asked Bowman, who was rather dull of hearing. Bowman's voice, being therefore loud, had been heard by the vicar within.

'I said, "Thanks, villagers!" ' cried the vicar again.

'Beg yer pardon; didn't hear ye the first time!' cried Bowman.

'Now don't for heaven's sake spoil the young man's temper by answering like that!' said the tranter.

'You won't do that, my friends!' the vicar shouted.

'Well to be sure, what ears!' said Mr. Penny in a whisper. 'Beats any horse or dog in the parish, and depend upon't, that's a sign he's a proper clever chap.'[8]

'We shall see that in time,' said the tranter.

Old William, in his gratitude for such thanks from a comparatively new inhabitant, was anxious to play all the tunes over again; but renounced his desire on being reminded by Reuben that it would be best to leave well alone.

'Now putting two and two together,' the tranter continued, as they wended their way to the other portion of the village, 'that is, in the form of that young vision we seed just now, and this young tinner-voiced parson, my belief is she'll wind en round her finger, and twist the pore young feller about like the figure of 8 – that she will so, my sonnies.'[9]

CHAPTER VI

Christmas Morning[1]

The choir at last reached their beds, and slept like the rest of the parish. Dick's slumbers, through the three or four hours remaining for rest, were disturbed and slight; an exhaustive variation upon the incidents that had passed that night in connection with the school-window going on in his brain every moment of the time.

In the morning, do what he would – go upstairs, downstairs, out of doors, speak of the wind and weather, or what not – he could not refrain from an unceasing renewal, in imagination, of that interesting enactment. Tilted on the edge of one foot he stood beside the fireplace, watching his mother grilling rashers; but there was nothing in grilling, he thought, unless the Vision grilled. The limp rasher hung down between the bars of the gridiron like a cat in a child's arms; but there was nothing in similes. He looked at the daylight shadows of a yellow hue, dancing with the firelight shadows in blue on the whitewashed chimney-corner, but there was nothing in shadows. 'Perhaps the new young wom – sch – Miss Fancy Day will sing in church with us this morning,' he said.

The tranter looked a long time before he replied, 'I fancy she will; and yet I fancy she won't.'

Dick implied that such a remark was rather to be tolerated than admired; though the slight meagreness observable in the information conveyed disappointed him less than may be expected, deliberateness in speech being known to have, as a rule, more to do with the machinery of the tranter's throat than with the matter enunciated.

They made preparations for going to church as usual; Dick with extreme alacrity, though he would not definitely consider why he was so religious. His wonderful nicety in brushing and cleaning his best light boots had features which elevated it to the rank of an art. Every particle and speck of last week's mud was scraped and brushed from toe and heel; new blacking from the packet was carefully mixed and made use of, regardless of expense. A coat was laid on and polished; then another coat for increased blackness; and lastly a third, to give the perfect and mirror-like jet which the hoped-for rencontre demanded.

It being Christmas-day, the tranter prepared himself with Sunday particularity. Loud sousing and snorting noises were heard to proceed from the back quarters of the dwelling, proclaiming that he was there performing his great Sunday wash, lasting half an hour, to which his washings on working-day mornings were mere flashes in the pan. Vanishing into the outhouse with a large brown basin, and the above-named bubblings and snortings being carried on for about twenty minutes, the tranter would appear round the edge of the door, smelling like a summer fog, and looking as if he had just narrowly escaped a watery grave with the loss of hat and neckerchief, having since been weeping bitterly till his eyes were red; a crystal drop of water hanging ornamentally at the bottom of each ear, one at the tip of his nose, and others in the form of spangles about his hair.

After a great deal of crunching upon the sanded stone floor by the feet of father, son, and grandson as they moved to and fro in these preparations, the bass-viol and fiddles were taken from their nook, and the strings examined and screwed a little above concert pitch, that they might keep their tone when service commenced, to obviate the awkward contingency of having to retune them at the back of the gallery during a cough, sneeze, or amen – an inconvenience which had been known to arise in damp wintry weather.

The three left the door and paced down Mellstock-lane, bearing under their arms the instruments in faded green-baize bags, and old brown music-books in their hands; Dick continually finding himself in advance of the other two, and the tranter moving on with toes turned outwards to an enormous angle.

Seven human heads in a row were now observable over a hedge of laurel, which proved to be the choristers waiting; sitting occasionally on the churchyard-wall and letting their heels dangle against it, to pass the time. The musicians being now in sight, the youthful party scampered off and rattled up the old wooden stairs of the gallery like a regiment of cavalry; the other boys of the parish waiting outside looking at birds, cats, and other creatures till the vicar entered, when they suddenly subsided into sober church-goers, and passed down the aisle with echoing heels.

The gallery of Mellstock Church had a status and sentiment of its own.[2] A stranger there was regarded with a feeling altogether differing from that of the congregation below towards him. Banished from the nave as an intruder whom no originality could make interesting, he was received above as a curiosity that no unfitness could render dull. The gallery, too, looked down upon and knew the habits of the nave to its remotest peculiarity, and had an extensive stock of exclusive information about it; whilst the nave knew nothing of the gallery people, as gallery people, beyond their loud-sounding minims and chest notes. Such topics as that the clerk was always chewing tobacco except at the moment of crying amen; that he had a dust-hole in his pew; that during the sermon certain young daughters of the village had left off caring to read anything so mild as the marriage service for some years, and now regularly studied the one which chronologically follows it;[3] that a pair of lovers touched fingers through a knot-hole between their pews in the manner ordained by their great exemplars, Pyramus and Thisbe;[4] that Mrs. Ledlow, the farmer's wife,[5] counted her money and reckoned her week's marketing expenses during the first lesson – all news to those below – were stale subjects here.

Old William sat in the centre of the front row, his violoncello between his knees, and two singers on each hand. Behind him, on the left, came the treble singers and Dick; and on the right the tranter and the tenors. Farther back was old Mail with the altos and supernumeraries.

But before they had taken their places, and whilst they were standing in a circle at the back of the gallery practising a psalm or two, Dick cast his eyes over his grandfather's shoulder, and saw the vision of the past night enter the porch-door as methodically as if she had never been a vision at all. A new atmosphere seemed suddenly to be puffed into the ancient edifice by her movement, which made Dick's body and soul tingle with novel sensations. Directed by Shinar, the churchwarden, she proceeded to the short aisle on the north side of the chancel, a spot now allotted to a throng of Sunday-school girls, and distinctly visible from the gallery-front by looking under the curve of the furthermost arch on that side.

Before this moment the church had seemed comparatively empty – now it was thronged; and as Miss Fancy rose from her knees and looked around her for a permanent place in which to deposit herself – finally choosing the remotest corner – Dick began to breathe more freely the warm new air she had brought with her; to feel rushings of blood, and to have impressions that there was a tie between her and himself visible to all the congregation.

Ever afterwards the young man could recollect individually each part of the service of that bright Christmas morning, and the minute occurrences which took place as its hours slowly drew along;[6] the duties of that day dividing themselves by a complete line from the services of other times. The tunes they that morning essayed remained with him for years, apart from all others; also the text; also the appearance of the layer of dust upon the capitals of the piers; that the holly-bough in the chancel archway was hung a little out of the centre – all the ideas, in short, that creep into the mind when reason is only exercising its lowest activity through the eye.

By chance or by fate, another young man who attended Mellstock Church on that Christmas morning had towards the end of the service the same instinctive perception of an interesting presence, in the shape of the same bright maiden, though his emotion reached a far less-developed stage. And there was this difference, too, that the person in question was surprised at his condition, and sedulously endeavoured to reduce himself to his normal state of mind. He was the young vicar, Mr. Maybold.[7]

The music on Christmas mornings was frequently below the standard of church-performances at other times. The boys were sleepy from the heavy exertions of the night; the men were slightly wearied; and now, in addition to these constant reasons, there was a dampness in the atmosphere that still farther aggravated the evil. Their strings, from the recent long exposure to the night air, rose whole semitones, and snapped with a loud twang at the most silent moment; which necessitated more retiring than ever to the back of the gallery, and made the gallery throats quite husky with the quantity of coughing and hemming required for tuning in. The vicar looked cross.[8]

When the singing was in progress, there was suddenly discovered to be a strong and shrill reinforcement from some point, ultimately found to be the school-girls' aisle.[9] At every attempt it grew bolder and more distinct. At the third time of singing, these intrusive feminine voices were as mighty as those of the regular singers; in fact, the flood of sound from this quarter assumed such an individuality, that it had a time, a key, almost a tune of its own, surging upwards when the gallery plunged downwards, and the reverse.

Now this had never happened before within the memory of man. The girls, like the rest of the congregation, had always been humble and respectful followers of the gallery; singing at sixes and sevens if without gallery leaders; never interfering with the ordinances of these practised artists – having no will, union, power, or proclivity except it was given them from the established choir enthroned above them.

A good deal of desperation became noticeable in the gallery throats and strings, which continued throughout the musical portion of the service. Directly the fiddles were laid down, Mr. Penny's spectacles put in their sheath, and the text had been given out, an indignant whispering began.

'Did ye hear that, souls?' Mr. Penny said in a groaning breath.

'Brazen-faced hussies!' said Bowman.

'Trew; why, they were every note as loud as we, fiddles and all, if not louder.'

'Fiddles and all,' echoed Bowman bitterly.

'Shall anything bolder be found than united woman?' Mr. Spinks murmured.

'What I want to know is,' said the tranter (as if he knew already, but that civilisation required the form of words), 'what business people have to tell maidens to sing like that when they don't sit in a gallery, and never have entered one in their lives? That's the question, my sonnies.'

''Tis the gallery have got to sing, all the world knows,' said Mr. Penny. 'Why, souls, what's the use o' the ancients spending scores of pounds to build galleries if people down in the lowest depths of the church sing like that at a moment's notice?'

'Really, I think we useless ones had better march out of church, fiddles and all!' said Mr. Spinks, with a laugh which, to a stranger, would have sounded mild and real. Only the initiated body of men he addressed could understand the horrible bitterness of irony that lurked under the quiet words 'useless ones,' and the ghastliness of the laughter apparently so natural.

'Never mind! Let 'em sing too – 'twill make it all the louder – hee, hee!' said Leaf.

'Thomas Leaf, Thomas Leaf! Where have you lived all your life?' said grandfather William sternly.

The quailing Leaf tried to look as if he had lived nowhere at all.

'When all's said and done, my sonnies,' Reuben said, 'there'd have been no real harm in their singing if they had let nobody hear 'em, and only jined in now and then.'

'None at all,' said Mr. Penny. 'But though I don't wish to accuse people wrongfully, I'd say before my lord judge that I could hear every note o' that last psalm come from 'em as much as from us – every note as if 'twas their own.'

'Know it! ah, I should think I did know it!' Mr. Spinks was heard to observe at this moment, without reference to his fellow-creatures – shaking his head at some idea he seemed to see floating before him, and smiling as if he were attending a funeral at the time. 'Ah, do I or don't I know it!'

No one said 'Know what?' because all were aware from experience that what he knew would declare itself in process of time.

'I could fancy last night that we should have some trouble wi' that young man,' said the tranter, pending the continuance of Spinks's speech, and looking towards the unconscious Mr. Maybold in the pulpit.

'*I* fancy,' said old William, rather severely, 'I fancy there's too much whispering going on to be of any spiritual use to gentle or simple.' Then folding his lips and concentrating his glance on the vicar, he implied that none but the ignorant would speak again; and accordingly there was silence in the gallery, Mr. Spinks's telling speech remaining for ever unspoken.

Dick had said nothing, and the tranter little, on this episode of the morning; for Mrs. Dewy at breakfast expressed it as her intention to invite the youthful leader of the culprits to the small party it was customary with them to have on Christmas-night – a piece of knowledge which had given a particular brightness to Dick's reflections since he had received it. And in the tranter's slightly cynical nature, party feeling was weaker than in the other members of the choir, though friendliness and faithful partnership still sustained in him a hearty earnestness on their account.

CHAPTER VII

The Tranter's Party

During the afternoon unusual activity was seen to prevail about the precincts of tranter Dewy's house. The flagstone floor was swept of dust, and a sprinkling of the finest yellow sand from the innermost stratum of the adjoining sand-pit lightly scattered thereupon. Then were produced large knives and forks, which had been shrouded in darkness and grease since the last occasion of the kind, and bearing upon their sides, 'Shear-steel, warranted,' in such emphatic letters of assurance, that the cutler's name was not required as further proof, and not given. The key was left in the tap of the cider-barrel, instead of being carried in a pocket. And finally the tranter had to stand up in the room and let his wife wheel him round like a turnstile, to see if anything discreditable was visible in his appearance.

'Stand still till I've been for the scissors,' said Mrs. Dewy.

The tranter stood as still as a sentinel at the challenge.

The only repairs necessary were a trimming of one or two whiskers that had extended beyond the general contour of the mass; a like trimming of a slightly frayed edge visible on his shirt-collar; and a final tug at a gray hair – to all of which operations he submitted in resigned silence, except the last, which produced a mild 'Come, come, Ann,' by way of expostulation.

'Really, Reuben, 'tis quite a disgrace to see such a man,' said Mrs. Dewy, with the severity justifiable in a long-tried companion, giving him another turn round, and picking several of Smiler's hairs from the shoulder of his coat. Reuben's thoughts seemed engaged elsewhere, and he yawned. 'And the collar of your coat is a shame to behold – so plastered with dirt, or dust, or grease, or something. Why, wherever could you have got it?'

"Tis my warm nater in summer-time, I suppose. I always did get in such a heat when I bustle about.'

'Ay, the Dewys always were such a coarse-skinned family. There's your brother Bob – as fat as a porpoise – just as bad – wi' his low, mean, "How'st do, Ann?" whenever he meets me. I'd "How'st do" him, indeed! If the sun only shines out a minute, there be you all streaming in the face – I never see!'[1]

'If I be hot week-days, I must be hot Sundays.'

'If any of the girls should turn after their father 'twill be a poor look-out for 'em, poor things! None of my family was sich vulgar perspirers, not one of 'em. But, Lord-a-mercy, the Dewys! I don't know how ever I came into such a family.'

'Your woman's weakness when I asked ye to jine us. That's how it was, I suppose;' but the tranter appeared to have heard some such words from his wife before, and hence his answer had not the energy it might have possessed if the inquiry had possessed the charm of novelty.

'You never did look so well in a pair o' trousers as in them,' she continued in the same unimpassioned voice, so that the unfriendly criticism of the Dewy family seemed to have been more normal[2] than spontaneous. 'Such a cheap pair as 'twas too. As big as any man could wish to have, and lined inside, and double-lined in the lower parts, and an extra piece of stiffening at the bottom. And 'tis a nice high cut that comes up right under your armpits, and there's enough turned down inside the seams to make half a pair more, besides a piece of stuff left that will make an honest waistcoat – all by my contriving in buying the stuff at a bargain, and having it made up under my eye. It only shows what may be done by taking a little trouble, and not going straight to the rascally tailors.'

The discourse was cut short by the sudden appearance of Charley on the scene with a face and hands of hideous blackness, and a nose guttering like a candle. Why, on that particularly cleanly afternoon, he should have discovered that the chimney-crook and chain from which the hams were suspended should have possessed more merits and general interest as playthings than any other article in the house, is a question for nursing mothers to decide. However, the humour seemed to lie in the result being, as has been seen, that any given player with these articles was in the long-run daubed with soot. The last that was seen of Charley by daylight after this piece of ingenuity was when in the act of vanishing from his father's presence round the corner of the house, – looking back over his shoulder with an expression of great sin on his face, like Cain as the Outcast in Bible pictures.

The guests had all assembled, and the tranter's party had reached that degree of development which accords with ten o'clock P.M. in rural assemblies. At that hour the sound of a fiddle in process of tuning was heard from the inner pantry.

'That's Dick,' said the tranter. 'That lad's crazy for a jig.'

'Dick! Now I cannot – really, I cannot allow any dancing at all till Christmas-day is out,' said old William emphatically. 'When the clock ha' done striking twelve, dance as much as ye like.'

'Well, I must say there's reason in that, William,' said Mrs. Penny. 'If you do have a party on Christmas-day-night, 'tis only fair and honourable to the Church of England[3] to have it a sit-still party. Jigging parties be all very well, and this, that, and therefore; but a jigging party looks suspicious. O, yes; stop till the clock strikes, young folk – so say I.'

It happened that some warm mead accidentally got into Mr. Spinks's head about this time.

'Dancing,' he said, 'is a most strengthening, enlivening, and courting movement, especially with a little beverage added! And dancing is good. But why disturb what is ordained, Richard and Reuben, and the company zhinerally? Why, I ask, as far as that goes?'

'Then nothing till after twelve,' said William.

Though Reuben and his wife ruled on social points, religious questions were mostly disposed of by the old man, whose firmness on this head quite counterbalanced a certain weakness in his handling of domestic matters. The hopes of the younger members of the household were therefore relegated to a distance of one hour and three-quarters – a result that took visible shape in them by a remote and listless look about the eyes – the singing of songs being permitted in the interim.

At five minutes to twelve the soft tuning was again heard in the back quarters; and when at length the clock had whizzed forth the last stroke, Dick appeared ready primed, and the instruments were boldly handled; old William very readily taking the bass-viol from its accustomed nail, and touching the strings as irreligiously as could be desired.

The country-dance called the 'Triumph, or Follow my Lover,' was the figure with which they opened.[4] The tranter took for his partner Mrs. Penny, and Mrs. Dewy was chosen by Mr. Penny, who made so much of his limited height by a judicious carriage of the head, straightening of the back, and important flashes of his spectacle-glasses, that he seemed almost as tall as the tranter. Mr. Shinar, age about thirty-five, farmer and churchwarden, a character principally composed of watch-chain, with a mouth always hanging on a smile but never smiling,[5] had come quite willingly to the party, and showed a wondrous obliviousness of all his antics on the previous night. But the comely, slender, prettily-dressed prize Fancy Day fell to Dick's lot, in spite of some private machinations of the farmer, for the reason that Mr. Shinar, as a richer man, had shown too much assurance in asking the favour, whilst Dick had been duly courteous.

We gain a good view of our heroine[6] as she advances to her place in the ladies' line. She belonged to the taller division of middle height. Flexibility was her first characteristic, by which she appeared to enjoy the most easeful rest when she was in gliding motion. Her dark eyes – arched by brows of so keen, slender, and soft a curve, that they resembled nothing so much as two slurs in music[7] – showed primarily a bright sparkle each. This was softened by a frequent thoughtfulness, yet not so frequent as to do away, for more than a few minutes at a time, with a certain coquettishness; which in its turn was never so decided as to banish honesty. Her lips imitated her brows in their clearly-cut outline and softness of curve; and her nose was well shaped – which is saying a great deal, when it is remembered that there are a hundred pretty mouths and eyes for one pretty nose. Add to this, plentiful knots of dark-brown hair, a gauzy dress of white, with blue facings; and the slightest idea may be gained of the young maiden who showed, amidst the rest of the dancing-ladies, like a flower among vegetables. And so the dance proceeded. Mr. Shinar, according to the interesting rule laid down, deserted his own partner, and made off down the middle with this fair one of Dick's – the pair appearing from the top of the room like two persons tripping down a lane to be married. Dick trotted behind with what was intended to be a look of composure, but which was, in fact, a rather silly expression of feature – implying, with too much earnestness, that such an elopement could not be tolerated. Then they turned and came back, when Dick grew more rigid around his mouth, and blushed with ingenuous ardour as he joined hands with the rival and formed the arch over his lady's head;[8] relinquishing her again at setting to partners, when Mr. Shinar's new chain quivered in every link, and all the loose flesh upon the tranter – who here came into action again – shook like jelly. Mrs. Penny, being always rather concerned for her personal safety when she danced with the tranter, fixed her face to a chronic smile of timidity the whole time it lasted – a peculiarity which filled her features with wrinkles, and reduced her eyes to little straight lines like hyphens, as she jigged up and down opposite him; repeating in her own person not only his proper movements, but also the minor flourishes which the richness of the tranter's imagination led him to introduce from time to time – an imitation which had about it something of slavish obedience, not unmixed with fear.

The ear-rings of the ladies now flung themselves wildly about, turning violent summersaults, banging this way and that, and then swinging quietly against the ears sustaining them. Mrs. Crumpler – a heavy woman, who, for some reason which nobody ever thought worth inquiry, danced in a clean apron – moved so smoothly through the figure that her feet were never seen; conveying to imaginative minds the idea that she rolled on castors.

Minute after minute glided by, and the party reached the period when ladies' back-hair begins to look forgotten and dissipated; when a perceptible dampness makes itself apparent upon the faces even of delicate girls – a ghastly dew having for some time rained from the features of their masculine partners; when skirts begin to be torn out of their gathers; when elderly people, who have stood up to please their juniors, begin to feel sundry small tremblings in the region of the knees, and to wish the interminable dance was at Jericho; when (at country parties) waistcoats begin to be unbuttoned, and when the fiddlers' chairs have been wriggled, by the frantic bowing of their occupiers, to a distance of about two feet from where they originally stood.[9]

Fancy was dancing with Mr. Shinar. Dick knew that Fancy, by the law of good manners, was bound to dance as pleasantly with one partner as with another; yet he could not help suggesting to himself that she need not have put *quite* so much spirit into her steps, nor smiled *quite* so frequently whilst in the farmer's hands.

'I'm afraid you didn't cast off,' said Dick mildly to Mr. Shinar, before the latter man's watch-chain had done vibrating from a recent whirl.

Fancy made a motion of accepting the correction; but her partner took no notice, and proceeded with the next movement, with an affectionate bend towards her.

'That Shinar's too fond of her,' the young man said to himself as he watched them. They came to the top again, Fancy smiling warmly towards her partner, and went to their places.

'Mr. Shinar, you didn't cast off,' said Dick, for want of something else to demolish him with; casting off himself, and being put out at the farmer's irregularity.

'Perhaps I sha'n't cast off for any man,' said Mr. Shinar.

'I think you ought to, sir.'

Dick's partner, a young lady of the name of Lizzy – called Lizz for short – tried to mollify.

'I can't say that I myself have much feeling for casting off,' she said.

'Nor I,' said Mrs. Penny, following up the argument; 'especially if a friend and naibour is set against it. Not but that 'tis a terrible tasty thing in good hands and well done; yes, indeed, so say I.'

'All I meant was,' said Dick, rather sorry that he had spoken correctly to a guest, 'that 'tis in the dance; and a man has hardly any right to hack and mangle what was ordained by the regular dance-maker, who, I daresay, got his living by making 'em, and thought of nothing else all his life.'

'I don't like casting off: then very well; I cast off for no dance-maker that ever lived.'

Dick now appeared to be doing mental arithmetic, the act being really an effort to present to himself, in an abstract form, how far an argument with a formidable rival ought to be carried, when that rival was his mother's guest. The dead-lock was put an end to by the stamping arrival up the middle of the tranter, who, despising minutiæ on principle, started a theme of his own.

'I assure you, naibours,' he said, 'the heat of my frame no tongue can tell!' He looked around, and endeavoured to give, by a forcible gaze of self-sympathy, some faint idea of the truth.

Mrs. Dewy formed one of the next couple.

'Yes,' she said in an auxiliary tone, 'Reuben always was such a hot man.'

Mrs. Penny implied the correct species of sympathy that such a class of affliction required, by trying to smile and to look grieved at the same time.

'If he only walk round the garden of a Sunday morning, his shirt-collar is as limp as no starch at all,' continued Mrs. Dewy, her countenance lapsing parenthetically into a housewifely expression of concern at the reminiscence.

'Come, come, you wimmen-folk; 'tis hands-across[10] – come, come!' said the tranter; and the conversation ceased for the present.

CHAPTER VIII

They Dance More Wildly

Dick had at length secured Fancy for that most delightful of country-dances, beginning with six-hands-round.[1]

'Before we begin,' said the tranter, 'my proposal is, that 'twould be a right and proper plan for every martel man in the dance to pull off his jacket, considering the heat.'

'Such low notions as you have, Reuben! Nothing but strip will go down with you when you are a-dancing. Such a hot man as he is!'

'Well, now, look here, my sonnies,' he argued to his wife, whom he often addressed in the plural masculine for convenience of epithet merely; 'I don't see that. You dance and get hot as fire; therefore you lighten your clothes. Isn't that nater and reason for gentle and simple? If I strip by myself and not necessary, 'tis rather pot-housey, I own; but if we stout chaps strip one and all, why, 'tis the native manners of the country, which no man can gainsay. Hey – what do you say, my sonnies?'

'Strip we will!' said the three other heavy men; and their coats were accordingly taken off and hung in the passage, whence the four sufferers from heat soon reappeared, marching in close column, with flapping shirt-sleeves, and having, as common to them all, a general glance of being now a match for any man or dancer in England or Ireland. Dick, fearing to lose ground in Fancy's good opinion, retained his coat; and Mr. Shinar did the same from superior knowledge.

And now a further phase of rural revelry had disclosed itself. It was the time of night when a guest may write his name in the dust upon the tables and chairs, and a bluish mist pervades the atmosphere, becoming a distinct halo round the candles; when people's nostrils, wrinkles, and crevices in general, seem to be getting gradually plastered up; when the very fiddlers as well as the dancers get red in the face, the dancers having advanced farther still towards incandescence, and entered the cadaverous phase; the fiddlers no longer sit down, but kick back their chairs and saw madly at the strings, with legs firmly spread and eyes closed, regardless of the visible world. Again and again did Dick share his Love's hand with another man, and wheel round; then, more delightfully, promenade in a circle with her all to himself, his arm holding her waist more firmly each time, and his elbow getting farther and farther behind her back, till the distance reached was rather noticeable; and, most blissful, swinging to places shoulder to shoulder, her breath curling round his neck like a summer zephyr that had strayed from its proper date. Threading the couples one by one they reached the bottom, when there arose in Dick's mind a minor misery lest the tune should end before they could work their way to the top again, and have anew the same exciting run down through. Dick's feelings on actually reaching the top in spite of his doubts were supplemented by a mortal fear that the fiddling might even stop at this supreme moment; which prompted him to convey a stealthy whisper to the far-gone musicians, to the effect that they were not to leave off till he and his partner had reached the bottom of the dance once more, which remark was replied to by the nearest of those convulsed and quivering men by a private nod to the anxious young man between two semiquavers of the tune, and a simultaneous 'All right, ay, ay,' without opening his eyes. Fancy was now held so closely, that Dick and she were practically one person. The room became to Dick like a picture in a dream; all that he could remember of it afterwards being the look of the fiddlers going to sleep, as humming-tops sleep – by increasing their motion and hum, together with the figures of grandfather James and old Simon Crumpler sitting by the chimney-corner, talking and nodding in dumb-show, and beating the air to their emphatic sentences like people in a railway train.[2]

The dance ended. 'Piph-h-h-h!' said tranter Dewy, blowing out his breath in the very finest stream of vapour that a man's lips could form. 'A regular tightener, that one, sonnies!' He wiped his forehead, and went to the cider-mug[3] on the table.

'Well!' said Mrs. Penny, flopping into a chair, 'my heart haven't been in such a thumping state of uproar since I used to sit up on old Midsummer-eves[4] to see who my husband was going to be.'

'And that's getting on for a good few years ago now, from what I've heard you tell,' said the tranter without lifting his eyes from the cup he was filling. Being now engaged in the business of handing round refreshments, he was warranted in keeping his coat off still, though the other heavy men had resumed theirs.

'And a thing I never expected would come to pass, if you'll believe me, cam to pass then,' continued Mrs. Penny. 'Ah, the first spirit ever I see on a Midsummer-eve was a puzzle to me when he appeared, a hard puzzle, so say I!'

'So I should have imagined; as far as that goes,' said Elias Spinks.

'Yes,' said Mrs. Penny, throwing her glance into past times, and talking on in a running tone of complacent abstraction, as if a listener were not a necessity. 'Yes; never was I in such a taking as on that Midsummer-eve! I sat up, quite determined to see if John Wildway was going to marry me or no. I put the bread-and-cheese and cider quite ready, as the witch's book ordered, and I opened the door, and I waited till the clock struck twelve, my nerves all alive, and so distinct that I could feel every one of 'em twitching like bell-wires. Yes, sure! and when the clock had struck, lo and behold, I could see through the door a *little small* man in the lane wi' a shoe-maker's apron on.'

Here Mr. Penny stealthily enlarged himself half an inch.

'Now John Wildway,' Mrs. Penny continued, 'who courted me at that time, was a shoe-maker, you see, but he was a very fair-sized man, and I couldn't believe that any such a little small man had anything to do wi' me, as anybody might. But on he came, and crossed the threshold – not John, but actually the same little small man in the shoe-maker's apron –'

'You needn't be so mighty particular about little and small!' said her husband, pecking the air with his nose.

'In he walks, and down he sits, and O my goodness me, didn't I flee upstairs, body and soul hardly hanging together! Well, to cut a long story short, by-long and by-late, John Wildway and I had a miff and parted; and lo and behold, the coming man[5] came! Penny asked me if I'd go snacks with him, and afore I knew what I was about a'most, the thing was done.'

'I've fancied you never knew better in your life; but I may be mistaken,' said Mr. Penny in a murmur.

After Mrs. Penny had spoken, there being no new occupation for her eyes, she still let them stay idling on the past scenes just related, which were apparently visible to her in the candle-flame.[6] Mr. Penny's remark received no reply.

During this discourse the tranter and his wife might have been observed standing in an unobtrusive corner, in mysterious closeness to each other, a just perceptible current of intelligence passing from each to each, which had apparently no relation whatever to the conversation of their guests, but much to their sustenance.[7] A conclusion of some kind having at length been drawn, the palpable confederacy of man and wife was once more obliterated, the tranter marching off into the pantry, humming a tune that he couldn't quite recollect, and then breaking into the words of a song of which he could remember about one line and a quarter. Mrs. Dewy mentioned a few words about preparations for a bit of supper.

That portion of the company which loved eating and drinking then put on a look to signify that till that moment they had quite forgotten that it was customary to eat suppers in this climate; going even farther than this politeness of feature, and abruptly starting irrelevant subjects, the exceeding flatness and forced tone of which rather betrayed their object. The younger members said they were quite hungry, and that supper would be delightful though it was so late.

Good luck attended Dick's love-passes during the meal. He sat next Fancy, and had the thrilling pleasure of using permanently a glass which had been taken by Fancy in mistake; of letting the outer edge of the sole of his boot touch the lower verge of her skirt; and to add to these delights, a cat, which had lain unobserved in her lap for several minutes, crept across into his own, touching him with the same portion of fur that had touched her hand a moment before. Besides these, there were some little pleasures in the shape of helping her to vegetable she didn't want, and when it had nearly alighted on her plate, taking it across for his own use, on the plea of waste not, want not. He also, from time to time, sipped sweet sly glances at her profile; noticing the set of her head, the curve of her throat, and other artistic properties of the lively goddess, who the while kept up a rather free, not to say too free, conversation with Mr. Shinar sitting opposite; which, after some uneasy criticism, and much shifting of argument backwards and forwards in Dick's mind, he decided not to consider of alarming significance.

'A new music greets our ears now,' said Miss Fancy, alluding, with the sharpness that her position as village sharpener demanded, to the contrast between the rattle of knives and forks and the late notes of the fiddlers.

'Ay; and I don't know but that 'tis sweeter in tone when you get above forty,' said the tranter; 'except, in faith, 'tis as regards father there: never such a martel man as he for tunes. They move his soul; don't 'em, father?'

The eldest Dewy smiled across from his distant chair an assent to Reuben's remark.

'Spaking of being moved in soul,' said Mr. Penny, 'I shall never forget the first time I heard the "Dead March."[8] 'Twas at poor Corp'l Nineman's funeral at Casterbridge. It fairly made my hair creep and fidget about like a flock of sheep – ah, it did, souls! And when they had done, and the last trump had sounded, and the guns was fired over the dead hero's grave, an icy-cold drop of moist sweat hung upon my forehead, and another upon my jawbone. Ah, 'tis a very solemn thing!'

'Well, as to father in the corner there,' the tranter said, pointing to old William, who was in the act of filling his mouth; 'he'd starve to death for music's sake now, as much as when he was a boy-chap of fifteen.'

'Truly, now,' said Michael Mail, clearing the corner of his throat in the manner of a man who meant to be convincing; 'there's a friendly tie of some sort between music and eating.'[9] He lifted the cup to his mouth, and drank himself gradually backwards from a perpendicular position to a slanting one, during which time his looks performed a circuit from the wall opposite him to the ceiling overhead. Then clearing the other corner of his throat: 'Once I was sitting in the little kitchen of the Three Choughs at Casterbridge,[10] having a bit of dinner, and a brass band struck up in the street. Sich a beautiful band as that were! I was sitting eating fried liver and lights, I well can mind – ah, I was! and to save my life, I couldn't help chawing to the tune. Band played six-eight time; six-eight chaws I, willynilly. Band plays common; common time went my teeth among the fried liver and lights as true as a hair. Beautiful 'twere! Ah, I shall never forget that there band!'

'That's as musical a circumstance as ever I heard of,' said grandfather James, with the absent gaze which accompanies profound criticism.

'I don't like Michael's musical circumstances then,' said Mrs. Dewy. 'They are quite coarse to a person of decent taste.'

Old Michael's mouth twitched here and there, as if he wanted to smile but didn't know where to begin, which gradually settled to an expression that it was not displeasing for a nice woman like the tranter's wife to correct him.

'Well, now,' said Reuben, with decisive earnestness, 'that coarseness that's so upsetting to Ann's feelings is to my mind a recommendation; for it do always prove a story to be true. And for the same reason, I like a story with a bad moral. My sonnies, all true stories have a coarseness or a bad moral, depend upon't. If the story-tellers could have got decency and good morals from true stories, who'd ha' troubled to invent parables?'[11] Saying this the tranter arose to fetch a new stock of cider, mead, and home-made wines.

Mrs. Dewy sighed, and appended a remark (ostensibly behind her husband's back, though that the words should reach his ears distinctly was understood by both): 'Such a man as Dewy is! nobody do know the trouble I have to keep that man barely respectable. And did you ever hear too – just now at supper-time – talking about "taties" with Michael in such a labourer's way. Well, 'tis what I was never brought up to! With our family 'twas never less than "taters," and very often "pertatoes" outright; mother was so particular and nice with us girls: there was no family in the parish that kept theirselves up more than we.'

The hour of parting came. Fancy could not remain for the night, because she had engaged a woman to wait up for her.[12] She disappeared temporarily from the flagging party of dancers, and then came downstairs wrapped up and looking altogether a different person from whom she had been hitherto; in fact (to Dick's sadness and disappointment), a woman somewhat reserved and of a phlegmatic temperament – nothing left in her of the romping girl that she had been but a short quarter-hour before, who had not minded the weight of Dick's hand upon her waist, nor shirked the purlieus of the mistletoe.

'What a contradiction!'[13] thought the young man – hoary cynic *pro tem.* 'What a miserable delusive contradiction between the manners of a maid's life at dancing times and at others! Look at this idol Fancy! during the whole past evening touchable, pressable – even kissable. For whole half-hours I held her so close to me that not a sheet of paper could have been slipped between us; and I could feel her heart only just outside my own, her existence going on so close to mine, that I was aware of every breath in it. A flit is made to the bedroom – a hat and a cloak put on – and I no more dare to touch her than –'[14] Thought failed him, and he returned to life.

But this was an endurable misery in comparison with what followed. Mr. Shinar and his watch-chain, taking the intrusive advantage that ardent males who are going homeward along the same road as a pretty young female always do take of that circumstance, came forward to assure Fancy – with a total disregard of Dick's emotions, and in tones which were certainly not frigid – that he (Shinar) was not the man to go to bed before seeing his Lady Fair safe within her own door – not he: nobody should say he was that; – and that he would not leave her side an inch till the thing was done – drown him if he would.[15] The proposal was assented to by Miss Day, in Dick's foreboding judgment with one degree – or at any rate, an appreciable fraction of a degree – of warmth beyond that required by a disinterested desire for protection from the dangers of the night.

All was over; and Dick surveyed the chair she had last occupied, looking now like a setting from which the gem has been torn. There stood her glass, and the romantic teaspoonful of elder wine at the bottom that she couldn't drink by trying ever so hard, in obedience to the mighty arguments of the tranter (his hand coming down upon her shoulder the while, like a Nasmyth hammer[16]); but the drinker was there no longer. There were the nine or ten pretty little crumbs she had left on her plate; but the eater was no more seen.

There seemed to be a disagreeable closeness of relationship between himself and the members of his family, now that they were left alone again face to face. His father seemed quite offensive for appearing to be in just as high spirits as when the guests were there; and as for grandfather James (who had not yet left), he was quite fiendish in being rather glad they were gone.

'Really,' said the tranter, in a tone of placid satisfaction, 'I've had so little time to attend to myself all the evenen, that I mane to enjoy a quiet meal now! A slice of this here ham – neither too fat nor too lane – so; and then a drop of this vinegar and pickles – there, that's it – and I shall be as fresh as a lark again! And to tell the truth, my sonny, my inside 've a-been as dry as a lime-basket all night.'

'I like a party very well,' said Mrs. Dewy, leaving off the adorned tones she had been bound to use throughout the evening, and returning to the natural marriage voice; 'but, lord, 'tis such a sight of heavy work next day! And what with the plates, and knives and forks, and bits kicked off your furniture, and I don't know what-all, why a body could a'most wish there were no such things as Christmases. Ah-h dear!' she yawned, till the clock in the corner had ticked several beats. She cast her eyes round upon the dust-laden furniture, and sank down overpowered at the sight.

'Well, I be getting all right by degrees, thank the Lord for't!' said the tranter cheerfully through a mangled mass of ham and bread, without lifting his eyes from his plate, and chopping away with his knife and fork as if he were felling trees. 'Ann, you may as well go on to bed at once, and not bide there making such sleepy faces; you look as long-favoured as a fiddle, upon my life, Ann. There, you must be wearied out, 'tis true. I'll do the doors and wind up the clock;[17] and you go on, or you'll be as white as a sheet to-morrow.'

'Ay; I don't know whether I sha'n't or no.' The matron passed her hand across her eyes to brush away the film of sleep till she got upstairs.

Dick wondered how it was that when people were married they could be so blind to romance; and was quite certain that if he ever took to wife that dear impossible Fancy, he and she would never be so dreadfully practical and undemonstrative of the Passion as his father and mother were. The most extraordinary thing was, that all the fathers and mothers he knew were just as undemonstrative as his own.

CHAPTER IX

Dick Calls at the School [1]

The early days of the year drew on, and Fancy, having passed the holiday weeks at home, returned again to Mellstock.

Every spare minute of the week following her return was spent by Dick in accidentally passing the school-house in his journeys about the neighbourhood; but not once did she make herself visible. A handkerchief belonging to her had been providentially found by his mother in clearing the rooms the day after that of the dance; and by much contrivance Dick got it handed over to him, to leave with her at any time he was passing the school after her return. But he delayed taking the extreme measure of calling with it lest, had she really no sentiment of interest in him, it might be regarded as a slightly absurd errand, the reason guessed; and the sense of the ludicrous, which was rather keen in her, might do his dignity considerable injury in her eyes; and what she thought of him, even apart from the question of her loving, was all the world to him now.

But the hour came when the patience of love at twenty-one could endure no longer. One Saturday he approached the school with a mild air of indifference, and had the satisfaction of seeing the object of his quest at the farther end of her garden, trying, by the aid of a spade and gloves, to root a bramble that had intruded itself there.

He disguised his feelings from some suspicious-looking cottage-windows opposite, by endeavouring to appear like a man in a great hurry of business, who wished to leave the handkerchief and have done with such trifling errands. [2]

This endeavour signally failed; for on approaching the gate, he found it locked to keep the children, who were playing prisoner's base [3] in the front, from running into her private grounds.

She did not see him; and he could only think of one thing to be done, which was to shout her name.

'Miss Day!'

The words were uttered with a jerk and a look, which were meant to imply to the cottages opposite that he was simply a young man who liked shouting, as being a pleasant way of passing his time, without any reference at all to persons in gardens. The name died away, and the unconscious Miss Day continued digging and pulling as before.

He screwed himself up to enduring the cottage-windows yet more stoically, and shouted again. Fancy took no notice whatever.

He shouted again the third time, with desperate vehemence; then turned suddenly about and retired a little distance, as if he had no connection with the school, but was standing there by chance.

This time she heard him, came down the garden, and entered the school at the back. Footsteps echoed across the interior, the door opened, and three-quarters of the blooming young schoolmistress's face and figure stood revealed before him; a perpendicular slice on her left-hand side being cut off by the edge of the door she held ajar. Having surveyed and recognised him, she came to the gate.

At sight of him had the pink of her cheeks increased, lessened, or did it continue to cover its normal area of ground? It was a question meditated several hundreds of times by her visitor in after-hours – the meditation, after wearying involutions, always ending in one way, that it was impossible to say.

'Your handkerchief: Miss Day: I called with.' He held it out spasmodically and awkwardly. 'Mother found it: under a chair.'

'O, thank you very much for bringing it, Mr. Dewy. I couldn't think where I had dropped it.'

Now Dick, not being an experienced lover – indeed, never before having been engaged in the practice of love-making at all, except in a small schoolboy way – could not take advantage of the situation; and out came the blunder, which afterwards cost him so many bitter moments and three sleepless nights: –

'Good-morning, Miss Day.'

'Good-morning, Mr. Dewy.'

The gate was closed; she was gone; and Dick was standing outside, unchanged in his condition from what he had been before he called. Of course the Angel was not to blame – a young woman living alone in a house could not ask him indoors unless she had known him better – he should have kept her outside.[4] He wished that before he called he had realised more fully than he did the pleasure of being about to call; and turned away.

PART II

Spring

CHAPTER I

Passing by the School[1]

It followed that as the spring advanced, Dick walked abroad much more frequently than had hitherto been usual with him, and was continually finding that his nearest way to or from home lay across the field at the corner of the school. The first-fruits of his perseverance were that, on turning the angle on the nineteenth journey that way, he saw Miss Fancy's figure, clothed in a dark-gray dress, looking from a high open window upon the crown of his hat. The friendly greeting, which was the result of this rencounter, was considered so valuable an elixir that Dick passed still oftener; and by the time he had trodden a little path in the grass where never a path was before, he was rewarded with an actual meeting face to face on the open ground. This brought another meeting, and another, Fancy faintly showing by her bearing that it was a pleasure to her of some kind to see him there; but the sort of pleasure she derived, whether exultation at the hope her exceeding fairness inspired, or the true feeling which was alone Dick's concern, he could not anyhow decide, although he meditated on her every little movement for hours after it was made.

CHAPTER II

A Meeting of the Choir[1]

It was the evening of a fine spring day. The descending sun appeared as a nebulous blaze of amber light, its outline being lost in cloudy masses hanging round it, like wild locks of hair.

The chief members of Mellstock parish choir were standing in a group in front of Mr. Penny's workshop in the lower village. They were all brightly illuminated, and each was backed up by a shadow as long as a steeple; the lowness of the source of light rendering the brims of their hats of no use at all as a protection to the eyes.[2]

Mr. Penny's was the last house in that portion of the parish, and stood in a hollow by the road-side; so that cart-wheels and horses' feet were about level with the sill of his shop-window. This was low and wide, and was open from morning till evening, Mr. Penny himself being invariably seen working inside, like a framed portrait of a shoe-maker by some modern Moroni.[3] He sat facing the road, with a boot on his knees and the awl in his hand, only looking up for a moment as he stretched out his arms and bent forward at the pull, when his spectacles flashed in the passer's face with a shine of flat whiteness, and then returned again to the boot as usual. Rows of lasts, small and large, stout and slender, covered the wall which formed the background, in the extreme shadow of which a kind of dummy was seen sitting, in the shape of an apprentice with a string tied round his hair (probably to keep it out of his eyes). He smiled at remarks that floated in from the outside, but was never known to answer them in Mr. Penny's presence. Outside the window, the upper-leather of a Wellington-boot[4] was usually hung, pegged to a board as if to dry. No sign was over his door; in fact – as with old banks and mercantile houses – advertising in any shape was scorned; and it would have been felt as beneath his dignity to paint, for the benefit of strangers, the name of an establishment the trade of which came solely by connection based on personal respect.[5]

His visitors now stood on the outside of his window, sometimes leaning against the sill, sometimes moving a pace or two backwards and forwards in front of it. They talked with deliberate gesticulations to Mr. Penny, enthroned in the shadow of the interior.

'I do like a man to stick to men who be in the same line o' life – o' Sundays, any way – that I do so.'

''Tis like all the doings of folk who don't know what a day's work is, that's what I say.'

'My belief is the man's not to blame; 'tis *she* – she's the bitter weed.'

'No, not altogether. He's a poor gawk-hammer. Look at his sermon yesterday.'

'His sermon was well enough, a very excellent sermon enough, only he couldn't put it into words and speak it. That's all was the matter wi' the sermon. He hadn't been able to get it past his pen.'

'Well – ay, the sermon might be good enough; for, ye see, the sermon of Old Ecclesiastes himself lay in Old Ecclesiastes's ink-bottle afore he got it out.'[6]

Mr. Penny, being in the act of drawing the last stitch tight, could afford time to look up and throw in a word at this point.

'He's no spouter – that must be said, 'a b'lieve.'

''Tis a terrible muddle sometimes with the man, as far as that goes,' said Spinks.

'Well, we'll say nothing about that,' the tranter answered; 'for I don't believe 'twill make a penneth o' difference to we poor martels here or hereafter whether his sermons be good or bad, my sonnies.'

Mr. Penny made another hole with his awl, pushed in the thread, and looked up and spoke again at the extension of arms.

''Tis his goings-on, souls, that's what it is.' He clenched his features for an Herculean addition to the ordinary pull, and went on, 'The first thing he do when he cam here was to be hot and strong about church business.'

'Trew,' said Spinks; 'that was the very first thing he do.'

Mr. Penny, having now been offered the ear of the assembly, accepted it, ceased stitching, swallowed an unimportant quantity of air as if it were a pill, and continued:

'The next thing he do is to think about altering the church, until he found 'twould be a matter o' cost and what not, and then not to think no more about it.'

'Trew: that was the next thing he do.'

'And the next thing was to tell the young chaps that they were not on no account to put their hats in the font during service.'

'Trew.'

'And then 'twas this, and then 'twas that, and now 'tis –'

Words were not forcible enough to conclude the sentence, and Mr. Penny gave a huge pull to signify the concluding word.

'Now 'tis to turn us out of the quire neck and crop,' said the tranter after a silent interval of half a minute, not at all by way of explaining the pause and pull, which had been quite understood, but simply as a means of keeping the subject well before the meeting.

Mrs. Penny came to the door at this point in the discussion. Like all good wives, however much she was inclined to play the Tory to her husband's Whiggism,[7] and *vice versâ*, in times of peace, she coalesced with him heartily enough in time of war.

'It must be owned he's not all there,' she replied, in a general way, to the fragments of talk she had heard from indoors. 'Far below poor Mr. Grinham' (the late vicar).

'Ay, there was this to be said for him, that you were quite sure he'd never come mumbudgeting to see ye, just as you were in the middle of your work, and put you out with his anxious trouble about you – so say I.'

'Never. But as for this new Mr. Maybold, he's a very singular, well-intentioned party in that respect, but unbearable; for as to sifting your cinders, scrubbing your floors, or emptying your soap-suds, why you can't do it. I assure you I've not been able to empt them for several days, unless I throw 'em up the chimley or out of winder; for as sure as the sun you meet him at the door, coming to ask how you be, and 'tis such a confusing thing to meet a gentleman at the door when ye are in the mess o' washing.'

''Tis only for want of knowing better, poor gentleman,' said the tranter. 'His maning's good enough. Ay, your parson comes by fate: 'tis heads or tails, like pitch-halfpenny, and no choosing; so we must take en as he is, my sonnies, and thank God he's no worse, I suppose.'

'I fancy I've seen him look across at Miss Day in a warmer way than Christianity required,' said Mrs. Penny musingly; 'but I don't quite like to say it.'

'O, no; there's nothing in that,' said grandfather William.

'If there's nothing, we shall see nothing,' Mrs. Penny replied, in the tone of a woman who might possibly have private opinions still.

'Ah, Mr. Grinham was the man!' said Bowman. 'Why, he never troubled us wi' a visit from year's end to year's end. You might go anywhere, do anything: you'd be sure never to see him.'

''A was a right sensible parson,' said Michael. 'He never entered our door but once in his life, and that was to tell my poor wife – ay, poor soul, dead and gone now, as we all shall! – that as she was such a old aged person, and lived so far from the church, he didn't at all expect her to come any more to the service.'

'And 'a was a very jinerous gentleman about choosing the psalms and hymns o' Sundays. "Confound ye," says he, "blare and scrape what ye like, but don't bother me!"'

'And he was a very honourable good man in not wanting any of us to come and hear him if we were all on-end for a jaunt or spree, or to bring the babies to be christened if they were inclined to squalling. There's virtue in a man's not putting a parish to spiritual trouble.'

'And there's this man never letting us have a bit of peace; but wanting us to be good and upright till 'tis carried to such a shameful pitch as I never see the like afore nor since!'[8]

'Still, for my part,' said old William, 'though he's arrayed against us, I like the hearty borus-snorus ways of the new pa'son.'

'You, ready to die for the quire,' said Bowman reproachfully, 'to stick up for the quire's enemy, William!'

'Nobody will feel the loss of our occupation so much as I,' said the old man firmly; 'that you d'all know. I've been in the quire man and boy ever since I was a chiel of eleven. But for all that 'tisn't in me to call the man a bad man, because I truly and sincerely believe en to be a good young feller.'

Some of the youthful sparkle that used to reside there animated William's eye as he uttered the words, and a certain nobility of aspect was also imparted to him by the setting sun, which gave him a Titanic shadow at least thirty feet in length, stretching away to the east in outlines of imposing magnitude, his head finally terminating upon the trunk of a grand old oak-tree.

'Mayble's a hearty feller,' the tranter replied, 'and will spak to you be you dirty or be you clane. The first time I met en was in a drong, and though 'a didn't know me no more than the dead, 'a passed the time of day. "D'ye do?" he said, says he, nodding his head, "A fine day." Then the second time I met en was full-buff in town street, when my breeches were tore all to strents and lippets by getting through a copse of thorns and brimbles for a short cut home-along; and not wanting to disgrace the man by spaking in that state, I fixed my eye on the weathercock to let en pass me as a stranger. But no: "How d'ye do, Reuben?" says he, right hearty. If I'd been dressed in silver spangles from top to toe, the man couldn't have been civiller.'

At this moment Dick was seen coming up the village-street, and they turned and watched him.

CHAPTER III

A Turn in the Discussion

'I'm afraid Dick's a lost man,' said the tranter.

'What? – no!' said Mail, implying by his manner that it was a far commoner thing for his ears to report what was not said than that his judgment should be at fault.

'Ay,' said the tranter, still looking at Dick's unconscious advance. 'I don't at all like what I see! There's too many o' them looks out of the winder without noticing anything; too much shining of boots; too much peeping round corners; too much looking at the clock; telling about clever things She did till you be sick of it, and then upon a hint to that effect a horrible silence about her. I've walked the path once in my life and know the country, naibours; and Dick's a lost man!' The tranter turned a quarter round and smiled a smile of miserable satire at the rising new moon,[1] which happened to catch his eye.

The others' looks became far too serious at this announcement to allow them to speak; and they still regarded Dick in the distance.

''Twas his mother's fault,' the tranter continued, shaking his head two-and-half times, 'in asking the young woman to our party last Christmas. When I eyed the blue frock and light heels o' the maid, I had my thoughts directly. "God bless thee, Dicky my sonny," I said to myself, "there's a delusion for thee!"'

'They seemed to be rather distant in manner last Sunday, I thought,' said Mail tentatively, as became one who was not a member of the family.

'Ay, that's a part of the illness. Distance belongs to it, slyness belongs to it, quarest things on earth belongs to it. There, 'tmay as well come early as late s'far as I know. The sooner begun, the sooner over; for come it will.'

'The question I ask is,' said Mr. Spinks, connecting into one thread the two subjects of discourse, as became a man learned in rhetoric, and beating with his hand in a way which signified that the manner rather than the matter of his speech was to be observed, 'how did Mr. Maybold know she could play the organ? You know we had it from her own lips, as far as that goes, that she has never, first or last, breathed such a thing to him; much less that she ever would play.'

In the midst of this puzzle Dick joined the party, and the news which had caused such a convulsion among the ancient musicians was unfolded to him. 'Well,' he said, blushing at the allusion to Miss Day, 'I know by some words of hers that she has particularly wished not to play, because she is a friend of ours; and how the alteration comes, I don't know.'

'Now, this is my plan,' said the tranter, turning from Dick and reviving the spirit of the discussion by the infusion of new ideas, as was his custom. 'This is my plan; if you don't like it, no harm's done. We all know one another very well, don't we, naibours?'

That they knew one another very well was received as a statement of much relevance to the present subject, and one which, though very familiar, should not in the nature of things be omitted in introductory speeches.

'Then I say this' – and the tranter in his emphasis suddenly slapped down his hand on Mr. Spinks's shoulder with a momentum of several pounds, upon which Mr. Spinks tried to look not in the least startled by what had sent his nerves flying in all directions – 'I say that we all move down-along straight as a line to Pa'son Mayble's when the clock have gone six to-morrow night. There we one and all stand in the passage, then one or two of us go in and spak to en, man and man; and say, "Pa'son Mayble, every tradesman d'like to have his own way in his workshop, and Mellstock Church is yours. Instead of turning us out neck and crop, let us stay on till Christmas, and we'll gie way to the young woman, Mr. Mayble, and make no more ado about it. And we shall always be quite willing to touch our hats when we meet ye, Mr. Mayble, just as before." That sounds very well? Hey?'

'Excellent well in faith, Reuben Dewy.'

'And we won't sit down in his house; 'twould be looking too familiar when only just reconciled.'

'No need at all to sit down. Just do our duty man and man, turn round, and march out – he'll think all the more of us for it.'

'I hardly think Leaf had better go wi' us?' said Michael, turning to Leaf and taking his measure from top to bottom by the eye. 'He's so terrible silly that he might ruin the concern.'

'He don't want to go much; do ye, Thomas Leaf?' said William.

'Hee-hee! no; I don't want to.'[2]

'I be martal afeard, Leaf, that you'll never be able to tell how many cuts d'take to sharpen a spar,'³ said Mail.

'I never had no head, never! that's how it happened to happen, hee-hee!'

They all assented to this, not with any sense of humiliating Leaf by disparaging him after an open confession, but because it was an accepted thing that Leaf didn't in the least mind having no head, that he habitually walked about without one being an unimpassioned matter of parish history.

'But I can sing my treble!' continued Thomas Leaf, quite delighted at being called a fool in such a friendly way; 'I can sing my treble as well as any maid, or married woman either, and better!⁴ And if Jim had lived, I should have had a clever brother! To-morrow is poor Jim's birthday. He'd ha' been twenty-six if he'd lived till to-morrow.'

'You always seem very sorry for Jim,' said old William musingly.

'Ah! I do. Such a stay to mother as he'd always ha' been! She'd never have had to work in her old age if he had continued strong, poor Jim!'

'What was his age when 'a died?'

'Four hours and twenty minutes, poor Jim. 'A was born as might be at night; and 'a didn't last as might be till the morning. No, 'a didn't last. Mother called en Jim on the day that would ha' been his christening day if he had lived; and she's always thinking about en. You see he died so very young.'

'Well, 'twas rather youthful,' said Michael.

'Now to my mind that woman is very imaginative⁵ on the subject of children,' said the tranter, his eye precisely sweeping his audience as he spoke.

'Ah, well she may be,' said Leaf. 'She had twelve regularly one after another, and they all, except myself, died very young; either before they was born or just afterwards.'

'Pore feller too. I suppose th'st want to come wi' us?' the tranter murmured.

'Well, Leaf, you shall come wi' us as yours is such a melancholy family,' said old William rather sadly.

'I never see such a melancholy family as that afore in my life,' said Reuben. 'There's Leaf's mother, pore woman! Every morning I see her eyes mooning out through the panes of glass like a pot-sick winder-flower; and as Leaf sings a very high treble, and we don't know what we should do without en for upper G, we'll let en come as a trate, pore feller.'

'Ay, we'll let en come 'a b'lieve,' said Mr. Penny, looking up, as the pull happened to be at that moment.

'Now,' continued the tranter, dispersing by a new tone of voice this digression about Leaf; 'as to going to see the pa'son, one of us might just call and ask en his maning, and 'twould be just as well done; but it will add a bit of a flourish to the cause if the quire waits on him as a body. Then the great thing to mind is, not for any of our fellers to be nervous; so before starting we'll one and all come to my house and have a rasher of bacon; then every man-jack het a pint of cider into his inside; then we'll warm up an extra drop wi' some mead and a bit of ginger; every man take a thimbleful – just a glimmer of a drop, mind ye, no more, to finish off his inner man – and march off to Pa'son Mayble. Why, sonnies, a man's not himself till he is fortified wi' a bit and a drop? We shall be able to look any gentleman in the face then without sin or shame.'

Mail just recovered from a deep meditation and downward glance into the earth in time to give a cordial approval to this line of action, and the meeting adjourned.

CHAPTER IV

The Interview with the Vicar

At six o'clock the next day, the whole body of men in the choir emerged from the tranter's door, and advanced with a firm step down the lane. This dignity of march gradually became obliterated as they went on, and by the time they reached the hill behind the vicarage, a faint resemblance to a flock of sheep might have been discerned in the venerable party. A word from the tranter, however, set them right again; and as they descended the hill, the regular tramp, tramp, tramp of the united feet was clearly audible from the vicarage garden. At the opening of the gate there was another short interval of irregular shuffling, caused by a rather peculiar habit the gate had, when swung open quickly, of striking against the bank and slamming back into the opener's face.

'Now keep step again, will ye?' said the tranter solemnly. 'It looks better,

and more becomes the high class of errand which has brought us here.'
Thus they advanced to the door.

At Reuben's ring the more modest of the group turned aside, adjusted
their hats, and looked critically at any shrub that happened to lie in the
line of vision; endeavouring thus to give any one who chanced to look
out of the windows the impression that their request, whatever it was
going to be, was rather a casual thought occurring whilst they were
inspecting the vicar's shrubbery and grass-plot than a predetermined
thing. The tranter, who, coming frequently to the vicarage with luggage,
coals, firewood, &c., had none of the awe for its precincts that filled the
breasts of most of the others, fixed his eyes with much strong feeling on
the knocker during this interval of waiting. The knocker having no
characteristic worthy of notice, he relinquished it for a knot in one of the
door-panels, and studied the winding lines of the grain.[1]

'O, sir, please, here's tranter Dewy, and old William Dewy, and young
Richard Dewy, O, and all the quire too, sir, except the boys, a-come to
see you!' said Mr. Maybold's maid-servant to Mr. Maybold, the pupils of
her eyes dilating like circles in a pond.

'All the choir?' said the astonished vicar (who may be shortly described
as a good-looking young man with courageous eyes, timid mouth, and
neutral nose), looking fixedly at his parlour-maid after speaking, like
a man who fancied he had seen her face before but couldn't recollect
where.

'And they looks very firm, and tranter Dewy do turn neither to the
right hand nor to the left,[2] but looked quite straight and solemn with his
mind made up!'

'O, all the choir,' repeated the vicar to himself, trying by that simple
device to trot out his thoughts on what the choir could come for.

'Yes; every man-jack of 'em, as I be alive!' (The parlour-maid was
rather local in manner, having in fact been raised in the same village.)
'Really, sir, 'tis thoughted by many in town and country that –'

'Town and country! – Heavens, I had no idea that I was public property
in this way!' said the vicar, his face acquiring a hue somewhere between
that of the rose and the peony. 'Well, "It is thought in town and country
that –"'

'It is thought that you are going to get it hot and strong! – excusen my
incivility, sir.'

The vicar suddenly recalled to his recollection that he had long ago settled it to be decidedly a mistake to encourage his servant Jane in giving personal opinions. The servant Jane saw by the vicar's face that he suddenly recalled this fact to his mind; and removing her forehead from the edge of the door, and rubbing away the indent that edge had made, vanished into the passage as Mr. Maybold remarked, 'Show them in, Jane.'

A few minutes later a shuffling and jostling (reduced to as refined a form as was compatible with the nature of shuffles and jostles) was heard in the passage; then an earnest and prolonged wiping of shoes, conveying the notion that volumes of mud had to be removed; but the roads being so clean that not a particle of dirt appeared on the choir's boots (those of all the elder members being newly oiled, and Dick's brightly polished), this wiping must be set down simply as a desire to show that these respectable men had no intention or wish to take a mean advantage of clean roads for curtailing proper ceremonies. Next there came a powerful whisper from the same quarter:–

'Now stand stock-still there, my sonnies, one and all! and don't make no noise; and keep your backs close to the wall, that company may pass in and out easy if they want to without squeezing through ye: and we two be enough to go in.' . . . The voice was the tranter's.

'I wish I could go in, too, and see the sight!' said a reedy voice – that of Leaf.

''Tis a pity Leaf is so terrible silly, or else he might,' another said.

'I never in my life seed a quire go into a study to have it out about the playing and singing,' pleaded Leaf; 'and I should like, too, to see it just once!'

'Very well; we'll let en come in,' said the tranter feelingly. 'You'll be like chips in porridge,[3] Leaf – neither good nor hurt. All right, my sonny, come along;' and immediately himself, old William, and Leaf appeared in the room.

'We've took the liberty to come and see ye, sir,' said Reuben, letting his hat hang in his left hand, and touching with his right the brim of an imaginary one on his head. 'We've come to see ye, sir, man and man, and no offence, I hope?'

'None at all,' said Mr. Maybold.

'This old aged man standing by my side is father; William Dewy by name, sir.'

'Yes; I see it is,' said the vicar, nodding aside to old William, who smiled.

'I thought ye mightn't know en without his bass-viol,' said the tranter apologetically. 'You see, he always wears his best clothes and his bass-viol a-Sundays, and it do make such a difference in a old man's look.'

'And who's that young man?' the vicar said.

'Tell the pa'son yer name,' said the tranter, turning to Leaf, who stood with his elbows nailed back to a bookcase.

'Please, Thomas Leaf, your holiness!' said Leaf, trembling.

'I hope you'll excuse his looks being so very thin,' continued the tranter deprecatingly, turning to the vicar again. 'But 'tisn't his fault, pore feller. He's rather silly by nater, and could never get fat; though he's a excellent tribble,[4] and so we keep him on.'

'I never had no head, sir,' said Leaf, eagerly grasping at this opportunity for being forgiven his existence.

'Ah, poor young man!' said Mr. Maybold.

'Bless you, he don't mind it a bit, if you don't, sir,' said the tranter assuringly. 'Do ye, Leaf?'

'Not I – not a morsel – hee, hee! I was afeard it mightn't please your holiness, sir, that's all.'

The tranter, finding Leaf get on so very well through his negative qualities, was tempted in a fit of generosity to advance him still higher, by giving him credit for positive ones. 'He's very clever for a silly chap, good-now,[5] sir. You never knowed a young feller keep his smock-frocks so clane; very honest too. His ghastly looks is all there is against en, pore feller; but we can't help our looks, you know, sir.'

'True: we cannot. You live with your mother, I think, Leaf?'

The tranter looked at Leaf to express that the most friendly assistant to his tongue could do no more for him now, and that he must be left to his own resources.

'Yes, sir: a widder, sir. Ah, if brother Jim had lived she'd have had a clever son to keep her without work!'

'Indeed! poor woman. Give her this half-crown. I'll call and see your mother.'

'Say, "Thank you, sir,"' the tranter whispered imperatively towards Leaf.

'Thank you, sir!' said Leaf.

'That's it, then; sit down, Leaf,' said Mr. Maybold.

'Y-yes, sir!'

The tranter cleared his throat after this accidental parenthesis about Leaf, rectified his bodily position, and began his speech.

'Mr. Mayble,' he said, 'I hope you'll excuse my common way, but I always like to look things in the face.'

Reuben made a point of fixing this sentence in the vicar's mind by giving a smart nod at the conclusion of it, and then gazing hard out of the window.

Mr. Maybold and old William looked in the same direction, apparently under the impression that the things' faces alluded to were there visible.

'What I have been thinking' – the tranter implied by this use of the past tense that he was hardly so discourteous as to be positively thinking it then – 'is that the quire ought to be gie'd a little time, and not done away wi' till Christmas, as a fair thing between man and man. And, Mr. Mayble, I hope you'll excuse my common way?'

'I will, I will. Till Christmas,' the vicar murmured, stretching the two words to a great length, as if the distance to Christmas might be measured in that way. 'Well, I want you all to understand that I have no personal fault to find, and that I don't wish to change the church music in a forcible way, or in a way which should hurt the feelings of any parishioners. Why I have at last spoken definitely on the subject is that a player has been brought under – I may say pressed upon – my notice several times by one of the churchwardens. And as the organ I brought with me is here waiting' (pointing to a cabinet-organ standing in the study), 'there is no reason for longer delay.'

'We made a mistake I suppose then, sir? But we understood the young lady didn't want to play particularly?' The tranter arranged his countenance to signify that he did not want to be inquisitive in the least.

'No, nor did she. Nor did I definitely wish her to just yet; for your playing is very good. But as I said, one of the churchwardens has been so anxious for a change, that as matters stand, I couldn't consistently refuse my consent.'

Now for some reason or other, the vicar at this point seemed to have an idea that he had prevaricated; and as an honest vicar, it was a thing he determined not to do. He corrected himself, blushing as he did so, though why he should blush was not known to Reuben.

'Understand me rightly,' he said: 'the churchwarden proposed it to me, but I had thought myself of getting – Miss Day to play.'[6]

'Which churchwarden might that be who proposed her, sir? – excusing my common way.' The tranter intimated by his tone, that so far from being inquisitive he did not even wish to ask a single question.

'Mr. Shinar, I believe.'

'Clk, my sonny! – beg your pardon, sir, that's only a form of words of mine, sir, and slipped out accidental – sir, he nourishes enmity against us for some reason or another; perhaps because we played rather hard upon en Christmas night. I don't know; but 'tis certain-sure that Mr. Shinar's rale love for music of a particular kind isn't his reason. He've no more ear than that chair. But let that pass.'

'I don't think you should conclude that, because Mr. Shinar wants a different music, he has any ill-feeling for you. I myself, I must own, prefer organ-music to any other. I consider it most proper, and feel justified in endeavouring to introduce it; but then, although other music is better, I don't say yours is not good.'

'Well then, Mr. Mayble, since death's to be, we'll die like men any day you names, (excusing my common way).'

Mr. Maybold bowed his head.

'All we thought was, that for us old ancient singers to be finished off quietly at no time in particular, as now, in the Sundays after Easter, would seem rather mean in the eyes of other parishes, sir. But if we fell glorious with a bit of a flourish at Christmas, we should have a respectable end, and not dwindle away at some nameless paltry second-Sunday-after or Sunday-next-before something, that's got no name of his own.'

'Yes, yes, that's reasonable; I own it's reasonable.'

'You see, Mr. Mayble, we've got – do I keep you inconveniently long, sir?'

'No, no.'

'We've got our feelings – father there especially, Mr. Mayble.'

The tranter, in his eagerness to explain, had advanced his person to within six inches of the vicar's.

'Certainly, certainly!' said Mr. Maybold, retreating a little for convenience of seeing. 'You are all enthusiastic on the subject, and I am all the more gratified to find you so. A Laodicean lukewarmness[7] is worse than wrongheadedness itself.'

'Exactly, sir. In fact now, Mr. Mayble,' Reuben continued, more impressively, and advancing a little closer still to the vicar, 'father there is a perfect figure of wonder, in the way of being fond of music!'

The vicar drew back a little farther, the tranter suddenly also standing back a foot or two, to throw open the view of his father, and pointing to him at the same time.

Old William moved uneasily in the large chair, and constructing a minute smile on the mere edge of his lips, for good-manners, said he was indeed very fond of tunes.

'Now, sir, you see exactly how it is,'[8] Reuben continued, appealing to Mr. Maybold's sense of justice by looking sideways into his eyes. The vicar seemed to see how it was so well, that the gratified tranter walked up to him again with even vehement eagerness, so that his waistcoat-buttons almost rubbed against the vicar's as he continued: 'As to father, if you or I, or any man or woman of the present generation, at the time music is playing, was to shake your fist in father's face, as might be this way, and say, "Don't you be delighted with that music!" ' – the tranter went back to where Leaf was sitting, and held his fist so close to Leaf's face, that the latter pressed his head back against the wall: 'All right, Leaf, my sonny, I won't hurt you; 'tis just to show my maning to Mr. Mayble. – As I was saying, if you or I, or any man, was to shake your fist in father's face this way, and say, "William, your life or your music!" he'd say, "My life!" Now that's father's nater all over; and you see, sir, it must hurt the feelings of a man of that kind, for him and his bass-viol to be done away wi' neck and crop.'

The tranter went back to the vicar's front, and looked earnestly at a very minute point in his face.

'True, true, Dewy,' Mr. Maybold answered, trying to withdraw his head and shoulders without moving his feet; but finding this impracticable, edging back another inch. These frequent retreats had at last jammed Mr. Maybold between his easy-chair and the edge of the table.

And at the moment of the announcement of the choir, Mr. Maybold had just re-dipped the pen he was using; at their entry, instead of wiping it, he had laid it on the table with the nib overhanging. At the last retreat his coat-tails came in contact with the pen, and down it rolled, first against the back of the chair; thence turning a summersault into the seat; thence rolling to the floor with a rattle.

The vicar stooped for his pen, and the tranter, wishing to show that, however great their ecclesiastical differences, his mind was not so small as to let this affect his social feelings, stooped also.

'And have you anything else you want to explain to me, Dewy?' said Mr. Maybold from under the table.

'Nothing, sir. And, Mr. Mayble, you be not offended? I hope you see our desire is reason?' said the tranter from under the chair.

'Quite, quite; and I shouldn't think of refusing to listen to such a reasonable request,' the vicar replied. Seeing that Reuben had secured the pen, he resumed his vertical position, and added, 'You know, Dewy, it is often said how difficult a matter it is to act up to our convictions and please all parties. It may be said with equal truth, that it is difficult for a man of any appreciativeness to have convictions at all. Now in my case, I see right in you, and right in Shinar. I see that violins are good, and that an organ is good; and when we introduce the organ, it will not be that fiddles were bad, but that an organ was better. That you'll clearly understand, Dewy?'

'I will; and thank you very much for such feelings, sir. Piph-h-h-h! How the blood do get into my head to be sure, whenever I quat down like that!' said Reuben, having also risen to his feet, sticking the pen vertically in the inkstand and almost through the bottom, that it might not roll down again under any circumstances whatever.

Now the ancient body of minstrels in the passage felt their curiosity surging higher and higher as the minutes passed. Dick, not having much affection for this errand, soon grew tired, and went away in the direction of the school. Yet their sense of propriety would probably have restrained them from any attempt to discover what was going on in the study, had not the vicar's pen fallen to the floor. The conviction that the movement of chairs, &c. necessitated by the search, could only have been caused by the catastrophe of a bloody fight, overpowered all other considerations; and they advanced to the door, which had only just fallen to. Thus, when Mr. Maybold raised his eyes after the stooping, he beheld glaring through the door Mr. Penny in full-length portraiture, Mail's face and shoulders above Mr. Penny's head, Spinks's forehead and eyes over Mail's crown, and a fractional part of Bowman's countenance under Spinks's arm – crescent-shaped portions of other heads and faces being visible behind these – the whole dozen and odd eyes bristling with eager inquiry.

Mr. Penny, as is the case with excitable bootmakers and men, on seeing the vicar look at him, and hearing no word spoken, thought it incumbent upon himself to say something of any kind. Nothing suggested itself till he had looked for about half a minute at the vicar.

'You'll excuse my naming it, sir,' he said, regarding with much commiseration the mere surface of the vicar's face; 'but perhaps you don't know, sir, that your chin have bust out a-bleeding where you cut yourself a-shaving this morning, sir.'

'Now, that was the stooping, depend upon't, Mr. Mayble,' the tranter suggested, also looking with much interest at the vicar's chin. 'Blood always will bust out again if you hang down the member that ha' been bleeding.'

Old William raised his eyes and watched the vicar's bleeding chin likewise; and Leaf advanced two or three paces from the bookcase, absorbed in the contemplation of the same phenomenon, with parted lips and delighted eyes.

'Dear me, dear me!' said Mr. Maybold hastily, looking very red, and brushing his chin with his hand, then taking out his handkerchief and wiping the place.

'That's it, sir; all right again now, 'a b'lieve – a mere nothing,' said Mr. Penny. 'A little bit of fur off your hat will stop it in a minute if it should bust out again.'

'I'll let ye have a bit of fur off mine,' said Reuben, to show his good feeling; 'my hat isn't so new as yours, sir, and 'twon't hurt mine a bit.'

'No, no; thank you, thank you,' Mr. Maybold again nervously replied.

''Twas rather a deep cut seemingly, sir?' said Reuben, thinking these the kindest and best remarks he could make.

'O, no; not particularly.'

'Well, sir, your hand will shake sometimes a-shaving, and just when it comes into your head that you may cut yourself, there's the blood.'

'I have been revolving in my mind that question of the time at which we make the change,' said Mr. Maybold, 'and I know you'll meet me half-way. I think Christmas-day as much too late for me as the present time is too early for you. I suggest Michaelmas[9] or thereabout as a convenient time for both parties; for I think your objection to a Sunday which has no name is not one of any real weight.'

'Very good, sir. I suppose martel men mustn't expect their own way entirely; and I express in all our names that we'll make shift and be satisfied with what you say.' The tranter touched the brim of his imaginary hat again, and all the choir did the same. 'About Michaelmas, then, as far as you be concerned, sir, and then we make room for the next generation.'

'About Michaelmas,' said the vicar.

CHAPTER V

Returning Homeward

''A took it very well, then?' said Mail, as they all walked up the hill.

'He behaved like a man, 'a did so,' said the tranter.[1] 'Supposing this tree here was Pa'son Mayble as might be, and here be I standing, and that large stone is father sitting in the easy-chair. "Dewy," says he, "I don't wish to change the church music in a forcible way."'

'Now, that was very nice o' the man.'[2]

'Proper nice – out and out nice. The fact is,' said Reuben confidentially, ''tis how you take a man. Everybody must be managed. Queens must be managed: kings must be managed; for men want managing almost as much as women, and that's saying a good deal.'

''Tis truly!' murmured the husbands.

'Pa'son Mayble and I were as good friends all through it as if we'd been sworn brothers. Ay, the man's well enough; 'tis what's in his head that spoils him.'

'There's really no believing half you hear about people nowadays.'

'Bless ye, my sonnies! 'tisn't the pa'son's move at all. That gentleman over there' (the tranter nodded in the direction of Shinar's farm) 'is at the root of the mischief.'

'What! Shinar?'

'Ay; and I see what the pa'son don't see. Why, Shinar is for putting forward that young woman that only last night I was saying was our Dick's sweetheart, but I suppose can't be, and making much of her in the sight of the congregation, and thinking he'll win her by showing her off; well, perhaps 'a will.'

'Then the music is second to the woman, the other churchwarden is second to Shinar, the pa'son is second to the churchwardens, and God A'mighty is nowhere at all.'

'That's true; and you see,' continued Reuben, 'at the very beginning it put me in a stud as to how to quarrel wi' en. In short, to save my soul, I couldn't quarrel wi' such a civil man without belying my conscience. Says he to father there, in a voice as quiet as a lamb's, "William, you are a old aged man, William, as all shall be," says he, "and sit down in my easy-chair, and rest yourself." And down father set. I could fain ha' laughed at thee, father; for thou'st take it so unconcerned at first, and then looked so frightened when the chair-bottom sunk in.'

'Ye see,' said old William, hastening to explain, 'I was alarmed to find the bottom gie way – what should I know o' spring bottoms? – and thought I had broke it down: and of course as to breaking down a man's chair, I didn't wish any such thing.'

'And, naibours, when a feller, ever so much up for a miff, d'see his own father sitting in his enemy's easy-chair, and a pore chap like Leaf made the best of, as if he almost had brains – why, it knocks all the wind out of his sail at once: it did out of mine.'

'If that young figure of fun – Fance Day, I mean,' said Bowman, 'hadn't been so mighty forward wi' showing herself off to Shinar and Dick and the rest, 'tis my belief we should never ha' left the gallery.'

''Tis my belief that though Shinar fired the bullets, the parson made 'em,' said Mr. Penny. 'My wife sticks to it that he's in love wi' her.'

'That's a thing we shall never know. I can't translate[3] her, nohow.'

'Thou'st ought to be able to translate such a little chiel as she,' the tranter observed.

'The littler the maid, the bigger the riddle, to my mind. And coming of such a stock, too, she may well be a twister.'

'Yes; Geoffrey Day is a clever man if ever there was one. Never says anything: not he.'

'Never.'

'You might live wi' that man, my sonnies, a hundred years, and never know there was anything in him.'

'Ay; one o' these up-country London ink-bottle fellers would call Geoffrey a fool.'

'Ye never find out what's in that man: never. Silent? ah, he is silent! He can keep silence well. That man's silence is wonderful to listen to.'[4]

'There's so much sense in it. Every moment of it is brimming over with sound understanding.'

''A can keep a very clever silence – very clever truly,' echoed Leaf. ''A looks at me as if 'a could see my thoughts running round like the works of a clock.'

'Well, all will agree that the man can pause well in conversation, be it a long time or be it a short time. And though we can't expect his daughter to inherit his silence, she may have a few dribblets from his sense.'

'And his pocket, perhaps.'

'Yes; the nine hundred pound that everybody says he's worth; but I call it four hundred and fifty; for I never believe more than half I hear.'

'Well, 'tis to be believed he've made a pound or two, and I suppose the maid will have it, since there's nobody else. But 'tis rather sharp upon her, if she's born to fortune, to make her become as if not born for it, by using her to work so hard.'

''Tis all upon his principle. A long-headed feller!'

'Ah,' murmured Spinks, ''twould be sharper upon her if she were born for fortune, and not to it! I suffer from that affliction.'

CHAPTER VI

Yalbury Wood and the Keeper's House

A mood of blitheness rarely experienced even by young men was Dick's on the following Monday morning. It was the week after the Easter holidays, and he was journeying along with Smart the mare and the light spring-cart, watching the damp slopes of the hill-sides as they steamed[1] in the warmth of the sun, which at this unsettled season shone on the grass with the freshness of an occasional inspector rather than as an accustomed proprietor. His errand was to fetch Fancy, and some additional household goods, to her dwelling at Mellstock. The distant view was darkly shaded with clouds; but the nearer parts of the landscape were whitely illumined by the visible rays of the sun streaming down across the heavy gray shade behind.

The tranter had not yet told his son of the state of Shinar's heart, that had been suggested to him by Shinar's movements. He preferred to let such delicate affairs right themselves; experience having taught him that the uncertain phenomenon of love, as it existed in other people, was not a groundwork upon which a single action of his own life could be founded.

The game-keeper, Geoffrey Day,[2] lived in the depths of Yalbury Wood; but the wood was intersected by a lane at a place not far from the house, and some trees had of late years been felled, to give the solitary cottager a glimpse of the occasional passers-by.

It was a satisfaction to walk into the keeper's house, even as a stranger, on a fine spring morning like the present. A curl of wood-smoke came from the chimney, and drooped over the roof like a blue feather in a lady's hat;[3] and the sun shone obliquely upon the patch of grass in front, which reflected its brightness through the open doorway and up the staircase opposite, lighting up each riser with a shiny green radiance, and leaving the top of each step in shade.

The window-sill of the front room was between four and five feet from the floor, dropping inwardly to a broad low bench, over which, as well as over the whole surface of the wall beneath, there always hung a deep shade, which was considered objectionable on every ground save one, namely, that the perpetual sprinkling of seeds and water by the caged canary above was not noticed as an eyesore by visitors. The window was set with thickly-leaded diamond glazing, formed, especially in the lower panes, of knotty glass of various shades of green. Nothing was better known to Fancy than the extravagant manner in which these circular knots or eyes distorted everything seen through them from the outside – lifting hats from heads, shoulders from bodies; scattering the spokes of cartwheels, and bending the straight fir-trunks into semicircles. The ceiling was carried by a huge beam traversing its midst, from the side of which projected a large nail, used solely and constantly as a peg for Geoffrey's hat; the nail was arched by a rainbow-shaped stain, imprinted by the brim of the said hat when it was hung there dripping wet.

The most striking point about the room was the furniture. This was a repetition upon inanimate objects of the old principle introduced by Noah, consisting for the most part of two articles of every sort. The duplicate system of furnishing owed its existence to the forethought of Fancy's mother, exercised from the date of Fancy's birthday onwards. The arrangement spoke for itself; nobody who knew the tone of the household could look at the goods without being aware that the second set was a provision for Fancy, when she should marry and have a house of her own. The most noticeable instance was a pair of green-faced eight-day clocks, ticking alternately, which were severally two and half minutes and three minutes striking the hour of twelve, one proclaiming, in Italian flourishes, Thomas Wood as the name of its maker, and the other – arched at the top and altogether of more cynical appearance – that of Ezekiel Sparrowgrass.[4]

These were two departed clockmakers of Casterbridge, whose desperate rivalry throughout their lives was nowhere more emphatically perpetuated than here at Geoffrey's. These chief specimens of the marriage provision were supported on the right by a couple of kitchen dressers, each fitted complete with their cups, dishes, and plates, in their turn followed by two dumb-waiters, two family Bibles, two warming-pans, and two intermixed sets of chairs.

But the position last reached – the chimney-corner – was, after all, the most attractive side of the parallelogram. It was large enough to admit, in addition to Geoffrey himself, Geoffrey's wife, her chair, and her work-table, entirely within the line of the mantel, without danger or even inconvenience from the heat of the fire; and was spacious enough overhead to allow of the insertion of wood poles for the hanging of bacon, which were cloaked with long shreds of soot, floating on the draught like the tattered banners on the walls of ancient aisles.

These points were common to most chimney-corners of the neighbour-hood; but one feature there was which made Geoffrey's fireside not only an object of interest to casual aristocratic visitors – to whom every cottage fireside was more or less a curiosity – but the admiration of friends who were accustomed to fireplaces of the ordinary hamlet model. This peculiarity was a little window in the chimney-back, almost over the fire, around which the smoke crept caressingly when it left the perpendicular course. The window-board was curiously stamped with black circles, burnt thereon by the heated bottoms of drinking-cups, which had rested there after previously standing on the hot ashes of the hearth for the purpose of warming their contents, the result giving to the ledge the look of an envelope which has passed through innumerable post-offices.

Fancy was gliding about the room preparing dinner, her head inclining now to the right, now to the left, and singing the tips and ends of tunes that sprang up in her mind like mushrooms. The footsteps of Mrs. Day could be heard in the room overhead. Fancy went finally to the door.

'Father! Dinner.'

A tall spare figure was seen advancing by the window with periodical steps, and the keeper entered from the garden. He appeared to be a man who was always looking down, as if trying to recollect something he said yesterday. The surface of his face was fissured rather than wrinkled, and over and under his eyes were folds which seemed as a kind of exterior eyelids. His nose had been thrown backwards by a blow in a poaching fray, so that when the sun was low and shining in his face, people could see far into his head. There was in him a quiet grimness, which would in his moments of displeasure have become surliness, had it not been tempered by honesty of soul, and which was often wrong-headedness because not allied with subtlety.

Although not an extraordinarily taciturn man among friends slightly richer than he, he never wasted words upon outsiders, and to his trapper Enoch his ideas were seldom conveyed by any other means than nods and shakes of the head. Their long acquaintance with each other's ways, and the nature of their labours, rendered words between them almost superfluous as vehicles of thought, whilst the coincidence of their horizons, and the astonishing equality of their social views, by startling the keeper from time to time as very damaging to the theory of master and man, strictly forbade any indulgence in words as courtesies.

Behind the keeper came Enoch (who had been assisting in the garden) at the well-considered chronological distance of three minutes – an interval of non-appearance on the trapper's part not arrived at without some reflection. Four minutes had been found to express indifference to indoor arrangements, and simultaneousness had implied too great an anxiety about meals.

'A little earlier than usual, Fancy,' the keeper said, as he sat down and looked at the clocks. 'That Ezekiel Sparrowgrass o' thine is tearing on afore Thomas Wood again.'

'I kept in the middle between them,' said Fancy, also looking at the two clocks.

'Better stick to Thomas,' said her father. 'There's a healthy beat in Thomas that would lead a man to swear by en offhand. He is as true as the Squire's time.[5] How is it your stap-mother isn't here?'

As Fancy was about to reply, the rattle of wheels was heard, and 'Weh-hey, Smart!' in Mr. Richard Dewy's voice rolled into the cottage from round the corner of the house.

'Hullo! there's Dewy's cart come for thee, Fancy – Dick driving – afore time, too. Well, ask the lad to have a bit and a drop with us.'

Dick on entering made a point of implying by his general bearing that he took an interest in Fancy simply as in one of the same race and country as himself; and they all sat down. Dick could have wished her manner had not been so entirely free from all apparent consciousness of those accidental meetings of theirs;[6] but he let the thought pass. Enoch sat diagonally at a table afar off, under the corner cupboard, and drank his cider from a long perpendicular pint cup, having tall fir-trees done in brown on its sides. He threw occasional remarks into the general tide of conversation, and with this advantage to himself, that he participated in the pleasures of a talk (slight as it was) at meal-times, without saddling himself with the responsibility of sustaining it.

'Why don't your stap-mother come down, Fancy?' said Geoffrey. 'You'll excuse her, Mister Dick, she's a little quare sometimes.'

'O yes, – quite,' said Richard, as if he were in the habit of excusing several people every day.

'She d'belong to that class of womankind that become second wives: a rum class rather.'[7]

'Indeed,' said Dick, with sympathy for an indefinite something.

'Yes; and 'tis trying to a female, especially if you've been a first wife, as she hev.'

'Very trying it must be.'

'Yes: you see her first husband was a young man, who let her go too far; in fact, she used to kick up Bob's-a-dying at the least thing in the world. And when I'd married her and found it out, I thought, thinks I, "'Tis too late now to begin to cure ye;" and so I let her bide. But she's quare, – very quare, at times!'

'I'm sorry to hear that.'

'Yes: there; wives be such a provoking class of society, because though they be never right, they be never more than half wrong.'

Fancy seemed uneasy under the infliction of this household moralising, which might tend to damage the airy-fairy nature that Dick, as maiden shrewdness told her, had accredited her with. Her dead silence impressed Geoffrey with the notion that something in his words did not agree with her educated ideas, and he changed the conversation.

'Did Fred Shinar send the cask o' drink, Fancy?'[8]

'I think he did: O yes, he did.'

'Nice solid feller, Fred Shinar!' said Geoffrey to Dick as he helped himself to gravy, bringing the spoon round to his plate by way of the potato-dish, to obviate a stain on the cloth in the event of a spill.

Geoffrey's eyes had been fixed upon his plate for the previous four or five minutes, and in removing them he had only carried them to the spoon, which, from its fulness and the distance of its transit, necessitated a steady watching through the whole of the route. Just as intently as the keeper's eyes had been fixed on the spoon, Fancy's had been fixed on her father's, without premeditation or the slightest phase of furtiveness; but there they were fastened. This was the reason why:

Dick was sitting next to her on the right side, and on the side of the table opposite to her father. Fancy had laid her right hand lightly down upon the table-cloth for an instant, and to her alarm Dick, after dropping his fork and brushing his forehead as a reason, flung down his own left hand, overlapping a third of Fancy's with it, and keeping it there. So the innocent Fancy, instead of pulling her hand from the trap, settled her eyes on her father's, to guard against his discovery of this perilous game of Dick's. Dick finished his mouthful; Fancy finished her crumb, and nothing was done beyond watching Geoffrey's eyes. Then the hands slid apart; Fancy's going over six inches of cloth, Dick's over one. Geoffrey's eye had risen.

'I said Fred Shinar is a nice solid feller,' he repeated, more emphatically.

'He is; yes, he is,' stammered Dick; 'but to me he is little more than a stranger.'

'True. There, I know en as well as any man can be known. And you know en very well too, don't ye, Fancy?'

Geoffrey put on a tone expressing that these words signified at present about one hundred times the amount of meaning they conveyed literally.

Dick looked anxious.

'Will you pass me some bread?' said Fancy in a flurry, the red of her face becoming slightly disordered, and looking as solicitous as a human being could look about a piece of bread.

'Ay, that I will,' replied the unconscious Geoffrey. 'Ay,' he continued, returning to the displaced idea, 'we be likely to remain friendly wi' Mr. Shinar if the wheels d'run smooth.'

'An excellent thing – a very capital thing, as I should say,' the youth answered with exceeding relevance, considering that his thoughts, instead of following Geoffrey's remark, were nestling at a distance of about two feet on his left the whole time.

'A young woman's face will turn the north wind, Master Richard: my heart if 'twon't.' Dick looked more anxious and was attentive in earnest at these words. 'Yes; turn the north wind,' added Geoffrey after an emphatic pause. 'And though she's one of my own flesh and blood . . .'

'Will you fetch down a bit of raw-mil' cheese from pantry-shelf,' Fancy interrupted, as if she were famishing.

'Ay, that I will, chiel, chiel, says I, and Mr. Shinar only asking last Saturday night . . . cheese you said, Fancy?'

Dick controlled his emotion at these mysterious allusions to Mr. Shinar, – the better enabled to do so by perceiving that Fancy's heart went not with her father's – and spoke like a stranger to the affairs of the neighbourhood. 'Yes, there's a great deal to be said upon the power of maiden faces in settling your courses,' he said as the keeper retreated for the cheese.

'The conversation is taking a very strange turn: nothing that *I* have ever done warrants such things being said,' murmured Fancy with emphasis, just loud enough to reach Dick's ears.[9]

'You think to yourself, 'twas to be,' cried Enoch from his distant corner, by way of filling up the vacancy caused by Geoffrey's momentary absence. 'And so you marry her, Master Dewy, and there's an end o't.'

'Pray don't say such things, Enoch,' said Fancy severely, upon which Enoch relapsed into servitude.

'If we are doomed to marry, we marry; if we are doomed to remain single, we do,' replied Dick.

Geoffrey had by this time sat down again, and he now made his lips thin by severely straining them across his gums, and looked out of the fireplace window to the end of the paddock with solemn scrutiny. 'That's not the case with some folk,' he said at length, as if he read the words on a board at the farther end of the paddock.

Fancy looked interested, and Dick said, 'No?'

'There's that wife o' mine. It was her doom not to be nobody's wife at all in the wide universe. But she made up her mind that she would, and did it twice over. Doom? Doom is nothing beside a elderly woman – quite a chiel in her hands.'

A movement was now heard along the upstairs passage and footsteps descending. The door at the foot of the stairs opened and the second Mrs. Day appeared in view, looking fixedly at the table as she advanced towards it, with apparent obliviousness of the presence of any other human being than herself. In short, if the table had been the personages, and the persons the table, her glance would have been the most natural imaginable.

She showed herself to possess an ordinary woman's face, iron-gray hair, hardly any hips, and a great deal of cleanliness in a broad white apron-string, as it appeared upon the waist of her dark stuff dress.

'People will run away with a story now, I suppose,' she began saying, 'that Jane Day's table-cloths be as poor and ragged as any union beggar's!'

Dick now perceived that the table-cloth was a little the worse for wear, and reflecting for a moment, concluded that 'people' in step-mother language probably meant himself. On lifting his eyes he found that Mrs. Day had vanished again upstairs, and presently returned with an armful of new damask-linen table-cloths, folded square and hard as boards by long compression. These she flounced down into a chair; then took one, shook it out from its folds, and spread it on the table by instalments, transferring the plates and dishes one by one from the old to the new cloth.

'And I suppose they'll say, too, that she hasn't a decent knife and fork in her house!'

'I shouldn't say any such ill-natured thing, I am sure –' began Dick. But Mrs. Day had vanished into the next room. Fancy appeared distressed.

'Very strange woman, isn't she?' said Geoffrey, quietly going on with his dinner. 'But 'tis too late to attempt curing. My heart! 'tis so growed into her that 'twould kill her to take it out. Ay, she's very quare: you'd be amazed to see what valuable goods we've got stowed away upstairs.'

Back again came Mrs. Day with a box of bright steel horn-handled knives, silver forks, carver, and all complete. These were wiped of the preservative oil which coated them, and then a knife and fork were laid down to each individual with a bang, the carving knife and fork thrust into the meat dish, and the old ones they had hitherto used tossed away.

Geoffrey placidly cut a slice with the new knife and fork, and asked Dick if he wanted any more.

The table had been spread for the mixed midday meal of dinner and tea, which is common among cottagers.[10] 'The parishioners about here,' continued Mrs. Day, not looking at any living being, but snatching up the brown delf tea-things, 'be the laziest, gossipest, poachest, jailest[11] set of any ever I come among. And they'll talk about my teapot and tea-things next, I suppose!' She vanished with the teapot, cups, and saucers, and reappeared with a tea-service in white china, and a packet wrapped in brown paper. This was removed, together with folds of tissue-paper underneath; and a brilliant silver teapot appeared.

'I'll help to put the things right,' said Fancy soothingly, and rising from her seat. 'I ought to have laid out better things, I suppose. But' (here she enlarged her looks so as to include Dick) 'I have been away from home a good deal, and I make shocking blunders in my housekeeping.' Smiles and suavity were then dispensed all around by the bright little bird.

After a little more preparation and modification, Mrs. Day took her seat at the head of the table, and during the latter or tea division of the meal, presided with much composure. It may cause some surprise to learn that, now her vagary was over, she showed herself to be an excellent person with much common sense, and even a religious seriousness of tone on matters pertaining to her afflictions.

CHAPTER VII

Dick Makes Himself Useful

The effect of Geoffrey's incidental allusions to Mr. Shinar was to restrain a considerable quantity of spontaneous chat that would otherwise have burst from young Dewy along the drive homeward. And a certain remark he had hazarded to her, in rather too blunt and eager a manner, kept the young lady herself even more silent than Dick. On both sides there was an unwillingness to talk on any but the most trivial subjects, and their sentences rarely took a larger form than could be expressed in two or three words.

Owing to Fancy being later in the day than she had promised, the charwoman had given up expecting her; whereupon Dick could do no less than stay and see her comfortably tided through the disagreeable time of entering and establishing herself in an empty house after an absence of a week. The additional furniture and utensils that had been brought (a canary and cage among the rest) were taken out of the vehicle, and the horse was unharnessed and put in the school plot, where there was some tender grass. Dick lighted the fire; and activity began to loosen their tongues a little.

'There!' said Fancy, 'we forgot to bring the fire-irons!'

She had originally found in her house, to bear out the expression 'nearly furnished' which the school-manager had used in his letter to her, a table, three chairs, a fender, and a piece of carpet. This 'nearly' had been supplemented hitherto by a kind friend, who had lent her fire-irons and crockery until she should fetch some from home.

Dick attended to the young lady's fire, using his whip-handle for a poker till it was spoilt, and then flourishing a hurdle stick for the remainder of the time.

'The kettle boils, now you shall have a cup of tea,' said Fancy, diving into the hamper she had brought.

'Thank you,' said Dick, whose drive had made him ready for a cup, especially in her company.

'Well, here's only one cup and saucer, as I breathe! Whatever could mother be thinking about. Do you mind making shift, Mr. Dewy?'

'Not at all, Miss Day,' said that civil person.

'And only having a cup by itself? or a saucer by itself?'

'Don't mind in the least.'

'Which do you mean by that?'

'I mean the cup, if you like the saucer.'

'And the saucer, if I like the cup?'

'Exactly, Miss Day.'

'Thank you, Mr. Dewy, for I like the cup decidedly. Stop a minute; there are no spoons now!' She dived into the hamper again, and at the end of two or three minutes looked up and said, 'I suppose you don't mind if I can't find a spoon?'

'Not at all,' said the agreeable Richard.

'The fact is, the spoons have slipped down somewhere; right under the other things. O yes, here's one, and only one. You would rather have one than not, I suppose, Mr. Dewy?'

'Rather not. I never did care much about spoons.'

'Then I'll have it. I do care about them. You must stir up your tea with a knife. Would you mind lifting the kettle off, that it may not boil dry?'

Dick leaped to the fireplace, and earnestly removed the kettle.

'There! you did it so wildly that you have made your hand black. We always use kettle-holders; didn't you learn housewifery as far as that, Mr. Dewy? Well, never mind the soot on your hand. Come here. I am going to rinse mine, too.'

They went to a basin she had placed in the back room. 'This is the only basin I have,' she said. 'Turn up your sleeves, and by that time my hands will be washed, and you can come.'

Her hands were in the water now. 'O, how vexing!' she exclaimed.

'There's not a drop of water left for you, unless you draw it, and the well is I don't know how many feet deep; all that was in the pitcher I used for the kettle and this basin. Do you mind dipping the tips of your fingers in the same?'

'Not at all. And to save time I won't wait till you have done, if you have no objection?'

Thereupon he plunged in his hands, and they paddled together. It being the first time in his life that he had touched female fingers under water, Dick duly registered the sensation as rather a nice one.[1]

'Really, I hardly know which are my own hands and which are yours, they have got so mixed up together,' she said, withdrawing her own very suddenly.

'It doesn't matter at all,' said Dick, 'at least as far as I am concerned.'

'There! no towel! Whoever thinks of a towel till the hands are wet?'

'Nobody.'

'"Nobody." How very dull it is when people are so friendly! Come here, Mr. Dewy. Now do you think you could lift the lid of that box with your elbow, and then, with something or other, take out a towel you will find under the clean clothes. Be *sure* don't touch any of them with your wet hands, for the things at the top are all Starched and Ironed.'

Dick managed, by the aid of a knife and fork, to extract a towel from under a muslin dress without wetting the latter; and for a moment he ventured to assume a tone of criticism.

'I fear for that dress,' he said, as they wiped their hands together.

'What?' said Miss Day, looking into the box at the dress alluded to. 'O, I know what you mean – that the vicar will never let me wear muslin?'

'Yes.'

'Well, I know it is condemned by all parties in the church as flaunting, and unfit for common wear for girls below clerical condition; but we'll see.'

'In the interest of the church, I hope you don't speak seriously.'

'Yes, I do; but we'll see.' There was a comely determination on her lip, very pleasant to a beholder who was neither bishop, priest, nor deacon. 'I think I can manage any vicar's views about me if he's under forty.'

Dick rather wished she had never thought of managing vicars.[2]

'I certainly shall be glad to get some of your delicious tea,' he said in rather a free way, yet modestly, as became one in a position between that of visitor and inmate, and looking wistfully at his lonely saucer.

'So shall I. Now is there anything else we want, Mr. Dewy?'

'I really think there's nothing else, Miss Day.'

She prepared to sit down, looking musingly out of the window at Smart's enjoyment of the rich grass. 'Nobody seems to care about me,' she murmured, with large lost eyes fixed upon the sky beyond Smart.

'Perhaps Mr. Shinar does,' said Dick, in the tone of a slightly injured man.

'Yes, I forgot – he does, I know.' Dick precipitately regretted that he had suggested Shinar, since it had produced such a miserable result as this.

'I'll warrant you'll care for somebody very much indeed another day, won't you, Mr. Dewy?' she continued, looking very feelingly into the mathematical centre of his eyes.

'Ah, I'll warrant I shall!' said Dick, feelingly too, and looking back into her dark pupils, whereupon they were turned aside.

'I meant,' she went on, preventing him from speaking just as he was going to narrate a forcible story about his feelings; 'I meant that nobody comes to see if I have returned – not even the vicar.'

'If you want to see him, I'll call at the vicarage directly we have had some tea.'

'No, no! Don't let him come down here, whatever you do, whilst I am in such a state of disarrangement. Vicars look so miserable and awkward when one's house is in a muddle; walking about, and making impossible suggestions in quaint academic phrases till your flesh creeps and you wish them dead. Do you take sugar?'

Mr. Maybold was at this instant seen coming up the path.

'There! That's he coming! How I wish you were not here! – that is, how awkward – dear, dear!' she exclaimed, with a quick ascent of blood to her face, and irritated with Dick rather than the vicar, as it seemed.

'Pray don't be alarmed on my account, Miss Day – good-afternoon!' said Dick in a huff, putting on his hat, and leaving the room hastily by the back-door.

The horse was put in, and on mounting the shafts to start, he saw through the window the vicar standing upon some books piled in a chair, and driving a nail into the wall; Fancy, with a demure glance, holding the canary-cage up to him, as if she had never in her life thought of anything but vicars and canaries.

CHAPTER VIII

Dick Meets His Father

For several minutes Dick drove along homeward, with the inward eye of reflection so anxiously set on his passages at arms with Fancy,[1] that the road and scenery were as a thin mist over the real pictures of his mind. Was she a coquette? The balance between the evidence that she did love him and that she did not was so nicely struck, that his opinion had no stability. She had let him put his hand upon hers; she had allowed her eyes to drop plump into the depths of his – his into hers – three or four times; her manner had been very free with regard to the basin and towel; she had appeared vexed at the mention of Shinar. On the other hand, she had driven him about the house like a quiet dog or cat, said Shinar cared for her, and seemed anxious that Mr. Maybold should do the same.

Thinking thus as he turned the corner at Mellstock Cross, sitting on the front board of the spring cart – his legs on the outside, and his whole frame jigging up and down like a candle-flame to the time of Smart's trotting – who should he see coming down the hill but his father in the light wagon, quivering up and down on a smaller scale of shakes, those merely caused by the stones in the road. They were soon crossing each other's front.

'Weh-hey!' said the tranter to Smiler.

'Weh-hey!' said Dick to Smart, in an echo of the same voice.

'Th'st hauled her over, I suppose?' Reuben inquired peaceably.

'Yes,' said Dick, with such a clinching period at the end that it seemed he was never going to add another word. Smiler, thinking this the close of the conversation, prepared to move on.

'Weh-hey!' said the tranter. 'I tell thee what it is, Dick. That there maid is taking up thy thoughts more than's good for thee, my sonny. Thou'rt never happy now unless th'rt making thyself miserable about her in one way or another.'

'I don't know about that, father,' said Dick rather stupidly.

'But I do – Wey, Smiler! – 'Od rot the women, 'tis nothing else wi' 'em nowadays but getting young men and leading 'em astray.'

'Pooh, father! you just repeat what all the common world says; that's all you do.'

'The world's a very sensible feller on things in jineral, Dick; a very sensible party indeed.'

Dick looked into the distance at a vast expanse of mortgaged estate. 'I wish I was as rich as a lord when he's as poor as a crow,' he murmured; 'I'd soon ask Fancy something.'

'I wish so too, wi' all my heart, sonny; that I do. Well, mind what beest about, that's all.'

Smart moved on a step or two. 'Supposing now, father – We-hey, Smart! – I did think a little about her, and I had a chance, which I ha'n't; don't you think she's a very good sort of – of – one?'

'Ay, good; she's good enough. When you've made up your mind to marry, take the first respectable body that comes to hand – she's as good as any other; they be all alike in the groundwork: 'tis only in the flourishes there's a difference. She's good enough; but I can't see what the nation a young feller like you – wi' a comfortable house and home, and father and mother to take care o' thee, and who sent 'ee to a school so good that 'twas hardly fair to the other children – should want to go hollering after a young woman for, when she's quietly making a husband in her pocket, and not troubled by chick nor chiel, to make a poverty-stric' wife and family of her, and neither hat, cap, wig, nor waistcoat to set 'em up wi': be drowned if I can see it, and that's the long and short o't, my sonny!'

Dick looked at Smart's ears, then up the hill; but no reason was suggested by any object that met his gaze.

'For about the same reason that you did, father, I suppose.'

'Dang it, my sonny, thou'st got me there!' and the tranter gave vent to a grim admiration, with the mien of a man who was too magnanimous not to appreciate a slight rap on the knuckles, even if they were his own.

'Whether or no,' said Dick, 'I asked her a thing going along the road.'

'Come to that, is it? Turk! won't thy mother be in a taking! Well, she's ready, I don't doubt?'

'I didn't ask her anything about having me; and if you'll let me speak, I'll tell 'ee what I want to know. I just said, Did she care about me?'

'Piph-ph-ph!'

'And then she said nothing for a quarter of a mile, and then she said she didn't know. Now, what I want to know is, what was the meaning of that speech?' The latter words were spoken resolutely, as if he didn't care for the ridicule of all the fathers in creation.

'The maning of that speech is,' the tranter replied deliberately, 'that the maning is rather hid at present.² Well, Dick, as an honest father to thee, I don't pretend to deny what you d'know well enough; that is, that her father being rather better in the world than we, I should welcome her ready enough if it must be somebody.'

'But what d'ye think she really did mean?' said Dick.

'I'm afeard I ben't o' much account in guessing, especially as I was not there when she said it, and seeing that your mother was the only woman I ever cam into such close quarters as that wi'.'

'And what did mother say to you when you asked her?' said Dick musingly.

'I don't see that that will help ye.'

'The principle is the same.'

'Well – ay: what did she say? Let's see. I was oiling my working-day boots without taking 'em off, and wi' my head hanging down, when she just brushed on by the garden hatch like a flittering leaf. "Ann," I said, says I, and then, – but, Dick, I be afeard 'twill be no help to thee; for we were such a rum couple, your mother and I, leastways one half was, that is myself – and your mother's charms was more in the manner than the material.'

'Never mind! "Ann," said you.'

'"Ann," said I, as I was saying . . . "Ann," I said to her when I was oiling my working-day boots wi' my head hanging down, "Woot hae me?" . . . What came next I can't quite call up at this distance o' time. Perhaps your mother would know, – she's a better memory for her little triumphs than I. However, the long and the short o' the story is that we were married somehow, as I found afterwards. 'Twas on White Tuesday, – Mellstock Club walked the same day,³ every man two and two, and a fine day 'twas, – hot as fire, – the sun did strik' down upon my back going to church! I well can mind what a bath o' sweating I was in, body and mind! But Fance will ha' thee, Dick – she won't walk wi' another chap – no such good luck.'

'I don't know about that,' said Dick, whipping at Smart's flank in a fanciful way, which, as Smart knew, meant nothing in connection with going on. 'There's Pa'son Maybold, too – that's all against me.'

'What about he? She's never been stuffing into thy innocent heart that he's in love wi' her? Lord, the vanity o' maidens!'

'No, no. But he called, and she looked at him in such a way, and at me in such a way – quite different the ways were, – and as I was coming off, there was he hanging up her birdcage.'

'Well, why shouldn't the man hang up her birdcage? Turk seize it all, what's that got to do wi' it? Dick, that thou beest a white-lyvered chap I don't say, but if thou beestn't as mad as a cappel-faced bull, let me smile no more.'

'O, ay.'

'And what's think now, Dick?'

'I don't know.'

'Here's another pretty kettle o' fish for thee. Who d'ye think's the bitter weed in our being turned out? Did our party tell'ee?'

'No. Why, Pa'son Maybold, I suppose.'

'Shinar, – because he's in love with thy young woman, and d'want to see her young figure sitting up at that quare instrume't, and her young fingers rum-strumming upon the keys.'

A sharp ado of sweet and bitter was going on in Dick during this communication from his father. 'Shinar's a fool! – no, that's not it; I don't believe any such thing, father. Why, Shinar would never take a determined step like that, unless she'd been a little made up to, and had taken it kindly. Pooh!'

'Who's to say she didn't?'

'I do.'

'The more fool you.'

'Why, father of me?'

'Has she ever done more to thee?'

'No.'

'Then she has done as much to he – rot 'em! Now, Dick, this is how a maiden is. She'll swear she's dying for thee, and she is dying for thee, and she will die for thee; but she'll fling a look over t'other shoulder at another young feller, though never leaving off dying for thee just the same.'

'She's not dying for me, and so she didn't fling a look at him.'

'But she may be dying for him, for she looked at thee.'

'I don't know what to make of it at all,' said Dick gloomily.

'All I can make of it is,' the tranter said, raising his whip, arranging his different joints and muscles, and motioning to the horse to move on, 'that if you can't read a maid's mind by her motions, nater d'seem to say thou'st ought to be a bachelor. Clk, clk! Smiler!' And the tranter moved on.

Dick held Smart's rein firmly, and the whole concern of horse, cart, and man remained rooted in the lane. How long this condition would have lasted is unknown, had not Dick's thoughts, after adding up numerous items of misery, gradually wandered round to the fact, that as something must be done, it could not be done by staying there all night.

Reaching home he went up to his bedroom, shut the door as if he were going to be seen no more in this life, and taking a sheet of paper and uncorking the ink-bottle, he began a letter. The dignity of the writer's mind was so powerfully apparent in every line of this effusion, that it obscured the logical sequence of facts and intentions to such an appreciable degree that it was not at all clear to a reader whether he there and then left off loving Miss Fancy Day; whether he had never loved her seriously, and never meant to; whether he had been dying up to the present moment, and now intended to get well again; or whether he had hitherto been in good health, and intended to die for her forthwith.

He put this letter in an envelope, sealed it up, directed it in a stern handwriting of straight firm dashes – easy flourishes being rigorously excluded. He walked with it in his pocket down the lane in strides not an inch less than three feet and a half long. Reaching her gate he put on a resolute expression – then put it off again, turned back homeward, tore up his letter, and sat down.

That letter was altogether in a wrong tone – that he must own. A heartless man-of-the-world tone was what the juncture required. That he rather wanted her, and rather did not want her – the latter for choice; but that as a member of society he didn't mind making a query in plain terms,[4] which could only be answered in the same plain terms: did she mean anything by her bearing towards him, or did she not?

This letter was considered so satisfactory in every way that, being put into the hands of a little boy, and the order given that he was to run with it to the school, he was told in addition not to look behind him if Dick called after him to bring it back, but to run along with it just the same. Having taken this precaution against vacillation, Dick watched his messenger down the road, and turned into the house whistling an air in such ghastly jerks and starts, that whistling seemed to be the act the very farthest removed from that which was instinctive in such a youth.

The letter was left as ordered: the next morning came and passed –

and no answer. The next. The next. Friday night came. Dick resolved that if no answer or sign were given by her the next day, on Sunday he would meet her face to face, and have it all out by word of mouth.

'Dick,' said his father, coming in from the garden at that moment – in each hand a hive of bees tied in a cloth to prevent their egress – 'I think you'd better take these two swarms of bees to Mrs. Maybold's to-morrow, instead o' me, and I'll go wi' Smiler and the wagon.'

It was a relief; for Mrs. Maybold, the vicar's mother, who had just taken into her head a fancy for keeping bees (pleasantly disguised under the pretence of its being an economical wish to produce her own honey), lived at a watering-place fourteen miles off,[5] and the business of transporting the hives thither would occupy the whole day, and to some extent annihilate the vacant time between this evening and the coming Sunday. The best spring-cart was washed throughout, the axles oiled, and the bees placed therein for the journey.

PART III

Summer

CHAPTER I

Driving out of Budmouth

An easy bend of neck and graceful set of head; full and wavy bundles of dark-brown hair; light fall of little feet; pretty devices on the skirt of the dress; clear deep eyes; in short, a bunch of sweets: it was Fancy! Dick's heart went round to her with a rush.

The scene was the corner of the front street at Budmouth, at which point the angle of the last house in the row cuts perpendicularly a wide expanse of nearly motionless ocean – to-day, shaded in bright tones of green and opal.[1] Dick and Smart had just emerged from the street, and there, against the brilliant sheet of liquid colour, stood Fancy Day; and she turned and recognised him.

Dick suspended his thoughts of the letter and wonder at how she came there by driving close to the edge of the parade – displacing two chairmen, who had just come to life for the summer in new clean shirts and revivified clothes, and being almost displaced in turn by a rigid boy advancing with a roll under his arm,[2] and looking neither to the right nor the left – and asking if she were going to Mellstock that night.

'Yes, I'm waiting for the carrier,' she replied, seeming, too, to suspend thoughts of the letter.

'Now I can drive you home nicely, and you save an hour. Will you come with me?'

As Fancy's power to will anything seemed to have departed in some mysterious manner at that moment, Dick settled the matter by getting out and assisting her into the vehicle without another word.

The temporary flush upon her cheek changed to a lesser hue, which was permanent, and at length their eyes met; there was present between them a certain feeling of embarrassment, which arises at such moments when all the instinctive acts dictated by the position have been performed. Dick, being engaged with the reins, thought less of this awkwardness than did Fancy, who had nothing to do but to feel his presence, and to be more and more conscious of the fact, that by accepting a seat beside him in this way she succumbed to the tone of his note. Smart jogged along, and Dick jogged, and the helpless Fancy necessarily jogged too; and she felt that she was in a measure captured and made a prisoner.

'I am so much obliged to you for your company, Miss Day.'[3]

To Miss Day, crediting him with the same consciousness of mastery – a consciousness of which he was perfectly innocent – this remark sounded like a magnanimous intention to soothe her, the captive.

'I didn't come for the pleasure of obliging you with my company,' she said.

The answer had an unexpected manner of incivility in it that must have been rather surprising to young Dewy. At the same time it may be observed, that when a young woman returns a rude answer to a young man's civil remark, her heart is in a state which argues rather hopefully for his case than otherwise.

There was silence between them till they had passed about twenty of the equidistant elm-trees that ornamented the road leading up out of the town.[4]

'Though I didn't come for that purpose either, I would have,' said Dick at the twenty-first tree.

'Now, Mr. Dewy, no flirtation, because it's wrong, and I don't wish it.'

Dick seated himself afresh just as he had been sitting before, and arranged his looks very emphatically, then cleared his throat.

'Really, anybody would think you had met me on business and were just going to begin,' said the lady intractably.

'Yes, they would.'

'Why, you never have, to be sure!'

This was a shaky beginning. He chopped round, and said cheerily, as a man who had resolved never to spoil his jollity by loving one of womankind,

'Well, how are you getting on, Miss Day, at the present time? Gaily, I don't doubt for a moment.'

'I am not gay, Dick; you know that.'

'Gaily doesn't mean decked in gay dresses.'

'I didn't suppose gaily was gaily dressed. Mighty me, what a scholar you've grown!'

'Lots of things have happened to you this spring, I see.'

'What have you seen?'

'O, nothing; I've heard, I mean!'

'What have you heard?'

'The name of a pretty man, with brass studs and a copper ring and a tin watch-chain, a little mixed up with your own. That's all.'

'That's a very unkind picture of Mr. Shinar, for that's who you mean. The studs are gold, as you know, and it's a real silver chain; the ring I can't conscientiously defend, and he only wore it once.'

'He might have worn it a hundred times without showing it half so much.'

'Well, he's nothing to me,' she serenely observed.

'Not any more than I am?'

'Now, Mr. Dewy,' said Fancy severely, 'certainly he isn't any more to me than you are!'

'Not so much?'

She looked aside to consider the precise compass of that question. 'That I can't exactly answer,' she replied with soft archness.[5]

As they were going rather slowly, another spring-cart, containing a farmer, farmer's wife, and farmer's man, jogged past them; and the farmer's wife and farmer's man eyed the couple very curiously. The farmer never looked up from the horse's tail.

'Why can't you exactly answer?' said Dick, quickening Smart a little, and jogging on just behind the farmer and farmer's wife and man.

As no answer came, and as their eyes had nothing else to do, they both contemplated the picture presented in front, and noticed how the farmer's wife sat flattened between the two men, who bulged over each end of the seat to give her room, till they almost sat upon their respective wheels; and they looked too at the farmer's wife's silk mantle, inflating itself between her shoulders like a balloon, and sinking flat again, at each jog of the horse. The farmer's wife, feeling their eyes sticking into her back, looked over her shoulder. Dick dropped ten yards farther behind.

'Fancy, why can't you answer?' he repeated.

'Because how much you are to me depends upon how much I am to you,' said she in low tones.

'Everything,' said Dick, putting his hand towards hers, and casting emphatic eyes upon the upper curve of her cheek.

'Now, Richard Dewy, no touching me. I didn't say in what way your thinking of me affected the question – perhaps inversely, don't you see? No touching, sir! Look; goodness me, don't, Dick!'

The cause of her sudden start was the unpleasant appearance over Dick's right shoulder of an empty timber-wagon and four journeymen-carpenters reclining in lazy postures inside it, their eyes directed upwards at various oblique angles into the surrounding world, the chief object of their existence being apparently to criticise to the very backbone and marrow every animate object that came within the compass of their vision. This difficulty of Dick's was overcome by trotting on till the wagon and carpenters were beginning to look reduced in size and rather misty, by reason of a film of dust that accompanied their wagon-wheels, and rose around their heads like a fog.

'Say you love me, Fancy.'

'No, Dick, certainly not; 'tisn't time to do that yet.'

'Why, Fancy?'

' "Miss Day" is better at present – don't mind my saying so; and I ought not to have called you Dick.'

'Nonsense! when you know that I would do anything on earth for your love. Why, you make any one think that loving is a thing that can be done and undone, and put on and put off at a mere whim.'

'No, no, I don't,' she said gently; 'but there are things which tell me I ought not to give way to much thinking about you, even if –'

'But you want to, don't you? Yes, say you do; it is best to be truthful, Fancy. Whatever they may say about a woman's right to conceal where her love lies, and pretend it doesn't exist, and things like that, it is not best; I do know it, Fancy. And an honest woman in that, as well as in all her daily concerns, shines most brightly, and is thought most of in the long-run.'

'Well then, perhaps, Dick, I do love you a little,' she whispered tenderly; 'but I wish you wouldn't say any more now.'

'I won't say any more now, then, if you don't like it. But you do love me a little, don't you?'

'Now you ought not to want me to keep saying things twice; I can't say any more now, and you must be content with what you have.'

'I may at any rate call you Fancy? There's no harm in that.'

'Yes, you may.'

'And you'll not call me Mr. Dewy any more?'

'Very well.'

CHAPTER II

Farther along the Road

Dick's spirits having risen in the course of these admissions of his sweet-heart, he now touched Smart with the whip; and on Smart's neck, not far behind his ears. Smart, who had been lost in thought for some time, never dreaming that Dick could reach so far with a whip which, on this particular journey, had never been extended farther than his flank, tossed his head, and scampered along with exceeding briskness, which was very pleasant to the young couple behind him till, turning a bend in the road, they came instantly upon the farmer, farmer's man, and farmer's wife with the flapping mantle, all jogging on just the same as ever.

'Bother those people! Here we are upon them again.'

'Well, of course. They have as much right to the road as we.'

'Yes, but it is provoking to be overlooked so. I like a road all to myself. Look what a lumbering affair theirs is!' The wheels of the farmer's cart, just at that moment, jogged into a depression running across the road, giving the cart a twist, whereupon all three nodded to the left, and on coming out of it all three nodded to the right, and went on jerking their backs in and out as usual. 'We'll pass them when the road gets wider.'

When an opportunity seemed to offer itself for carrying this intention into effect, they heard light flying wheels behind, and on quartering, there whizzed along past them a brand-new gig, so brightly polished that the spokes of the wheels sent forth a continual quivering light at one point in their circle, and all the panels glared like mirrors in Dick and Fancy's eyes. The driver, and owner as it appeared, was really a handsome man; his companion was Shinar. Both turned round as they passed Dick and Fancy, and stared steadily in her face till they were obliged to attend to the operation of passing the farmer. Dick glanced for an instant at Fancy while she was undergoing their scrutiny; then returned to his driving with rather a sad countenance.

'Why are you so silent?' she said, after a while, with real concern.

'Nothing.'

'Yes, it is, Dick. I couldn't help those people passing.'

'I know that.'

'You look offended with me. What have I done?'

'I can't tell without offending you.'

'Better out.'

'Well,' said Dick, who seemed longing to tell, even at the risk of offending her, 'I was thinking how different you in love are from me in love. Whilst those men were staring, you dismissed me from your thoughts altogether, and –'

'You can't offend me farther now; tell all.'

'And showed upon your face a flattered consciousness of being attractive to them.'

'Don't be silly, Dick! You know very well I didn't.'

Dick shook his head sceptically, and smiled.

'Dick, I always believe flattery *if possible* – and it was possible then. Now there's an open confession of weakness. But I showed no consciousness of it.'[1]

Dick, perceiving by her look that she would adhere to her statement, charitably forbore saying anything that could make her prevaricate. The sight of Shinar, too, had recalled another branch of the subject to his mind; that which had been his greatest trouble till her company and words had obscured its probability.

'By the way, Fancy, do you know why our choir is to be dismissed?'

'No: except that it is Mr. Maybold's wish for me to play the organ.'

'Do you know how it came to be his wish?'

'That I don't.'

'Mr. Shinar, being churchwarden, has persuaded the vicar; who, however, was willing enough before. Shinar, I know, is crazy to see you playing every Sunday; I suppose he'll turn over your music, for the organ will be close to his pew. But – I know you have never encouraged him?'

'Never once!' said Fancy emphatically, and with eyes full of earnest truth. 'I don't like him indeed, and I never heard of his doing this before! I have always felt that I should like to play in a church, but I never wished to turn you and your choir out; and I never even said that I could play till I was asked. You don't think for a moment that I did, surely, do you?'

'I know you didn't, Fancy.'

'Or that I care the least morsel of a bit for him?'

'I know you don't.'

The distance between Budmouth and Mellstock was eighteen miles, and there being a good inn six miles out of Budmouth, Dick's custom in driving thither was to divide his journey into three stages by resting at this inn, going and coming, and not troubling the Budmouth stables at all, whenever his visit to the town was a mere call and deposit, as to-day.

Fancy was ushered into a little tea-room, and Dick went to the stables to see to the feeding of Smart. In face of the significant twitches of feature that were visible in the ostler and odd men idling around, Dick endeavoured to look unconscious of the fact that there was any sentiment between him and Fancy beyond a tranter's desire to carry a passenger home. He presently entered the inn and opened the door of Fancy's room.

'Dick, do you know, it has struck me that it is rather awkward, my being here alone with you like this. I don't think you had better come in with me.'

'That's rather unpleasant.'

'Yes, it is, and I wanted you to have some tea as well as myself too, because you must be tired.'

'Well, let me have some with you, then. I was denied once before, if you recollect, Fancy.'

'Yes, yes, never mind! And it seems unfriendly of me now, but I don't know what to do.'

'It shall be as you say, then,' said Dick, beginning to retreat with a dissatisfied wrinkling of face, and giving a farewell glance at the cosy tea-tray.

'But you don't see how it is, Dick, when you speak like that,' she said, with more earnestness than she had ever shown before. 'You do know, that even if I care very much for you, I must remember that I have a difficult position to maintain. The vicar would not like me, as his schoolmistress, to indulge in *tête-à-têtes* anywhere with anybody.'

'But I am not *any* body!' exclaimed Dick.

'No, no, I mean with a young man;' and she added softly, 'unless I were really engaged to be married to him.'

'Is that all? then, dearest, dearest, why we'll be engaged at once, to be sure we will, and down I sit! There it is, as easy as a glove!'

'Ah! but suppose I won't! And, goodness me, what have I done!' she faltered, getting very red and confused. 'Positively, it seems as if I meant you to say that!'

'Let's do it! I mean get engaged,' said Dick. 'Now, Fancy, will you be my wife?'

'Do you know, Dick, it was rather unkind of you to say what you did coming along the road,' she remarked, as if she had not heard the latter part of his speech; though an acute observer might have noticed about her breast, as the word 'wife' fell from Dick's lips, soft motions consisting of a silent escape of pants,[2] with very short rests between each.

'What did I say?'

'About my trying to look attractive to those men in the gig.'

'You couldn't help looking so, whether you tried or no. And, Fancy, you do care for me?'

'Yes.'

'Very much?'

'Yes.'

'And you'll be my own wife?'

Her heart grew boisterous, adding to and withdrawing from the cheek varying tones of red to match each varying thought.[3] Dick looked expectantly at the ripe tint of her delicate mouth, waiting for what was coming forth.

'Yes – if father will let me.'

Dick drew himself close to her, compressing his lips and pouting them out, as if he were about to whistle the softest melody known.

'O no!' said Fancy solemnly; and the modest Dick drew back a little.

'O Dick, Dick, kiss me, and let me go instantly! here's somebody coming!' she exclaimed.[4]

* * * * * *

Half an hour afterwards Dick emerged from the inn, and if Fancy's lips had been real cherries, Dick's would have appeared deeply stained. The landlord was standing in the yard.

'Heu-heu! hay-hay, Master Dewy! Ho-ho!' he laughed, letting the laugh slip out gently and by degrees, that it might make little noise in its exit, and smiting Dick under the fifth rib at the same time. 'This will never do, upon my life, Master Dewy! calling for tay for a passenger, and then going in and sitting down and having some too!'

'But surely you know?' said Dick, with great apparent surprise. 'Yes, yes! Ha-ha!' smiting the landlord under the ribs in return.

'Why, what? Yes, yes; ha-ha!'

'You know, yes; ha-ha, of course!'

'Yes, of course! But – that is – I don't.'

'Why about – between that young lady and me?' nodding to the window of the room that Fancy occupied.

'No; not I!' bringing his eyes into mathematical circles.

'And you don't!'

'Not a word, I'll take my oath!'

'But you laughed, when I laughed.'

'Ay, that was me sympathy; so did you when I laughed!'

'Really, you don't know? Goodness – not knowing that!'

'I'll take my oath I don't!'

'O yes,' said Dick, with frigid rhetoric of pitying astonishment, 'we're engaged to be married, you see, and I naturally look after her.'

'Of course, of course! I didn't know that, and I hope ye'll excuse any little freedom of mine. But it is a very odd thing; I was talking to your father very intimate about family matters, only last Friday in the world, and who should come in but keeper Day, and we all then fell a-talking o' family matters; but neither one o' them said a mortal word about it; known me too so many years, and I at your father's own wedding. 'Tisn't what I should have expected from a old naibour.'

'Well, to tell the truth, we hadn't told father of the engagement at that time; in fact, 'twasn't settled.'

'Ah! the business was done Sunday. Yes, yes, Sunday's the courting day. Heu-heu!'

'No, 'twasn't done Sunday in particular.'

'After school-hours this week? Well, a very good time, a very proper good time.'

'O no, 'twasn't done then.'

'Coming along the road to-day then, I suppose?'

'Not at all; I wouldn't think of getting engaged in a cart.'

'Dammy – might as well have said at once, the *when* be blowed! Anyhow, 'tis a fine day, and I hope next time you'll come as one.'

Fancy was duly brought out and assisted into the vehicle, and the newly-affianced youth and maiden passed over the bridge, and vanished in the direction of Mellstock.

CHAPTER III

A Confession[1]

It was a morning of the latter summer-time; a morning of lingering dews, when the grass is never dry in the shade. Fuchsias and dahlias were laden till eleven o'clock with small drops and dashes of water, changing the colour of their sparkle at every movement of their air, or hanging on twigs like small silver fruit. The threads of garden spiders appeared thick and polished. In the dry and sunny places, dozens of long-legged crane-flies whizzed off the grass at every step the passer took.

Fancy Day and her friend Susan Dewy were in such a spot as this, pulling down a bough laden with early apples. Three months had elapsed since Dick and Fancy had journeyed together from Budmouth, and the course of their love had run on vigorously during the whole time. There had been just enough difficulty attending its development, and just enough finesse required in keeping it private, to lend the passion an ever-increasing freshness on Fancy's part, whilst, whether from these accessories or not, Dick's heart had been at all times as fond as could be desired. But there was a cloud on Fancy's horizon now.

'She is so well off – better than any of us,' Susan Dewy was saying. 'Her father farms five hundred acres, and she might marry a doctor or curate or anything of that kind, if she contrived a little.'

'I don't think Dick ought to have gone to that gipsy-party at all when he knew I couldn't go,' replied Fancy uneasily.

'He didn't know that you would not be there till it was too late to decline the invitation,' said Susan.

'And what was she like? Tell me.'

'Well, she was rather pretty, I must own.'

'Tell straight on about her, can't you! Come, do, Susan. How many times did you say he danced with her?'

'Once.'

'Twice, I think you said?'

'Indeed, I'm sure I didn't.'

'Well, and he wanted to again, I expect.'

'No; I don't think he did. She wanted to dance with him again badly enough, I know. Everybody does with Dick, because he's so handsome and such a clever courter.'[2]

'O, I wish! – How did you say she wore her hair?'

'In long curls, – and her hair is light, and it curls without being put in paper: that's how it is she's so attractive.'

'She's trying to get him away! yes, yes, she is! And through keeping this miserable school I mustn't wear my hair in curls! But I will; I don't care if I leave the school and go home, I will wear my curls! Look, Susan, do: is her hair as soft and long as this?' Fancy pulled from its coil under her hat a twine of her own hair, and stretched it down her shoulder to show its length, eagerly looking at Susan to catch her opinion from her eyes.

'It is about the same length as that, I think,' said Miss Dewy.

Fancy paused hopelessly. 'I wish mine was lighter, like hers!' she continued mournfully. 'But hers isn't so soft, is it? Tell me, now.'

'I don't know.'

Fancy abstractedly extended her vision to survey a yellow butterfly and a red-and-black butterfly, that were flitting along in company, and then became aware that Dick was advancing up the garden.

'Susan, here's Dick coming; I suppose that's because we've been talking about him.'

'Well, then, I shall go indoors now – you won't want me;' and Susan turned practically and walked off.

Enter the single-minded Dick, whose only fault at the gipsying, or picnic, had been that of loving Fancy too exclusively, and depriving himself of the innocent pleasure the gathering might have afforded him, by sighing regretfully at her absence, – who had danced with the rival in sheer despair of ever being able to get through that stale, flat, and unprofitable[3] afternoon in any other way; but this she would not believe.

Fancy had settled her plan of emotion. To reproach Dick? O no, no. 'I am in great trouble,' said she, taking what was intended to be a hopelessly melancholy survey of a few small apples lying under the tree; yet a critical ear might have noticed in her voice a tentative tone as to the effect of the words upon Dick when she uttered them.

'What are you in trouble about? Tell me of it,' said Dick earnestly. 'Darling, I will share it with you and help you.'

'No, no: you can't! Nobody can!'

'Why not? You don't deserve it, whatever it is. Tell me, dear.'

'O, it isn't what you think! It is dreadful: my own sin!'

'Sin, Fancy! as if you could sin! I know it can't be.'

''Tis, 'tis!' said the young lady, in a pretty little frenzy of sorrow. 'I have done wrong, and I don't like to tell it! Nobody will forgive me, nobody! and you above all will not! ... I have allowed myself to – to – fl –'

'What, – not flirt!' he said, controlling his emotion as it were by a sudden pressure inward from his surface. 'And you said only the day before yesterday that you hadn't flirted in your life!'

'Yes, I did; and that was a wicked story! I have let another love me, and –'

'Good G—! Well, I'll forgive you, – yes, if you couldn't help it, – yes, I will!' said the now miserable Dick. 'Did you encourage him?'

'O, O, O, – I don't know, – yes – no. O, I think so!'

'Who was it?'

A pause.

'Tell me!'

'Mr. Shinar.'

After a silence that was only disturbed by the fall of an apple, a long-checked sigh from Dick, and a sob from Fancy, he said with real austerity,

'Tell it all; – every word!'

'He looked at me, and I looked at him, and he said, "Will you let me show you how to catch bullfinches down here by the stream?" And I – wanted to know very much – I did so long to have a bullfinch! I couldn't help that! – and I said, "Yes!" and then he said, "Come here." And I went with him down to the lovely river, and then he said to me, "Look and see how I do it, and then you'll know: I put this birdlime round this twig, and then I go here," he said, "and hide away under a bush; and presently clever Mister Bird comes and perches upon the twig, and flaps his wings, and you've got him before you can say Jack" – something! O, O, O, I forget what!'

'Jack Sprat,' mournfully suggested Dick through the cloud of his misery.

'No, not Jack Sprat,' she sobbed.

'Then 'twas Jack Robinson!' he said, with the emphasis of a man who had resolved to discover every iota of the truth, or die.

'Yes, that was it! And then I put my hand upon the rail of the bridge to get across, and – That's all.'

'Well, that isn't much, either,' said Dick critically, and more cheerfully.

'Not that I see what business Shinar has to take upon himself to teach you anything. But it seems – it seems there must have been more than that to set you up in such a dreadful taking?'

He looked into Fancy's eyes. Misery of miseries! – guilt was written there still.

'Now, Fancy, you've not told me all!' said Dick, rather sternly for a quiet young man.

'O, don't speak so cruelly! I am afraid to tell now! If you hadn't been harsh, I was going on to tell all; now I can't!'

'Come, dear Fancy, tell: come. I'll forgive; I must, – by heaven and earth, I must, whether I will or no; I love you so!'

'Well, when I put my hand on the bridge, he touched it – '

'A scamp!' said Dick, grinding an imaginary human frame to powder.

'And then he looked at me, and at last he said, "Are you in love with Dick Dewy?" And I said, "Perhaps I am;" and then he said, "I wish you weren't then, for I want to marry you, with all my soul." '

'There's a villain now! Want to marry you!' And Dick quivered with the bitterness of satirical laughter. Then suddenly remembering that he might be reckoning without his host: 'Unless, indeed, you are willing to have him, – perhaps you are,' he said, with the wretched indifference of a castaway.

'No, indeed I am not!' she said, her sobs just beginning to take a favourable turn towards cure.

'Well, then,' said Dick, coming a little to his senses, 'you've been exaggerating very much in giving such a dreadful beginning to such a mere nothing. And I know what you've done it for, – just because of that gipsy-party!' He turned away from her and walked five paces decisively, as if he were alone in a strange country and had never known her.[4] 'You did it to make me jealous, and I won't stand it!' He flung the words to her over his shoulder and then stalked on, apparently very anxious to walk to the colonies that very minute.

'O, O, O, Dick – Dick!' she cried, trotting after him like a pet lamb,[5] and really seriously alarmed at last, 'you'll kill me! My impulses are bad – miserably wicked, – and I can't help it;[6] forgive me, Dick! And I love you always; and those times when you look silly and don't seem quite good enough for me, – just the same, I do, Dick! And there is something more serious, though not concerning that walk with him.'

'Well, what is it?' said Dick, altering his mind about walking to the colonies; in fact, passing to the other extreme, and standing so rooted to the road that he was apparently not even going home.

'Why this,' she said, drying the beginning of a new flood of tears she had been going to shed, 'this is the serious part. Father has told Mr. Shinar that he would like him for a son-in-law, if he could get me; – that he has his right hearty consent to come courting me!'

CHAPTER IV

An Arrangement

'That *is* serious,' said Dick, more intellectually than he had spoken for a long time.

The truth was that Geoffrey knew nothing about his daughter's continued walks and meetings with Dick. When a hint that there were symptoms of an attachment between them had first reached Geoffrey's ears, he stated so emphatically that he must think the matter over before any such thing could be allowed, that, rather unwisely on Dick's part, whatever it might have been on the lady's, the lovers were careful to be seen together no more in public; and Geoffrey, forgetting the report, did not think over the matter at all. So Mr. Shinar resumed his old position in Geoffrey's brain by mere flux of time. Even Shinar began to believe that Dick existed for Fancy no more, – though that remarkably easy-going man had taken no active steps on his own account as yet.

'And father has not only told Mr. Shinar that,' continued Fancy, 'but he has written me a letter, to say he should wish me to encourage Mr. Shinar, if 'twas convenient!'

'I must start off and see your father at once!' said Dick, taking two or three vehement steps to the east, recollecting that Mr. Day lived to the west, and coming back again.

'I think we had better see him together. Not tell him what you come for, or anything of the kind, until he likes you, and so win his brain through his heart, which is always the way to manage people. I mean in this way: I am going home on Saturday week to help them in the honey-taking. You might come there to me, have something to eat and drink, and let him guess what your coming signifies, without saying it in so many words.'

'We'll do it, dearest. But I shall ask him for you, flat and plain; not wait for his guessing.' And the lover then stepped close to her, and attempted to give her one little kiss on the cheek, his lips alighting, however, on an outlying tract of her back hair, by reason of an impulse that had caused her to turn her head with a jerk. 'Yes, and I'll put on my second-best suit and a clean collar, and black my boots as if 'twas a Sunday. 'Twill have a good appearance, you see, and that's a great deal to start with.'

'You won't wear that old waistcoat, will you, Dick?'

'Bless you, no! Why I –'

'I didn't mean to be personal, dear Dick,' she said apologetically, fearing she had hurt his feelings. ''Tis a very nice waistcoat, but what I meant was, that though it is an excellent waistcoat for a settled-down man, it is not quite one for' (she waited, and a blush expanded over her face, and then she went on again)[1] – 'for going courting in.'

'No, I'll wear my best winter one, with the leather lining, that mother made. It is a beautiful, handsome waistcoat inside, yes, as ever anybody saw. In fact, only the other day, I unbuttoned it to show a chap that very lining, and he said it was the strongest, handsomest lining you could wish to see on the king's waistcoat himself.'

'*I* don't quite know what to wear,' she said, as if her habitual indifference alone to dress had kept back so important a subject till now.

'Why, that blue dress you wore last week.'

'Doesn't set well round the neck. I couldn't wear that.'

'But I sha'n't care.'

'No, you won't mind.'

'Well, then it's all right. Because you only care how you look to me, do you, dear? I only dress for you, that's certain.'

'Yes, but you see I couldn't appear in it again very well.'

'Any strange gentleman you may meet in your journey might notice the set of it, I suppose. Fancy, men in love don't think so much about how they appear to other women.' It is difficult to say whether a tone of playful banter or of gentle reproach prevailed in the speech.

'Well then, Dick,' she said, with good-humoured frankness, 'I'll own it. I shouldn't like a stranger to see me dressed badly, even though I am in love. 'Tis our nature, I suppose.'

'You perfect woman!'[2]

'Yes; if you lay the stress on "woman,"' she murmured, looking at a group of hollyhocks in flower, round which a crowd of butterflies had gathered like females round a bonnet-shop.

'But about the dress. Why not wear the one you wore at our party?'

'That sets well, but a girl of the name of Bet Taylor, who lives near our house, has had one made almost like it (only in pattern, though of miserably cheap stuff), and I couldn't wear it on that account. Dear me, I am afraid I can't go now.'

'O yes, you must; I know you will!' said Dick, with dismay. 'Why not wear what you've got on?'

'What! this old one! After all, I think that by wearing my gray one Saturday, I can make the blue one do for Sunday. Yes, I will. A hat or a bonnet, which shall it be? Which do I look best in?'

'Well, I think the bonnet is nicest, more quiet and matronly.'

'What's the objection to the hat? Does it make me look old?'

'O no; the hat is well enough; but it makes you look rather too – you won't mind me saying it, dear?'

'Not at all, for I shall wear the bonnet.'

'– Rather too coquettish and flirty for an engaged young woman.'

She reflected a minute. 'Yes, yes. Still, after all, the hat would do best; hats are best, you see. Yes, I must wear the hat, dear Dicky, because I ought to wear a hat, you know.'

PART IV

Autumn

CHAPTER I

Going Nutting[1]

Dick, dressed in his 'second-best' suit, burst into Fancy's sitting-room with a glow of pleasure on his face.

It was two o'clock on Friday, the day before Fancy's contemplated visit to her father, and for some reason connected with cleaning the school, the children had had given them this Friday afternoon for pastime, in addition to the usual Saturday.

'Fancy! it happens just right that it is a leisure half day with you. Smart is lame in his near-foot-afore, and so, as I can't do anything, I've made a holiday afternoon of it, and am come for you to go nutting with me!'

She was sitting by the window, with a blue dress lying across her lap, and the scissors in her hand.

'Go nutting! Yes. But I'm afraid I can't go for an hour or so.'

'Why not? 'Tis the only spare afternoon we may both have together for weeks.'

'This dress of mine, that I am going to wear on Sunday at Yalbury; – I find it sets so badly that I must alter it a little, after all. I told the dressmaker to make it by a pattern I gave her at the time; instead of that, she did it her own way, and made me look a perfect fright.'

'How long will you be?' he inquired, looking rather disappointed.

'Not long. Do wait and talk to me; come, do, dear.'

Dick sat down. The talking progressed very favourably, amid the snipping and sewing, till about half-past two, at which time his conversation began to be varied by a slight tapping upon his toe with a walking-stick he had cut from the hedge as he came along. Fancy talked and answered him, but sometimes the answers were so negligently given, that it was evident her thoughts lay for the greater part in her lap with the blue dress.

The clock struck three. Dick arose from his seat, walked round the room with his hands behind him, examining all the furniture, then sounded a few notes on the harmonium, then looked inside all the books he could find, then smoothed Fancy's head with his hand. Still the snipping and sewing went on.

The clock struck four. Dick fidgeted about, yawned privately; counted the knots in the table, yawned publicly; counted the flies on the ceiling, yawned horribly; went into the scullery, and so thoroughly studied the principle upon which the pump was constructed, that he could have delivered a lecture on the subject. Stepping back to Fancy, and finding still that she had not done, he went into her garden and looked at her cabbages and potatoes, and reminded himself that they seemed to him to wear a decidedly feminine aspect; then pulled up several weeds, and came in again. The clock struck five, and still the snipping and sewing went on.

Dick attempted to kill a fly, peeled all the rind off his walking-stick, then threw the stick into the scullery because it was spoilt, produced hideous discords from the harmonium, and accidentally overturned a vase of flowers, the water from which ran in a rill across the table and dribbled to the floor, where it formed a lake, the shape of which, after the lapse of a few minutes, he began to modify considerably with his foot, till it was like a map of England and Wales.

'Well, Dick, you needn't have made quite such a mess.'

'Well, I needn't, I suppose.' He walked up to the blue dress, and looked at it with a rigid gaze. Then an idea seemed to cross his brain.

'Fancy.'

'Yes.'

'I thought you said you were going to wear the gray dress all day to-morrow on your trip to Yalbury, and in the evening too, when I shall be with you, and ask your father for you.'

'So I am.'

'And the blue one only on Sunday?'

'And the blue one Sunday.'

'Well, dear, I sha'n't be there Sunday to see it.'

'No, but such lots of people will be looking at me Sunday, you know, and it did set so badly round the neck.'[2]

'I never noticed it, and probably nobody else would.'

'They might.'

'Then why not wear the gray one on Sunday as well? 'Tis as pretty as the blue one.'

'I might make the gray one do, certainly. But it isn't so good; it didn't cost half so much as this one, and besides, it would be the same I wore Saturday.'

'Then wear the striped one, dear.'

'I might.'

'Or the dark one.'

'Yes, I might; but I want to wear a fresh one they haven't seen.'

'I see, I see,' said Dick, in a voice in which the tones of love were decidedly inconvenienced by a considerable emphasis, his thoughts meanwhile running as follows: 'I, the man she loves best in the world, as she says, am to understand that my poor half-holiday is to be lost, because she wants to wear on Sunday a dress there is not the slightest necessity for wearing, simply, in fact, to appear more striking than usual in the eyes of Yalbury young men; and I not there, either.'

'Then there are three dresses good enough for my eyes, but neither is good enough for the youth of Yalbury,' he said.

'No, not that exactly, Dick. Still, you see, I do want – to look pretty to them – there, that's honest. But I sha'n't be much longer.'

'How much?'

'A quarter of an hour.'

'Very well; I'll come in in a quarter of an hour.'

'Why go away?'

'I may as well.'

He went out, walked down the road, and sat upon a gate. Here he meditated and meditated, and the more he meditated, the more decidedly did he begin to fume, and the more positive was he that his time had been scandalously trifled with by Miss Fancy Day – that, so far from being the simple girl who had never had a sweetheart before, as she had solemnly assured him time after time, she was, if not a flirt, a woman who had had no end of admirers; a girl most certainly too anxious about her dresses; a girl whose feelings, though warm, were not deep; a girl who cared a great deal too much how she appeared in the eyes of other men. 'What she loves best in the world,' he thought, with an incipient spice of his father's grimness, 'are her hair and complexion. What she loves next best, her dresses; what she loves next best, myself, perhaps.'

Suffering great anguish at this disloyalty in himself, and harshness to his darling, yet disposed to persevere in it, a horribly cruel thought crossed his mind. He would not call for her, as he had promised, at the end of a quarter of an hour! Yes, it would be a punishment she well deserved! Although the best part of the afternoon had been wasted, he would go nutting as he had intended, and go by himself.

He leaped over the gate, and pushed along the path for nearly two miles, till it sloped up a hill, and entered a hazel copse by a hole like a rabbit's burrow. In he plunged, vanished among the bushes, and in a short time there was no sign of his existence upon earth, save an occasional rustling of boughs and snapping of twigs in divers points of the wood.

Never man nutted as Dick nutted that day. He worked like a galley slave. Hour after hour passed away,[3] and still he gathered without ceasing. At last, when the sun had set, and bunches of nuts could not be distinguished from the leaves which nourished them, he shouldered his bag, containing about two pecks of the finest produce of the wood, and which were about as much use to him as two pecks of stones from the road, and strolled along a bridle-path leading into open ground, whistling as he went.

Probably, Miss Fancy Day never before or after stood so low in Mr. Dewy's opinion as on that afternoon. In fact, it is just possible that a few more blue dresses on the Yalbury young men's account would have clarified Dick's brain entirely, and made him once more a free man.

But Venus had planned other developments, at any rate for the present. The path he pursued passed over a ridge which rose keenly against the western sky, about fifty yards in his van. Here, upon the bright after-glow about the horizon, was now visible an irregular outline, which at first he conceived to be a bush standing a little beyond the line of its neighbours. Then it seemed to move, and as he advanced still farther, there was no doubt that it was a living being of some species or other. The grassy path entirely prevented his footsteps from being heard, and it was not till he was close, that the figure recognised him. Up it sprang, and he was face to face with Fancy.

'Dick, Dick! O, is it you, Dick!'

'Yes, Fancy,' said Dick, in a rather repentant tone, and lowering his nuts.

She ran up to him, flung her parasol on the grass, put her little head against his breast, and then there began a narrative, disjointed by such a hysterical weeping as was never surpassed for intensity in the whole history of love.

'O Dick,' she sobbed out, 'where have you been, away from me! O, I have suffered agony, and thought you would never come any more! 'Tis cruel, Dick; no 'tisn't, it is justice! I've been walking miles and miles up and down this wood, trying to find you, till I was wearied and worn out, and I could walk no farther. O Dick, directly you were gone, I thought I had offended you, and I put down the dress; 'tisn't finished now, Dick, and I never will finish it, and I'll wear an old one Sunday! Yes, Dick, I will, because I don't care what I wear when you are not by my side – ah, you think I do, but I don't! – and I ran after you, and I saw you go up the hill and not look back once, and then you plunged in, and I after you; but I was too far behind. O, I did wish the horrid bushes had been cut down, so that I could see your dear shape again!⁴ And then I called out to you, and nobody answered, and I was afraid to call very loud, lest anybody else should hear me. Then I kept wandering and wandering about, and it was dreadful misery, Dick. And then I shut my eyes and fell to picturing you looking at some other woman, very pretty and nice, but with no affection or truth in her at all, and then imagined you saying to yourself, "Ah, she's as good as Fancy, for Fancy told me a story, and was a flirt, and cared for herself more than me, so now I'll have this one for my sweetheart." O, you won't, will you, Dick, for I do love you so!'

It is scarcely necessary to add that Dick renounced his freedom there and then, and kissed her ten times over, and promised that no pretty woman of the kind alluded to should ever engross his thoughts; in short, that though he had been vexed with her, all such vexation was past, and that henceforth and for ever it was simply Fancy or death for him. And then they set about proceeding homewards, very slowly on account of Fancy's weariness, she leaning upon his shoulder, and in addition receiving support from his arm round her waist; though she had sufficiently recovered from her desperate condition to sing to him 'Why are you wandering here, I pray?'⁵ during the latter part of their walk. Nor is it necessary to describe in detail how the bag of nuts was quite forgotten until three days later, when it was found by an underkeeper and restored empty to Mrs. Dewy, her initials being marked thereon in red cotton; and how she puzzled herself till her head ached, upon the question of how on earth her meal-bag could have got into Mellstock copse.

CHAPTER II

Honey-Taking, and Afterwards

Saturday evening saw Dick Dewy journeying on foot to Yalbury Wood, according to the arrangement with Fancy.

The landscape was concave, and at the going down of the sun[1] everything suddenly assumed a uniform robe of shade. The evening advanced from sunset to dusk long before Dick's arrival, and his progress during the latter portion of his walk through the trees was indicated by the flutter of terrified birds that had been roosting over the path. And in crossing the glades, masses of hot dry air, that had been formed on the hills during the day, greeted his cheeks alternately with clouds of damp night air from the valleys. He reached the keeper's house, where the grass-plot and the garden in front appeared light and pale against the unbroken darkness of the grove from which he had emerged, and paused at the garden gate.

He had scarcely been there a minute when he beheld a sort of procession advancing from the door in his front. It consisted first of Enoch the trapper, carrying a spade on his shoulder and a lantern dangling in his hand; then came Mrs. Day, the light of the lantern revealing that she bore in her arms curious objects about a foot long, in the form of Latin crosses (made of lath and brown paper dipped in brimstone, – called matches by bee-fanciers); next came Miss Day, with a shawl thrown over her head; and behind all, in the gloom, Mr. Frederic Shinar.

Dick, in his consternation at finding Shinar present, was at a loss how to proceed, and retired under a tree to collect his thoughts.

'Here I be, Enoch,' said a voice; and the procession advancing farther, the lantern's rays illuminated the figure of Geoffrey, awaiting their arrival beside a row of beehives, in front of the path. Taking the spade from Enoch, he proceeded to dig two holes in the earth beside the hives, the others standing round in a circle, except Mrs. Day, who deposited her matches in the fork of an apple-tree, and returned to the house. The party remaining were now lit up in front by the lantern in their midst, their shadows radiating each way upon the garden-plot like the spokes of a wheel. An apparent embarrassment of Fancy at the presence of Shinar caused a silence in the assembly, during which the preliminaries of execution were arranged, the matches fixed, the stake kindled, the two hives placed over the two holes, and the earth stopped round the edges. Geoffrey then stood erect, and rather more, to straighten his backbone after the digging.

'They were a peculiar family,' said Mr. Shinar, regarding the hives reflectively.

Geoffrey nodded.

'Those holes will be the grave of thousands!' said Fancy. 'I think 'tis rather a cruel thing to do.'

Her father shook his head. 'No,' he said, tapping the hives to shake the dead bees from their cells, 'if you suffocate 'em this way, they only die once: if you fumigate 'em in the new way, they come to life again, and so the pangs o' death be twice upon 'em.'

'I incline to Fancy's notion,' said Mr. Shinar, laughing lightly.

'The proper way to take honey, so that the bees be neither starved nor murdered, is not so much an amusing as a puzzling matter,' said the keeper steadily.

'I should like never to take it from them,' said Fancy.

'But 'tis the money,' said Enoch musingly. 'For without money man is a shadder!'[2]

The lantern-light had disturbed several bees that had escaped from hives destroyed some days earlier, and who were now getting a living as marauders about the doors of other hives. Several flew round the head and neck of Geoffrey; then darted upon him with an irritated bizz.

Enoch threw down the lantern, and ran off and pushed his head into a currant bush; Fancy scudded up the path; and Mr. Shinar floundered away helter-skelter among the cabbages. Geoffrey stood his ground unmoved, and firm as a rock. Fancy was the first to return, followed by Enoch picking up the lantern. Mr. Shinar still remained invisible.

'Have the craters stung ye?' said Enoch to Geoffrey.

'No, not much – only a little here and there,' he said with leisurely solemnity, shaking one bee out of his shirt sleeve, pulling another from among his hair, and two or three more from his neck. The others looked on during this proceeding with a complacent sense of being out of it, – much as a European nation in a state of internal commotion is watched by its neighbours.[3]

'Are those all of them, father?' said Fancy, when Geoffrey had pulled away five.

'Almost all, – though I feel a few more sticking into my shoulder and side. Ah! there's another just begun again upon my backbone. You lively young martels, how did you get inside there? However, they can't sting me many times more, poor things, for they must be getting weak. They may as well stay in me till bedtime now, I suppose.'

As he himself was the only person affected by this arrangement, it seemed satisfactory enough; and after a noise of feet kicking against cabbages in a blundering progress among them, the voice of Mr. Shinar was heard from the darkness in that direction.

'Is all quite safe again?'

No answer being returned to this query, he apparently assumed that he might venture forth, and gradually drew near the lantern again. The hives were now removed from their position over the holes, one being handed to Enoch to carry indoors, and one being taken by Geoffrey himself.

'Bring hither the lantern, Fancy: the spade can bide.'

Geoffrey and Enoch then went towards the house, leaving Shinar and Fancy standing side by side on the garden-plot.

'Allow me,' said Shinar, stooping for the lantern and seizing it at the same time with Fancy.

'I can carry it,' said Fancy, religiously repressing all inclination to trifle. She had thoroughly considered that subject after the tearful explanation of the bird-catching adventure to Dick, and had decided that it would be dishonest in her, as an engaged young woman, to trifle with men's eyes and hands any more. Finding that Shinar still retained his hold of the lantern, she relinquished it, and he, having found her retaining it, also let go. The lantern fell, and was extinguished. Fancy moved on.

'Where is the path?' said Mr. Shinar.

'Here,' said Fancy. 'Your eyes will get used to the dark in a minute or two.'

'Till that time will ye lend me your hand?'

Fancy gave him the extreme tips of her fingers, and they stepped from the plot into the path.

'You don't accept attentions very freely.'

'It depends upon who offers them.'

'A fellow like me, for instance.'

A dead silence.

'Well, what do you say, Missie?'

'It then depends upon how they are offered.'

'Not wildly, and yet not indifferently; not intentionally, and yet not by chance; not actively nor idly; quickly nor slowly.'

'How then?' said Fancy.

'Coolly and practically,' he said. 'How would that kind of love be taken?'

'Not anxiously, and yet not carelessly; neither quickly nor slowly; neither redly nor palely; not religiously nor yet quite wickedly.'

'Well, how?'

'Not at all.'[4]

Geoffrey Day's storehouse at the back of his dwelling was hung with bunches of dried horehound, mint, and sage; brown-paper bags of thyme and lavender; and long ropes of clean onions. On shelves were spread large red and yellow apples, and choice selections of early potatoes for seed next year; – vulgar crowds of commoner kind lying beneath in heaps. A few empty beehives were clustered around a nail in one corner, under which stood two or three barrels of new cider of the first crop, each bubbling and squirting forth from the yet open bunghole.

Fancy was now kneeling beside the two inverted hives, one of which rested against her lap, for convenience in operating upon the contents. She thrust her sleeves above her elbows, and inserted her small pink hand edgewise between each white lobe of honey-comb, performing the act so adroitly and gently as not to unseal a single cell. Then cracking the piece off at the crown of the hive by a slight backward and forward movement, she lifted each portion as it was loosened into a large blue platter, placed on a bench at her side.

'Bother them little martels!' said Geoffrey, who was holding the light to her, and giving his back an uneasy twist. 'I really think I may so well go indoors and take 'em out, poor things! for they won't let me alone. There's two a-stinging wi' all their might now. I'm sure I wonder their strength can last so long.'

'All right, friend; I'll hold the candle whilst you are gone,' said Mr. Shinar, leisurely taking the light, and allowing Geoffrey to depart, which he did with his usual long paces.

He could hardly have gone round to the cottage-door when other footsteps were heard approaching the outhouse; the tip of a finger appeared in the hole through which the wood latch was lifted, and Dick Dewy came in, having been all this time walking up and down the wood, vainly waiting for Shinar's departure.

Fancy looked up and welcomed him rather confusedly. Shinar grasped the candlestick more firmly, and, lest doing this in silence should not imply to Dick with sufficient force that he was quite at home and cool, he sang invincibly,

'King Arthur he had three sons.'[5]

'Father here?' said Dick.

'Indoors, I think,' said Fancy, looking pleasantly at him.

Dick surveyed the scene, and did not seem inclined to hurry off just at that moment. Shinar went on singing,

'The miller was drown'd in his pond,
  The weaver was hung in his yarn,
And the d— ran away with the little tailór,
  With the broadcloth under his arm.'

'That's a terrible crippled rhyme, if that's your rhyme!' said Dick, with a grain of superciliousness in his tone, and elevating his nose an inch or thereabout.

'It's no use your complaining to me about the rhyme!' said Mr. Shinar. 'You must go to the man that made it.'

Fancy by this time had acquired confidence.

'Taste a bit, Mr. Dewy,' she said, holding up to him a small circular piece of honeycomb that had been the last in the row of lobes, and remaining still on her knees, and flinging back her head to look in his face; 'and then I'll taste a bit too.'

'And I, if you please,' said Mr. Shinar. Nevertheless the farmer looked superior, as if he could even now hardly join the trifling from very importance of station; and after receiving the honeycomb from Fancy, he turned it over in his hand till the cells began to be crushed, and the liquid honey ran down from his fingers in a thin string.

Suddenly a faint cry from Fancy caused them to gaze at her.

'What's the matter, dear?' said Dick.

'It is nothing, but O-o! a bee has stung the inside of my lip! He was in one of the cells I was eating!'

'We must keep down the swelling, or it may be serious!' said Shinar, stepping up and kneeling beside her. 'Let me see it.'

'No, no!'

'Just let *me* see it,' said Dick, kneeling on the other side; and after some hesitation she pressed down her lip with one finger to show the place. 'I hope 'twill soon be better. I don't mind a sting in ordinary places, but it is so bad upon your lip,' she added, with tears in her eyes, and writhing a little from the pain.

Shinar held the light above his head and pushed his face close to Fancy's, as if the lip had been shown exclusively to himself, upon which Dick pushed closer, as if Shinar were not there at all.

'It is swelling,' said Dick to her right aspect.

'It isn't swelling,' said Shinar to her left aspect.

'Is it dangerous on the lip?' cried Fancy. 'I know it is dangerous on the tongue.'

'O no, not dangerous!' answered Dick.

'Rather dangerous,' had answered Shinar simultaneously.

'It doesn't hurt me so much now,'[6] said Fancy, turning again to the hives.

'Hartshorn and oil is a good thing to put to it, Miss Day,' said Shinar with great concern.

'Sweet oil and hartshorn I've found to be a good thing to cure stings, Miss Day,' said Dick with greater concern.

'We have some mixed indoors; would you kindly run and get it for me?' she said.

Now, whether by inadvertence, or whether by mischievous intention, the individuality of the *you* was so carelessly denoted that both Dick and Shinar sprang to their feet like twin acrobats, and marched abreast to the door; both seized the latch and lifted it, and continued marching on, shoulder to shoulder, in the same manner to the dwelling-house. Not only so, but entering the room, they marched as before straight up to Mrs. Day's chair, letting the door in the old oak partition slam so forcibly, that the rows of pewter on the dresser rang like a bell.

'Mrs. Day, Fancy has stung her lip, and wants you to give me the hartshorn, please,' said Mr. Shinar, very close to Mrs. Day's face.

'O, Mrs. Day, Fancy has asked me to bring out the hartshorn, please, because she has stung her lip!' said Dick, a little closer to Mrs. Day's face.

'Well, men alive! that's no reason why you should eat me, I suppose!' said Mrs. Day, drawing back.

She searched in the corner-cupboard, produced the bottle, and began to dust the cork, the rim, and every other part very carefully, Dick's hand and Shinar's hand waiting side by side.

'Which is head man?' said Mrs. Day. 'Now, don't come mumbudgeting so close again. Which is head man?'

Neither spoke; and the bottle was inclined towards Shinar. Shinar, as a high-class man,[7] would not look in the least triumphant, and turned to go off with it as Geoffrey came downstairs after the search in his linen for concealed bees.

'O – that you, Master Dewy?'

Dick assured the keeper that it was; and the young man then determined upon a bold stroke for the attainment of his end, forgetting that the worst of bold strokes is the disastrous consequences they involve if they fail.

'I've come o' purpose to speak to you very particularly, Mr. Day,' he said, with a crushing emphasis intended for the ears of Mr. Shinar, who was vanishing round the door-post at that moment.

'Well, I've been forced to go upstairs and unrind myself, and shake some bees out o' me,' said Geoffrey, walking slowly towards the open door, and standing on the threshold. 'The young rascals got into my shirt and wouldn't be quiet nohow.'

Dick followed him to the door.

'I've come to speak a word to you,' he repeated, looking out at the pale mist creeping up from the gloom of the valley. 'You may perhaps guess what it is about.'

The keeper lowered his hands into the extreme depths of his pockets, twirled his eyes, balanced himself on his toes, looked perpendicularly downward as if his glance were a plumb-line, then scrupulously horizontal, gradually collecting together the cracks that lay about his face till they were all in the neighbourhood of his eyes.

'Maybe I don't know,' he replied.

Dick said nothing; and the stillness was disturbed only by some small bird that was being killed by an owl in the adjoining copse, whose cry passed into the silence without mingling with it.

'I've left my hat in the chammer,' said Geoffrey; 'wait while I step up and get en.'

'I'll be in the garden,' said Dick.

He went round by a side wicket into the garden, and Geoffrey went upstairs. It was the custom in Mellstock and its vicinity to discuss matters of pleasure and ordinary business inside the house, and to reserve the

garden for very important affairs: a custom which, as is supposed, origin-
ated in the desirability of getting away at such times from the other
members of the family, when there was only one room for living in,
though it was now quite as frequently practised by those who suffered
from no such limitation to the size of their domiciles.

The keeper's form appeared in the dusky garden, and Dick walked
towards him. The keeper paused, turned, and leant over the rail of a
piggery that stood on the left of the path, upon which Dick did the same;
and they both contemplated a whitish shadowy form that was moving
about and grunting among the straw of the interior.

'I've come to ask for Fancy,' said Dick.

'I'd as lief you hadn't.'

'Why should that be, Mr. Day?'

'Because it makes me say that you've come to ask for what ye be'n't
likely to have. Have ye come for anything else?'

'Nothing.'

'Then I'll just tell ye you've come on a very foolish errand. D'ye know
what her mother was?'

'No.'

'A governess in a county family, who was foolish enough to marry the
keeper of the same establishment.[8] D'ye think Fancy picked up her good
manners, the smooth turn of her tongue, her musical skill, and her
knowledge of books, in a homely hole like this?'

'No.'

'D'ye know where?'

'No.'

'Well, when I went a-wandering after her mother's death, she lived
with her aunt, who kept a boarding-school, till her aunt married Lawyer
Green – a man as sharp as a needle – and the school was broken up. Did
ye know that then she went to the training-school, and that her name
stood first among the Queen's scholars[9] of her year?'

'I've heard so.'

'And that when she sat for her certificate as Government teacher, she
had the highest of the first class?'

'Yes.'

'Well, and do ye know what I live in such a miserly way for when I've
got enough to do without it, and why I make her work as a schoolmistress
instead of living here?'

'No.'

'That if any gentleman, who sees her to be his equal in polish, should want to marry her, and she want to marry him, he sha'n't be superior to her in pocket. Now do ye think after this that you be good enough for her?'

'No.'

'Then good-night t'ye, Master Dewy.'

'Good-night, Mr. Day.'

Modest Dick's reply had faltered upon his tongue, and he turned away wondering at his presumption in asking for a woman whom he had seen from the beginning to be so superior to him.

CHAPTER III

Fancy in the Rain

The next scene is a tempestuous afternoon in the following month, and Fancy Day is discovered walking from her father's home towards Mellstock.

A single vast gray cloud covered all the country, from which the small rain and mist had just begun to blow down in wavy sheets, alternately thick and thin. The trees of the old brown plantation writhed like miserable men as the air wended its way swiftly among them: the lowest portions of their trunks, that had hardly ever been known to move, were visibly rocked by the fiercer gusts, distressing the mind by its painful unwontedness, as when a strong man is seen to shed tears. Low-hanging boughs went up and down; high and erect boughs went to and fro; the blasts being so irregular, and divided into so many cross-currents, that neighbouring branches of the same tree swept the skies in independent motions, crossed each other, passed, or became entangled. Across the open spaces flew flocks of green and yellowish leaves, which, after travelling a long distance from their parent trees, reached the ground, and lay there with their under-sides upward.

As the rain and wind increased, and Fancy's bonnet-ribbons leapt more and more snappishly against her chin, she paused to consider her latitude, and the distance to a place of shelter. The nearest house was Elizabeth Endorfield's,[1] whose cottage and garden stood at the junction of the lane with the high road. Fancy hastened onward, and in five minutes entered a gate, which shed upon her toes a flood of water-drops as she opened it.

'Come in, chiel!' a voice exclaimed, before Fancy had knocked: a promptness that would have surprised her, had she not known that Mrs. Endorfield was an exceedingly and exceptionally sharp woman in the use of her eyes and ears.

Fancy went in and sat down. Elizabeth was paring potatoes for her husband's supper.

Scrape, scrape, scrape; then a toss, and splash went a potato into a bucket of water.

Now, as Fancy listlessly noted these proceedings of the dame, she began to reconsider an old subject that lay uppermost in her heart. Since the interview between her father and Dick, the days had been melancholy days for her. Geoffrey's firm opposition to the notion of Dick as a son-in-law was more than she had expected. She had frequently seen her lover since that time, it is true, and had loved him more for the opposition than she would have otherwise dreamt of doing[2] – which was a happiness of a certain kind. Yet, though love is thus an end in itself, it must be believed to be the means to another end if it is to assume the rosy hues of an unalloyed pleasure. And such a belief Fancy and Dick were emphatically denied just now.

Elizabeth Endorfield had a repute among women which was in its nature something between distinction and notoriety. It was founded on the following items of character. She was shrewd and penetrating; her house stood in a lonely place; she never went to church; she always retained her bonnet indoors; and she had a pointed chin. Thus far her attributes were distinctly Satanic; and those who looked no further called her, in plain terms, a witch. But she was not gaunt, nor ugly in the upper part of her face, nor particularly strange in manner; so that, when her more intimate acquaintances spoke of her, the term was softened, and she became simply a Deep Body, who was as long-headed as she was high. It may be stated that Elizabeth belonged to a class of people who were gradually losing their mysterious characteristics under the administration of the young vicar; though, during the long reign of Mr. Grinham, the parish of Mellstock had proved extremely favourable to the growth of witches.[3]

While Fancy was revolving all this in her mind, and putting it to herself whether it was worth while to tell her troubles to Elizabeth, and ask her advice in getting out of them, the witch spoke.

'You are down – proper down,' she said suddenly, dropping another potato into the bucket.

Fancy took no notice.

'About your young man.'

Fancy reddened. Elizabeth seemed to be watching her thoughts. Really, one would almost think she must have the powers people ascribed to her.

'Father not in the humour for't, hey?' Another potato was finished and flung in. 'Ah, I know about it. Little birds tell me things that people don't dream of my knowing.'

Fancy was desperate about Dick, and here was a chance – O, such a wicked chance! – of getting help; but what was goodness beside love!

'I wish you'd tell me how to put him in the humour for it?' she said.

'That I could soon do,' said the witch quietly.

'Really? O, do; anyhow – I don't care – so that it is done! How could I do it, Mrs. Endorfield?'

'Nothing so mighty wonderful in it.'

'Well, but how?'

'By witchery, of course!' said Elizabeth.

'No!' said Fancy.

''Tis, I assure ye. Didn't you ever hear I was a witch?'

'Well,' said Fancy hesitatingly, 'I have heard you called so.'

'And you believed it?'

'I can't say that I did exactly believe it, for 'tis very horrible and wicked; but, O, how I do wish it was possible for you to be one!'

'So I am. And I'll tell ye how to bewitch your father, to let you marry Dick Dewy.'

'Will it hurt him, poor thing?'

'Hurt who?'

'Father.'

'No; the charm is worked by common sense, and the spell can only be broke by your acting stupidly.'

Fancy looked rather perplexed, and Elizabeth went on:

'This fear of Lizz – whatever 'tis –
  By great and small;
She makes pretence to common sense,
  And that's all.'[4]

You must do it like this.' The witch laid down her knife and potato, and then poured into Fancy's ear a long and detailed list of directions, glancing up from the corner of her eye into Fancy's face with an expression of sinister humour. Fancy's face brightened, clouded, rose and sank, as the narrative proceeded. 'There,' said Elizabeth at length, stooping for the knife and another potato, 'do that, and you'll have him by-long and by-late, my dear.'

'And do it I will!' said Fancy.

She then turned her attention to the external world once more. The rain continued as usual, but the wind had abated considerably during the discourse. Judging that it was now possible to keep an umbrella erect, she pulled her hood again over her bonnet, bade the witch good-bye, and went her way.

CHAPTER IV

The Spell

Mrs. Endorfield's advice was duly followed.

'I be proper sorry that your daughter isn't so well as she might be,' said a Mellstock man to Geoffrey one morning.

'But is there anything in it?' said Geoffrey uneasily. He shifted his hat slightly to the right. 'I can't understand the report. She didn't complain to me at all, when I seed her.'

'No appetite at all, they say.'

Geoffrey called at the school that afternoon. Fancy welcomed him as usual, and asked him to stay and take tea with her.

'I be'n't much for tea, this time o' day,' he said, but stayed.

During the meal he watched her narrowly. And to his great consternation, discovered the following unprecedented change in the healthy girl – that she cut herself only a diaphanous slice of bread-and-butter, and laying it on her plate, passed the meal in breaking it into pieces, but eating no more than about one-tenth of the slice. Geoffrey hoped she would say something about Dick, and finish up by weeping, as she had done after the decision against him a few days subsequent to the interview in the garden. But nothing was said, and in due time Geoffrey departed again for Yalbury Wood.

''Tis to be hoped poor Miss Fancy will be able to keep on her school,' said Geoffrey's man Enoch to Geoffrey the following week, as they were shovelling up ant-hills in the wood.

Geoffrey stuck in the shovel, swept seven or eight ants from his sleeve, and killed another that was prowling round his ear, then looked perpendicularly into the earth, waiting for Enoch to say more. 'Well, why shouldn't she?' said the keeper at last.

'The baker told me yesterday,' continued Enoch, shaking out another emmet that had run merrily up his thigh, 'that the bread he've left at that there school-house this last month would starve any mouse in the three creations;[1] that 'twould so. And afterwards I had a pint o' small at the Old Souls, and there I heard more.'

'What might that ha' been?'

'That she used to have half a pound o' the best rolled butter a week, regular as clockwork, from Dairyman Quenton's; but now the same quantity d'last her three weeks, and then 'tis thought she throws it away sour.'

'Finish doing the emmets, and carry the bag home-along.' The keeper resumed his gun, tucked it under his arm, and went on without whistling to the dogs, who however followed, with a bearing meant to imply that they did not expect any such attentions when their master was reflecting.

On Saturday morning a note came from Fancy. He was not to trouble about sending her the couple of early young rabbits, as was intended, because she feared she should not want them. Later in the day, Geoffrey went to Casterbridge, and called upon the butcher who served Fancy with fresh meat, which was put down to her father's account.

'I've called to pay up our little bill, naibour Sabley, and you can gie me the chiel's account at the same time.'

Mr. Sabley turned round three quarters of a circle in the midst of a heap of joints, altered the expression of his face from meat to money, went into a little office consisting only of a door and a window, looked very vigorously into a book which possessed length but no breadth; and then, seizing a piece of paper and scribbling thereupon, handed the bill.

Probably it was the first time in the history of commercial transactions that the quality of shortness in a butcher's bill was a cause of tribulation to the debtor. 'Why this isn't all she've had in a whole month!' said Geoffrey.

'Every mossel,' said the butcher – '(now, Dan, take that leg and shoulder to Mrs. White's, and this eleven pound here to Mr. Martin's) – you've been trating her to smaller joints lately, to my thinking, Mr. Day?'

'Only two or three little scram rabbits this last week, as I be alive – I wish I had.'

'Well, my wife said to me – (Dan! not too much, not too much at a time; better go twice) – my wife said to me as she posted up the books: "Sabley," she ses, "Miss Day must have been affronted this summer during that hot muggy weather that spoilt so much for us; for depend upon't," she ses, "she've been trying Joe Grimmett unknown to us: see her account else." 'Tis little, of course, at the best of times, being only for one, but now 'tis next kin to nothing.'

'I'll inquire,' said Geoffrey despondingly.

He returned by way of Mellstock, and called upon Fancy, in fulfilment of a promise. It being Saturday, the children were enjoying a holiday, and on entering the residence Fancy was nowhere to be seen. Nan, the charwoman, was sweeping the kitchen.

'Where's my da'ter?' said the keeper.

'Well, you see she was tired with the week's work, and this morning she said, "Nan, I sha'n't get up till the evening." You see, Mr. Day, if people don't eat, they can't work; and as she've gie'd up eating, she must gie up working.'

'Have ye carried up any dinner to her?'

'No; she don't want any. There, we all know that such things don't come without good reason – not that I wish to say anything about a broken heart, or anything of the kind.'

Geoffrey's own heart felt inconveniently large just then. He went to the staircase and ascended to his daughter's door.

'Fancy!'

'Come in, father.'

To see a person in bed from any cause whatever, on a fine afternoon, is depressing enough; and here was his only child Fancy, not only in bed, but looking very pale. Geoffrey was visibly disturbed.

'Fancy, I didn't expect to see thee here, chiel,' he said. 'What's the matter?'

'I'm not well, father.'

'How's that?'

'Because I think of things.'

'What things can you have to think o' so martel much?'

'You know, father.'

'You think I've been cruel to thee in saying that that penniless Dick o' thine sha'n't marry thee, I suppose?'

No answer.

'Well, you know, Fancy, I do it for the best, and he isn't good enough for thee. You know that well enough.' Here he again looked at her as she lay. 'Well, Fancy, I can't let my only chiel die; and if you can't live without en, you must ha' en, I suppose.'

'O, I don't want him like that; all against your will, and everything so disobedient!' sighed the invalid.

'No, no; 'tisn't against my will. My wish is, now I d'see how 'tis hurten thee to live without en, that he shall marry thee as soon as we've considered a little. That's my wish flat and plain, Fancy. There, never cry, my little maid! You ought to ha' cried afore; no need o' crying now 'tis all over. Well, howsoever, try to stap over and see me and mother-law to-morrow, and ha' a bit of dinner wi' us.'

'And – Dick too?'

'Ay, Dick too, 'far's I know.'

'And *when* do you think you'll have considered, father, and he may marry me?' she coaxed.

'Well, there, say next Midsummer; that's not a day too long to wait.'

On leaving the school, Geoffrey went to the tranter's. Old William opened the door.

'Is your grandson Dick in 'ithin, William?'

'No, not just now, Geoffrey. Though he've been at home a good deal lately.'

'O, how's that?'

'What wi' one thing, and what wi' 'tother, he's all in a mope, as m't be said. Don't seem the feller 'a used to. Ay, 'a will sit studding and thinking as if 'a were going to turn chapel-member, and then 'a don't do nothing but traypsing and wambling about. Used to be such a chatty feller, too, Dick did; and now 'a don't spak at all. But won't ye stap inside? Reuben will be home soon, 'a b'lieve.'

'No, thank you, I can't stay now. Will ye just ask Dick if he'll do me the kindness to stap over to Yalbury to-morrow with my da'ter Fancy, if she's well enough? I don't like her to come by herself, now she's not so terrible topping in health.'

'So I've heard. Ay, sure, I'll tell'n without fail.'

CHAPTER V

After Gaining Her Point[1]

The visit to Geoffrey passed off as delightfully as a visit might have been expected to pass off when it was the first day of smooth experience in a hitherto obstructed love-course. And then came a series of several happy days, of the same undisturbed serenity. Dick could court her when he chose; stay away when he chose, – which was never; walk with her by winding streams and waterfalls and autumn scenery till dews and twilight sent them home. And thus they drew near the day of the Harvest Thanksgiving, which was also the time chosen for opening the organ in Mellstock Church.[2]

It chanced that Dick on that very day was called away from Mellstock. A young acquaintance had died of consumption at Stoneley, a neighbouring village, on the previous Monday, and Dick, in fulfilment of a long-standing promise, was to assist in carrying him to the grave. When, on Tuesday, Dick went towards the school to acquaint Fancy of the fact, it is difficult to say whether his own disappointment, at being denied the sight of her triumphant *début* as organist, was greater than his vexation that his pet should on this great occasion be deprived of the pleasure of his presence. However, the intelligence was communicated. She bore it as she best could, not without many expressions of regret, and convictions that her performance would be nothing to her now.

Just before eleven o'clock on Sunday he set out upon his sad errand. The funeral was to be immediately after the morning service, and as there were four good miles to walk, it became necessary to start comparatively early. Half an hour later would certainly have answered his purpose quite as well, yet nothing would content his ardent mind but that he must go a mile out of his way, in the direction of the school, in the hope of getting a glimpse of his Love as she started for church.

Striking into the path between the church and the school, he proceeded towards the latter spot, and arrived opposite her door as his goddess emerged.

If ever a woman looked a divinity, Fancy Day appeared one that morning as she floated down those school steps, in the form of a nebulous collection of colours inclining to blue. With an audacity unparalleled in the whole history of schoolmistresses[3] – partly owing, no doubt, to papa's respectable accumulation of cash, which rendered her profession not altogether one of necessity – she had actually donned a hat and feather, and lowered her hitherto plainly looped-up hair, which now fell about her shoulders in a profusion of curls.[4] Poor Dick was astonished: he had never seen her look so distractingly beautiful before, save on Christmas-eve, when her hair was in the same luxuriant condition of freedom. But his first burst of delighted surprise was followed by less comfortable feelings, as soon as his brain recovered its power to think.

Fancy had blushed; – was it with confusion? She had also involuntarily pressed back her curls. She had not expected him.

'Fancy, you didn't know me for a moment in my funeral clothes, did you?'

'Good-morning, Dick – no, really I didn't recognise you for an instant.'

He looked again at the gay tresses and hat. 'You've never dressed so charmingly before, dearest.'

'I like to hear you praise me in that way, Dick,' she said, smiling archly. 'It is meat and drink to a woman. Do I look nice really?'

'Fancy, – fie! you know it. Did you remember, – I mean didn't you remember about my going away to-day?'

'Well, yes, I did, Dick; but, you know, I wanted to look well; – forgive me.'

'Yes, darling; yes, of course, – there's nothing to forgive. No, I was only thinking that when we talked on Tuesday and Wednesday and Thursday and Friday about my absence to-day, and I regretted it so, you said, Fancy, so did you regret it, and almost cried, and said it would be no pleasure to you to be the attraction of the church to-day, since I could not be there.'

'My dear one, neither will it be so much pleasure to me ... But I do take a little delight in my life, I suppose,' she pouted.

'Apart from mine?'

She looked at him with perplexed eyes. 'I know you are vexed with me, Dick, and it is because the first Sunday I have curls and a hat and feather since I have been here happens to be the very day you are away and won't be with me. Yes, say it is, for that is it! And you think that all this week I ought to have remembered you wouldn't be here, and not have cared to be better dressed than usual. Yes, you do, Dick, and it is rather unkind!'

'No, no,' said Dick earnestly and simply, 'I didn't think so badly of you as that. I only thought that, if you had been going away, I shouldn't have adopted new attractions for the eyes of other people.[5] But then of course you and I are different, naturally.'

'Well, perhaps we are.'

'Whatever will the vicar say, Fancy?'

'I don't fear what he says in the least!' she answered proudly. 'But he won't say anything of the sort you think. No, no.'

'He can hardly have conscience to, indeed.'

'Now come, you say, Dick, that you quite forgive me, for I must go,' she said with sudden gaiety, and skipped backwards into the porch. 'Come here, sir! – say you forgive me, and then you shall kiss me; – you never have yet when I have worn curls, you know. Yes, in the very middle of my mouth, where you want to so much, – yes, you may.'

Dick followed her into the inner corner, where he was not slow in availing himself of the privilege offered.

'Now that's a treat for you, isn't it?' she continued. 'Good-bye, or I shall be late. Come and see me to-morrow: you'll be tired to-night.'

Thus they parted, and Fancy proceeded to the church. The organ stood on one side of the chancel, close to and under the immediate eye of the vicar when he was in the pulpit, and also in full view of the whole congregation. Here she sat down, for the first time in such a conspicuous position, her seat having previously been in a remote spot in the aisle. 'Good heavens – disgraceful! Curls and a hat and feather!' said the daughters of the small gentry, who had either only curly hair without a hat and feather, or a hat and feather without curling hair. 'A bonnet for church always!' said sober matrons.

That Mr. Maybold was conscious of her presence close beside him during his sermon; that he was not at all angry at her development of costume; that he admired her, she perceived. But she did not see that he loved her during that sermon-time as he had never loved a woman before; that her proximity was a strange delight to him; and that he gloried in her musical success that morning in a spirit quite beyond a mere cleric's glory at the inauguration of a new order of things.

The old choir, with humbled hearts, no longer took their seats in the gallery as heretofore (which was now given up to the school-children who were not singers, and a pupil-teacher), but were scattered about with their wives in different parts of the church. Having nothing to do with conducting the service for almost the first time in their lives, they all felt awkward, out of place, abashed, and inconvenienced by their hands. The tranter had proposed that they should stay away to-day and go nutting, but grandfather William would not hear of such a thing for a moment. 'No,' he replied reproachfully, and quoted a verse: ' "Though this has come upon us, let not our hearts be turned back, or our steps go out of the way." '6 So they stood and watched the curls of hair trailing down the back of the successful rival, and the waving of her feather, as she swayed her head. After a few timid notes and uncertain touches her playing became markedly correct, and towards the end full and free. But, whether from prejudice or unbiassed judgment, the venerable body of musicians could not help thinking that the simpler notes they had been wont to bring forth were more in keeping with the simplicity of their old church than the crowded chords and interludes it was her pleasure to produce.

CHAPTER VI

Into Temptation¹

The day was done, and Fancy was again in the school-house. About five o'clock it began to rain, and in rather a dull frame of mind she wandered into the schoolroom, for want of something better to do. She was thinking – of her lover Dick Dewy? not precisely. Of how weary she was of living alone; how unbearable it would be to return to Yalbury under the rule of her strange-tempered step-mother; that it was far better to be married to anybody than do that; that eight or nine long months had yet to be lived through ere the wedding could take place.

At the end of the room was a high window, upon the sill of which she could sit by first mounting a desk and using it as a footstool. As the evening advanced, here she perched herself, as was her custom on such wet and gloomy occasions, put on a light shawl and bonnet, opened the window, and looked out at the rain.

The window overlooked a field and footpath across it, and it was the position from which she used to survey the crown of Dick's hat in the early days of their acquaintance and meetings. Not a living soul was now visible anywhere; the rain kept all people indoors who were not forced abroad by necessity, and necessity was less importunate on Sundays than during the week.

Sitting here and thinking again – of her lover, or of the sensation she had created at church that day? – well, it is unknown – thinking and thinking she saw a dark masculine figure arising into distinctness at the farther end of the path – a man without an umbrella. Nearer and nearer he came, and she perceived that he was in deep mourning, and then that it was Dick. Yes, in the fondness and foolishness of his young heart, after walking four miles in a drizzling rain without overcoat or umbrella, and in face of a remark from his love that he was not to come because he would be tired, he had made it his business to wander this mile out of his way again, from sheer love of spending ten minutes in her beloved presence.

'O Dick, how wet you are!' she said, as he drew up under the window. 'Why, your coat shines as if it had been varnished, and your hat – my goodness, there's a streaming hat!'

'O, I don't mind, darling!' said Dick cheerfully. 'Wet never hurts me, though I am rather sorry for my best clothes. However, it couldn't be helped; they lent all the umbrellas to the women.'[2]

'And look, there's a nasty patch of something just on your shoulder.'

'Ah, that's japanning; it rubbed off the clamps of poor Jack's coffin when we lowered him from our shoulders upon the bier! I don't care about that, for 'twas the last deed I could do for him; and 'tis hard if you can't afford a coat to an old friend.'

Fancy put her hand to her mouth for half a minute. Underneath the palm of that little hand there existed for that half-minute a little yawn.

'Dick, I don't like you to stand there in the wet. Go home and change your things. Don't stay another minute.'

'One kiss after coming so far,' he pleaded.

'If I can reach, then.'

He looked rather disappointed at not being invited round to the door. She left her seated position and bent herself downwards, but not even by standing on the plinth was it possible for Dick to get his mouth into contact with hers as she held it. By great exertion she might have reached a little lower; but then she would have exposed her head to the rain.

'Never mind, Dick; kiss my hand,' she said, flinging it down to him. 'Now, good-bye.'[3]

'Good-bye!'

He walked slowly away, turning and turning again to look at her till he was out of sight. During the retreat she said to herself, almost involuntarily, and still conscious of that morning's triumph,[4]

'I like Dick, and I love him; but how poor and mean a man looks in the rain,[5] with no umbrella, and wet through!'

As he vanished, she made as if to descend from her seat; but glancing in the other direction she saw another form coming along the same path. It was also that of a man. He, too, was in black from top to toe; but he carried an umbrella.

He drew nearer, and the direction of the rain caused him so to slant his umbrella, that from her height above the ground his head was invisible, as she was also to him. He passed in due time directly beneath her, and in looking down upon the exterior of his umbrella her feminine eyes instinctively perceived[6] it to be of superior silk,[7] and of elegant make. He reached the angle of the building, and Fancy suddenly lost sight of him. Instead of pursuing the straight path, as Dick had done, he had turned sharply round to her own door.

She jumped to the floor, hastily flung off the shawl and bonnet, smoothed and patted her hair till the curls hung in passable condition, and listened. No knock. Nearly a minute passed, and still there was no knock. Then there arose a soft series of raps, no louder than the tapping of a distant woodpecker, and barely distinct enough to reach her ears. She composed herself and flung open the door.

In the porch stood Mr. Maybold.

There was a warm flush upon his face, and a bright flash in his eyes, which made him look handsomer than she had ever seen him before.

'Good-evening, Miss Day.'

'Good-evening, Mr. Maybold,' she said, in a strange state of mind. She had noticed, beyond the ardent hue of his face, that his voice had a singular tremor in it, and that his hand shook like an aspen leaf when he laid his umbrella in the corner of the porch. Without another word being spoken by either he came into the schoolroom, shut the door, and moved close to her. Once inside, the expression of his face was no more discernible, by reason of the increasing dusk of evening.

'I want to speak to you,' he then said; 'seriously – on a perhaps unexpected subject, but one which is all the world to me – I don't know what it may be to you, Miss Day.'

No reply.

'Fancy, I have come to ask you if you will be my wife?'

As a person who has been idly amusing himself with rolling a snowball might start at finding he had set in motion an avalanche, so did Fancy start at these words from the vicar. And in the dead silence which followed them, the breathings of the man and of the woman could be distinctly and separately heard; and there was this difference between them – his respirations gradually grew quieter and less rapid after the enunciation; hers, from having been low and regular, increased in quickness and force, till she almost panted.

'I cannot, I cannot, Mr. Maybold – I cannot. Don't ask me!' she said.

'Don't answer in a hurry!' he entreated. 'And do listen to me. This is no sudden feeling on my part. I have loved you for more than six months! Perhaps my late interest in teaching the children here has not been so single-minded as it seemed. You will understand my motive – like me better, perhaps – for honestly telling you that I have struggled against my emotion continually, because I have thought that it was not well for me to love you! But I resolve to struggle no longer; I have examined the feeling; and the love I bear you is as genuine as that I could bear any woman! I see your great beauty;[8] I respect your natural talents, and the refinement they have brought into your nature – they are quite enough, and more than enough for me! They are equal to anything ever required of the mistress of a quiet parsonage-house – the place in which I shall pass my days, wherever it may be situated. O Fancy, I have watched you, criticised you even severely, brought my feelings to the light of judgment, and still have found them rational, and such as any man might have expected to be inspired with by a woman like you! So there is nothing hurried, secret, or untoward in my desire to make you my wife! Fancy, will you marry me?'

No answer was returned.

'Don't refuse; don't,' he implored. 'It would be foolish of you – I mean cruel! Of course we would not live here, Fancy. I have had for a long time the offer of an exchange of livings with a friend in Yorkshire, but I have hitherto refused on account of my mother. There we would go. Your musical powers shall be still further developed; you shall have whatever piano you like; you shall have anything, Fancy! anything to make you happy – pony-carriage, flowers, birds, pleasant society; yes, you have enough in you for any society, after a few months of travel with me! Will you, Fancy, marry me?'

Another pause ensued, varied only by the surging of the rain against the window-panes, and then Fancy spoke, in a faint and broken voice.

'Yes, I will,' she said.

'God bless you, my own!' He advanced quickly, and put his arm out to embrace her. She drew back hastily. 'No, no, not now!' she said in an agitated whisper.

'There are things; – but the temptation is, O, too strong, and I can't resist it; I can't tell you now, but I must tell you! Don't, please, don't come near me now! I want to think. I can scarcely get myself used to the idea of what I have promised yet.' The next minute she turned to a desk, buried her face in her hands, and burst into a hysterical fit of weeping. 'O, leave me!' she sobbed, 'leave me! O, leave me!'

'Don't be distressed; don't, dearest!' It was with visible difficulty that he restrained himself from approaching her. 'You shall tell me at your leisure what it is that grieves you so; I am happy – beyond all measure happy! – at having your simple promise.'

'And do leave me now!'

'But I must not, in justice to you, leave for a minute, until you are yourself again.'

'There then,' she said, controlling her emotion, and standing up; 'I am not disturbed now.'

He reluctantly moved towards the door. 'Good-bye!' he murmured tenderly. 'I'll come to-morrow about this time.'

CHAPTER VII

A Crisis[1]

The next morning the vicar rose early. The first thing he did was to write a long and careful letter to his friend in Yorkshire. Then, partaking of a little breakfast, he crossed the dale and heath in the direction of Casterbridge, bearing his letter in his pocket, that he might post it at the town office, and obviate the loss of one day in its transmission that would have resulted had he left it for the foot-post through the village.

It was a foggy morning, and the trees shed in noisy water-drops the moisture they had collected from the thick air, an acorn occasionally falling from its cup to the ground, in company with the drippings. In the heath, sheets of spiders'-web, almost opaque with wet, hung in folds over the furze-bushes, and the ferns appeared in every variety of brown, green, and yellow hues.

A low and merry whistling was heard on the other side of the hedge, then the light footsteps of a man going in the same direction as himself. On reaching the gate which divided the two enclosures, the vicar beheld Dick Dewy's open and cheerful face. Dick lifted his hat, and came through the gate into the path the vicar was pursuing.

'Good-morning, Dewy. How well you are looking!' said Mr. Maybold.

'Yes, sir, I am well – quite well! I am going to Casterbridge now, to get Smart's collar; we left it there Saturday to be repaired.'

'I am going to Casterbridge, so we'll walk together,' the vicar said. Dick gave a hop with one foot to put himself in step with Mr. Maybold, who proceeded: 'I fancy I didn't see you at church yesterday, Dewy. Or were you behind the pier?'

'No: I went to Stoneley. Poor John Dunford chose me to be one of his bearers a long time before he died, and yesterday was the funeral. Of course I couldn't refuse, though I should have liked particularly to have been at home on this occasion.'

'Yes, you should have been. The musical portion of the service was successful – very successful indeed; and what is more to the purpose, no ill-feeling whatever was evinced by any of the members of the old choir. They joined in the singing with the greatest good-will.'

''Twas natural enough that I should want to be there, I suppose,' said Dick, smiling a private smile; 'considering who the organist was.'

At this the vicar reddened a little, and said, 'Yes, yes,' though not at all comprehending Dick's true meaning, who, as he received no further reply, continued hesitatingly, and with another smile denoting his pride as a lover,

'I suppose you know what I mean, sir? You've heard about me and – Miss Day?'

The red in Maybold's countenance went away: he turned and looked Dick in the face.

'No,' he said constrainedly, 'I've heard nothing whatever about you and Miss Day.'

'Why, she's my sweetheart, and we are going to be married next Midsummer. We are keeping it rather close just at present, because it is a good many months to wait; but it is her father's wish that we don't marry before, and of course we must submit. But the time will soon slip along.'

'Yes, the time will soon slip along. Time glides away every day – yes.'

Maybold said these words, but he had no idea of what they were. He was conscious of a cold and sickly thrill throughout him; and all he reasoned was this, that the young creature whose graces had intoxicated him into making the most imprudent resolution of his life, was less an angel than a woman.[2]

'You see, sir,' continued the ingenuous Dick, ''twill be better in one sense. I shall by that time be the regular manager of a branch of my father's business,[3] which has very much increased lately, and we expect next year to keep an extra couple of horses. We've already our eye on one – brown as a berry, neck like a rainbow, fifteen hands, and not a gray hair in her – offered us at twenty-five want a crown.[4] And to keep pace with the times, I have had some cards printed,[5] and I beg leave to hand you one, sir.'

'Certainly,' said the vicar, mechanically taking the card that Dick offered him.

'I turn in here by the river,' said Dick. 'I suppose you go straight up the town?'

'Yes.'

'Good-morning, sir.'

'Good-morning, Dewy.'

Maybold stood still upon the bridge, holding the card as it had been put into his hand, and Dick's footsteps died away. The vicar's first voluntary action was to read the card: –

DEWY AND SON,

𝕿ranters and 𝕳auliers,

MELLSTOCK.

N.B. Furniture, Coals, Potatoes, Live and Dead Stock,
removed to any distance on the shortest notice.

Mr. Maybold leant over the parapet of the bridge and looked into the river. He saw – without heeding – how the water came rapidly from beneath the arches, glided down a little steep, then spread itself over a pool in which dace, trout, and minnows sported at ease among the long green locks of weed, that lay heaving and sinking with their roots towards the current. At the end of ten minutes spent leaning thus, he stood erect, drew the letter from his pocket, tore it deliberately into such minute fragments that scarcely two syllables remained in juxtaposition, and sent the whole handful of shreds fluttering into the water. Here he watched them eddy, dart, and turn, as they were carried downwards towards the ocean and gradually disappeared from his view. Finally he moved off, and pursued his way at a rapid pace towards Mellstock Vicarage.

Nerving himself by a long and intense effort, he sat down in his study and wrote as follows:

Dear Miss Day, – The meaning of your words, 'the temptation is too strong,' of your sadness and your tears, has been brought home to me by an accident. I know to-day what I did not know yesterday – that you are not a free woman.

Why did you not tell me – why didn't you? Did you suppose I knew? No. Had I known, my conduct in coming to you as I did would have been reprehensible.

But I don't chide you! perhaps no blame attaches to you – I can't tell. Fancy, though my opinion of you is assailed and disturbed in a way which cannot be expressed, I love you still, and my word to you holds good yet. But will you, in justice to an honest man who relies upon your word to him, consider whether, under the circumstances, you can honourably forsake him?

Yours ever sincerely,
ARTHUR MAYBOLD.

He rang the bell. 'Tell Charles to take these copybooks and this note to the school at once.'

The maid took the parcel and the letter, and in a few minutes a boy was seen to leave the vicarage gate, with the one under his arm, and the other in his hand. The vicar sat with his hand to his brow, watching the lad as he climbed the hill and entered the little field that intervened between that spot and the school.

Here he was met by another boy, and after a salutation and pugilistic frisk had passed between the two, the second boy came on his way to the vicarage, and the other vanished out of sight.

The boy came to the door, and a note for Mr. Maybold was brought in.

He knew the writing. Opening the envelope with an unsteady hand, he read the subjoined words:

Dear Mr. Maybold, – I have been thinking seriously and sadly through the whole of the night of the question you put to me last evening; and of my answer. That answer, as an honest woman, I had no right to give.

It is my nature – perhaps all women's – to love refinement of mind and manners; but even more than this, to be ever fascinated with the idea of surroundings more elegant and luxurious than those which have been customary. And you praised me, and praise is life to me. It was alone my sensations at these things which prompted my reply. Ambition and vanity they would be called; perhaps they are so.

After this explanation, I hope you will generously allow me to withdraw the answer I too hastily gave.

And one more request. To keep the meeting of last night, and all that passed between us there, for ever a secret. Were it to become known, it would for ever blight the happiness of a trusting and generous man, whom I love still, and shall love always.

Yours sincerely,
FANCY DAY.

The last written communication that ever passed from the vicar to Fancy, was a note containing these words only:

Tell him everything; it is best. He will forgive you.

PART V

Conclusion

CHAPTER I

'The Knot There's No Untying'[1]

The last day of the story is dated just subsequent to that point in the development of the seasons when country people go to bed among nearly naked trees, and awake next morning among green ones; when the landscape appears embarrassed with the sudden weight and brilliancy of its leaves; when the night-jar[2] comes and commences for the summer his tune of one note; when the apple-trees have bloomed, and the roads and orchards become spotted with fallen petals; when the faces of the delicate flowers are darkened, and their heads weighed down by the throng of honey-bees, which increase their humming till humming is too mild a term for the all-pervading sound; and when cuckoos, blackbirds, and sparrows, that have hitherto been merry and respectful neighbours, become noisy and persistent intimates.[3]

The exterior of Geoffrey Day's house in Yalbury Wood appeared exactly as was usual at that season, but a frantic barking of the dogs at the back told of unwonted movements somewhere within. Inside the door the eyes beheld a gathering, which was a rarity indeed for the dwelling of the solitary keeper.

About the room were sitting and standing, in various gnarled attitudes, our old acquaintance, grandfathers James and William, the tranter, Mr. Penny, two or three children, including Jimmy and Charley, besides three or four country ladies and gentlemen who do not require any distinction by name. Geoffrey was seen and heard stamping about the outhouse and among the bushes of the garden, attending to details of daily routine before the proper time arrived for their performance, in order that they might be off his hands for the day. He appeared with his shirt-sleeves rolled up; his best new nether garments, in which he had arrayed himself that morning, being temporarily disguised under a week-day apron whilst these proceedings were in operation. He occasionally glanced at the hives in passing, to see if the bees were swarming, ultimately rolling down his shirt-sleeves and going indoors, talking to tranter Dewy whilst buttoning the wrist-bands, to save time; next going upstairs for his best waistcoat, and coming down again to make another remark whilst buttoning that, during the time looking fixedly in the tranter's face, as if he were a looking-glass.

The furniture had undergone attenuation to an alarming extent, every duplicate piece having been removed, including the clock by Ezekiel Sparrowgrass; Thomas Wood[4] being at last left sole referee in matters of time.

Fancy was stationary upstairs, receiving her layers of clothes and adornments, and answering by short fragments of laughter, which had more fidgetiness than mirth in them, remarks that were made from time to time by Mrs. Dewy and Mrs. Penny, who were assisting her at the toilet, Mrs. Day having pleaded a queerness in her head as a reason for shutting herself up in an inner bedroom for the whole morning. Mrs. Penny appeared with nine corkscrew curls on each side of her temples, and a back comb stuck upon her crown like a castle on a steep.

The conversation just now going on was concerning the banns, the last publication of which had been on the Sunday previous.

'And how did they sound?' Fancy subtly inquired.

'Very beautiful indeed,' said Mrs. Penny. 'I never heard any sound better.'

'But *how?*'

'O, *so* natural and elegant, didn't they, Reuben!' she cried, through the chinks of the unceiled floor, to the tranter downstairs.

'What's that?' said the tranter, looking up inquiringly at the floor above him for an answer.

'Didn't Dick and Fancy sound well when they were called home in church last Sunday?' came downwards again in Mrs. Penny's voice.

'Ay, that they did, my sonnies! – especially the first time. There was a terrible whispering piece of work in the congregation, wasn't there, naibour Penny?' said the tranter, taking up the thread of conversation on his own account, and, in order to be heard in the room above, speaking very loudly to Mr. Penny, who sat at the distance of two feet from him, or rather less.

'I never remember seeing such a whispering as there was,' said Mr. Penny, also loudly, to the room above. 'And such sorrowful envy on the maidens' faces; really, I never see such envy as there was!'

Fancy's lineaments varied in innumerable little flushes, and her heart palpitated innumerable little tremors of pleasure. 'But perhaps,' she said, with assumed indifference, 'it was only because no religion was going on just then.'

'O, no; nothing to do with that. 'Twas because of your high standing. It was just as if they had one and all caught Dick kissing and coling ye to death, wasn't it, Mrs. Dewy?'

'Ay; that 'twas.'

'How people will talk about people!' Fancy exclaimed.

'Well, if you make songs about yourself, my dear, you can't blame other people for singing 'em.'

'Mercy me! how shall I go through it?' said the young lady again, but merely to those in the bedroom, with a breathing of a kind between a sigh and a pant, round shining eyes, and warm face.

'O, you'll get through it well enough, child,' said Mrs. Dewy placidly. 'The edge of the performance is taken off at the calling home; and when once you get up to the chancel end o' the church, you feel as saucy as you please. I'm sure I felt as brave as a sodger all through the deed – though of course I dropped my face and looked modest, as was becoming to a maid. Mind you do that, Fancy.'

'And I walked into the church as quiet as a lamb, I'm sure,' subjoined Mrs. Penny. 'There, you see Penny is such a little small man. But certainly, I was flurried in the inside o' me. Well, thinks I, 'tis to be, and here goes! And do you do the same: say, "'Tis to be, and here goes!"'

'Is there such a wonderful virtue in your "'Tis to be, and here goes!"' inquired Fancy.

'Wonderful! 'Twill carry a body through it all from wedding to church-ing, if you only let it out with spirit enough.'[5]

'Very well, then,' said Fancy, blushing. "'Tis to be, and here goes!'

'That's a girl for a husband!'[6] said Mrs. Dewy.

'I do hope he'll come in time!' continued the bride-elect, inventing a new cause of affright, now that the other was demolished.

"'Twould be a thousand pities if he didn't come, now you be so brave,' said Mrs. Penny.

Grandfather James, having overheard some of these remarks, said downstairs with mischievous loudness:

'I've heard that at some weddings the men don't come.'

'They've been known not to, before now, certainly,' said Mr. Penny, cleaning one of the glasses of his spectacles.

'O, do hear what they're saying downstairs,' whispered Fancy. 'Hush, hush!'

She listened.

'They have, haven't they, Geoffrey?' continued grandfather James, as Geoffrey entered.

'Have what?' said Geoffrey.

'The men have been known not to come.'

'That they have,' said the keeper.

'Ay; I've knowed times when the wedding had to be put off through his not appearing, being tired of the woman. And another case I knowed when the man was catched in a man-trap[7] crossing Mellstock Wood, and the three months had run out before he got well, and the banns had to be published over again.'

'How horrible!' said Fancy.

'They only say it on purpose to tease you, my dear,' said Mrs. Dewy.

''Tis quite sad to think what wretched shifts poor maids have been put to,' came again from downstairs. 'Ye should hear Clerk Wilkins, my brother-law, tell his experiences in marrying couples these last thirty years: sometimes one thing, sometimes another – 'tis quite heart-rending – enough to make your hair stand on end.'

'Those things don't happen very often, I know,' said Fancy, with smouldering uneasiness.

'Well, really 'tis time Dick was here,' said the tranter.

'Don't keep on at me so, grandfather James and Mr. Dewy, and all you down there!' Fancy broke out, unable to endure any longer. 'I am sure I shall die, or do something, if you do.'

'Never you hearken to these old chaps, Miss Day!' cried Nat Callcome, the best man, who had just entered, and threw his voice upward through the chinks of the floor as the others had done. ''Tis all right; Dick's coming on like a wild feller; he'll be here in a minute. The hive o' bees his mother gie'd en for his new garden swarmed jist as he was starting, and he said, "I can't afford to lose a stock o' bees; no, that I can't, though I fain would; and Fancy wouldn't wish it on any account." So he jist stopped to ting to 'em and shake 'em.'

'A genuine wise man,' said Geoffrey.

'To be sure, what a day's work we had yesterday!' Mr. Callcome continued, lowering his voice as if it were not necessary any longer to include those in the room above among his audience, and selecting a remote corner of his best clean handkerchief for wiping his face. 'To be sure!'

'Things so heavy, I suppose,' said Geoffrey, as if reading through the chimney-window from the far end of the paddock.

'Ay,' said Nat, looking round the room at points from which furniture had been removed. 'And so awkward to carry, too. 'Twas ath'art and across Dick's garden; in and out Dick's door; up and down Dick's stairs; round and round Dick's chammers till legs were worn to stumps: and Dick is so particular, too. And the stores of victuals and drink that lad has laid in: why, 'tis enough for Noah's ark! I'm sure I never wish to see a choicer half-dozen of hams than he's got there in his chimley; and the cider I tasted was a very pretty drop, indeed; – never could desire a prettier tasted cider.'

'They be for the love and the stalled ox both.[8] Ah, the greedy martels!' said grandfather James.

'Well, may-be they be. "Surely," says I, "that couple between 'em have heaped up so much furniture and victuals, that anybody would think they were going to take hold the big end of married life first, and begin wi' a grown-up family." Ah, what a bath of heat we two chaps were in, to be sure, a-getting that furniture in order!'

'I do so wish the room below was ceiled,' said Fancy, as the dressing went on; 'they can hear all we say and do up here.'[9]

'Hark! Who's that?' exclaimed a small pupil-teacher, who also assisted this morning, to her great delight. She ran half-way down the stairs, and peeped round the bannister. 'O, you should, you should, you should!' she exclaimed, scrambling up to the room again.

'What?' said Fancy.

'See the bridesmaids! They've just come! 'Tis wonderful, really! 'tis wonderful how muslin can be brought to it. There, they don't look a bit like themselves, but like some very rich sisters o' theirs that nobody knew they had!'

'Make 'em come up to me, make 'em come up!' cried Fancy ecstatically; and the four damsels appointed, namely, Miss Susan Dewy, Miss Bessie Dewy, Miss Vashti Sniff, and Miss Mercy Onmey, surged upstairs, and floated along the passage.

'I wish Dick would come!' was again the burden of Fancy.

The same instant a small twig and flower from the creeper outside the door flew in at the open window, and a masculine voice said, 'Ready, Fancy dearest?'

'There he is, he is!' cried Fancy, tittering spasmodically, and breathing as it were for the first time that morning.

The bridesmaids crowded to the window and turned their heads in the direction pointed out, at which motion eight ear-rings all swung as one: – not looking at Dick because they particularly wanted to see him, but with an important sense of their duty as obedient ministers of the will of that apotheosised being – the Bride.

'He looks very taking!' said Miss Vashti Sniff, a young lady who blushed cream-colour and wore yellow bonnet-ribbons.

Dick was advancing to the door in a painfully new coat of shining cloth, primrose-coloured waistcoat, hat of the same painful style of newness, and with an extra quantity of whiskers shaved off his face, and his hair cut to an unwonted shortness in honour of the occasion.

'Now I'll run down,' said Fancy, looking at herself over her shoulder in the glass, and flitting off.

'O Dick!' she exclaimed, 'I am so glad you are come! I knew you would, of course, but I thought, O if you shouldn't!'

'Not come, Fancy! Het or wet, blow or snow, here come I to-day! Why, what's possessing your little soul? You never used to mind such things a bit.'

'Ah, Mr. Dick, I hadn't hoisted my colours and committed myself then!' said Fancy.

''Tis a pity I can't marry the whole five of ye!' said Dick, surveying them all round.

'Heh-heh-heh!' laughed the four bridesmaids, and Fancy privately touched Dick and smoothed him down behind his shoulder, as if to assure herself that he was there in flesh and blood as her own property.[10]

'Well, whoever would have thought such a thing?' said Dick, taking off his hat, sinking into a chair, and turning to the elder members of the company.

The elder members of the company arranged their eyes and lips to signify that in their opinion nobody could have thought such a thing, whatever it was.

'That my bees should have swarmed just then, of all times and seasons!'[11] continued Dick, throwing a comprehensive glance like a net over the whole auditory. 'And 'tis a fine swarm, too: I haven't seen such a fine swarm for these ten years.'

'An excellent sign,' said Mrs. Penny, from the depths of experience. 'An excellent sign.'

'I am glad everything seems so right,' said Fancy with a breath of relief.

'And so am I,' said the four bridesmaids with much sympathy.

'Well, bees can't be put off,' observed grandfather James.[12] 'Marrying a woman is a thing you can do at any moment; but a swarm of bees won't come for the asking.'

Dick fanned himself with his hat. 'I can't think,' he said thoughtfully, 'whatever 'twas I did to offend Mr. Maybold, – a man I like so much too. He rather took to me when he came first, and used to say he should like to see me married, and that he'd marry me, whether the young woman I chose lived in his parish or no. I slightly reminded him of it when I put in the banns, but he didn't seem to take kindly to the notion now, and so I said no more. I wonder how it was.'

'I wonder,' said Fancy, looking into vacancy with those beautiful eyes of hers – too refined and beautiful for a tranter's wife; but, perhaps, not too good.[13]

'Altered his mind, as folk will, I suppose,' said the tranter. 'Well, my sonnies, there'll be a good strong party looking at us to-day as we go along.'

'And the body of the church,' said Geoffrey, 'will be lined with feymells, and a row of young fellers' heads, as far down as the eyes, will be noticed just above the sills of the chancel-winders.'

'Ay, you've been through it twice,' said Reuben, 'and well may know.'

'I can put up with it for once,' said Dick, 'or twice either, or a dozen times.'

'O Dick!' said Fancy reproachfully.

'Why, dear, that's nothing, – only just a bit of a flourish. You are as nervous as a cat to-day.'

'And then, of course, when 'tis all over,' continued the tranter, 'we shall march two and two round the parish.'

'Yes, sure,' said Mr. Penny: 'two and two: every man hitched up to his woman, 'a b'lieve.'

'I never can make a show of myself in that way!' said Fancy, looking at Dick to ascertain if he could.

'I'm agreed to anything you and the company likes, my dear!' said Mr. Richard Dewy heartily.

'Why, we did when we were married didn't we, Ann?' said the tranter; 'and so do everybody, my sonnies.'

'And so did we,' said Fancy's father.

'And so did Penny and I,' said Mrs. Penny: 'I wore my best Bath clogs, I remember, and Penny was cross because it made me look so tall.'

'And so did father and mother,' said Miss Mercy Onmey.

'And I mane to, come next Christmas!' said Nat the bridesman vigorously, and looking towards the person of Miss Vashti Sniff.

'Respectable people don't nowadays,' said Fancy. 'Still, since poor mother did, I will.'[14]

'Ay,' resumed the tranter, ''twas on a White Tuesday when I committed it. Mellstock Club walked the same day, and we new-married folk went a-gaying round the parish behind 'em. Everybody used to wear summat white at Whitsuntide in them days. My sonnies, I've got they very white trousers that I wore, at home in box now. Ha'n't I, Ann?'

'You had till I cut 'em up for Jimmy,' said Mrs. Dewy.

'And we ought, by rights, to go round Galligar-lane, by Quenton's,' said Mr. Penny, recovering scent of the matter in hand. 'Dairyman Quenton is a very respectable man, and so is Farmer Crocker, and we ought to show ourselves to them.'

'True,' said the tranter, 'we ought to go round Galligar-lane to do the thing well. We shall form a very striking object walking along: good-now, naibours?'

'That we shall: a proper pretty sight for the nation,' said Mrs. Penny.

'Hullo!' said the tranter, suddenly catching sight of a singular human figure standing in the doorway, and wearing a long smock-frock of pillow-case cut and of snowy whiteness. 'Why, Leaf! whatever dost thou do here?'

'I've come to know if so be I can come to the wedding – hee-hee!' said Leaf in an uneasy voice of timidity.

'Now, Leaf,' said the tranter reproachfully, 'you know we don't want ye here to-day: we've got no room for ye, Leaf.'

'Thomas Leaf, Thomas Leaf, fie upon ye for prying!' said old William.

'I know I've got no head, but I thought, if I washed and put on a clane shirt and smock-frock, I might just call,' said Leaf, turning away disappointed and trembling.

'Pore feller!' said the tranter, turning to Geoffrey. 'Suppose we must let en come? His looks is rather against en, and 'a is terrible silly; but 'a have never been in jail, and 'a won't do no harm.'

Leaf looked with gratitude at the tranter for these praises, and then anxiously at Geoffrey, to see what effect they would have in helping his cause.

'Ay, let en come,' said Geoffrey decisively. 'Leaf, th'rt welcome, 'st know;' and Leaf accordingly remained.

They were now all ready for leaving the house, and began to form a procession in the following order: Fancy and her father, Dick and Susan Dewy, Nat Callcome and Vashti Sniff, Ted Waywood and Mercy Onmey, and Jimmy and Bessy Dewy. These formed the executive, and all appeared in strict wedding attire. Then came the tranter and Mrs. Dewy, and last of all, Mr. and Mrs. Penny; – the tranter conspicuous by his enormous gloves, size eleven and three-quarters, which appeared at a distance like boxing gloves bleached, and sat rather awkwardly upon his brown hands; this hall-mark of respectability having been set upon himself to-day (by Fancy's special request) for the first time in his life.

'The proper way is for the bridesmaids to walk together,' suggested Fancy.

'What? 'Twas always young man and young woman, arm in crook, in my time!' said Geoffrey, astounded.

'And in mine!' said the tranter.

'And in ours!' said Mr. and Mrs. Penny.

'Never heard o' such a thing as woman and woman!' said old William; who, with grandfather James and Mrs. Day, was to stay at home.

'Whichever way you and the company likes, my dear!' said Dick, who being on the point of securing his right to Fancy, seemed willing to renounce all other rights in the world with the greatest pleasure. The decision was left to Fancy.

'Well, I think I'd rather have it the way mother had it,' she said, and the couples moved along under the trees, every man to his maid.

'Ah!' said grandfather James to grandfather William, as they retired, 'I wonder which she thinks most about, Dick or her wedding raiment!'

'Well, 'tis their nater,' said grandfather William. 'Remember the words of the prophet Jeremiah: "Can a maid forget her ornaments, or a bride her attire?"' [15]

Now among dark perpendicular firs, like the shafted columns of a cathedral; now under broad beeches in bright young leaves, they threaded their way: then through a hazel copse, matted with primroses and wild hyacinths, into the high road, which dipped at that point directly into the village of Yalbury; and in the space of a quarter of an hour, Fancy found herself to be Mrs. Richard Dewy, though, much to her surprise, feeling no other than Fancy Day still.

On the circuitous return walk through the lanes and fields, amid much chattering and laughter, especially when they came to stiles, Dick discerned a brown spot far up a turnip field.

'Why, 'tis Enoch!' he said to Fancy. 'I thought I missed him at the house this morning. How is it he's left you?'

'He drank too much cider, and it got into his head, and they put him in the stocks[16] for it. Father was obliged to get somebody else for a day or two, and Enoch hasn't had anything to do with the woods since.'

'We might ask him to call down tonight. Stocks are nothing for once, considering 'tis our wedding-day.' The bridal party was ordered to halt.

'Eno-o-o-o-ch!' cried Dick at the top of his voice.

'Y-a-a-a-a-a-as!' said Enoch from the distance.

'D'ye know who I be-e-e-e-e-e?'

'No-o-o-o-o-o-o!'

'Dick Dew-w-w-w-wy!'

'O-h-h-h-h-h!'

'Just a-ma-a-a-a-a-arried!'

'O-h-h-h-h-h!'

'This is my wife, Fa-a-a-a-a-ancy!' (holding her up to Enoch's view as if she had been a nosegay.)

'O-h-h-h-h-h!'

'Will ye come down to the party to-ni-i-i-i-i-i-ight!'

'Ca-a-a-a-a-ant!'

'Why n-o-o-o-o-ot?'

'Don't work for the family no-o-o-o-ow!'

'Not nice of Master Enoch,' said Dick, as they resumed their walk.

'You mustn't blame en,' said Geoffrey; 'the man's not himself now; he's in his morning frame of mind. When he's had a gallon o' cider or ale, and a pint or two of mead, the man's well enough, and his manners be as good as anybody's in the kingdom.'

CHAPTER II

Under the Greenwood Tree[1]

The point in Yalbury Wood which abutted on the end of Geoffrey Day's premises was closed with an ancient beech-tree,[2] horizontally of enormous extent, though having no great pretensions to height. Many hundreds of birds had been born amidst the boughs of this single tree; tribes of rabbits and hares had nibbled at its bark from year to year; quaint tufts of fungi had sprung from the cavities of its forks; and countless families of moles and earthworms had crept about its roots. Beneath its shade spread a carefully-tended grass-plot, its purpose being to supply a healthy exercise-ground for young chicken and pheasants; the hens, their mothers, being enclosed in coops placed upon the same green flooring.

All these encumbrances were now removed, and as the afternoon advanced, the guests gathered on the spot, where music, dancing, and the singing of songs went forward with great spirit throughout the evening. The propriety of every one was intense, by reason of the influence of Fancy, who, as an additional precaution in this direction, had strictly charged her father and the tranter to carefully avoid saying 'thee' and 'thou' in their conversation, on the plea that those ancient words sounded so very humiliating to persons of decent taste;[3] also that they were never to be seen drawing the back of the hand across the mouth after drinking, – a local English custom of extraordinary antiquity, but stated by Fancy to be decidedly dying out among the upper classes of society.

In addition to the local musicians present, a man who had a thorough knowledge of the tambourine was invited from the village of Tantrum Clangley,[4] – a place long celebrated for the skill of its inhabitants as performers on instruments of percussion. These important members of the assembly were relegated to a height of two or three feet from the ground, upon a temporary erection of planks supported by barrels. Whilst the dancing progressed, the older persons sat in a group under the trunk of the beech, – the space being allotted to them somewhat grudgingly by the young ones, who were greedy of pirouetting room, – and fortified by a table against the heels of the dancers. Here the gaffers and gammers, whose dancing days were over, told stories of great impressiveness, and at intervals surveyed the advancing and retiring couples from the same retreat, as people on shore might be supposed to survey a naval engagement in the bay beyond; returning again to their tales when the pause was over. Those of the whirling throng, who, during the rests between each figure, turned their eyes in the direction of these seated ones, were only able to discover, on account of the music and bustle, that a very striking circumstance was in course of narration – denoted by an emphatic sweep of the hand, snapping of the fingers, close of the lips, and fixed look into the centre of the listener's eye for the space of a quarter of a minute, which raised in that listener such a reciprocating working of face as to sometimes make the distant dancers half wish to know what such an interesting tale could refer to.

Fancy caused her looks to wear as much matronly expression as was obtainable out of six hours' experience as a wife, in order that the contrast between her own state of life and that of the unmarried young women present might be duly impressed upon the company: occasionally stealing glances of admiration at her left hand, but this quite privately; for her ostensible bearing concerning the matter was intended to show that, though she undoubtedly occupied the most wondrous position in the eyes of the world that had ever been attained,[5] she was almost unconscious of the circumstance, and that the somewhat prominent position in which that wonderfully-emblazoned left hand was continually found to be placed, when handing cups and saucers, knives, forks, and glasses, was quite the result of accident. As to wishing to excite envy in the bosoms of her maiden companions, by the exhibition of the shining ring, every one was to know it was quite foreign to the dignity of such an experienced married woman. Dick's imagination in the mean time was far less capable of drawing so much wontedness from his new condition. He had been for two or three hours trying to feel himself merely a newly-married man, but had been able to get no farther in the attempt than to realise that he was Dick Dewy, the tranter's son, at a party at the keeper's, dancing and chatting with Fancy Day.

Five country dances, including 'Haste to the Wedding,' two reels, and three fragments of hornpipes, brought them to the time for supper, which, on account of the dampness of the grass from the immaturity of the summer season, was spread indoors. At the conclusion of the meal, Dick went out to put the horse in; and Fancy, with the elder half of the four bridesmaids, retired upstairs to dress for the journey to Dick's new cottage near Mellstock.

'How long will you be putting on your bonnet, Fancy?' Dick inquired at the foot of the staircase. Being now a man of business and married, he was strong on the importance of time, and doubled the emphasis of his words in conversing, and added vigour to his nods.[6]

'Only a minute.'

'How long is that?'

'Well, dear, five.'

'Ah, sonnies!' said the tranter, as Dick retired, ''tis a talent of the female race that low numbers should stand for high, more especially in matters of waiting, matters of age, and matters of money.'

'True, true, upon my body,' said Geoffrey.

'Ye spak with feeling, Geoffrey, seemingly.'

'Anybody that d'know my experience might guess that.'

'What's she doing now, Geoffrey?'

'Claning out all the upstairs drawers and cupboards, and dusting the second-best chainey – a thing that's only done once a year. "If there's work to be done, I must do it," says she, "wedding or no."'

''Tis my belief she's a very good woman at bottom.'

'She's terrible deep, then.'

Mrs. Penny turned round. 'Well, 'tis humps and hollers with the best of us; but still and for all that, Dick and Fancy stand as fair a chance of having a bit of sunsheen as any married pair in the land.'

'Ay, there's no gainsaying it.'

Mrs. Dewy came up, talking to one person and looking at another. 'Happy, yes,' she said. ''Tis always so when a couple is so exactly in tune with one another as Dick and she.'

'When they be'n't too poor to have time to sing,' said grandfather James.

'I tell ye, naibours, when the pinch comes,' said the tranter: 'when the oldest daughter's boots be only a size less than her mother's, and the rest o' the flock close behind her. A sharp time for a man that, my sonnies; a very sharp time! Chanticleer's comb is a-cut then,[7] 'a b'lieve.'

'That's about the form o't,' said Mr. Penny. 'That'll put the stuns upon a man, when you must measure mother and daughter's lasts to tell 'em apart.'

'You've no cause to complain, Reuben, of such a close-coming flock,' said Mrs. Dewy; 'for ours was a straggling lot enough, God knows.'

'I d'know it, I d'know it,' said the tranter. 'You be a well-enough woman, Ann.'

Mrs. Dewy put her mouth in the form of a smile, and put it back again without smiling.

'And if they come together, they go together,' said Mrs. Penny, whose family was the reverse of the tranter's; 'and a little money will make either fate tolerable. And money can be made by our young couple, I know.'

'Yes, that it can!' said the impulsive voice of Leaf, who had hitherto humbly admired the proceedings from a corner. 'It can be done – all that's wanted is a few pounds to begin with. That's all! I know a story about it!'

'Let's hear thy story, Leaf,' said the tranter. 'I never knowed you were clever enough to tell a story. Silence, all of ye! Mr. Leaf will tell a story.'

'Tell your story, Thomas Leaf,' said grandfather William in the tone of a schoolmaster.

'Once,' said the delighted Leaf, in an uncertain voice, 'there was a man who lived in a house! Well, this man went thinking and thinking night and day. At last he said to himself, as I might, "If I had only ten pound, I'd make a fortune." At last, by hook or by crook, behold he got the ten pounds!'

'Only think of that!' said Nat Callcome satirically.

'Silence!' said the tranter.

'Well, now comes the interesting part of the story! In a little time he made that ten pounds twenty. Then a little time after that he doubled it, and made it forty. Well, he went on, and a good while after that he made it eighty, and on to a hundred. Well, by and by he made it two hundred! Well, you'd never believe it, but – he went on and made it four hundred! He went on, and what did he do? Why, he made it eight hundred! Yes, he did,' continued Leaf, in the highest pitch of excitement, bringing down his fist upon his knee with such force that he quivered with the pain; 'yes, and he went on and made it A THOUSAND!'

'Hear, hear!' said the tranter. 'Better than the history of England, my sonnies!'

'Thank you for your story, Thomas Leaf,' said grandfather William; and then Leaf gradually sank into nothingness again.[8]

*

Amid a medley of laughter, old shoes, and elder-wine, Dick and his bride took their departure, side by side in the excellent new spring-cart which the young tranter now possessed. The moon was just over the full, rendering any light from lamps or their own beauties quite unnecessary to the pair. They drove slowly along Wilderness Bottom, where the lane passed between two copses. Dick was talking to his companion.

'Fancy,' he said, 'why we are so happy is because there is such entire confidence between us. Ever since that time you confessed to that little flirtation with Shinar by the river (which was really no flirtation at all), I have thought how artless and good you must be to tell me of such a trifling thing, and to be so frightened about it as you were. It has won me to tell you my every movement since then. We'll have no secrets from each other, darling, will we ever? – no secret at all.'

'None from to-day,' said Fancy. 'Hark! what's that?'

From a neighbouring thicket was suddenly heard to issue in a loud, musical, and liquid voice,

'Tippiwit! swe-e-et! ki-ki-ki! Come hither, come hither, come hither!'[9]

'O, 'tis the nightingale,' murmured she, and thought of a secret she should never tell.[10]

Hardy's Prefaces to Later Editions

PREFACE TO THE 1896 EDITION

This story of the Mellstock Quire and its old established west-gallery musicians, with some supplementary descriptions of similar officials in *Two on a Tower, A Few Crusted Characters*, and other places,[1] is intended to be a fairly true picture, at first hand, of the personages, ways, and customs which were common among such orchestral bodies in the villages of fifty years ago.[2]

One is inclined to regret the displacement of these ecclesiastical bandsmen by an isolated organist (often at first a barrel-organist) or harmonium player; and despite certain advantages in point of control and accomplishment which were, no doubt, secured by installing the single artist, the change has tended to stultify the professed aims of the clergy, its direct result being to curtail and extinguish the interest of parishioners in church doings. Under the old plan, from half a dozen to ten full-grown players, in addition to the numerous more or less grown-up singers, were officially occupied with the Sunday routine, and concerned in trying their best to make it an artistic outcome of the combined musical taste of the parish.[3] With a musical executive limited, as it mostly is limited now, to the parson's wife or daughter and the school-children, or to the school-teacher and the children, an important union of interests has disappeared.

The zest of these bygone instrumentalists must have been keen and staying, to take them, as it did, on foot every Sunday after a toilsome week through all weathers to the church, which often lay at a distance from their homes. They usually received so little payment for their performances that their efforts were really a labour of love. In the parish I had in my mind when writing the present tale, the gratuities received yearly by the musicians at Christmas were somewhat as follows: From the manor-house ten shillings and a supper; from the vicar ten shillings; from the farmers five shillings each; from each cottage-household one shilling; amounting altogether to not more than ten shillings a head annually – just enough, as an old executant told me, to pay for their fiddle-strings, repairs, rosin, and music-paper (which they mostly ruled themselves). Their music in those days was all in their own manuscript, copied in the evenings after work, and their music-books were home-bound.

It was customary to inscribe a few jigs, reels, hornpipes, and ballads in the same book, by beginning it at the other end, the insertions being continued from front and back till sacred and secular met together in the middle, often with bizarre effect, the words of some of the songs exhibiting that ancient and broad humour which our grandfathers, and possibly grandmothers, took delight in, and is in these days unquotable.

The aforesaid fiddle-strings, rosin, and music-paper were supplied by a pedlar, who travelled exclusively in such wares from choir to choir,[4] coming to each village about every six months. Tales are told of the consternation once caused among the church fiddlers when, on the occasion of their producing a new Christmas anthem, he did not come to time, owing to being snowed up on the downs, and the straits they were in through having to make shift with whip cord and twine for strings. He was generally a musician himself and sometimes a composer in a small way, bringing his own new tunes, and tempting each choir to adopt them for a consideration. Some of these compositions which now lie before me, with their repetitions of lines, half-lines, and half-words, their fugues and their intermediate symphonies,[5] are good singing still though they would hardly be admitted into such hymn-books as are popular in the churches of fashionable society at the present time.

August 1896

PREFACE TO THE 1912 EDITION

Under the Greenwood Tree was first brought out in the summer of 1872 in two volumes. The name of the story was originally intended to be, more appropriately, *The Mellstock Quire*, and this has been appended as a sub-title since the early editions, it having been thought unadvisable to displace for it the title by which the book first became known.[6]

In rereading the narrative after a long interval there occurs the inevitable reflection that the realities out of which it was spun were material for another kind of study of this little group of church musicians than is found in the chapters here penned so lightly, even so farcically and flippantly at times. But circumstances would have rendered any aim at a deeper, more essential, more transcendent handling unadvisable at the date of writing; and the exhibition of the Mellstock Quire in the following pages must remain the only extant one, except for the few glimpses of that perished band which I have given in verse elsewhere.

April 1912
T.H.

Notes

1 See chapter ii of *Two on a Tower* (1882), 'Absent-Mindedness in a Parish Choir' (*Life's Little Ironies* [1894], see Appendix III, 'The Fiddler of the Reels' (*LLI*), and chapter xvii of *Tess of the D'Urbervilles*. The choir appears more frequently in work published by Hardy after he wrote this Preface in 1896: 'The Grave by the Handpost' (*A Changed Man and Other Tales* [1913]), and especially in several poems (the excerpt from *Tess*, 'Absent-Mindedness' and the poetry are reproduced in Appendix III).

2 Hardy here places the story between 1835 and 1845. In one of the manuscript music-books owned by his father, Hardy wrote: 'The Carol Book of T.H.II (used on the rounds on Xmas Eve in "Mellstock Quire" down to about 1842)'. As he did in other novels, Hardy revised this dated Preface in 1912, where he wrote 'fifty or sixty' years.

3 Hardy wrote 'congregation' in 1912.

4 Hardy wrote 'parish to parish' in 1812.

5 Opening or closing instrumental passages in a song.

6 The subtitle was in fact not appended until 1906. In the *Life*, Hardy restates that he originally intended to call the novel *The Mellstock Quire*, but altered it 'because titles from poetry were in fashion just then' (p. 88). He was probably thinking of Rhoda Broughton's *Cometh up as a Flower* and *Not wisely, but too well* (1867). In 1879, the *Saturday Review* suggested that the novel 'received less attention than [it] deserved' because of this 'unpromising' name (though of course one of Hardy's most famous titles, *Far from the Madding Crowd*, is also borrowed from poetry).

An Overview of Topographical Changes
in Under the Greenwood Tree

Hardy extensively revised the topography of *Under the Greenwood Tree* in both his revisions of the novel – for Osgood, McIlvaine's collected edition of 1896 and the Macmillan 1912 Wessex Edition. The model for Mellstock parish is the village of Stinsford and the hamlets of Higher and Lower Bockhampton two miles east of Dorchester (the fictional Casterbridge). Stinsford Church, where Hardy's family, his first wife, Emma Lavinia Hardy, and his own heart are buried, is located just east of the A35 Dorchester to London highway near the intersection of the B3150 (the course of the Roman road). Keeper Day's lodge is based on the keeper's lodge in Yellowham Wood, a mile or so to the north of Higher Bock-hampton, the hamlet where Hardy was born. Fancy's school and Shinar's house are on Bockhampton Lane in Lower Bockhampton, which runs virtually north–south between the A35 and the village of West Stafford.[1]

The Mellstock of this edition (based on the first edition of 1872) differs considerably from the cluster of hamlets, natural features, roads and pathways with which readers would be familiar from the versions of the novel widely available today. Close parallels between the fictional Mellstocks and Stinsford and the Bockhamptons – accentuated in 1896 and 1912 – are disguised in this edition, partly because the villages and hamlets function as a picturesque backdrop for a 'landscape with figures' (as suggested in the subtitle, 'A Rural Painting of the Dutch School'), and partly because Mellstock was imagined as a sort of pastoral realm (Hardy signals this by invoking the Forest of Arden in his title from *As You Like It*). The later conception of Mellstock, on the other hand, is governed by Hardy's desire to draw the novel into the internally coherent imaginative realm that is the 'Wessex' of the collected editions (this is dominant in the 1896 revisions), and to locate it much more precisely as the parish of his own childhood (his principal concern in 1912). Of course, the 1896 revisions were probably concluded some time late in 1894, and the Preface was being written in 1895, when *Jude* was still unfinished, so these topographical concerns go hand in hand with Hardy's mood and preoccupations during these critical years. In 1912, Hardy's revisions attempt to make the narrative more respectful of the choir (and more regretful of its passing), and less the 'burlesque' that Hardy rued having written in 1872, and the topographical changes do some of this work by relocating *Under the Greenwood Tree* to the immediate neighbourhood of graver novels: the addition of Bloom's End, for example, sets up a faint allusion to *The Return of the Native*; the alteration of the 'Three Choughs' to the 'Dree Mariners' echoes *The Mayor of Casterbridge*; and the introduction of Weatherbury and Longpuddle fixes the story firmly within the country of the 'Novels of Character and Environment'.

The focus of the 'Mellstock choir' plot – Stinsford Church with its west gallery – is in this edition located in West Mellstock (changed to 'Mellstock' in 1896). It is 'half a mile from the main village', East Mellstock (Lower Bockhampton: 'Lower Mellstock' in 1896). The school-house, though characters approach it from different directions and along differently named pathways, remains in the same place in all editions. The Dewy cottage, however, is situated in Lewgate in this edition, not Upper Mellstock as later: Pinion argues that Lewgate 'was used for Upper Mellstock in the early editions of *UGT*', being the name 'often suggested for Hardy's home at Higher Bockhampton during his lifetime, but never adopted'.[2] However, later editions retain Lewgate as the hamlet next to Upper Mellstock, perhaps because Hardy was loath to dispense with it altogether. In spite of this ambiguity, the 1872 Dewy cottage is positioned in relation to East and West Mellstock precisely as it is in relation to Lower Mellstock and Mellstock in later editions, and thus corresponds on the map to Higher Bockhampton. Hardy extensively revised his description of this cottage in 1896 and 1912, enlarging it to correspond more closely to his birthplace. A detailed discussion of these changes can be found in I, ii, note 2.

Geoffrey Day's cottage in Yalbury Wood (Yellowham Wood) is likewise altered in later editions to reflect Day's changed social status (he is no longer the lowly keeper, but head keeper to the Earl of Wessex, with many added responsibilities). The cottage is also repositioned slightly. It is close to a lane that intersects with the wood in this edition (marked as the Yellowham Wood Keeper's Lodge on today's Ordnance Survey maps), but in 1896 Hardy moved it much closer to the Casterbridge–London highway. Consequently, Day's fireplace window, which looks out on a

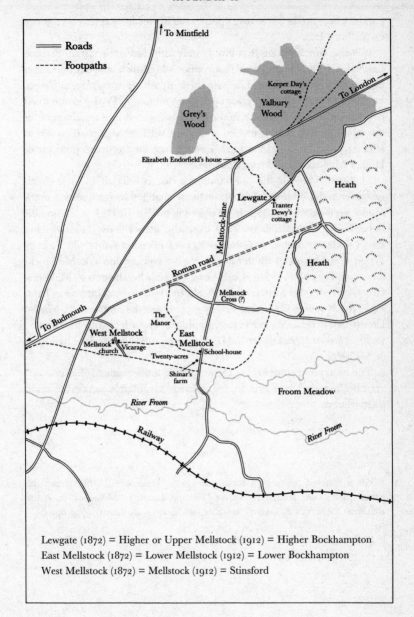

Lewgate (1872) = Higher or Upper Mellstock (1912) = Higher Bockhampton

East Mellstock (1872) = Lower Mellstock (1912) = Lower Bockhampton

West Mellstock (1872) = Mellstock (1912) = Stinsford

paddock here, looks out in 1912 upon a vista of the highway as it disappears up Yalbury Hill.

It is also worth noting that Hardy only introduced the name 'Cuckoo Lane' (for the segment of road that connects Mellstock-lane with the main highway) in later editions. Likewise the footpath known as 'Snail Creep' in later editions – the lane Dick takes to go nutting in IV, i – is unnamed here. Elizabeth Endorfield's house is also relocated in later changes: in this edition it 'lies at the junction of the lane with the high road', whereas after 1896 it stands a little further south, not far from the junction of Higher Mellstock and Mellstock-lane.

Mellstock Cross is the one landmark that is difficult to locate with certainty in this edition, and is accordingly qualified with a question mark on the accompanying map. In chapter viii of Part II, Dick is leading his horse and spring-cart homeward from the school-house, after driving Fancy and some household belongings back from her father's in Yalbury Wood, when he meets tranter Dewy. He is travelling north on Mellstock-lane from East Mellstock towards Lewgate, yet when he gets to Mellstock Cross, he turns the corner, which ought by rights to lead him away from Lewgate. It seems likely that Hardy recognized the ambiguity when he later strove to make the novel topographically consistent with his Wessex, for he altered this passage so that Dick more plausibly 'neared the handpost at Mellstock Cross'.

The most comprehensive of the remaining topographical changes concern Budmouth, which is more immediately identifiable as Weymouth in later editions.

Notes

1 For a detailed account of correspondences between the fictional and the actual places, see Jeanne Howard's 'Thomas Hardy's "Mellstock" and the Registrar General's Stinsford', *Literature and History* 6 (Autumn 1977), pp. 179–202.
2 Pinion, 389.

The Mellstock Choir in Hardy's Later Writings: A Selection[1]

EXCERPT FROM THE FIRST EDITION OF *TESS OF THE D'URBERVILLES* (1891)

'Oh yes; there's nothing like a fiddle,' said the dairyman. 'Though I do think that bulls are more moved by a tune than cows – at least that's my experience. Once there was a old aged man over at Mellstock – William Dewy by name – one of the family that used to do a good deal of business as tranters over there, Jonathan, do ye mind? – I knowed the man by sight as well as I know my own brother, in a manner of speaking. Well, this man was a coming home along from a wedding where he had been playing his fiddle, one fine moonlight night, and for shortness' sake he took a cut across Forty-acres, a field lying that way, where a bull was out to grass. The bull seed William, and took after him, horns aground, begad; and though William runned his best, and hadn't much drink in him (considering 'twas a wedding, and the folks well off), he found he'd never reach the fence and get over in time to save himself. Well, as a last thought, he pulled out his fiddle as he runned, and struck up a jig, turning to the bull, and backing towards the corner. The bull softened down, and stood still, looking hard at William Dewy, who fiddled on and on; till a sort of a smile stole over the bull's face. But no sooner did William stop his playing and turn to get over hedge than the bull would stop his smiling and lower his horns to the seat of William's breeches. Well, William had to turn about and play on, willy-nilly; and 'twas only three o'clock in the world, and 'a knowed that nobody would come that way for hours, and he so leery and tired that 'a didn't know what to do. When he had scraped till about four o'clock he felt that he verily would have to give over soon, and he said to himself, "There's only this last tune between me and eternal welfare! Heaven save me, or I'm a done man." Well, then he called to mind how he'd seed the cattle kneel o' Christmas Eves in the dead o' the night. It was not Christmas Eve then, but it came into his head to play a trick upon the bull. So he broke into the 'Tivity Hymn, just as at Christmas carol-singing: when, lo and behold, down went the bull on his bended knees, in his ignorance, just as if 'twere the true 'Tivity night and hour. As soon as his horned friend were down, William turned, clinked off like a long-dog, and jumped safe over hedge, before the praying bull had got on his feet again to take after him. William used to say that he'd seen a man look a fool a good many times, but never such a fool as that bull looked when he found his pious feelings had been played upon, and 'twas not Christmas Eve. . . Yes, William Dewy, that was the man's name; and I can tell ye to a foot where he's a-lying in Mellstock Churchyard at this very moment – just between the second yew-tree and the north aisle' [chapter xvii].

ABSENT-MINDEDNESS IN A PARISH CHOIR (1894)[2]

'It happened on Sunday after Christmas – the last Sunday ever they played in Longpuddle church gallery, as it turned out, though they didn't know it then. As you may know, sir, the players formed a very good band – almost as good as the Mellstock parish players that were led by the Dewys; and that's saying a great deal. There was Nicholas Puddingcome, the leader, with the first fiddle; there was Timothy Thomas, the bass-viol man; John Biles, the tenor fiddler; Dan'l Hornhead, with the serpent; Robert Dowdle, with the clarionet; and Mr. Nicks, with the oboe – all sound and powerful musicians, and strong-winded men – they that blowed. For that reason they were very much in demand Christmas week for little reels and dancing parties; for they could turn a jig or a hornpipe out of hand as well as ever they could turn out a psalm, and perhaps better, not to speak irreverent. In short, one half-hour they could be playing a Christmas carol in the squire's hall to the ladies and gentlemen, and drinking tay and coffee with 'em as modest as saints; and the next, at The Tinker's Arms, blazing away like wild horses with the "Dashing White Sergeant" to nine couple of dancers and more, and swallowing rum-and-cider hot as flame.

'Well, this Christmas they'd been out to one rattling randy after another every night, and had got next to no sleep at all. Then came the Sunday after Christmas, their fatal day. 'Twas so mortal cold that year that they could hardly sit in the gallery; for though the congregation down in the body of the church had a stove to keep off the frost, the players in the gallery had nothing at all. So Nicholas said at morning service, when 'twas freezing an inch an hour, "Please the Lord I won't stand this numbing weather no longer: this afternoon we'll have something in our insides to make us warm, if it cost a king's ransom."

'So he brought a gallon of hot brandy and beer, ready mixed, to church with him in the afternoon, and by keeping the jar well wrapped up in Timothy Thomas's bass-viol bag it kept drinkably warm till they wanted it, which was just a thimbleful in the Absolution, and another after the Creed, and the remainder at the beginning of the sermon. When they'd had the last pull they felt quite comfortable and warm, and as the sermon went on – most unfortunately for 'em it was a long one that afternoon – they fell asleep, every man jack of 'em; and there they slept on as sound as rocks.

"Twas a very dark afternoon, and by the end of the sermon all you could see of the inside of the church were the pa'son's two candles alongside of him in the pulpit, and his spaking face behind 'em. The sermon being ended at last, the pa'son gie'd out the Evening Hymn. But no choir set about sounding up the tune, and the people began to turn their heads to learn the reason why, and then Levi Limpet, a boy who sat in the gallery, nudged Timothy and Nicholas, and said, "Begin! begin!"

' "Hey? what?" says Nicholas, starting up; and the church being so dark and his head so muddled he thought he was at the party they had played at all the night before, and away he went, bow and fiddle, at "The Devil among the Tailors," the favourite jig of our neighbourhood at that time. The rest of the band, being in the same state of mind and nothing doubting, followed their leader with all their strength, according to custom. They poured out that there tune till the lower bass notes of "The Devil among the Tailors" made the cobwebs in the roof shiver like ghosts; then Nicholas, seeing nobody moved, shouted out as he scraped (in his usual commanding way at dances when the folk didn't know the figures), "Top couples cross hands! And when I make the fiddle squeak at the end, every man kiss his pardner under the mistletoe!"

'The boy Levi was so frightened that he bolted down the gallery stairs and out homeward like lightning. The pa'son's hair fairly stood on end when he heard the evil tune raging through the church, and thinking the choir had gone crazy he held up his hand and said: "Stop, stop, stop! Stop, stop! What's this?" But they didn't hear'n for the noise of their own playing, and the more he called the louder they played.

'Then the folks came out of their pews, wondering down to the ground, and saying: "What do they mean by such wickedness! We shall be consumed like Sodom and Gomorrah!"

'Then the squire came out of his pew lined wi' green baize, where lots of lords and ladies visiting at the house were worshipping along with him, and went and stood in front of the gallery, and shook his fist in the musicians' faces, saying, "What! In this reverent edifice! What!"

'And at last they heard'n through their playing, and stopped.

' "Never such an insulting, disgraceful thing – never!" says the squire, who couldn't rule his passion.

' "Never!" says the pa'son, who had come down and stood beside him.

' "Not if the Angels of Heaven," says the squire (he was a wickedish man, the squire was, though now for once he happened to be on the Lord's side) – "not if the Angels of Heaven come down," he says, "shall one of you villanous players ever sound a note in this church again; for the insult to me, and my family, and my visitors, and God Almighty, that you've a-perpetrated this afternoon!"

'Then the unfortunate church band came to their senses, and remembered where they were; and 'twas a sight to see Nicholas Pudding-come and Timothy Thomas and John Biles creep down the gallery stairs with their fiddles under their arms, and poor Dan'l Hornhead with his serpent, and Robert Dowdle with his clarionet, all looking as little as ninepins; and out they went. The pa'son might have forgi'ed 'em when he learned the truth o't, but the squire would not. That very week he sent for a barrel-organ that would play two-and-twenty new psalm-tunes, so exact and particular that, however sinful inclined you was, you could play nothing but psalm-tunes whatsomever. He had a really respectable man to turn the winch, as I said, and the old players played no more.'

FROM *Wessex Poems and Other Verses* (1898)

Friends Beyond

William Dewy, Tranter Reuben, Farmer Ledlow late at plough,
   Robert's kin, and John's, and Ned's,
And the Squire, and Lady Susan, lie in Mellstock churchyard now!

'Gone,' I call them, gone for good, that group of local hearts and heads;
   Yet at mothy curfew-tide,
And at midnight when the noon-heat breathes it back from walls and
      leads,

They've a way of whispering to me — fellow-wight who yet abide —
   In the muted, measured note
Of a ripple under archways, or a lone cave's stillicide:

'We have triumphed: this achievement turns the bane to antidote,
   Unsuccesses to success,
Many thought-worn eves and morrows to a morrow free of thought.

'No more need we corn and clothing, feel of old terrestrial stress;
   Chill detraction stirs no sigh;
Fear of death has even bygone us: death gave all that we possess.'

W.D. – 'Ye mid burn the old bass-viol that I set such value by.'
   Squire. – 'You may hold the manse in fee,
You may wed my spouse, may let my children's memory of me die.'

Lady S. – 'You may have my rich brocades, my laces; take each household
      key;
   Ransack coffer, desk, bureau;
Quiz the few poor treasures hid there, con the letters kept by me.'

Far. – 'Ye mid zell my favourite heifer, ye mid let the charlock grow,
   Foul the grinterns, give up thrift.'
Far. Wife. – 'If ye break my best blue china, children, I shan't care or ho.'

All. – 'We've no wish to hear the tidings, how the people's fortunes shift;
   What your daily doings are;
Who are wedded, born, divided; if your lives beat slow or swift.

'Curious not the least are we if our intents you make or mar,
   If you quire to our old tune,
If the City stage still passes, if the weirs still roar afar.'

– Thus, with very gods' composure, freed those crosses late and soon
   Which, in life, the Trine allow
(Why, none witteth), and ignoring all that haps beneath the moon,

William Dewy, Tranter Reuben, Farmer Ledlow late at plough,
   Robert's kin, and John's, and Ned's,
And the Squire, and Lady Susan, murmur mildly to me now.

FROM *Time's Laughingstocks and Other Verses* (1909)

A Church Romance

(Mellstock, *circa* 1835)

She turned in the high pew, until her sight
Swept the west gallery, and caught its row
Of music-men with viol, book, and bow
Against the sinking sad tower-window light.

She turned again; and in her pride's despite
One strenuous viol's inspirer seemed to throw
A message from his string to her below,
Which said: 'I claim thee as my own forthright!'

Thus their hearts' bond began, in due time signed.
And long years thence, when Age had scared Romance,
At some old attitude of his or glance
That gallery-scene would break upon her mind,
With him as minstrel, ardent, young, and trim,
Bowing 'New Sabbath' or 'Mount Ephraim'.

The Rash Bride
An Experience of the Mellstock Quire

I

We Christmas-carolled down the Vale, and up the Vale, and round the Vale,
We played and sang that night as we were yearly wont to do –
A carol in a minor key, a carol in the major D,
Then at each house: 'Good wishes: many Christmas joys to you!'

II

Next, to the widow's John and I and all the rest drew on. And I
Discerned that John could hardly hold the tongue of him for joy.
The widow was a sweet young thing whom John was bent on marrying,
And quiring at her casement seemed romantic to the boy.

III

'She'll make reply, I trust,' said he, 'to our salute? She must!' said he,
'And then I will accost her gently – much to her surprise! –
For knowing not I am with you here, when I speak up and call her dear
A tenderness will fill her voice, a bashfulness her eyes.'

IV

So, by her window-square we stood; ay, with our lanterns there we stood,
And he along with us, – not singing, waiting for a sign;
And when we'd quired her carols three a light was lit and out looked she,
A shawl about her bedgown, and her colour red as wine.

V

And sweetly then she bowed her thanks, and smiled, and spoke aloud her
    thanks;
When lo, behind her back there, in the room, a man appeared.
I knew him – one from Woolcomb way – Giles Swetman – honest as the day,
But eager, hasty; and I felt that some strange trouble neared.

VI

'How comes he there? . . . Suppose', said we, 'she's wed of late! Who
    knows?' said we.
– 'She married yester-morning – only mother yet has known
The secret o't!' shrilled one small boy. 'But now I've told, let's wish 'em joy!'
A heavy fall aroused us: John had gone down like a stone.

VII

We rushed to him and caught him round, and lifted him, and brought
    him round,
When, hearing something wrong had happened, oped the window she:
'Has one of you fallen ill?' she asked, 'by these night labours overtasked?'
None answered. That she'd done poor John a cruel turn felt we.

VIII

Till up spoke Michael: 'Fie, young dame! You've broke your promise, sly
    young dame,
By forming this new tie, young dame, and jilting John so true,
Who trudged to-night to sing to 'ee because he thought he'd bring to 'ee
Good wishes as your coming spouse. May ye such trifling rue!'

IX

Her man had said no word at all; but being behind had heard it all,
And now cried: 'Neighbours, on my soul I knew not 'twas like this!'
And then to her: 'If I had known you'd had in tow not me alone,
No wife should you have been of mine. It is a dear bought bliss!'

X

She changed death-white, and heaved a cry: we'd never heard so grieved
    a cry
As came from her at this from him: heartbroken quite seemed she;
And suddenly, as we looked on, she turned, and rushed; and she was gone,
Whither, her husband, following after, knew not; nor knew we.

XI

We searched till dawn about the house; within the house, without the house,
We searched among the laurel boughs that grew beneath the wall,
And then among the crocks and things, and stores for winter junketings,
In linhay, loft, and dairy; but we found her not at all.

XII

Then John rushed in: 'O friends,' he said, 'hear this, this, this!' and bends
    his head:
'I've – searched round by the – *well*, and find the cover open wide!
I am fearful that – I can't say what. . . . Bring lanterns, and some cords
    to knot.'
We did so, and we went and stood the deep dark hole beside.

XIII

And then they, ropes in hand, and I – ay, John, and all the band, and I
Let down a lantern to the depths – some hundred feet and more;
It glimmered like a fog-dimmed star; and there, beside its light, afar,
White drapery floated, and we knew the meaning that it bore.

XIV

The rest is naught . . . We buried her o' Sunday. Neighbours carried her;
And Swetman – he who'd married her – now miserablest of men,
Walked mourning first; and then walked John; just quivering, but
    composed anon;
And we the quire formed round the grave, as was the custom then.

XV

Our old bass player, as I recall – his white hair blown – but why recall! –
His viol upstrapped, bent figure – doomed to follow her full soon –
Stood bowing, pale and tremulous; and next to him the rest of us. . . .
    We sang the Ninetieth Psalm to her – set to 'Saint Stephen's' tune.

The Dead Quire

I

    Beside the Mead of Memories,
    Where Church-way mounts to Moaning Hill,
    The sad man sighed his phantasies:
        He seems to sigh them still.

II

    ''Twas the Birthtide Eve, and the hamleteers
    Made merry with ancient Mellstock zest,
    But the Mellstock quire of former years
        Had entered into rest.

III

    'Old Dewy lay by the gaunt yew tree,
    And Reuben and Michael a pace behind,
    And Bowman with his family
        By the wall that the ivies bind.

IV

'The singers had followed one by one,
Treble, and tenor, and thorough-bass;
And the worm that wasteth had begun
   To mine their mouldering place.

V

'For two-score years, ere Christ-day light,
Mellstock had throbbed to strains from these;
But now there echoed on the night
   No Christmas harmonies.

VI

'Three meadows off, at a dormered inn,
The youth had gathered in high carouse,
And, ranged on settles, some therein
   Had drunk them to a drowse.

VII

'Loud, lively, reckless, some had grown,
Each dandling on his jigging knee
Eliza, Dolly, Nance, or Joan –
   Livers in levity.

VIII

'The taper flames and hearthfire shine
Grew smoke-hazed to a lurid light,
And songs on subjects not divine
   Were warbled forth that night.

IX

'Yet many were sons and grandsons here
Of those who, on such eves gone by,
At that still hour had throated clear
   Their anthems to the sky.

X

'The clock belled midnight; and ere long
One shouted, "Now 'tis Christmas morn;
Here's to our women old and young,
   And to John Barleycorn!"

XI

'They drink the toast and shout again:
The pewter-ware rings back the boom,
And for a breath-while follows then
   A silence in the room.

XII

'When nigh without, as in old days,
The ancient quire of voice and string
Seemed singing words of prayer and praise
   As they had used to sing:

XIII

'*While shepherds watch'd their flocks by night,* –
Thus swells the long familiar sound
In many a quaint symphonic flight –
   To, *Glory shone around.*

XIV

'The sons defined their fathers' tones,
The widow his whom she had wed,
And others in the minor moans
   The viols of the dead.

XV

'Something supernal has the sound
As verse by verse the strain proceeds,
And stilly staring on the ground
   Each roysterer holds and heeds.

XVI

'Towards its chorded closing bar
Plaintively, thinly, waned the hymn,
Yet lingered, like the notes afar
   Of banded seraphim.

XVII

'With brows abashed, and reverent tread,
The hearkeners sought the tavern door:
But nothing, save wan moonlight, spread
   The empty highway o'er.

XVIII

'While on their hearing fixed and tense
The aerial music seemed to sink,
As it were gently moving thence
 Along the river brink.

XIX

'Then did the Quick pursue the Dead
By crystal Froom that crinkles there;
And still the viewless quire ahead
 Voiced the old holy air.

XX

'By Bank-walk wicket, brightly bleached,
It passed, and 'twixt the hedges twain,
Dogged by the living; till it reached
 The bottom of Church Lane.

XXI

'There, at the turning, it was heard
Drawing to where the churchyard lay:
But when they followed thitherward
 It smalled, and died away.

XXII

'Each headstone of the quire, each mound,
Confronted them beneath the moon;
But no more floated therearound
 That ancient Birth-night tune.

XXIII

'There Dewy lay by the gaunt yew tree,
There Reuben and Michael, a pace behind,
And Bowman with his family
 By the wall that the ivies bind. . . .

XXIV

'As from a dream each sobered son
Awoke, and musing reached his door:
'Twas said that of them all, not one
 Sat in a tavern more.'

XXV
– The sad man ceased; and ceased to heed
His listener, and crossed the leaze
From Moaning Hill towards the mead –
   The Mead of Memories.

FROM *Moments of Vision and Miscellaneous Verses* (1917)

Afternoon Service at Mellstock
(*Circa* 1850)

On afternoons of drowsy calm
   We stood in the panelled pew,
Singing one-voiced a Tate-and-Brady psalm
   To the tune of 'Cambridge New'.

We watched the elms, we watched the rooks,
   The clouds upon the breeze,
Between the whiles of glancing at our books,
   And swaying like the trees.

So mindless were those outpourings! –
   Though I am not aware
That I have gained by subtle thought on things
   Since we stood psalming there.

FROM *Late Lyrics and Earlier with Many Other Verses* (1922)

The Country Wedding
(A Fiddler's Story)

Little fogs were gathered in every hollow,
But the purple hillocks enjoyed fine weather
As we marched with our fiddles over the heather
– How it comes back! – to their wedding that day.

Our getting there brought our neighbours and all, O!
Till, two and two, the couples stood ready.
And her father said: 'Souls, for God's sake, be steady!'
And we strung up our fiddles, and sounded out 'A'.

The groomsman he stared, and said, 'You must follow!'
But we'd gone to fiddle in front of the party,
(Our feelings as friends being true and hearty)
And fiddle in front we did – all the way.

Yes, from their door by Mill-tail-Shallow,
And up Styles-Lane, and by Front-Street houses,
Where stood maids, bachelors, and spouses,
Who cheered the songs that we knew how to play.

I bowed the treble before her father,
Michael the tenor in front of the lady,
The bass-viol Reub – and right well played he! –
The serpent Jim; ay, to church and back.

I thought the bridegroom was flurried rather,
As we kept up the tune outside the chancel,
While they were swearing things none can cancel
Inside the walls to our drumstick's whack.

'Too gay!' she pleaded. 'Clouds may gather,
And sorrow come.' But she gave in, laughing,
And by supper-time when we'd got to the quaffing
Her fears were forgot, and her smiles weren't slack.

A grand wedding 'twas! And what would follow
We never thought. Or that we should have buried her
On the same day with the man that married her,
A day like the first, half hazy, half clear.

Yes: little fogs were in every hollow,
Though the purple hillocks enjoyed fine weather,
When we went to play 'em to church together,
And carried 'em there in an after year.

FROM *Human Shows, Far Phantasies, Songs and Trifles* (1925)

Winter Night in Woodland
(Old Time)

The bark of a fox rings, sonorous and long:–
Three barks, and then silentness; 'wong, wong, wong!'
In quality horn-like, yet melancholy,
As from teachings of years; for an old one is he.
The hand of all men is against him, he knows; and yet, why?
That he knows not, – will never know, down to his death-halloo cry.

With clap-nets and lanterns off start the bird-baiters,
In trim to make raids on the roosts in the copse,
Where they beat the boughs artfully, while their awaiters
Grow heavy at home over divers warm drops.
The poachers, with swingels, and matches of brimstone, outcreep
To steal upon pheasants and drowse them a-perch and asleep.

Out there, on the verge, where a path wavers through,
Dark figures, filed singly, thrid quickly the view,
Yet heavily laden: land-carriers are they
In the hire of the smugglers from some nearest bay.
Each bears his two 'tubs', slung across, one in front, one behind,
To a further snug hiding, which none but themselves are to find.

And then, when the night has turned twelve, the air brings
From dim distance, a rhythm of voices and strings:
'Tis the quire, just afoot on their long yearly rounds,
To rouse by worn carols each house in their bounds;
Robert Penny, the Dewys, Mail, Voss, and the rest; till anon
Tired and thirsty, but cheerful, they home to their beds in the dawn.

The Paphian Ball
Another Christmas Experience of the Mellstock Quire

We went our Christmas rounds once more,
With quire and viols as theretofore.

Our path was near by Rushy-Pond,
Where Egdon-Heath outstretched beyond.

There stood a figure against the moon
Tall, spare, and humming a weirdsome tune.

'You tire of Christian carols,' he said:
'Come and lute at a ball instead.

''Tis to your gain, for it ensures
That many guineas will be yours.

'A slight condition hangs on't, true,
But you will scarce say nay thereto:

'That you go blindfold; that anon
The place may not be gossiped on.'

We stood and argued with each other:
'Why sing from one house to another

'These ancient hymns in the freezing night,
And all for nought? 'Tis foolish, quite!'

'– 'Tis serving God, and shunning evil:
Might not elsedoing serve the devil?'

'But grand pay!' . . . We were lured by his call,
Agreeing to go blindfold all.

We walked, he guiding, some new track,
Doubting to find the pathway back.

In a strange hall we found us when
We were unblinded all again.

Gilded alcoves, great chandeliers,
Voluptuous paintings ranged in tiers,

In brief, a mansion large and rare,
With rows of dancers waiting there.

We tuned and played; the couples danced;
Half-naked women tripped, advanced,

With handsome partners footing fast,
Who swore strange oaths, and whirled them past.

And thus and thus the hours onbore us:
While shone our guineas heaped before us.

Drowsy at length, in lieu of the dance
'*While Shepherds watched . . .*' we bowed by chance;

And in a moment, at a blink,
There flashed a change; ere we could think

The ball-room vanished and all its crew:
Only the well-known heath we view –

The spot of our crossing overnight,
When wheedled by the stranger's sleight.

There, east, the Christmas dawn hung red,
And dark Rainbarrow with its dead

Bulged like a sleeping negress' breast
Against Clyffe-Clump's faint far-off crest.

Yea; the rare mansion, gorgeous, bright,
The ladies, gallants, gone were quite.

The heaped-up guineas, too, were gone
With the gold table they were on.

'Why did not grasp we what was owed!'
Cried some, as homeward, shamed, we strode.

Now comes the marvel and the warning:
When we had dragged to church next morning,

With downcast heads and scarce a word,
We were astound at what we heard.

Praises from all came forth in showers
For how we'd cheered the midnight hours.

'We've heard you many times,' friends said,
'But like *that* never have you played!

'*Rejoice ye tenants of the earth,*
And celebrate your Saviour's birth,

'Never so thrilled the darkness through,
Or more inspired us so to do!' . . .

– The man who used to tell this tale
Was the tenor-viol, Michael Mail;

Yes; Mail the tenor, now but earth. –
I give it for what it may be worth.

Notes

1 The poems in this appendix have been edited on different principles from the main text: four-point ellipses, for instance, have been retained, and some variant spellings (e.g. 'further' for 'farther') have not been standardized.
2 'Absent-Mindedness in a Parish Choir' is one of nine linked sketches in 'A Few Crusted Characters' which Hardy wrote sometime in 1890 and 1891 (originally entitled 'Wessex Folk'), and which he included in *Life's Little Ironies* (1894). The sketches are narrated by characters who are passing the time as they travel together in a slow horse-drawn carrier's van. Because they are spoken they are enclosed in quotation marks. 'Absent-Mindedness' is narrated by the groceress.

The Stinsford Choir

FROM THOMAS HARDY, *THE LIFE AND WORK OF THOMAS HARDY*, ED. MICHAEL MILLGATE (LONDON: MACMILLAN, 1989)

In [Stinsford Church] ... the Hardys became well known as violinists, Thomas the Second, the poet and novelist's father aforesaid, after his early boyhood as chorister beginning as a youth with the 'counter' viol, and later taking on the tenor and treble.

They were considered among the best church-players in the neighbourhood, accident having helped their natural bent. This was the fact that in 1822, shortly after the death of the old vicar Mr Floyer, the Rev. Edward Murray, a connection of the Earl of Ilchester who was the patron of the living, was presented to it. Mr Murray was an ardent musician and performer on the violin himself, and the two younger Hardys and sometimes their father used to practise two or three times a week with him in his study at Stinsford House, where he lived instead of at the Vicarage.

Thus it was that the Hardy instrumentalists, though never more than four,[1] maintained an easy superiority over the larger bodies in parishes near. For while Puddletown west-gallery, for instance, could boast of eight players, and Maiden Newton of nine, these included wood-wind and leather – that is to say, clarionets and serpents – which were apt to be a little too sonorous, even strident, when zealously blown.[2] But the few and well-practised violists of Stinsford were never unduly emphatic, according to tradition.

Elaborate Canticle services – such as the noted 'Jackson in F', and in 'E flat' – popular in the West of England, possibly because Jackson had been an Exeter man[3] – Pope's Ode,[4] and anthems with portentous repetitions and 'mountainous fugues',[5] were carried through by the performers every Sunday, with what real success is not known, but to their own great satisfaction and the hearty approval of the musical vicar.

In their psalmody they adhered strictly to Tate-and-Brady[6] – upon whom, in truth, the modern hymn-book has been no great improvement – such tunes as the 'Old Hundredth', 'New Sabbath', 'Devizes', 'Wilton',

'Lydia', and 'Cambridge New'[7] being their staple ones; while Barthélémon and Tallis were played to Ken's Morning and Evening Hymns[8] respectively every Sunday throughout the year: a practice now obsolete, but a great stimulus to congregational singing.

As if the superintendence of the Stinsford choir were not enough distraction from business for Thomas Hardy the First, he would go whenever opportunity served and assist other choirs by performing with his violoncello in the galleries of their parish churches, mostly to the high contentment of the congregations. Although Thomas the Third had not come into the world soon enough to know his grandfather in person, there is no doubt that the description by Fairway in *The Return of the Native* of the bowing of Thomasin's father, when lending his services to the choir of Kinsgbere, is a humorous exaggeration of the traditions concerning Thomas Hardy the First's musical triumphs as locum-tenens.[9]

In addition it may be mentioned that he had been a volunteer till the end of the war, and lay in Weymouth with his company from time to time waiting for Bonaparte who never came.

Conducting the church choir all the year round involved carol-playing and singing at Christmas, which Thomas Hardy the Second loved as much as did his father. In addition to the ordinary practice, the work of preparing and copying carols a month of evenings beforehand was not light, and incidental expenses were appreciable. The parish being a large and scattered one it was the custom of Thomas Hardy the First to assemble the rather perfunctory rank-and-file of the choir at his house; and this necessitated suppers, and suppers demanded (in those days) plenty of liquor. This was especially the case on Christmas Eve itself, when the rule was to go to the northern part of the parish and play at every house before supper; then to return to Bockhampton and sit over the meal till twelve o'clock, during which interval a good deal was consumed at the Hardys' expense, the choir being mainly poor men and hungry. They then started for the other parts of the parish, and did not get home till all was finished at about six in the morning, the performers themselves feeling 'no more than malkins'* in church next day, as they used to declare. The practice was kept up by Thomas Hardy the Second, much as described in *Under the Greenwood Tree or the Mellstock Quire*, though its author Thomas Hardy the Third invented the personages, incidents, manners, etc., never having

---

* *Malkin*, a damp rag on a stem, for swabbing out ovens.

seen or heard the choir as such, they ending their office when he was about a year old. He was accustomed to say that on this account he had rather burlesqued them, the story not adequately reflecting as he could have wished in later years the poetry and romance that coloured their time-honoured observances.

This preoccupation of the Hardys with the music of the parish church and less solemn assemblies did not, to say the least, assist their building business, and it was somewhat of a relief to Thomas Hardy the Second's young wife – though musical herself to a degree – when ecclesiastical changes after the death of Thomas Hardy the First, including the cession of the living by Murray, led to her husband's abandoning in 1841 or 1842 all connection with the choir. The First Thomas's death having been quite unexpected – inasmuch as he was playing in the church one Sunday, and brought in for burial on the next – there could be no such quiring over his grave as he had performed over the graves of so many, owing to the remaining players being chief mourners. And thus ended his devoted musical services to Stinsford Church, in which he had occupied the middle seat of the gallery with his bass-viol on Sundays for a period of thirty-five year – to no worldly profit – far the reverse, indeed. [pp. 14–17]

Notes

1 That is, Thomas Hardy senior (1778–1837), Thomas Hardy junior (1811–92, i.e. 'the poet and novelist's father'), his elder brother James (1805–80), and the hay-dealer James Dart (1812–80).

2 In rural England during the first half of the nineteenth century, clarinets were played with the reed inverted. They were as a result much more raucous in tone and impossible to play in the demure position of today's orchestral players. In order to keep the vibrating reed away from the body, the clarinet had to be held away from the body, like a jazz trumpet. 'Clar'nets,' as Michail Mail exclaims, 'be bad at all times' (I, iv).

3 William Jackson (1730–1803) was organist at Exeter Cathedral. His *Te Deum* in F is described by Percy Scholes as 'a composition that rises to the height of a curious sublimity of commonplace' (*Oxford Companion to Music* [1970], p. 530).

4 Alexander Pope's *Ode to St Cecilia* (1713) was set to music by Maurice Green (1695–1755).

5 From Robert Browning, *Master Hugues of Saxe-Gotha* (1855). An interesting allusion since Browning's Master Hugues is no J. S. Bach, but rather a hack imitator of the form perfected by Bach.

6 Nahum Tate (1652–1715) and Nicholas Brady (1659–1726) collaborated on an edition of metrical versions of the Psalms (published in 1696). Their *Supplement to the New Version of the Psalms* (1700) gradually superseded the earlier metrical versions of Sternhold and Hopkins, and was dominant by the end of the eighteenth century.

7 These are the names of various tunes or measures to which hymns were set. The most popular of these, the 'Old Hundredth', was a musical setting of Sternhold and Hopkins's metrical version of Psalm 100: that is, it was dubbed 'Old' because it was not set to Tate and Brady's newer version.

8 Bishop Ken (1637–1711), Bishop of Bath and Wells, wrote the popular morning hymn 'Awake my soul'. His hymns were set to music by François Hippolyte Barthélémon (1741–1808), and in 1732 his 'Glory to Thee, my God, this night' was set to the music of Thomas Tallis (1505?–85).

9 *The Return of the Native*, I, v.

NOTES

Editions cited

1872: London: Tinsley, 1872

1873: London: Tinsley, 1873

1896: The Wessex Novels, London: Osgood, McIlvaine; New York: Harper Bros, 1896

1912: The Wessex Edition, London: Macmillan, 1912

1974: The New Wessex Edition, Geoffrey Grigson, ed., London: Macmillan, 1974

1978: The Penguin English Library, David Wright, ed., Harmondsworth: Penguin, 1978

1985: The World's Classics, Simon Gatrell, ed., Oxford: Oxford University Press, 1985

PART I: WINTER

CHAPTER I
Mellstock-lane

1 *To dwellers ... destroy its individuality*: In March 1871 Hardy noted in his 'Memoranda I' Notebook (*Notebooks*, 9) that lonely 'places in the country have each their own peculiar silences'; and in the following note, the sounds of the trees are likened to members of the church congregation, an apt image in the context of the Mellstock choir, and one which recurs in *An Indiscretion in the Life of an Heiress* (the 1878 story based on Hardy's unpublished first novel, *The Poor Man and the Lady*) and the poem 'Afternoon Service at Mellstock' (*Moments of Vision and Miscellaneous Verses* [1917] – see Appendix III). In *The Woodlanders* and the poem 'In a Wood' (*Wessex Poems and Other Verses* [1898], on the other hand, Hardy explores further the image of the blighted woodland, foreshadowed here in the sobbing and moaning fir-trees, the holly battling with itself, and the quivering ash. This opening image also contrasts markedly with the novel's concluding image of the ancient beech-tree: see note 2 of V, ii.

2 *less than a generation ago*: In 1896 and later the action is set 'within living memory'. The choir's Christmas Eve carolling (probably sometime after 1844) occurs fewer than thirty years before the narration in this edition, but more than fifty years before it in 1896. The interval between action and narration is widened further in the 1912 revisions, lending the novel much of the poignancy Hardy thought it lacked here.

3 *With the rose . . . a-sheep-shearing go*: From 'The Sheep-Shearing Song':

> Here's the rosebud in June, the sweet meadows in bloom,
> And the birds singing gaily on every green bough
> The pink and the lily the daffy down dilly
> To adorn the perfume the sweet meadows in June
> > Whilst out o' the plough the fat oxen go slow
> > And the lads and the lasses a-sheep-shearing go.

C. M. Jackson-Houlston, who has studied the formative influences of folk-song on Hardy, finds three versions of this song among those collected by Henry Hammond in the South-West of England between 1905 and 1908 ('Thomas Hardy's Use of Traditional Song', *Nineteenth-Century Literature* 44 [1989], pp. 324–5).

4 *all was dark as the grave*: Hardy also explores the idea of dark figures against a darker landscape elsewhere. See especially *The Return of the Native*, where 'beside anything less dark than the heath they themselves would have appeared as blackness' (V, viii). Stephen J. Spector suggests that from 'the perspective of realism' this image may be seen as 'a reference to the dead members of the Stinsford choir' ('Flights of Fancy: Characterization in Hardy's *Under the Greenwood Tree*', *ELH* 55 [1988], p. 474).

5 *The copsewood . . . so densely*: Dennis Taylor observes in Hardy 'a deepening sense of life-patterns which takes the form of a philosophical statement or an image. The most common images in the early novels are interlaced branches . . . and silhouetted outlines against a sky [see note 7 below] . . . in *Under the Greenwood Tree* . . . the image stands for the pastoral network of the novel' (*Hardy's Poetry, 1860–1928*, second edition [London: Macmillan, 1989], p. 82).

6 *like a ribbon jagged at the edges*: Images of a white road through a night landscape recur in Hardy, most notably as metaphors of 'the parting-line on a head of black hair' in *The Return of the Native*, I, ii, and *The Woodlanders*, I, i.

7 *portrait of a gentleman in black cardboard*: Tom Paulin has pointed out Hardy's fascination with 'sheer visibility', and the significance of dark outlines and 'mnemonic silhouettes' in both his fiction and poetry (*Thomas Hardy: The Poetry of Perception* [London: Macmillan, 1975], p. 111). However, this image, unlike the 'sky-backed pantomime of silhouettes' in *The Return of the Native* (I, ii), for example, or the memory of the effaced silhouette in 'The Whitewashed Wall' (*Late Lyrics and Earlier* [1922]), also draws attention to a strain of anti-naturalism in *Under the Greenwood Tree*. As J. B. Bullen argues, the novel is 'filled with glimpses of Mellstock society, seen not as it might be in life, but as it would be painted on canvas' (*The Expressive Eye: Fiction and Perception in the Work of Thomas Hardy* [Oxford: Clarendon Press, 1986], pp. 46–7). By flattening the rustics into silhouettes, Hardy momentarily divests them of their social identity and turns them into fashionable gentlemen (or, in the image of the procession in the following paragraph, representative figures in timeless rituals). These are 'not fragments of life but ... essentially verbal transcriptions of visual effects' (*The Expressive Eye*, p. 48). See also Spector, 'Flights of Fancy'.

8 *Assyrian or Egyptian incised work*: In the manuscript Hardy wrote 'Assyrian or Etruscan art'. In 1896, he changed it again, to 'some processional design on Greek or Etruscan pottery', which better serves the imagery here, since 'incised work' suggests relief sculpture and not the flat, abstracted figures of Keats's Grecian urn.

9 *Mr. Robert Penny*: When he presented the manuscript to his second wife, Hardy wrote in here, 'His real name was Robert Reason'. He later regretted not using Reason's real name, 'that being much better for his purpose than the one he had invented' (*Life*, 462).

10 *Thomas Leaf*: Leaf is aptly named, given the book's title. In addition, 'the phrase "to have a leaf out" [was] used of a half-witted person' (Firor, 249).

CHAPTER II
The Tranter's

1 *The Tranter's*: The manuscript's double numeration scheme (see 'A Note on the History of the Text') suggests that several pages were excised from the end of this chapter, probably as a result of Macmillan's reader John Morley's criticism of the tedious length of the episode in the ambiguous letter Hardy received in 1871. See also note 1 to the following chapter.

2 *It was a small low cottage ... the very midst*: Hardy radically modified this description of the cottage in 1896, and further refined it in 1912 to resemble the Hardy cottage at Higher Bockhampton more closely. It became a 'long low cottage with a hipped roof of thatch', and the one chimney in 1872 was changed to two in 1896 (one in the 'middle of the ridge and another at the further end'), and three in 1912 (one 'at each end'). These adjustments were not merely for the sake of a sentimental accuracy, however: in revision, the cottage was bigger, and subtly altered the social status of the Dewys. The shed was no longer attached to the end of the cottage, for example, but was 'a little way' from it in 1912; and the stables were likewise distanced from the house in 1896. Hardy was sensitive to misrepresentations of his family's social status, and did not consider the Bockhampton house to be a cottage at all. As Raymond Williams suggests, there is some justification in this, since Hardy's family (like so many of his characters) were not rural labourers but the artisans, traders and freeholders who represent 'the incomplete and ambiguous social mobility of the nineteenth century' (*The Country and the City* [London: Chatto and Windus, 1973], p. 200). It is significant that Hardy wrote *Under the Greenwood Tree* in the very cottage in which he later installed Tranter Dewy. Cf. Hardy's description of the cottage in the *Life* (7–8). See C. J. P. Beatty's extended note on the changes in 'The Tranter's Cottage in *Under the Greenwood Tree*', *Notes and Queries*, vol. 208 (Jan. 1963), p. 26. In addition, in the 1873 one-volume reprint a substantive error creeps into the text in this passage: see 'A Note on the History of the Text'.

3 *a 'tranter,' or irregular carrier*: Tranters were 'irregular' because their services, suitable for passengers or goods, were not time-tabled but were called upon as needed (cf. Mrs Dollery's van in *The Woodlander*, I, i). 'Naibour Sweatley', in the poem 'The Bride-Night Fire' (*Wessex Poems*), 'tranted, and moved people's things'.

4 *generally smiled . . . during conversations with friends*: Dennis Taylor has observed that Hardy's main characters are frequently 'subject to reveries which abstract them from the world around' (*Hardy's Poetry, 1860–1928*, p. 7), and this is the first of many examples here of what the narrator, in I, viii, calls 'the absent gaze'. In I, iv, Michael Mail regards 'nobody can tell what interesting old panoramas with an inward eye . . . letting his outward glance rest on the ground', and in I, viii, Mrs Penny talks on 'in a running tone of complacent abstraction, as if a listener were not a necessity'. Other examples occur later in this chapter, and in I, iii and I, viii.

5 *brightness had passed away . . . visible portions*: Hardy habitually worked verbal echoes of literary or other cultural texts into the most unlikely contexts. This phrase suggests a compound of Nashe's 'Brightness falls from the air' (*A Litany in Time of Plague* [1596]), and the glory that 'hath past away . . . from the earth' in Wordsworth's *Ode: Intimations of Immortality* (1807). See Hardy's early exercises in poetic composition, in Pamela Dalziel and Michael Millgate (eds.), *Thomas Hardy's 'Studies, Specimens &c.' Notebook* (Oxford: Clarendon Press, 1994).

6 *Horner's and Cadbury's*: The choice apples in 1896 and later are 'Sansoms, Stubbards, Five-corners, and such-like'.

7 *his eyes seemed to be . . . the scene before him*: A further example of the absent gazes of the older characters. See note 4 above. Hardy changed 'world' to 'case' in his study copy of the Wessex Edition.

8 *a smock-frock*: Leaf's dress identifies him as an agricultural labourer. His hesitant claim to join with the villagers here and elsewhere is attributed to their compassion for his feeble-mindedness, leaving unspoken the strict class distinctions otherwise in operation. Hardy clarified these in a letter to the English Folk Dance Society in 1926: 'down to the middle of the last century' villagers 'were divided into two distinct castes, one being the artisans, traders, "liviers" (owners of freeholds), and the manor-house upper servants; the other the "work-folk", i.e. farm-labourers . . . The two castes rarely intermarried, and did not go to each other's house-gatherings save exceptionally' (*Journal of the English Folk Dance Society*, second series [1927], p. 54).

9 *And how's your daughter, Mrs. Brownjohn?*: Interestingly, in the manuscript Mrs Dewy's question originally referred to Mrs Penny, not her daughter. If Hardy changed it because it seemed improbable, he retained other hints that women bore children into middle age. The Dewy children, for example, range in age from twenty to four, and there is some suggestion later that, for reasons only hinted at, Mrs Dewy has failed in her obligation to produce a large family.

10 *a maid yet*: In 1896, Hardy added: 'She do know the multiplication table onmistakable well.' One of many undercurrents in the novel hinting at the hardships of married life.

11 *Casterbridge*: Dorchester. In 1896, Hardy added 'jist below the King's Arms', to situate the action precisely for readers familiar with the hotel from *The Mayor of Casterbridge*, *The Trumpet-Major*, and other writings.

12 *with excruciating precision*: Omitted in 1896, presumably on the grounds of its facetiousness.

13 *bass-viol*: The bass-viol was properly the viola da gamba, though it is clear from I, vi that William's instrument is the successor to the viola da gamba, the violoncello.

CHAPTER III

The Assembled Choir

1 *The Assembled Choir*: This chapter was originally entitled 'By the Fireside' (Hardy may have changed it to avoid confusion with Browning's poem of that name). The numeration of the manuscript suggests that five leaves were cut from the end of this chapter very late in its composition (that is, after Hardy had completed the final numbering of the manuscript), probably in response to Morley's criticism (see 'A Note on the History of the Text'). In 1912, Hardy changed the spelling here, as elsewhere in the novel, to 'Quire', in keeping with the favoured subtitle. In 1872, however, 'quire' is used inconsistently.

2 *But to his neighbours . . . old William Dewy*: Cf. the description of Gabriel Oak in chapter i of *Far from the Madding Crowd*: 'to state his character as it stood in the scale of public opinion, when his friends and critics were in tantrums he was considered rather a bad man; when they were pleased, he was rather a good man; when they were neither he was a man whose moral colour was a kind of pepper and salt mixture'.

3 *John*: Since there is no John in the choir, this may indicate that Hardy lifted this passage from his unpublished first novel *The Poor Man and the Lady*.

4 *leg-wood*: Erroneously changed to 'log-wood' in the 1891 Chatto resetting of the novel, and not picked up in Hardy's revisions for the Wessex Edition. He marks it as an intended correction in his study copy of the Wessex Edition. Leg-wood is wood cut from long branches.

5 *a well-illuminated picture*: Another example of the self-conscious pictorialism which frames the rustics within a tradition of English rural genre painting.

6 *a heap . . . Christmas-carol books on a side table*: These 'home-bound' manuscript books, of great personal value to Hardy, are discussed in his Preface to the 1896 edition (reproduced in Appendix I), and in the *Life* (see Appendix IV).

7 *waving his head ominously*: Spinks's sententiousness is tempered somewhat in later editions, though it should be remarked that an aphoristic turn of phrase is characteristic of all the older villagers. In 1896 Hardy added: 'Mr. Spinks was considered to be a scholar, and always spoke up to that level'; and in 1912 he inserted the aside, 'having once kept a nightschool'. Pamela Dalziel and Michael Millgate suggest a possible source for the character of Spinks in a short sketch of a sanctimonious character in Hardy's 'Studies, Specimens &c.' Notebook: see Dalziel and Millgate (eds.), *Thomas Hardy's 'Studies, Specimens &c.' Notebook*, pp. xiii, 78.

8 *The new schoolmistress's!*: In the manuscript, this is a question asked by another of the choir; the following speech is therefore assumed in the manuscript to be spoken by Penny.

9 *figure of fun*: Not, as the phrase now suggests, a grotesque figure (compare, though, Geoffrey's bradded, bunioned last), but one ripe for courtship and its vagaries. Spector comments that because 'Fancy disrupts the text . . . because she seems to be a figure, not of some concept, but of the slippery playfulness of the figure', she is aptly named ('Flights of Fancy', p. 478).

10 *There between the cider-mug . . . a nature and a bias*: Typically of Hardy's heroines, Fancy is represented largely through different, often contradictory, paradigms and stereotypes of femininity: here, as Spector points out ('Flights of Fancy', p. 480), Cinderella is invoked. The suggestion of her fetishization here is also later reinforced in other conspicuously isolated descriptive details of her curls, dresses, and so on. Cf. George Melbury's preservation of his daughter Grace's footprint in *The Woodlanders* (I, iii): 'He took the candle from her hand, held it to the ground, and removed a tile which lay in the garden-path. " 'Tis the track of her shoe that she made when she ran down here the day before she went away all those months ago. I covered it up when she was gone; and when I come here and look at it, I ask myself again, why should she be sacrificed to a poor man?" ' Melbury's hostility to Giles Winterborne's suit recalls Geoffrey Day's ambitions for Fancy.

11 *I don't doubt . . . see it, perhaps*: Spinks's scepticism is more pronounced in 1896: he detects a 'fantastical' likeness, and Hardy removes the clause in which he gives Penny the benefit of the doubt. Hardy also later cancels or amends Spinks's characteristic phrase, 'as far as that goes'.

12 *perusing*: Spinks's use of this word 'comically accentuates its archaism' (Taylor, 182).

13 *observed Grandfather William . . . in the fire*: Another example of an absently gazing character.

CHAPTER IV

Going the Rounds

1 *Going the Rounds*: In the manuscript this chapter originally bore the title 'It was a Hearty Note and Strong'.

2 *dressed in snow-white smock-frocks . . . diamonds, and zigzags*: The smock-frocks identify these anonymous supernumeraries as agricultural labourers, like Leaf.

3 *second violins*: Hardy alters Mail's role to the more specific 'counter parts' (alto parts) in the changes to his own study copy of the Wessex Edition.

4 *Voss*: According to the *Life*, the only character named after a Stinsford villager of Hardy's childhood. He is mentioned again in 'Voices from Things Growing in a Churchyard' (*Late Lyrics and Earlier* [1922]).

5 *Barrel-organs, and they . . . you blow wi' your foot*: The barrel-organ was operated by handle: it revolved a pin-studded cylinder, which opened pipes and struck metal tongues. About ten popular metrical-psalm and hymn tunes could be played from one barrel. The barrel-organ was the most common replacement for church orchestras in the nineteenth century, and was itself replaced by the harmonium, which, as Mail describes, was a reed organ the volume and tone of which was controlled by pedals.

6 *musical religion*: In the manuscript, it is simply 'religion'. The distinction is an important one, since the choir differentiates religion, represented by Maybold, from its own brand of musical religion: likewise, the dead Sam Lawson, in I, ii, is described by Penny as 'Good, but not religious-good'.

7 *Clar'nets . . . at all times*: Percy Scholes, in his *Oxford Companion to Music* (1970), notes that, although some 'important orchestras do not seem to have had clarinets until the late 1780s or 1790s', the clarinet was 'one of the commonest instruments' in the 'hundreds of church orchestras that existed in England in the late eighteenth and early nineteenth centuries' (p. 191).

8 *Dibbeach*: Weatherbury (Puddletown) after 1896. 'Absent-Mindedness in a Parish Choir', in *Life's Little Ironies* (1894; see Appendix III), concerns this choir. In the *Life*, Hardy claimed that the family players, though never more than four, 'maintained an easy superiority over the larger bodies in the parishes near. For while Puddletown west-gallery, for instance, could boast of eight players, and Maiden Newton of nine, these included wood-wind and leather – that is to say, clarionets and serpents – which were apt to be a little too sonorous, even strident, when zealously blown' (see Appendix IV).

9 *High-Stoy Church*: Incorrectly typeset as 'High Story Church' in 1872 (Hardy wrote 'High Stoy' in the manuscript). In 1896 and later it is 'Chalk-Newton' (Maiden-Newton). This choir also features in 'The Grave by the Handpost' (*A Changed Man and Other Tales* [1913]).

10 *Your brass-man . . . good again*: In 1896, William's description is more colourful:

'Your brass-man is a rafting [rousing] dog . . . your reed-man is a dab at stirring ye . . . your drum-maker is a rare bowel-shaker.'

11 *harmoniums:* See note 5 above. These reed-organs were known by many different names, and Hardy changed the word to 'harmonions' in 1896.

12 *Miserable machines . . . music:* Hardy amends this to the more rusticated 'miserable dumbledores' (bumblebees) in 1896, in response to the criticism that his choir sometimes seems too well-educated. Horace Moule had isolated this phrase as incongruous in his review of the novel in the *Saturday Review*, 28 September 1872, arguing that the rustics speak 'in the language of the author's manner of thought, rather than their own'. However, as Dennis Taylor argues, 'Hardy knew that cottagers were influenced by newspapers, church sermons, the Bible, and some literature, and that when "wound up" they could speak in this manner, sometimes parodying the language of their betters, or using it with sudden efficiency. Hardy enjoys the interplay between standard and dialect when the rustics wind themselves up to speak in a high-falutin fashion' (Taylor, 183).

13 *opening the lanterns to get a clearer light:* The cow-horn used in the panels of these lanterns threw a soft, translucent light.

14 *Then passed . . . so earnestly:* This paragraph and the full text of the carol were added at proof-stage, emphasizing the importance Hardy attached to the background narrative of fall and redemption, death and resurrection, against which the demise of the choir is sketched. The paragraph is later modified: the hymn becomes 'time-worn' in 1896, and the words of the hymn do not simply 'befit' the picturesque choristers in 1896, but are 'orally transmitted from father to son through several generations down to the present'; and it is a species of 'quaint Christianity' in 1912 (transferring the quaintness from the characters themselves). The text of the carol is also slightly emended in 1896: 'Therefore to dwell' is corrected to 'There for to dwell'; 'Our hearts to aid' becomes 'Be not afraid'; the divine 'he' is capitalized; and 'heart-felt' is altered to 'heart-most'.

15 *Forty breaths . . . 'O, what unbounded goodness!' number fifty-nine:* It is unclear why Hardy has 'forty' breaths both here and in the manuscript. He amended it to 'four breaths' in 1896. In the Carol Book belonging to Hardy's grandfather (in the Dorset County Museum), this carol is on p. 59.

16 *thirty-nine and forty-three:* Old William speaks of these years as if they were long gone, but in the 1896 Preface Hardy placed the action 'fifty years ago' (emended to 'between fifty and sixty years ago' in 1912; see Appendix I). The novel is therefore probably set in 1845 or 1846 (or even conceivably a year or two later), since, if it were 1844, William is unlikely to refer to the previous Christmas by number.

CHAPTER V
The Listeners

1 *The Listeners*: Hardy originally entitled this chapter 'She was a Phantom of Delight', but he cancelled this and other allusions to Wordsworth's poem (see note 1 to IV, vi and note 2 to IV, vii) at some stage of the manuscript's composition. Covert reference to it does remain (see note 2 to III, iv and note 13 to V, i), and, as Gatrell argues, Fancy's character is clearly drawn with Wordsworth's phantom in mind (1985, p. xviii).

2 *Farmer Shinar's*: Shinar was not a farmer in early drafts of the novel but the keeper of the Old Soul's Inn, a 'queer lump of a house ... at the corner of a lane'. His name nicely suggests his new-moneyed ostentation, shining as he is with watch-chains and jewellery. Hardy seemed undecided about the spelling of his name (which Gatrell [1985, p. 207] notes is Dorset dialect for 'someone to have a flirtation with'): he is both 'Shiner' and 'Shinar' in the manuscript (and there are many examples where the -er spelling is overwritten). He settles on 'Shiner' in 1896, but, as Shinar, the farmer turns up again in *The Mayor of Casterbridge,* xiii and xvii.

3 *a churchwarden*: An elected lay representative of the parish. The stage at which Hardy decided to elevate Shinar to churchwarden is ambiguous in the manuscript, but it is likely to have occurred with his transformation from innkeeper to gentleman farmer (see previous note), which probably coincided with the introduction of Maybold's rival suit. This allowed Hardy to implicate Shinar in the conflict over the church music and link the churchwarden's attentions to Fancy with Maybold's later approaches. Because the manuscript includes (unrevised) material adverting to the belated Maybold–Fancy plot, this chapter must have been rewritten at the fair-copy stage; consequently grandfather William's reference to Shinar's position is not a late insertion; nor is the allusion to the wardenship at the tranter's party (I, vii), or the further reference in II, iv. But other references in the manuscript show the role to be an afterthought.

4 *What in the name . . . still more uneasily*: William suggests a rather ominous answer to his own question in 1896 and later: ' "Perhaps he's drownded!" '

5 *against a wall*: Dick leans (more poetically) against a beech-tree in 1896 and later. However, the 'greenwood tree' of the final chapter, 'an ancient beech-tree' in this edition, becomes simply 'an ancient tree' in 1896.

6 *The insult . . . murmured Mr. Spinks*: The epigrammatic Spinks seems rather too educated here. Accordingly, in 1896 Hardy changed his aside to ' "The stupidness lies in that point of it being nothing at all." ' See also note 11 to I, iii.

7 *Mr. Maybold*: In 1841, the vicar of Stinsford was a Londoner named Arthur Shirley (Jeanne Howard, 'Thomas Hardy's "Mellstock" and the Registrar General's Stinsford', *Literature and History* 6 [Autumn 1977], p. 186).

8 *that's a sign . . . clever chap*: Cf. the description of the other Mellstocker with sharp hearing, Mrs Endorfield, in IV, iii.

9 *like the figure of 8 . . . my sonnies*: The tranter's warning foreshadows the 'knot there's no untying' (V, i).

CHAPTER VI
Christmas Morning

1 *Christmas Morning*: In the manuscript Hardy originally conceived this chapter as two separate chapters – 'The Tranter's Toilet' and 'The Mellstock Chosen', the second of which had begun at the paragraph 'The three left the door and paced down Mellstock-lane'. From the manuscript numeration, it is clear that Hardy cut out some of the episode dealing with the tranter's elaborate toilet, in keeping with the diminished emphasis on the choir-members as the novel developed.

2 *The gallery of Mellstock Church . . . own*: Hardy included in the *Life* (p. 15) a plan of the west gallery of Stinsford Church, which he recalled was removed sometime in the 1840s (*Life*, 342). It has been argued, however, that the gallery was dismantled much later: see Denys Kay-Robinson, *Hardy's Wessex Re-appraised* (Newton Abbot: David and Charles, 1972), p. 40.

3 *chronologically follows it*: 'The Thanksgiving of Women after Childbirth'. See also note 5 to V, i.

4 *Pyramus and Thisbe*: These star-crossed lovers exchanged vows through a chink in the wall between their two houses. The scene is played by Bottom and his friends in *A Midsummer Night's Dream*.

5 *Mrs. Ledlow, the farmer's wife*: Old Dame Ledlow reappears as Shinar's aunt in *The Mayor of Casterbridge*, xiii.

6 *hours slowly drew along*: More plausibly, after 1896, 'as its minutes slowly . . .'

7 *By chance or by fate . . . Mr. Maybold*: Added on the verso of leaf 42 of the manuscript, this paragraph indicates that Hardy decided later in the process of composition to introduce Maybold as a rival to Dick.

8 *The music on Christmas mornings . . . looked cross*: In 'Absent-Mindedness in a Parish Choir' (*Life's Little Ironies*), Hardy tells the story of the Longpuddle choir's last performance on Christmas morning, when, similarly wearied after the night's carolling, and warmed with brandy-and-beer, they fall asleep in the gallery. Wakened suddenly, they strike up not a hymn but the dance tune 'The Devil Among the Tailors' (adverted to later in Shinar's song 'King Arthur he had three sons'). The choir is summarily replaced with a barrel-organ (see Appendix III).

9 *school-girls' aisle*: Hardy originally had 'school-children's aisle' here, but altered it presumably to emphasize the division between the sexes.

CHAPTER VII
The Tranter's Party

1 *If the sun only shines out . . . I never see!*: The perspiring Dewys are aptly named. Cf. George Crabbe's 'The Village' (1783), which describes how 'the mid-day sun, with fervid ray/On their bare heads and dewy temples play' (I, 43-4). Hardy's villagers are hardly Crabbe's 'laborious natives', of course, but the novel self-consciously foregrounds so many different conventions for representing rural life that Crabbe's anti-pastoral certainly may have been in Hardy's mind. In 1919 he claimed that Crabbe was 'one of the influences that led him towards his method – in his novels not in his poetry' (*Collected Letters*, V, 294). In the *Life*, likewise, he called Crabbe 'an apostle of realism . . . three-quarters of a century before the French realistic school had been heard of' (p. 351).

2 *normal*: Changed at proof-stage for the first edition from the more telling 'formular', which suggests that the Dewys have long since settled into patterned responses. The remainder of Ann's monologue is a later addition to the verso of the manuscript, indicating perhaps that Hardy felt that the women were not well-represented in the older rustics' dialogue.

3 *Church of England*: In his study copy of the Wessex Edition, Hardy changed this to 'sky-folk', at the same time altering the following sentence to read: 'Jigging parties be all very well on the Devil's holidays . . .'

4 *'Triumph, or Follow my Lover'*: In the 1896 Preface, Hardy wrote that it was 'customary to inscribe a few jigs, reels, hornpipes, and ballads' in the Sunday music-books, 'the insertions being continued from front and back till sacred and secular met together in the middle'. The Hardy family music book contains the music for this dance. See also the poems 'The Dance at the Phoenix' (*Wessex Poems* [1898]) and 'One We Knew' (*Time's Laughingstocks and Other Verses* [1909]).

5 *Mr. Shinar . . . but never smiling*: In 1896, Hardy added to this description, endowing Shinar with 'a crimson stare, vigorous breath' and a 'dark' smile.

6 *our heroine*: On the evidence of the manuscript's double numeration scheme, this leaf was inserted at a later stage of the composition, when Fancy takes over from the choir as the 'heroine' of the novel.

7 *two slurs in music*: In chapter xxxv of *The Hand of Ethelberta* (1876), the arch of Ethelberta's brows is also described as 'like a slur in music'.

8 *over his lady's head*: To which Hardy added in 1912: 'which presumably gave the figure its name'.

9 *when the fiddlers' chairs . . . originally stood*: In the *Life* Hardy described how as a child he had been stopped after three-quarters of an hour's unbroken fiddling, 'lest he should "burst a bloodvessel"' (p. 28).

10 *hands-across*: When the dancers join hands across the line.

CHAPTER VIII
They Dance More Wildly

1 *six-hands-round*: In 1926, Hardy wrote that the dance he was thinking of 'must have been "The College Hornpipe", as that is the only one I remember beginning with six-hands-round' (*English Folk Dance Society News* [Sept. 1926], p. 383). His letter also claimed that country dances such as the one described here were not folk dances at all, but more 'genteel' affairs, possibly derived from fashionable eighteenth-century London figures and tunes, an opinion that caused some controversy in the Folk Dance Society.

2 *people in a railway train*: In 1896, Hardy changed this simile to 'people near a threshing machine'. The latter is perhaps more appropriate to the rural West of England before 1850 (in the mid-century the railway was still seen as 'something foreign' and 'but dimly understood' [*Far from the Madding Crowd*, xvii]). The threshing machine reappears famously in chapter xlvii of *Tess of the d'Urbervilles*, and in *An Indiscretion in the Life of an Heiress*.

3 *cider-mug*: In 1912, Hardy amended this to 'cider and ale mugs', changing too Mrs Penny's Midsummer-eve offering of cider to 'beer', and later in the chapter adding 'ale' to the drinks the tranter replenishes after supper.

4 *sit up on old Midsummer-eves*: Old Midsummer-eve is 5 July. Cf. *The Woodlanders*, II, iv, *Jude the Obscure*, III, vii, and the poem 'On a Midsummer Eve' (*Moments of Vision*).

5 *the coming man*: An ironic pun on Mrs Penny's surrender to the portents of Midsummer-eve, and her appraisal of this small man's ambitions: the 'coming man' is the up-and-coming man, one likely to attain distinction.

6 *in the candle-flame*: Mrs Penny stares 'on the floor' in the manuscript, and in 'the centre of the room' in 1896 – another example of her complacent abstraction.

7 *but much to their sustenance*: The ambiguity of this passage suggests that the Dewys' uncharacteristic physical closeness is also a mystery: a further hint of life after marriage. In the manuscript, Hardy has cancelled the following: 'They were both seen to be taking mathematical measurements of the tables by the aid of the eye alone, and drawing imaginary pictures of these articles of furniture in any possible combinations [indecipherable] placed endwise to each other, or side to end, or side by side.'

8 *'Dead March'*: The march from Handel's oratorio *Saul* was frequently played at funerals.

9 *music and eating*: And, in keeping with the pastoral mood, music is the food of love in this chapter.

10 *Three Choughs at Casterbridge*: Choughs are red-legged crows. Changed to *The Mayor of Casterbridge*'s 'Dree Mariners' (based on Dorchester's 'The King of Prussia') in 1896.

11 *parables*: Changed in proof from 'fables'. The tranter's criterion for true stories raises inevitable questions about *Under the Greenwood Tree* itself, which is and is not what he would call a 'true story'. A 'coarseness' is modified to 'a coarse touch' in 1912.

12 *engaged a woman to wait up for her*: Presumably to ensure she arrives home safely. The novel registers here, and in Shinar's offering of 'protection from the dangers of the night', the hazards as well as the liberties for village women living alone. See also the finale of the nutting episode, IV, i.

13 *What a contradiction!*: Hardy changed 'contradiction' to 'difference' (and 'delusive contradiction' to 'deceiving difference') in 1896, perhaps because Dick's reaction seemed too educated for his social status.

14 *I no more dare to touch her than —*: Much is made in the novel, as elsewhere in Hardy, of erotic rituals of touching. The dancing over, Dick is prohibited from contact, and from this moment on, Fancy strictly regulates her suitors' touches (see the hand-washing episode, II, vii; Fancy's ' "No touching, sir!" ' in III, i; the two kissing scenes in III, ii and IV, v; and her physical rejection of Maybold, after accepting his offer in marriage, in IV, vi).

15 *Mr Shinar and his watch-chain . . . drown him if he would*: In the manuscript Shinar is not cast quite so obviously as the rival: 'Mr Shinar and his watch-chain – taking the cold-blooded advantage that people who are going homeward the same way with a young female always do take over those who are not . . .'; likewise, a few lines later, Fancy is not *his* Lady Fair in the manuscript but simply *a* Lady Fair.

16 *a Nasmyth hammer*: This simile, referring to the steam hammer invented by James Nasmyth in 1839, was added at proof-stage. In the manuscript, the tranter's hand is simply 'on her shoulder the while'.

17 *wind up the clock*: In his personal study copy of the Wessex Edition in the Dorset County Museum, Hardy emended this to 'draw up the clock'.

CHAPTER IX
Dick Calls at the School

1 *Dick Calls at the School*: Originally this was to have been the first chapter of Spring, not the last chapter of Winter (manuscript cancellation).

2 *He disguised . . . such trifling errands*: Gatrell (*Creator*, 13) points out the parallels between this paragraph and a passage in *An Indiscretion in the Life of an Heiress*, indicating possible borrowings from *The Poor Man and the Lady*, from which much of *An Indiscretion* is considered to derive: 'On a certain day he rang the bell with a mild air, and disguised his feelings by looking as if he wished to speak to her merely on copy-books, slates, and other school matters' (*The Excluded and Collaborative Stories*, Pamela Dalziel, ed. [Oxford: Clarendon Press, 1992], p. 103). See also Dalziel, 'Exploiting the *Poor Man*: The Genesis of Hardy's *Desperate*

Remedies', *Journal of English and Germanic Philology* 94 (1995), pp. 220–32. There is a similar scene in II, iv, when the choir assumes a forced casual air on arrival at the vicarage.

3 *prisoner's base*: Hardy may have intended this reference to suggest a comic counterpart to 'hands-across'. Two lines of players face one another, with at least one representative in each 'touching base'. 'Any player is free to leave the line and give an opponent chase; he who is touched first becomes the other's prisoner, and so on until the fixed number agreed on at the start of the game ... are safely "in prison"' (Firor, 161). Cf. *Far from the Madding Crowd*, xliv. Changed to 'cross-dadder' (the chasing game 'cross touch') in 1912.

4 *kept her outside*: In 1912, Hardy added: 'before floundering into that fatal farewell'.

PART II: SPRING

CHAPTER I
Passing by the School

1 *Passing by the School*: On the evidence of the double numeration of the manuscript, this chapter was added at a late stage of the composition.

CHAPTER II
A Meeting of the Choir

1 *A Meeting of the Choir*: In the manuscript there are two compositely numbered leaves in this chapter (and one in the next), both relating to the choir's discussion of Maybold. Hardy probably cut out material extraneous or irrelevant to the Maybold love plot when he added the vicar's suit at a late stage of the composition.

2 *They were all brightly illuminated ... a protection to the eyes*: The painstaking composition of the rustics here suggests again reference to Dutch and English genre painting, but the dramatic chiaroscuro denotes, as the earlier use of silhouettes and 'incised work' had, an intensification and abstraction at odds with the even light-effects characteristic of English painters such as Wilkie, Thomas Webster, or William Collins. Hardy is thinking, perhaps, of seventeenth-century Dutch landscape painters (Jakob van Ruysdael, for example, listed as one of the 'Dutch School' in Hardy's 'Schools of Painting' Notebook [Taylor, 113], for whom the nature of light was a scientific problem).

3 *some modern Moroni*: The *Portrait of a Man (The Tailor)* by Giambattista Moroni (*c.* 1525–78) is in the National Gallery. As J. B. Bullen explains, 'Mr Penny is depicted in the act of practising his trade', like Moroni's tailor, who stands in 'flannel jacket [and] red breeches . . . at his board with shears in his hand, about to cut a piece of black cloth' (*The Abridged Catalogue of the Pictures in the National Gallery: Foreign Schools* [1873], pp. 67–8; quoted in *The Expressive Eye*, p. 49). Hardy may have been unsure of his memory of the picture: in the manuscript he had 'a shoemaker by Moroni'.

4 *Wellington-boot*: Not the rubber waterproof boot common today, but a high leather boot covering the knee in front.

5 *No sign was . . . based on personal respect*: This practice comes to seem anachronistic even within the timespan of the narrative, when Dick has business cards printed: see note 5 of IV, vii, and the Introduction.

6 *the sermon . . . afore he got it out*: Changed at proof-stage from the slightly more risqué 'Solomon's Song lay in Solomon's ink-bottle afore he got it out', perhaps at Tinsley's suggestion.

7 *Tory to her husband's Whiggism*: Tories and Whigs were the forerunners of the Conservative and Liberal parties. The former sought the preservation of the social and political order, while the latter favoured reform. This paragraph, like other material added to enlarge the roles of Mrs Penny and Mrs Dewy, is an addition to the verso of the manuscript leaf (fo. 70).

8 *I never see . . . afore nor since*: Hardy was unsure at first how best to illustrate the 'spiritual trouble' to which Maybold was putting the village. This text is an addition to the verso of fo. 73 of the manuscript. Upside-down on the verso of the subsequent leaf (the compositely numbered fo. 74/75), moreover, Hardy has cancelled 'wanting any of us to come to church, or bring the little ones to be christened against our will'. The meaning here is quite different, and implies that the musicians and their families were even less 'hot and strong about church business' than the final text suggests. Maybold, in this context, would be seen as a proselytizing parson, too much given to looking out for the spiritual needs of his parishioners.

In 1912 Hardy added here the following anecdote:

'No sooner had he got here than he found the font wouldn't hold water, as it hadn't for years off and on; and when I told him that Mr Grinham never minded it, but used to spet upon his vinger and christen 'em just as well, 'a said, "Good Heavens! Send for a workman immediate. What place have I come to!" Which was no compliment to us, come to that.'

On the significance of church reform in the novel, see the Introduction.

CHAPTER III
A Turn in the Discussion

1 *the rising new moon*: In a letter to the Revd Arthur Moule on 19 October 1903, Hardy notes that 'I should have said "setting" of course: I have meant to correct it for years, but have always forgotten when a new edition has been required' (*Collected Letters*, III, 79). It was changed in 1912.

2 *Hee-hee! . . . want to*: To which Hardy added, in his study copy of the Wessex Edition, ' "Only a teeny bit!" '

3 *how many cuts . . . spar*: Mail's idiomatic expression for Leaf's weak-mindedness emphasizes again the kinds of manual skills the Mellstockers would have taken for granted. Consider Hardy's description of Marty South's spar-making in *The Woodlanders* (I, ii):

With a bill-hook in one hand and a leather glove, much too large for her, on the other, she was making spars, such as are used by thatchers, with great rapidity . . . On her left hand lay a bundle of the straight, smooth hazel rods called spar-gads – the raw material of her manufacture; on her right, a heap of chips and ends – the refuse – with which the fire was maintained; in front, a pile of the finished articles. To produce them she took up each gad, looked critically at it from end to end, cut it to length, split it into four, and sharpened each of the quarters with dexterous blows, which brought it to a triangular point precisely resembling that of a bayonet.

4 *I can sing my treble . . . and better!*: Like Christian Cantle in *The Return of the Native* – the 'slack-twisted, slim-looking maphrotight fool' – Leaf's treble voice signifies his ambiguous gender as well as his childishness.

5 *imaginative*: Hardy changed this to the more precise 'romantical' in 1896.

CHAPTER IV
The Interview with the Vicar

1 *studied . . . the winding lines of the grain*: This scene parallels that in I, ix. Hardy had originally inserted a chapter break – 'The Interview' – at this point.

2 *tranter Dewy do turn neither to the right hand nor to the left*: 'Be ye therefore very courageous to keep and to do all that is written in the book of the law of Moses, that ye turn not aside therefrom to the right hand or to the left' (Joshua 23:6).

3 *like chips in porridge*: 'The chip in the porridge which did neither good nor harm to the cooking itself is no doubt the "John-herb", or "John-indifferent" . . . It was commonly used to denote an absolutely insignificant person' (Firor, 219). In 1912, Hardy added an enigmatic footnote: 'This, a local expression, must be a corruption of something less questionable.'

4 *tribble*: Hardy inadvertently leaves this earlier manuscript dialect spelling intact here. In the previous chapter, Reuben used the word 'treble'.

5 *good-now*: 'Sure enough.' '[The] tone [of the expression] is one of conjectural assurance, its precise meaning being "You may be sure" and such phrases as "I'll warrant", "methinks", "sure enough" would be used as alternatives. The Americanism "I guess" is near it' (*Collected Letters*, I, 277).

6 *Now for some reason . . . getting – Miss Day to play*: Another late addition to the manuscript indicating that Hardy did not initially intend for Maybold to be a romantic rival to Dick. The vicar here joins Hardy's numerous blushing men (see note 1 to III, iv).

7 *A Laodicean lukewarmness*: Added on verso. One of Hardy's favourite expressions for half-heartedness, expressive here of the sociable church-going that he so admired (see, for example, 'Afternoon Service at Mellstock', reproduced in Appendix III).

8 *Now, sir, you see . . . it is*: In 1912, Hardy omitted the word 'sir' here, and once or twice later in the chapter, subtly suggesting the tranter's slight adjustment to his earlier automatically respectful mode of address.

9 *Michaelmas*: 29 September (the Feast of St Michael and All Angels). See also note 2 to IV,v.

CHAPTER V
Returning Homeward

1 *He behaved like . . . said the tranter*: In 1912, Hardy modified the scene to indicate that the tranter was well aware that they had lost the mock tournament with the vicar, adding here: '"And though, beyond that, we ha'n't got much by going, 'twas worth while. He won't forget it. Yes, he took it very well."'

2 *Now . . . nice o' the man*: The sarcasm here is more explicit in 1912, when Hardy added: '"even though words be wind"'.

3 *translate*: Changed to the more colloquial 'onriddle' in 1896, probably in response to Horace Moule's criticism (see note 12 to I, iv).

4 *That man's silence . . . to listen to*: In 1912, Hardy removed every instance of the word 'silence' from this conversation. The result is a more precise sense of Day's reserve, one that is linked more forcefully with his money: he is '"close"'; his '"dumbness"' is wonderful to listen to; and he can '"hold his tongue"'.

CHAPTER VI
Yalbury Wood and the Keeper's House

1 *steamed*: Erroneously set as 'streamed' in 1872.

2 *The game-keeper, Geoffrey Day*: In 1896, Day is not the 'game-keeper', but the more socially elevated 'head gamekeeper and general overlooker for this district', which is situated on the 'outlying estates of the Earl of Wessex'. In 1912, he is elevated further, his added duties including that of 'timber-steward'. He is mentioned again in chapter viii of *Far from the Madding Crowd*.

3 *A curl of wood-smoke . . . in a lady's hat*: Hardy first notes this simile in his 'Memoranda I' Notebook, dated Cornwall, August 1870 (*Notebooks*, 5). The convergence of nature and fashion here is significant: Fancy, like Hardy's later heroines, is associated simultaneously with stereotypes of woman's ineluctable 'nature' and her changefulness and enslavement to fashion. See too the later description of butterflies crowded around a group of hollyhocks 'like females round a bonnet-shop' (III, iv).

4 *The most noticeable instance . . . Ezekiel Sparrowgrass*: Eight-day clocks need be wound only every eight days. In 1896, 'Saunders' is substituted for 'Sparrowgrass'.

5 *true as the Squire's time*: By 1896, Geoffrey is more sophisticated, and less deferential to the big house: the Squire's time gives way to the national standard, 'town time'.

6 *Dick could have . . . theirs*: Another example of a close textual parallel with a sentence in *An Indiscretion in the Life of an Heiress* (see also note 2 to I, ix), which reads: 'Mayne could have wished that she had not been so thoroughly free from all apparent consciousness of the event of the previous week' (*The Excluded and Collaborative Stories*, p. 91). See *Creator*, 14.

7 *that class of womankind . . . a rum class rather*: Cf. *The Woodlanders* (II, xvi):

'I am an old man,' said Melbury, 'whom, somewhat late in life, God thought fit to bless with one child, and she a daughter. Her mother was a very dear wife to me; but she was taken away from us when the child was young; and the child became precious as the apple of my eye to me, for she was all I had left to love. For her sake entirely I married as second wife a homespun woman who had been kind as a mother to her.'

8 *Did Fred Shinar . . . cask o' drink, Fancy?*: Hardy evidently forgot that this question refers to Shinar's occupation in earlier stages of the composition, where he is keeper of the Old Souls' Inn.

9 *The conversation . . . reach Dick's ears*: An addition on the verso of the manuscript, to emphasize Fancy's resistance to her father's match-making, and play down what would otherwise seem like coquetry (as does Fancy's castigation of Enoch, also a later addition).

10 *which is common among cottagers*: In keeping with Day's higher social status in

1896, Hardy altered 'cottagers' to 'frugal countryfolk'. In 1912, significantly, he replaced 'is' with 'was' (see 'A Note on the History of the Text').

11 *gossipest, poachest, jailest*: Mrs Day's increasingly damning superlatives are invented words.

CHAPTER VII
Dick Makes Himself Useful

1 *Dick duly . . . rather a nice one*: See also 'Under the Waterfall' (*Satires of Circumstance, Lyrics and Reveries* [1914]) and the hand-washing scene in *Tess of the D'Urbervilles* (chapter xxxiv), noted in Rosemary L. Eakins, 'The Mellstock Quire and Tess in Hardy's Poetry', in Patricia Clements and Juliet Grindle (eds), *The Poetry of Thomas Hardy* (London: Vision, 1980), pp. 52–68; and William A. Davis, 'Hand Washing in Three Works by Thomas Hardy', *ELN* 24 (4), pp. 56–61.

2 *Dick rather wished . . . managing vicars*: Another late insertion of the Maybold plot into the manuscript. Cf. II, v, in which the tranter, who also feels that he has 'managed' his adversary, remarks that 'men want managing almost as much as women'.

CHAPTER VIII
Dick Meets His Father

1 *passages at arms with Fancy*: The vague allusions to courtly love and chivalry that surround the choir's rivalry with the vicar (most obvious in the comic 'tournament' of the interview) surface again in this phrase, which suggests, however, that Fancy is not the prize for the gallant victor, but a combatant herself.

2 *The maning . . . rather hid at present*: In 1896, Hardy changed the tranter's answer slightly to shift the emphasis from a woman's mystique to her connivance: the meaning is 'meant to be rather hid at present'.

3 *White Tuesday, – Mellstock Club walked the same day*: On the Tuesday of Whitsun-tide, members of parish clubs, or friendly societies, processed round the village soliciting contributions (see *Tess of the D'Urbervilles*, chapter ii). The tranter's association of the two events is significant, given the tension in the novel between the male fellowship of the choir and married life.

4 *plain terms*: Dick's second letter is less ingenuous in 1896; he inquires in 'jaunty terms, which could only be answered in the same way'.

5 *a watering-place fourteen miles off*: Named here as Budmouth Regis in 1896, which is ten, not fourteen, miles off in that edition. Hence Fancy will save not an hour but half an hour by travelling home with Dick when he offers her a lift in the following chapter. Cf. III, ii, which gives the distance between Budmouth and Mellstock as 'eighteen miles'.

PART III: SUMMER

CHAPTER I
Driving out of Budmouth

1 *The scene . . . green and opal*: The parallel with Weymouth is stressed in later editions. The street becomes 'Mary Street . . . near the King's statue' (the statue of George III on the Weymouth esplanade) in 1896; 'Regis' is added to the town's name in 1912, and Weymouth Bay is described as 'an embayed and nearly motionless expanse of salt water projected from the outer ocean – today lit in bright tones of green and opal'. In the following paragraph the parade becomes the 'Esplanade'.

2 *a roll under his arm*: The boy rattles along with a baker's cart in 1896 and later.

3 *I am so much obliged . . . company, Miss Day*: In 1896, this remark is followed by 'as they drove past the semicircular bays of the Royal Hotel'. The 1912 revisions, which tend to cast the action back into a more distant past, and which perhaps beg some explanation of the town's elevation to a 'Regis', alter this to the 'Old Royal Hotel, where His Majesty King George the Third had many a time attended the balls of the burgesses'.

4 *passed about twenty . . . out of the town*: Changed in 1896 to 'twenty of the trees . . . towards Casterbridge and Mellstock'. This landscape faintly recalls Hobbema's *The Avenue, Middelharnis* (in the National Gallery), one of numerous pictorial references to Dutch genre painting in the novel. See Bullen, *The Expressive Eye*, pp. 42–53; and Norman Page, 'Hardy's Dutch Painting: *Under the Greenwood Tree*', *Thomas Hardy Yearbook* 5 (1976), pp. 39–42.

5 *she replied with soft archness*: In proof for the first edition Hardy inserted several of these speech descriptors ('said she in low tones'; 'she said gently'; and 'she whispered tenderly'). They are reliable clues to Fancy's developing love of Dick in this critical scene.

CHAPTER II
Farther along the Road

1 *Dick, I always believe . . . no consciousness of it*: Fancy's fine distinction between flattery and her consciousness of flattery is added on the verso of the manuscript.

2 *a silent escape of pants*: Modified to 'a soft silent escape of breaths' in 1912.

3 *varying tones of red . . . varying thought*: Cf. *An Indiscretion in the Life of an Heiress*: 'the fresh, subtly-curved cheek, changing its tones of red with the fluctuation of each thought' (*The Excluded and Collaborative Stories*, p. 91). See note 1 to III, iv.

4 *O no! . . . she exclaimed*: Fancy's passionate submission to Dick's kiss seems to be a later addition to the manuscript. The modest screen of asterisks following this exclamation, the landlord's innuendoes, and the fact that, although Fancy commands Dick to let her go instantly, he emerges 'deeply stained' half an hour afterwards all hint that the lovers are indeed 'farther along the road'. Cf. Gatrell, who argues that 'Hardy at no stage intended [*Under the Greenwood Tree*] to have any sexual incident beyond the occasional kiss' (*Creator*, 132).

CHAPTER III
A Confession

1 *A Confession*: On the evidence of the manuscript numeration, the parts of this chapter relating to the 'gipsy-party' are later additions.

2 *handsome and such a clever courter*: Dick is simply 'so clever and handsome' in the manuscript. In a novel much more interested in Fancy's 'clever courting', this is an important claim of Susan's: the change, along with such later additions as the nutting chapter, makes Dick seem altogether less passive and artless. Fancy's ambiguous exclamation, ' "O, I wish!" ', suggests that she believes Dick's 'clever courting' to be nothing of the kind.

3 *stale, flat, and unprofitable*: 'How weary, stale, flat and unprofitable/ Seem to me all the uses of this world!' (*Hamlet*, I, ii, 133–4).

4 *as if he were alone . . . never known her*: In 1896, Hardy altered this analogy to read: 'as if he were tired of an ungrateful country and had never wanted her'. In 1912, it is altered again to read: 'as if he were tired of an ungrateful country, including herself'.

5 *like a pet lamb*: Cf. II, viii, in which Dick feels that Fancy had 'driven him about the house like a quiet cat or dog'. The scene of the vicar and the canary, and Fancy's anecdote about Shinar and the bullfinches, associate Fancy's coquetry with the domestication of animals, but here the simile points to Fancy's underlying vulnerability. The song by Thomas Campbell from which Hardy takes the title of V, i ('The Knot There's No Untying') also compares marriage to the capturing of birds: 'Love's wing moults when caged and captured,/ Only free he soars enraptured'.

6 *My impulses are bad . . . I can't help it*: Cf. Sue Bridehead in *Jude the Obscure*: ' "I should shock you by letting you know how I give way to my impulses, and how much I feel that I shouldn't have been provided with attractiveness unless it were meant to be exercised! Some women's love of being loved is insatiable; and so, often, is their love of loving" ' (IV, i); and later, ' "I am very bad and unprincipled – I know you think that!" ' (IV, v).

CHAPTER IV
An Arrangement

1 *she waited . . . she went on again*: In the manuscript Fancy's blush is more calculating: 'she waited till a blush expanded . . .' Hardy was always fascinated by the blushing of both women and men. In his 'Studies, Specimens &c.' Notebook *(1865), he first explores the idea of* 'thy {sweet cheek's/*facility* {in reds and whites: *facile* blushes' (*Thomas Hardy's 'Studies, Specimens &c.' Notebook*, p. 66).

2 *You perfect woman!*: An allusion to Wordsworth's 'She was a Phantom of Delight'. See also note 1 to I, v, note 1 to IV, vi, note 2 to IV, vii, and note 13 to V, i.

PART IV: AUTUMN

CHAPTER I
Going Nutting

1 *Going Nutting*: On the evidence of the manuscript numeration (see 'A Note on the History of the Text'), this entire chapter is a later addition, indicating that Hardy decided the lovers needed a climactic skirmish and reconciliation.

2 *such lots of people . . . round the neck*: This is clarified in 1896: Fancy explains that she will 'walk to Longpuddle church in the afternoon with father', where lots of people will see her. The following references to Yalbury are accordingly changed to Longpuddle.

3 *Hour after hour passed away*: Perhaps because summer is over, and Dick does not actually storm off until well after five o'clock, Hardy emends this to 'half-hour after half-hour' in 1896.

4 *O, I did wish the horrid . . . dear shape again!*: Cf. *The Woodlanders*, II, xvii, in which Grace Melbury and Felice Charmond become lost 'wandering' in the wood.

5 *'Why are you wandering here, I pray?'*: In the *Life* (p. 19) Hardy names this as one of his mother's favourite tunes. Gatrell (1985, p. 214) points out that it is a song of sexual innuendo about a maid who claims to be seeking poppies and nightingales in the wood, but is in fact waiting upon her lover.

CHAPTER II
Honey-Taking, and Afterwards

1 *at the going down of the sun*: 'Then the king, when he heard these words, was sore displeased with himself, and set his heart on Daniel to deliver him: and he laboured till the going down of the sun to deliver him' (Daniel 6:14).

2 *without money man is a shadder*: One of many aphorisms given by the villagers, this is also one of the conspicuous references to money in the novel (another is

Thomas Leaf's recasting of the parable of the talents as a parable of self-help and capitalist accumulation in the final chapter).

3 *much as a European nation . . . neighbours*: An unexpected simile, referring perhaps to the Commune in Paris, ruthlessly suppressed in 1871.

4 *Not wildly . . . Not at all*: Michael Millgate argues that this exchange reveals Fancy's affinity with Rosalind, Shakespeare's comic heroine in *As You Like It* (*Thomas Hardy: His Career as a Novelist* [London: The Bodley Head, 1971], pp. 44–5). However, the reviewer for the *Athenaeum* thought the witty dialogue too redolent of the drawing-room, and scarcely what might be expected of rustics (if Fancy and Shinar could be characterized as such). Hardy accordingly revised it in 1896, having Shinar declaim, ' "Not wildly, and yet not careless-like; not purposely, and yet not by chance; not too quick nor yet too slow" '; and having Fancy reply, ' "Not anxiously, and yet not indifferently; neither blushing nor pale; not religiously nor yet quite wickedly." ' In the manuscript, Shinar's 'idly' replaced 'stupidly', and his 'coolly and practically' replaced what looks like 'mildly'.

5 *King Arthur he had three sons*: A version of a ballad popular throughout England, and known also as 'Three Scamping Rogues':

> King Arthur he had three sons.
> Big rogues as ever did swing,
> He had three sons of wh—s
> And he kicked them all three out-of-doors
> Because they could not sing.

C. M. Jackson-Houlston ('Thomas Hardy's Use of Traditional Song', p. 324) points out that Hardy was familiar with this version of the ballad – it appears in a letter of September 1889 (*Collected Letters*, I, 198) – and he uses it here to expose Shinar's vulgarity.

6 *It doesn't hurt me so much now*: Hardy clearly felt that the flirtatious Fancy would not have admitted this to her eager suitors, so in 1896 he changed it to read: ' "I must try to bear it!" '

7 *a high-class man*: A late addition to the manuscript. Shinar the gentleman farmer is decidedly of a higher class than Shinar the innkeeper.

8 *A governess . . . same establishment*: In 1912, Fancy's mother is a 'teacher in a landed county-family's nursery' and Geoffrey is quick to point out that he didn't stay keeper for long: ' "I was only a keeper then, though now I've a dozen other irons in the fire as steward here for my lord, what with the timber sales and the yearly fellings, and the gravel and sand sales, and one thing and t'other." ' On similarities between Geoffrey and George Melbury, see note 7 to II, vi.

9 *Queen's scholars*: David Wright (1978) points out that Queen's Scholars were not instituted until 1846. In the 1896 Preface Hardy placed the events 'fifty years ago', and they certainly occur around the end of 1845 or later (see I, iv, note 16), so Geoffrey's claim is plausible.

CHAPTER III
Fancy in the Rain

1 *Elizabeth Endorfield's*: Named after the biblical witch of Endor (1 Samuel 28).
2 *loved him more . . . dreamt of doing*: A later addition to the manuscript. Hardy originally wrote simply that Fancy 'continued to' love him, only later altering the passage to indicate that Geoffrey's opposition heightens Fancy's passion.
3 *It may be stated . . . growth of witches*: Another allusion to Maybold added at a later stage to the manuscript.
4 *This fear of Lizz – . . . And that's all*: A later addition to the verso of fo. 162 of the manuscript. In proof for the first edition, Hardy changed the first two lines from 'Whatever blame and guilty name/Upon me fall'.

CHAPTER IV
The Spell

1 *the three creations*: Genesis 1 describes the creation of three groups: the fowls and fishes; cattle, creeping things and beasts of the earth; and man.

CHAPTER V
After Gaining Her Point

1 *After Gaining Her Point*: From the evidence of the double numeration scheme in the manuscript, the narrative from the beginning of this chapter to the end of chapter vii ('A Crisis') was a later addition, indicating that Maybold's suit was an afterthought. (See the 'Note on the History of the Text' to this edition, and *Creator*, pp. 8–9.) Hardy consequently altered earlier exchanges to prepare for these events.
2 *Harvest Thanksgiving . . . Mellstock Church*: If Maybold kept his word and allowed the choir's last performance to be 'about Michaelmas' (29 September), then Harvest Thanksgiving (usually in mid-September) is late. The implication in the vicar's decision at the end of the interview with the choir (II, iv) is that the singers will not fall 'glorious with a bit of a flourish' at all, and the timing of the organ opening seems to underline this. The vicar's choice of feast day is a very significant one: Alun Howkins has argued that in the mid-century, the rural clergy began to expropriate communal rituals like the harvest festival as part of the 'new paternalism' (*Reshaping Rural England: A Social History, 1850–1925* [London: Harper Collins, 1991], pp. 70–73). On Maybold as a representative figure in this paternalism, see the Introduction.
3 *the whole history of schoolmistresses*: A curiously specific note is struck in Hardy's 1912 revision to the 'whole history of village-schoolmistresses at this date'.
4 *she had actually donned . . . curls*: Interestingly, the narrator contends that Fancy

gets away with wearing her hair down in church because of her father's wealth and not, as she herself believes, because she is so attractive to vicars under forty.

5 *adopted new attractions . . . of other people*: Added in proof for the first edition. In the manuscript, it is simply: 'I shouldn't have cared about the other people.' The change emphasizes Fancy's sense of herself as an object of view.

6 *Though this . . . or our steps go out of the way*: 'All this is come upon us; yet we have not forgotten thee, neither have we dealt falsely in thy covenant. Our heart is not turned back, neither have our steps declined from thy way' (Psalm 44: 17–18). The manuscript cancellations suggest that Hardy altered what began as a more pleading tone in William's quote: 'Don't let [this come upon us] . . .'

CHAPTER VI
Into Temptation

1 *Into Temptation*: Changed in proof from 'A Creature Not Too Bright or Good' – a further allusion to Wordsworth's 'She was a Phantom of Delight'. Wordsworth's heroine, with her 'household motions light and free', is neither too bright nor good for 'human nature's daily food'. However, the novel insinuates that for Fancy (who is no paragon of housekeeping) the 'daily food' of her future married life may be less palatable when her sexual allure, like that of the older wives (the only other significant women in the novel, from whose lives we are obliged to project Fancy's future), will be all in the past. On the novel's exploration of sexual fascination and the grim materiality of marriage, see the Introduction.

2 *they lent . . . to the women*: Dick is made less 'poor and mean' in 1912: 'we lent all the umbrellas to the women. I don't know when I shall get mine back.'

3 *Now, good-bye*: Hardy uses the device of the woman at the high window again in *Jude the Obscure* (IV, i): 'Now that the high window-sill was between them, so that he could not get at her, [Sue] seemed not to mind indulging in a frankness she had feared at close quarters.'

4 *and still conscious . . . triumph*: Added in proof for the first edition. Without this memory of the morning to explain her sudden distaste for Dick's unglamorous figure, Fancy's love would seem to be in doubt.

5 *how poor and mean a man looks in the rain*: In 1896, Hardy changed this rather severe assessment of Fancy's to 'how plain and sorry a man looks'.

6 *feminine eyes instinctively perceived*: A late addition to the manuscript, which replaces the straightforward 'she saw' with the narrator's speculations on what is instinctive in a woman.

7 *of superior silk*: Lest readers in 1912 miss the contrast, Hardy added: 'less common at that date than since'.

8 *beauty*: Perhaps because of Maybold's character and position, this is modified to 'charm' in 1912.

CHAPTER VII
A Crisis

1 *A Crisis*: Retitled 'Second Thoughts' in 1896 and later.

2 *less an angel than a woman*: The manuscript cancellations show that Hardy was going to write 'not an angel, but a woman'. As its stands, however, it more closely alludes to Wordsworth's 'She was a Phantom of Delight', which describes a 'perfect Woman . . . /And yet a Spirit still, and bright/With something of angelic light'. Hardy's narrator is less dazzled by this 'lovely Apparition' than Wordsworth's speaker, however; and Dick impetuously, unconsciously, and ambiguously repeats Wordsworth's apostrophe in III, iv (see note 2).

3 *a branch of my father's business*: In 1912, Hardy added: 'which we think of starting elsewhere'. Dick, it seems, is now the 'coming man' (see note 5 to I, viii).

4 *twenty-five want a crown*. Twenty-five pounds minus a crown (five shillings): thus, twenty-four pounds fifteen shillings.

5 *to keep pace . . . printed*: Hardy renders Dick's speech more colloquial here in 1896 (and retains it in 1912), changing 'keep' to 'kip' and 'printed' to 'prented'. The effect is to ironize Dick's enterprise slightly in the presence of Maybold. Cf. Mr Penny's workshop door in II, ii.

PART V: CONCLUSION

CHAPTER I
'The Knot There's No Untying'

1 *'The Knot There's No Untying'*: From the song by Thomas Campbell (1777–1844). Later verses contain clues to the naming of Fancy – 'Love he comes, and Love he tarries,/Just as fate or fancy carries' – and to the novel's undertone of melancholy:

> Can you keep the bee from ranging
> Or the ringdove's neck from changing?
> No! nor fettered love from dying
> In the knot there's no untying.

Geoffrey Grigson (1974) calls these lines 'atrociously prophetic . . . about the love Hardy had begun and was engaged in at that time' (p. 24). Surely, though, they are more immediately prophetic of Fancy and Dick's future, as foreseen in the novel's other marriages. Significantly, Hardy makes use of the song again in *Jude the Obscure* (V, iii), where Sue Bridehead, feeling herself the ' "little bird . . . caught at last" ', quotes these lines as she and Jude retreat from the parish-clerk's door after putting off the posting of their marriage banns.

2 *night-jar*: The harsh cry of this night-flying bird, in folklore an evil omen, contrasts with the melodious song of the nightingale which escorts Dick and Fancy from their wedding.

3 *noisy and persistent intimates*: Dennis Taylor has argued that the imagery of this opening paragraph 'connects with the mainstream literary tradition of Tennyson's "Come down, O Maid" where "I, thy shepherd" calls his love to the valley where love goes "hand in hand with Plenty in the maize,/O red with spirited purple of the vats . . . and sweet is every sound". Tennyson's poem ends with the famous "murmuring of innumerable bees" ' (*Hardy's Poetry, 1860–1928*, p. 143).

4 *Thomas Wood*: The names are reversed in 1872, but as Simon Gatrell points out (1985, p. 215), Geoffrey Day says, ' "That Ezekiel Sparrowgrass o' thine" ' to Fancy in II, vi.

5 *from wedding to churching . . . spirit enough*: Fancy blushes at the sexual implications of Mrs Penny's advice, which also, however, insinuates that a married woman's sexual life – between the wedding and the thanksgiving service for the safe birth of her children – is one of unpleasant duties to be borne stoically. See also note 3 to I, vi.

6 *That's a girl . . . husband!*: The pre-nuptial sexual innuendos were originally compounded here by Mrs Dewy's: ' "That's a girl for a Dick!" ' (manuscript cancellation).

7 *a man-trap*: Man-traps were set by game-keepers to catch poachers. Here the allusion to marital entrapment is clear. Hardy later uses the man-trap to great melodramatic and symbolic effect in *The Woodlanders*, where Grace Melbury's dress becomes caught in one. It is described in detail in chapter xlvii of that novel:

There had been the toothless variety used by the softer-hearted landlords – quite contemptible in their clemency. The jaws of these resembled the jaws of an old woman to whom time has left nothing but gums. There were also the intermediate or half-toothed sorts, probably devised by the middle-natured squires, or those under the influence of their wives: two inches of mercy, two inches of cruelty, two inches of mere nip, two inches of probe, and so on, through the whole extent of the jaws. There were also, as a class apart, the bruisers, which did not lacerate the flesh, but only crushed the bone.

8 *the love and the stalled ox*: 'Better a dinner of herbs where love is, than a stalled ox and hatred therewith' (Proverbs 15:17).

9 *they can hear . . . up here*: Perhaps because of the intimation that the men overhear Fancy dressing, Hardy changed this in 1986 to: ' "we can hear all they say and do down there" '.

10 *as her own property*: Added at proof-stage for the first edition. An important addition, stressing that Fancy's acquisitiveness is still ascendant, even in choosing, as so many of Hardy's heroines do, the poor man.

11 *That my bees . . . times and seasons!*: Bees swarming on one's wedding day is a 'most delightful token of good luck' (Firor, 2).

12 *grandfather James*: Hardy calls him 'the inharmonious grandfather James' in 1912. Millgate associates him with *As You Like It*'s Jaques, 'his "inharmonious" note of cold realism . . . consistently disruptive of the idyllic surface' (*Thomas Hardy: His Career as a Novelist*, p. 48).

13 *those beautiful eyes of hers . . . not too good*: A further reference to Wordsworth's 'creature not too bright or good'. See note 1 of IV, vi.

14 *Respectable people . . . I will*: See also 'The Country Wedding' (*Late Lyrics and Earlier*) reproduced in Appendix III.

15 *Can a maid . . . bride her attire?*: Jeremiah 2:32. This aside was added on the verso of fo. 195. Its inclusion reinforces the idea that Fancy's vanity is, as she suggests in III, iv, simply part of a woman's nature.

16 *stocks*: 'Weatherbury stocks' (1912). Cf. *Far from the Madding Crowd*, xlvi, and 'In Weatherbury Stocks' (*Winter Words in Various Moods and Metres* [1928]). According to Firor, Dorset's 'last recorded case of this punishment was 1872' (Firor, 245).

CHAPTER II
Under the Greenwood Tree

1 *Under the Greenwood Tree*: From Amiens's song in *As You Like It* (II, v):

> Under the greenwood tree
>   Who loves to lie with me,
> And turn his merry note
>   Unto the sweet bird's throat,
> Come hither, come hither, come hither.
>   Here shall see no enemy
> But winter and rough weather.
>
> Who doth ambition shun
>   And loves to live i' th' sun,
> Seeking the food he eats,
>   And pleased with what he gets,
> Come hither, come hither, come hither.
>   Here shall see no enemy
> But winter and rough weather.

2 *an ancient beech-tree*: In this final chapter, the purely literary reference of the Shakespearian title is taken over by Hardy's bucolics, and the greenwood tree materializes in Yalbury Wood as the novel's principal pastoral symbol. Gatrell argues that the tree represents 'benevolent mutual cooperation in nature' and 'is matched by the sense of community founded upon similar relationships' (1985, p. xxii). The mournful or aggressive contending songs of the trees with which the novel had opened (reminiscent, perhaps, of the pastoral song contest) are here contrasted with an image of a single ancient encompassing tree. Hints of discord remain, however: the wedding may prove a 'healthy exercise ground for young chicken and pheasants', but 'the hens, their mothers' are 'enclosed in coops . . . upon the same green flooring'.

3 *persons of decent taste*: Changed to 'persons of newer taste' in 1896. The collisions of dialect and standard English pervade Hardy's work: see especially *The Mayor of Casterbridge*, xx; the representation of Tess in *Tess of the D'Urbervilles*; and Taylor, 82–6 and *passim*.

4 *Tantrum Clangley*: This percussive village obviously has no parallel in Hardy's Dorset.

5 *had ever been attained*: That 'feminine genius can attain' in the manuscript

6 *now . . . vigour to his nods*: This allusion to the new sense of time is an afterthought in the manuscript.

7 *Chanticleer's . . . a-cut then*: Without his flamboyant comb, the cock is reduced to nothing. Changed in proof for the first edition from 'Cock-a-doodle-doo's comb'.

8 *sank into nothingness again*: Barbara Hardy suggests that the 'pointlessness' of Leaf's story is used 'to instruct us in the ways of listening with generous love' (*Tellers and Listeners: The Narrative Imagination* [London: The Athlone Press, 1975], p. 205). See also the Introduction to this edition.

9 *come hither! . . . hither!*: A refrain from the song in *As You Like It*. See note 1 above.

10 *O, 'tis the nightingale . . . she should never tell*: If the nightingale's song harkens the lovers back to the pastoral realm, where their only enemies will be winter and rough weather, then Fancy clearly has her doubts, for this bird may be the harbinger of spring, but it does not live long in a cage. The nightingale's song also recalls the Greek legend of Philomela, who likewise bears 'a secret she should never tell' (she has her tongue cut out), and is finally turned into a nightingale. Fancy's is a secret she 'would' never tell in 1896 and later editions.

GLOSSARY

ath'art advb.	athwart.
awl sb.	small pointed tool used by shoemakers for pricking.
bass-viol sb.	viola da gamba, violoncello.
Bath clogs sb.pl.	women's overshoes with wooden soles.
beetle sb.	tool with a heavy head and handle for ramming wedges.
birdlime sb.	sticky substance made from holly bark for catching small birds.
Bob's-a-dying sb.	a row.
borus-snorus a.	spoken out in a bold or outspoken manner, without fear of consequences or people's opinions.
bradded p.p.	fastened with brads (shoemaker's thin small-headed nails).
brimbles sb.pl.	brambles.
broaching pr.p.	piercing the cask to draw the liquor.
cappel-faced a.	describes a white face dappled with red.
cast off vb.	alternate partners in a country-dance.
chairman sb.	someone who wheels a bath chair.
chammer sb.	chamber.

chancel sb.	eastern part of the church, usually set aside for the clergy or choir.
chest-notes sb.pl.	low notes.
chiel sb.	child.
chimley-corner sb.	chimney-corner, ingle-nook.
clink vb.	run away.
codlin-tree sb.	tree bearing long tapering cooking apples.
coling pr.p.	embracing.
common time sb.	two or four beats to the bar.
counter-boy sb.	alto voice.
crane-fly sb.	long-legged, two-winged fly.
crater sb.	creature.
dace sb.	small freshwater fish allied to carp.
dang it phr.	damn it.
delf a.	describes glazed earthenware made at Delft in Holland.
doorstone sb.	a flagstone laid at a door.
drong sb.	a lane between walls or hedges.
dumb waiter sb.	movable table with revolving shelves.
dust-hole sb.	hole or bin where dust and refuse are collected.
eight-day clock sb.	clock wound every eight days.
emmet sb.	ant.
feymell sb.	expression of disgust.
flitch sb.	salted and cured side of pork.
fourteen sb.	a small candle, named because fourteen weighed one pound.
full-buff a.	face to face.
full-butt a.	with full force.
furze sb.	spiny yellow-flowered evergreen shrub growing on waste-land.
fustian a.	describes thick twilled short-napped cotton cloth, usually dyed dark.
gaffers and gammers sb.pl.	old folks; grandfathers and grandmothers.
Gammer sb.	old woman.
gawk-hammer sb.	gaping fool.
gie vb.	give.
gig sb.	light two-wheeled one-horse carriage.
gipsy-party sb.	picnic.

good-now phr.	sure enough.
go snacks phr.	share anything; marry.
hard boy-chap sb.	robust boy
harmonium sb.	keyboard instrument in which notes are produced by air blown through reeds.
hartshorn sb.	distilled ammonium carbonate.
hedger and ditcher sb.	farm worker who cut hedges and cleared ditches.
het vb.	gulp.
hogshead sb.	fifty-gallon cask.
horn-lantern sb.	lantern with cow-horn rather than glass panels.
horsed a.	raised on legs.
husbird sb.	('hore's bird') bastard.
japanning sb.	surface coated with a hard varnish originally brought from Japan.
jimcrack a.	worthless, rickety.
last trump phr.	last note of the Last Post.
lath-like a.	thin as a strip of wood.
Latin crosses sb.	the horizontal beam of the cross used in the Christian church crosses the vertical beam two-thirds of the way up.
laurestinus sb.	evergreen winter flowering shrub, usually spelled 'laurustinus'.
leg-wood sb.	long branches cut from trees.
lights sb.pl.	lungs (of sheep, pigs, etc.).
lime-basket sb.	basket to keep lime dry and away from the skin.
linnet sb.	lint.
long-favoured a.	long-faced.
martel sb.	(mortal) individual.
meal-bag sb.	cloth bag for ground edible grain.
metheglin sb.	spiced mead.
minim sb.	note half as long as a semibreve.
mumbudget vb.	take by surprise.
nate a.	neat.
nation sb.	damnation.
near-foot-afore sb.	left forefoot.
'Od sb.	God.
on-end a.	ready, set.

peck sb.   a volume measure for dry goods equalling about two gallons.

pitch-halfpenny sb.   the tossing of a coin.

phlegmatic a.   cool and indifferent.

pothousey a.   vulgar

pro tem phr.   for the time being.

quarest a.   queerest.

quarter vb.   move off to the side of the road to allow a vehicle to pass.

quat vb.   squat.

raw-mil cheese sb.   rich cheese made from unskimmed milk.

ribstone-pippin sb.   red eating apple.

scram a.   emaciated, puny, despicable.

serpent sb.   wind instrument made of long leather-covered wooden tube with several bends.

settle sb.   a bench with high back and arms.

sharpener sb.   teacher.

shear-steel sb.   high-quality steel for shears and other cutting instruments.

slim-faced a.   sly.

small sb.   weak ale or beer.

snap sb.   a hasty meal.

sodger sb.   soldier.

spak vb.   speak.

spar sb.   a sharpened wooden peg for fastening thatch.

spet sb.   spit.

stocks sb.pl.   timber frames with holes for feet and occasionally hands in which petty offenders were confined in a sitting position in public.

strents sb.pl.   slits, tears.

stud sb.   quandary.

supernumeraries sb.pl.   extras.

thirtingill a.   wrong-headed, perverse.

ting vb.   make a noise with a key and a shovel or warming-pan to induce bees to swarm.

traypse vb.   walk about aimlessly.

Turk sb.   an exclamation indicating surprise or disbelief; here meaning something like 'Good God!'

union beggar sb.	a beggar from the workhouse.
unrind vb.	undress.
up-sides a.	equal.
varmit sb.	vermin.
wamble vb.	walk unsteadily or shakily.
warming pan sb.	flat, closed, long-handled pan which held coals or cinders and was used to warm the inside of a bed before it was occupied.
warn vb.	warrant.
water-cider sb.	weak cider from the second pressing of the apples.
white-lyvered a.	cowardly.
Woot hae me? phr.	Will you have me?
zhinerally advb.	generally.

READ MORE IN PENGUIN

In every corner of the world, on every subject under the sun, Penguin represents quality and variety – the very best in publishing today.

For complete information about books available from Penguin – including Puffins, Penguin Classics and Arkana – and how to order them, write to us at the appropriate address below. Please note that for copyright reasons the selection of books varies from country to country.

In the United Kingdom: Please write to *Dept. EP, Penguin Books Ltd, Bath Road, Harmondsworth, West Drayton, Middlesex UB7 ODA*

In the United States: Please write to *Consumer Sales, Penguin Putnam Inc., P.O. Box 12289 Dept. B, Newark, New Jersey 07101-5289.* VISA and MasterCard holders call 1-800-788-6262 to order Penguin titles

In Canada: Please write to *Penguin Books Canada Ltd, 10 Alcorn Avenue, Suite 300, Toronto, Ontario M4V 3B2*

In Australia: Please write to *Penguin Books Australia Ltd, P.O. Box 257, Ringwood, Victoria 3134*

In New Zealand: Please write to *Penguin Books (NZ) Ltd, Private Bag 102902, North Shore Mail Centre, Auckland 10*

In India: Please write to *Penguin Books India Pvt Ltd, 11 Community Centre, Panchsheel Park, New Delhi 110017*

In the Netherlands: Please write to *Penguin Books Netherlands bv, Postbus 3507, NL-1001 AH Amsterdam*

In Germany: Please write to *Penguin Books Deutschland GmbH, Metzlerstrasse 26, 60594 Frankfurt am Main*

In Spain: Please write to *Penguin Books S. A., Bravo Murillo 19, 1° B, 28015 Madrid* ·

In Italy: Please write to *Penguin Italia s.r.l., Via Benedetto Croce 2, 20094 Corsico, Milano*

In France: Please write to *Penguin France, Le Carré Wilson, 62 rue Benjamin Baillaud, 31500 Toulouse*

In Japan: Please write to *Penguin Books Japan Ltd, Kaneko Building, 2-3-25 Koraku, Bunkyo-Ku, Tokyo 112*

In South Africa: Please write to *Penguin Books South Africa (Pty) Ltd, Private Bag X14, Parkview, 2122 Johannesburg*

READ MORE IN PENGUIN

A CHOICE OF CLASSICS

READ MORE IN PENGUIN

A CHOICE OF CLASSICS

Charles Dickens	**American Notes for General Circulation**
	Barnaby Rudge
	Bleak House
	The Christmas Books (in two volumes)
	David Copperfield
	Dombey and Son
	Great Expectations
	Hard Times
	Little Dorrit
	Martin Chuzzlewit
	The Mystery of Edwin Drood
	Nicholas Nickleby
	The Old Curiosity Shop
	Oliver Twist
	Our Mutual Friend
	The Pickwick Papers
	Pictures from Italy
	Selected Journalism 1850–1870
	Selected Short Fiction
	Sketches by Boz
	A Tale of Two Cities
George Eliot	**Adam Bede**
	Daniel Deronda
	Felix Holt
	Middlemarch
	The Mill on the Floss
	Romola
	Scenes of Clerical Life
	Silas Marner
Fanny Fern	**Ruth Hall**
Elizabeth Gaskell	**Cranford/Cousin Phillis**
	The Life of Charlotte Brontë
	Mary Barton
	North and South
	Ruth
	Sylvia's Lovers
	Wives and Daughters